Fugitive Dreams

Library of the Indies

E. M. Beekman, General Editor

Fugitive Dreams

An Anthology of Dutch Colonial Literature

Edited, translated, with introductions

and notes by

E. M. Beekman

The University of Massachusetts Press

Amherst

1988

Preparation and publication of this work were supported by the Translation
Program of the National Endowment for the Humanities, the Foundation for the
Promotion of the Translation of Dutch Literary Works, the Prince Bernhard Fund,
and the Dutch Ministry of Welfare, Health, and Culture (Ministerie van Welzijn,
Volksgezondheid en Cultuur), Department for International Affairs, The
Netherlands, to which acknowledgment is gratefully made.

Set in Linotron Sabon at G & S Typesetters, Inc.
Printed by Cushing-Malloy and bound by John Dekker & Sons

Library of Congress Cataloging-in-Publication Data

Fugitive dreams.
(Library of the Indies)
1. Dutch prose literature—Indonesia—Translations
into English.   2. English prose literature—Translations
from Dutch.   3. Dutch—Indonesia—History—Sources.
4. Indonesia—History—Sources.   I. Beekman, E. M.,
1939– .   II. Series.
PT 5923.F8 1988   839.3'1808   87-19031
ISBN 0-87023-575-3 (alk. paper)

British Library Cataloguing in Publication data are available

Some portions of this book have appeared in different and abbreviated versions:
"Kartini: Letters from a Javanese Feminist, 1899–1902," *Massachusetts Review*
25, no. 4 (1984); "Against the Grain: A Dutch Soldier in Sumatra," *Translation*
(Columbia University) 24 (Spring 1985); "Bas Veth: A Colonial Muckraker," *Indonesia* (Cornell University) 42 (October 1986).

For Joost
My temoeshoelawak sobat

Contents

Preface to the Series

This volume is one of a series of literary works written by the Dutch about their lives in the former colony of the Dutch East Indies, now the Republic of Indonesia. This realm of 13,670 islands is roughly one quarter the size of the continental United States. It consists of the four Greater Sunda Islands—Sumatra, larger than California; Java, about the size of New York State; Borneo, about the size of France (presently called Kalimantan); and Celebes, about the size of North Dakota (now called Sulawesi). East from Java is a string of smaller islands called the Lesser Sunda Islands, which includes Bali, Lombok, Sumba, Sumbawa, Flores, and Timor. Further east from the Lesser Sunda Islands lies New Guinea, now called Irian Barat, which is the second largest island in the world. Between New Guinea and Celebes there is a host of smaller islands, often known as the Moluccas, that includes a group once celebrated as the Spice Islands.

One of the most volcanic regions in the world, the Malay archipelago is tropical in climate and has a diverse population. Some 250 languages are spoken in Indonesia, and it is remarkable that a population of such widely differing cultural and ethnic backgrounds adopted the Malay language as its *lingua franca* from about the fifteenth century, although that language was spoken at first only in parts of Sumatra and the Malay peninsula (now Malaysia).

Though the smallest of the Greater Sunda Islands, Java has always been the most densely populated, with about two-thirds of all Indonesians living there. In many ways a history of Indonesia is, first and foremost, the history of Java.

But in some ways Java's prominence is misleading, because it belies the great diversity of this island realm. For instance, the destination of the first Europeans who sailed to Southeast Asia was not Java but the Moluccas. It was that "odiferous pistil" (as Motley called the clove), as well as nutmeg and mace, that drew the Portuguese to a group of small islands in the Ceram and Banda Seas in the early part of the sixteenth century. Pepper was another profitable commodity, and attempts to obtain it brought the Portuguese into conflict with Atjeh, an Islamic sultanate in northern Sumatra, and with Javanese traders who, along with merchants from India, had been the traditional middlemen of the spice trade. The precedent of European intervention had been set and was to continue for nearly four centuries.

Although subsequent history is complicated in its causes and effects, one may propose certain generalities. The Malay realm was essentially a littoral one. Even in Java, the interior was sparsely populated and virtually unknown to the foreign intruders coming from China, India, and Europe. Whoever ruled the seas controlled the archipelago, and for the next three centuries the key needed to unlock the riches of Indonesia was mastery of the Indian Ocean. The nations who thus succeeded were, in turn, Portugal, Holland, and England, and one can trace the shifting of power in the prominence and decline of their major cities in the Orient. Goa, Portugal's stronghold in India, gave way to Batavia in the Dutch East Indies, while Batavia was overshadowed by Singapore by the end of the nineteenth century. Although all three were relatively small nations, they were maritime giants. Their success was partly due to the internecine warfare between the countless city-states, principalities, and native autocrats. The Dutch were masters at playing one against the other.

Religion was a major factor in the fortunes of Indonesia. The Portuguese expansion was in part a result of Portugal's crusade against Islam, which was quite as ferocious and intransigent as the holy war of the Mohammedans. Islam may be considered a unifying force in the archipelago; it cut across all levels of society and provided a rallying point for resistance to foreign intrusion. Just as the Malay language had done linguistically, Islam proved to be a syncretizing force when there was no united front. One of the causes of Portugal's demise was its inflexible antagonism to Islam, and later the Dutch found resistance to their rule fueled by religious fervor as well as political dissatisfaction.

THE DUTCH ventured to reach the tropical antipodes not only because their nemesis, Philip II of Spain, annexed Portugal and forbade them entry to Lisbon. The United Netherlands was a nation of merchants, a brokerage house for northern Europe, and it wanted to get to the source of tropical wealth itself. Dutch navigators and traders knew the location of the fabled Indies; they were well acquainted with Portuguese achievements at sea and counted among their members individuals who had worked for the Portuguese. Philip II simply accelerated a process that was inevitable.

At first, various individual enterprises outfitted ships and sent them to the Far East in a far from lucrative display of free enterprise. Nor was the first arrival of the Dutch in the archipelago auspicious, though it may have been symbolic of subsequent developments. In June 1596 a Dutch fleet of four ships anchored off the coast of Java. Senseless violence and a total disregard for local customs made the Dutch unwelcome on those shores.

During the seventeenth century the Dutch extended their influence in the archipelago by means of superior naval strength, by use of armed intervention which was often ruthless, and by shrewd politicking and exploitation of local differences. Their cause was helped by the lack of a cohesive force to withstand them. Yet the seventeenth century also saw a number of men who were eager to know the new realm, who investigated the language and the mores of the people they encountered, and who studied the flora and fauna. These were men who not only put the Indies on the map of trade routes, but who also charted riches of other than commercial value.

It soon became apparent to the Dutch that these separate ventures did little to promote welfare. In 1602 Johan van Oldenbarneveldt, the Advocate of the United Provinces, managed to negotiate a contract which in effect merged all these individual enterprises into one United East India Company, better known under its Dutch acronym as the voc. The merger ensured a monopoly at home, and the Company set out to obtain a similar insurance in the Indies. This desire for exclusive rights to the production and marketing of spices and other commodities proved to be a double-edged sword.

The voc succeeded because of its unrelenting naval vigilance in discouraging European competition and because the Indies were a politically unstable region. And even though the Company was only interested in its balance sheet, it soon found itself burdened with an expanding empire and an indolent bureaucracy which, in the eighteenth century, became not only unwieldy but tolerant of graft and extortion. Furthermore, even though its profits were far below what they were rumored to be, the Company kept its dividends artificially high and was soon forced to borrow money to pay the interest on previous loans. When Holland's naval supremacy was seriously challenged by the British in 1780, a blockade kept the Company's ships from reaching Holland, and the discrepancy between capital and expenditures increased dramatically until the Company's deficit was so large it had to request state aid. In 1798, after nearly two centuries, the Company ceased to exist. Its debt of 140 million guilders was assumed by the state, and the commercial enterprise became a colonial empire.

At the beginning of the nineteenth century, Dutch influence was still determined by the littoral character of the region. Dutch presence in the archipelago can be said to have lasted three and a half centuries, but if one defines colonialism as the subjugation of an *entire* area and dates it from the time when the last independent domain was conquered—in this case Atjeh in northern Sumatra—then the Dutch colonial empire lasted less than half a century. Effective government could only be claimed for the Moluccas, certain portions of Java (by no means the entire island), a southern portion of Celebes, and some coastal regions of Sumatra and Borneo. Yet it is also true that precisely because Indonesia was an insular realm, Holland never needed to muster a substantial army such as the one the British had to maintain in the large subcontinent of India. The extensive interiors of islands such as Sumatra, Borneo, or Celebes were not penetrated, because, for the seaborne empire of commercial interests, exploration of such regions was unprofitable, hence not desirable.

The nature of Holland's involvement changed with the tenure of Herman Willem Daendels as governor-general, just after the French revolution. Holland declared itself a democratic nation in 1795, allied itself with France—which meant a direct confrontation with England—and was practically a vassal state of France until 1810. Though reform, liberal programs, and the mandate of human rights were loudly proclaimed in Europe, they did not seem to apply to the Asian branch of the family of man. Daendels exemplified this double standard. He evinced reforms, either in fact or on paper, but did so in an imperious manner and with total disregard for native customs and law (known as *adat*). Stamford Raffles, who was the chief administrator of the British interim government from 1811 to 1816, expanded Daendels's innovations, which included tax reform and the introduction of the land-rent system, which was based on the assumption that all the land belonged to the colonial administration. By the time Holland regained its colonies in 1816, any resemblance to the erstwhile Company had vanished. In its place was a firmly established, paternalistic colonial government which ruled by edict and regulation, supported a huge bureaucracy, and sought to make the colonies turn a profit, as well as to legislate its inhabitants' manner of living.

It is not surprising that for the remainder of the nineteenth century, a centralized authority instituted changes from above that were often in direct conflict with Javanese life and welfare. One such change, which was supposed to increase revenues and improve the life of the Javanese peasant, was the infamous "Cultivation System" (*Cultuurstelsel*). This system required the Javanese to grow cash crops, such as sugar cane or indigo, which, although profitable on the world market, were of little practical use to the Javanese. In effect it meant compulsory labor and the exploitation of the entire island as if it were a feudal estate. The system proved profitable for the Dutch, and because it introduced varied crops such as tea and tobacco to local agriculture, it indirectly improved the living standard of some of the people. It also fostered distrust of colonial authority, caused uprisings, and provided the impetus for liberal reform on the part of Dutch politicians in the Netherlands.

Along with the increased demand in the latter half of the nineteenth century for liberal reform came an expansion of direct control over other areas of the archipelago. One of the reasons for this was an unprecedented influx of private citizens from Holland. Expansion of trade required expansion of territory that was under direct control of Batavia to insure stability. Colonial policy improved education, agriculture, and public hygiene and expanded the transportation network. In Java a paternalistic policy was not offensive, because its ruling class (the *prijaji*) had governed that way for centuries; but progressive politicians in The Hague demanded that the Indies be administered on a moral basis which favored the interests of the Indonesians rather than those of the Dutch government in Europe. This "ethical policy" became doctrine from about the turn of this century and followed on the heels of a renascence of scientific study of the Indies quite as enthusiastic as the one in the seventeenth century.

The first three decades of the present century were probably the most stable and prosperous in colonial history. This period was also the beginning of an emerging Indonesian national consciousness. Various nationalistic parties were formed, and the Indonesians demanded a far more representative role in the administration of their country. The example of Japan indicated to the Indonesians that European rulers were not invincible. The rapidity with which the Japanese conquered Southeast Asia during the Second World War only accelerated the process of decolonization. In 1945 Indonesia declared its independence, naming Sukarno the republic's first president. The Dutch did not accept this declaration, and between 1945 and 1949 they conducted several unsuccessful military campaigns to reestablish control. In 1950, with a new constitution, Indonesia became a sovereign state.

I OFFER here only a cursory outline. The historical reality is far more complex and infinitely richer, but this sketch must suffice as a backdrop for the particular type of literature that is presented in this series.

This is a literature written by or about European colonialists in Southeast Asia prior to the Second World War. Though the literary techniques may be Western, the subject matter is unique. This genre is also a self-contained unit that cannot develop further, because there are no new voices and because what was voiced no longer exists. Yet it is a literature that can still instruct, because it delineates the historical and psychological confrontation of East and West, it depicts the uneasy alliance of these antithetical forces, and it shows by prior example the demise of Western imperialism.

These are political issues, but there is another aspect of this kind of literature that is of equal importance. It is a literature of lost causes, of a past irrevocably gone, of an era that today seems so utterly alien that it is novel once again.

Tempo dulu it was once called—time past. But now, after two world wars and several Asian wars, after the passage of nearly half a century, this phrase presents more than a wistful longing for the prerogatives of imperialism; it gives as well a poignant realization that an epoch is past that will never return. At its worst the documentation of this perception is sentimental indulgence, but at its best it is the poetry of a vanished era, of the fall of an empire, of the passing of an age when issues moral and political were firmer and clearer, and when the drama of the East was still palpable and not yet reduced to a topic for sociologists.

In many ways, this literature of Asian colonialism reminds one of the literature of the American south—of Faulkner, O'Connor, John Crowe Ransom, and Robert Penn Warren. For that too was a "colonial" literature that was quite as much aware of its own demise and yet, not defiantly but wistfully, determined to record its own passing. One finds in both the peculiar hybrid of antithetical cultures, the inevitable defeat of the more recent masters, a faith in more traditional virtues, and that peculiar offbeat detail often called "gothic" or "grotesque." In both literatures loneliness is a central theme. There were very few who knew how to turn their mordant isolation into a dispassionate awareness that all things must pass and fail.

E. M. BEEKMAN

Foreword

This anthology, the twelfth and final volume of the Library of the Indies, contains examples of the work of eight writers. For various reasons it has not been possible to devote an entire book of the series to a work by any one of these authors, but the project would be incomplete without according each some representation.

Fugitive Dreams is intended to be a viable anthology of Dutch colonial literature, giving examples of the works of authors whose lives span the length of the Dutch colonial presence in Indonesia, from around 1600 (Willem Bontekoe) to just before the beginning of World War II (Willem Walraven). Each selection is introduced with an essay that gives an overview of the author, the times, and the colonial milieu in which he or she lived.

Of the eight authors, four have never been translated into English (Franz Wilhelm Junghuhn, Herman Neubronner van der Tuuk, Bas Veth, and Alexander Cohen), and Kartini's letters have only been available in a very unsatisfactory edition published in 1920. Walraven's story "The Clan" was translated, but "Borderline" was not, nor were the excerpts from his letters and his journalism that were woven into my introduction. There was an earlier translation of Bontekoe, but in my translation of his journal I have attempted to maintain the seventeenth-century style and flavor which I find essential to the text. Whether previous translations existed or not, all the translations in this anthology are my own. I take complete responsibility for them, as well as for the scholarly material in the introductions and notes.

ONCE again I have retained the older spelling of Indonesian words and phrases for both aesthetic and practical reasons. For one thing, because all secondary literature from before the Second World War was printed in the older spelling, it will make it easier for the nonspecialist to find the sources. For those who wish to know equivalents in modern Bahasa Indonesia, the following changes should be noted: the former spelling tj (tjemar) is now c (cemar); dj (djoeroek) is now j (jeruk); ch (chas) is now kh (khas); nj (njai) is now ny (nyai); sj (sjak) is now sy (syak), and oe (soedah) is now u (sudah). Of these, only the last change has been adopted because the ortography for that diphtong is not familiar to English readers.

Fugitive Dreams

Willem Bontekoe

Europe had to command the oceans before it could fully entertain the idea of empire. Its control began as exploration rather than possession, and Europe's first efforts were explorations in the original sense of the word—they were intended to search out and examine thoroughly. But the desire to expound soon turned into the temptation to impound, in a sequence all too familiar throughout history. What follows is a brief survey of the first half of European maritime development, with special emphasis on the Portuguese and Dutch contributions. Although I have included pertinent detail, this discussion is meant only as an outline; the scope of the subject and the limitations of the present work permit no more than a general orientation.[1]

The mariners of the fifteenth and sixteenth centuries gradually came to know that the land masses of the world were floating on a continuous ocean that could be traversed and encompassed. Their knowledge came from information furnished by men who had *returned* from their daring exploits. Only when one could be confident that a sea voyage was not a one-way journey into oblivion but instead a feat that could be duplicated did a feeling of confidence inspire the hope of compensation.

The discovery and mastery of the world's oceans was a European accomplishment. There were other maritime peoples, to be sure, but few sailed beyond their familiar naval domain. Only the Chinese could have preempted Europe's success. The junk—a Portuguese term adapted from the Javanese word *ajong* that means ship—was a sound vessel of commodious size and capable of long voyages. For instance, the seven voyages the Chinese admiral Chêng Ho made between 1405 and 1433 were astonishing achievements. His fleets then were far larger than those the Europeans would be able to assemble during the next hundred years. The fleet that left in 1405 for southern Asia and beyond had sixty-two ships and 40,000 men. Chêng Ho's treasure ships were 1,500 tons and up, a tonnage that dwarfed European vessels for at least a century more. This imperial argosy of the Ming Dynasty sailed as far as the Persian Gulf, explored the east coast of Africa, and managed to bring back a giraffe for the Imperial Court. But for political reasons China decided to forego following up on its remarkable ability, and by the end of the fifteenth century its maritime power had vanished.[2]

Europe's pelagic exploits were an incremental achievement that made good use of the European talent for adaptation and improvisation. It was a slow process, but that is not surprising when one realizes the great risks that were taken and remembers that seafaring is an eminently practical occupation. Theory holds no fascination when one is desperate, and by all accounts dire straits were the common lot of seamen far into the nineteenth century. Scientific advances recommended themselves only if they could be applied in a practical and pragmatic fashion; experience was far more valuable than experiment. This principle can be observed in the development of the type of ship that would be capable of long voyages on the open sea.

The *naos* the Iberian discoverers used in the late fifteenth and early sixteenth centuries were an amalgamation of the southern and northern traditions of European shipbuilding. According to Mediterranean fashion, the hull was carvel-built over a preconstructed frame. This means that the planks were attached to the frame edge to edge, flush, with caulked interstices. The method allowed for larger sizes than would have been possible with the northern European type of clinker-built ship with its overlapping planking, similar to the clapboard siding on some wooden houses. The typically Mediterranean, triangular, lateen sail was kept on the mizzen mast (the shorter mast near the stern), but the fore and main masts held the square sails derived from the northern tradition. Using the lateen sail is dangerous unless the weather is placid, but square sails are good for speed and a following wind (one coming from the stern), permit a larger area of canvas, and are easier to handle in foul weather—all important factors in long voyages on the high seas. The multiple masts—usually three, i.e., main, fore, and mizzen—derived from Mediterranean practice, though the use of more than one sail per mast most likely originated in the north. The north also contributed the *naos*'s straight keel and the sternpost that held the northern type of median, or stern, rudder. With its tiller extending into the ship, such a rudder was easier for the helmsman to maneuver, though it was always an arduous job. It could require a dozen or more men to control the tiller in bad weather. The steering wheel did not come into use until the late seventeenth century. A spritsail was added as well. This was the square sail rigged under the bowsprit—the spar that extends from the bow, or front—which allows, thereby, more control over the front part of the ship. The *naos* had a shallow draught, facilitated by the straight keel, which made it possible to run in closer to shore.

The evolution of navigational devices followed a similar pattern of incorporating what was useful and practical from both northern and southern traditions. The magnetic compass, essential for steering when out of sight of land or when deprived of clear weather, had a long Mediterranean tradition. The same is true of marine charts, though in the fifteenth century they "were essentially sailing directions drawn in chart form."[3] Northern seamen contributed their skill in pilotage, which was their expertise in steering a ship along a shore with its various tides, currents, shoals, and both land- and sea-marks. Pilotage included the practice of sounding, a skill necessary in northern waters with their fog, mist, varying depths, and turbid seas. The most common device for sounding was a simple graduated rod suspended from a long line, but for deeper seas a lead weight or plummet was used. It had some tallow in a cup-shaped indentation at its end, and whatever constituted the bottom, be it sand, mud, or shingle, stuck to the tallow and told the leadsman what type of seabed was beneath his ship. When it came up clean, it indicated rock. Clearly, sounding was a crucial skill to have when exploring strange coastal waters.

Although the northern sailors were expert pilots, written sailing directions (*portolani*) were a regular feature in the Mediterranean long before the northern European *rutters*. *Portolani* had been helping Mediterranean navigators since the Middle Ages: they provided directions for coastal sailing, marked and described coastlines, anchorages, hazards, and mentioned what kind of facilities were available in various ports. *Portolani* represented the collective experience of mindful sailors. Their drawback was that to use them one had to be able to read, and northern seamen were for the most part illiterate. *Rutters,* the northern equivalent of *portolani*, did not appear until the late fifteenth century. The first printed version in English was published in 1521. In Dutch, *portolani* were known as *leeskaarten* or "reading maps," which is precisely what they were. When sea charts came into being, they were called *paskaarten,* charts whereon was measured the miles traveled and the course steered since the last observation. The measure was made with what were called a "Pair of Compasses," a *passer* in Dutch. The habits of carefully noting the physical characteristics of a voyage, such as wind directions, currents, speeds, and soundings, were critical for voyages of discovery. These invaluable logs of information were jealously guarded by the Portuguese to keep rival nations from profiting from their laboriously assembled marine intelligence.

Besides capable ships, crews, and nautical devices, floating artillery turned out to be another decisive innovation. Ordnance under sail was a European invention that guaranteed a naval supremacy for several centuries. Before the middle of the sixteenth century, the best cannon was made in Italy, Holland, and Germany. Both Portugal and Spain had to rely on gun manufacturers from northern Europe, even if they were political enemies, as they were with the Dutch. The most experienced and skilled gunners were also recruited from the north. Holland became the prime mover of the continental armament industry. By the early seventeenth century, the Dutch had their own thriving gun foundries, and, during the entire seventeenth and early eighteenth centuries, Amsterdam became the most important European seller of arms and ammunition.[4]

At first, most cannon was made from an alloy of copper, tin, and zinc, but they were expensive to manufacture. Gradually the cast-iron cannon was perfected, primarily in England, so that by the end of the seventeenth century iron guns were the predominant ordnance on board European ships. Around 1500 it became feasible to cut gun ports in a ship's hull, thereby allowing cannon to be mounted on the main deck, later on separate gun-decks. The greater stability of ships permitted larger caliber (up to six and seven inches), and more pieces. Naval artillery had an important impact on ship construction. Ships became larger, not only to carry greater cargoes, but also to accommodate the cannon. With space at a premium, cargo ships kept increasing in tonnage, but at the expense of speed. It was the Dutch and the English who saw the wisdom of developing a separate class of swift ships that were heavily gunned, not only to protect their own shipping but also to raid the ponderous hulks of the Spanish and Portuguese treasure fleets. By the end of the sixteenth century, the Dutch and English shipwrights scored a success with the galleon, a warship that relied primarily on long-range broadsides from its impressive array of guns, thereby rendering boarding obsolete. The galleon's effectiveness was demonstrated against the Spanish Armada in 1588.

This Atlantic development of full-rigged and heavily armed ships made Europe invincible at sea and master of the world's oceans. However, until the eighteenth century, that unquestionable supremacy did not extend far inland. Except for the Spanish dominions in South America, the European presence was limited to being a primarily littoral one. But for Europe to reach those alien shores, it first had to be weaned from hugging its own coasts. The nursemaids of maritime independence were islands.

IF the Pacific Ocean had been the body of water the European mariners had to master first, the attempt would have taken a great deal more time. That vast marine desert, a third of the total area of the globe, with its few and widely scattered insular oases, presented an indomitable adversary. But in the Atlantic, the Portuguese could renew their courage from island to island. The first ones the Portuguese encountered on their southwesterly probe into the South Atlantic were the Madeira and Canary islands. They were settled during the fifteenth century and became important ports of call for the Iberian discoverers on their outward voyages to India. Favored by a northeast trade wind, Columbus used the Canary Islands as the final port of call on his way to the New World. Toward the end of the same century, the Cape Verde Islands became an additional haven on the long Atlantic track. On the return voyage, captains could rendezvous at the Azores, islands that were also colonized during the fifteenth century. They were known for quite a while as the Flemish Islands because of the large number of Netherlandic settlers. Farther south, below the equator and at approximately the same latitude as Angola, the island of St. Helena was not discovered until 1588 by Thomas Cavendish.

Being able to use the islands as landfalls depended on wind patterns and currents, and knowledge about them was passed from captain to captain during the three decades it took to establish a viable route to India. The Portuguese were familiar with the waters curving down the western coast of Africa because they had been in pursuit of the gold that was presumed to be on the Guinea coast. They crossed the equator in 1474. Bartholomeu Dias (1455?–1500) probed farther down into the South Atlantic and was the first European to round the southernmost point of Africa. In 1488 he made a landfall in Mossel Bay, 250 miles east of the Cape of Good Hope. Dias was the first European to establish that there was a continuous body of water connecting the Atlantic to the Indian Ocean. He also made the longest voyage (over 6,000 miles from Lisbon to the Cape) a European had ever completed up to that time, and set a precedent for negotiating the Cape of Good Hope by sailing south of it and then northeast in order to have enough searoom to clear that dangerous point. Dias returned to Portugal the same year to transmit his important information. He died in 1500, during the second Portuguese voyage to India by Pedro Cabral, in a tempest off the cape he had named so rightly the "Cape of Storms" (*Cabo Tormentoso*).

Four years after Dias's momentous discovery, Columbus established that the Atlantic, in terms of latitude, was finite. Just before the turn of the century, Vasco da Gama commanded the first successful return voyage to India. Da Gama (1460?–1524) left Lisbon in 1497 with a fleet of two stout, armed *naos,* a caravel, and a storeship. Dias had sailed down the coast of Africa, but da Gama had the courage to set a westerly course into the open ocean. The fleet was out of sight of land for three months, from the Cape Verde Islands down to South Africa, a longer sail than any European navigator had ever done before. This was the first European declaration of nautical independence; sailors had discovered that it was possible to venture into the vast "dead" seas, as unknown seas were called, out of sight of land, and return from the experience alive. After rounding the Cape, da Gama sailed up along the eastern coast of Africa in what were uncharted waters. He found thriving ports like Mozambique and Mombasa, both part of a bustling world of Arab traders who were not overly impressed by the Portuguese. In the coastal town of Malindi—just below the equator—da Gama found an Arab pilot willing to take him across the Indian Ocean to India. The crossing took only twenty-seven days; da Gama dropped anchor in Calicut on the western Malabar coast, on 20 May 1498. He returned home in September 1499 with a full cargo of spices. Da Gama had successfully established that there was indeed a great ocean to the east of the southernmost point of Africa, a body of water that provided a usable maritime route to the Orient. About half a year after da Gama's triumphant return, Portugal sent Pedro Cabral (1467?–1530) down the Tagus for the second voyage to India (1500–1501). Cabral established the first Portuguese and, therefore, the first European *factory* (or trading compound, from the word *fondaco*) in Calicut, and the foundation was thereby laid for the first European colonial empire in the East.

Cabral's settlement was attacked at the instigation of Arab traders. To avenge this, da Gama was sent to Calicut in 1502 with a fleet of twenty-five heavily armed ships. Due to his well-built vessels and superior fire power he was entirely successful in his attack. This marked the beginning of Europe's commercial war with the East, one that lasted for nearly four centuries. To complete the initial encompassing of the world, Ferdinand Magellan (1480?–1521), only two decades after da Gama's first assault on the Indian Ocean, circumnavigated the world, thereby proving that the globe's three great oceans were interconnected and navigable. This new and, most important, finite dimension of the world had been ascertained in less than half a century. It took another century before northern Europe could begin to exploit the achievements of the southern pioneers. By that time the European daredevils could boast with Satan in Job that they went "to and fro in the earth, and [sailed] up and down in it," but there were many who reaped nothing but the wind.

THE center of power began to shift from southern to northern Europe during the sixteenth century, a process completed by the beginning of the seventeenth. For the next three hundred years, northern Europe was the master of the world, a position of prominence that coincides with the advent and development of the modern era. The dominant nations were Holland and England, but, because we are primarily concerned with Dutch colonialism, the discussion will be limited to Holland's contribution to Europe's seaborne expansion and, more specifically, to Dutch colonization of the East Indies.

When, around 1600, the Dutch began seriously to challenge Iberian dominance in Asia, the Portuguese empire had been expanding for over a century. Yet certain qualities that had ensured Portugal's triumph were beginning to vitiate its welfare, a cycle that was repeated for every one of its successors.

Both Portugal and Spain began their conquest of the East and the New World for religious as well as commercial reasons. To be sure, religious conversion was often a mere pretext for seeking gold, but one cannot discount the missionary zeal and crusading mentality that motivated so much of the Iberian effort. While confronting Islam and other "pagan" religions, Portugal's intransigence was expressed by military ruthlessness. A Chinese scholar noted that "Buddha came to China on white elephants [but] Christ was borne on cannonballs."[5] The Portuguese "employed a policy of terror"[6] that earned them implacable enemies as well as Machiavellian allies. Spain pursued a similar course in South America, as did the Dutch in the Spice Islands. At first Holland prevailed in those islands because of a pragmatic civility and religious tolerance that contrasted favorably with its Catholic rivals. But such courtesy would have been merely foolhardy without the support of cannon, and the Dutch had to demonstrate to local potentates that the Portuguese were no longer dictating who could sail the oceans of the world. Only a European nation with equivalent, or superior, naval prowess could hope to best the Portuguese, and Holland proceeded to do so with superior craft, seamanship, and guns.

The Portuguese had overreached themselves. The *naos* had been allowed to expand beyond prudence or sense. Their enormous bulk, incompetent crews, and unprofessional commanders made the *naos da Carreira da India* vulnerable to attack and an easy prey to storms. A third of them never reached port. The practical sense and improvisational talent that had characterized the Portuguese in the fifteenth century had become moribund, sacrificed to cupidity and presumption. The advantage now went to the Dutch, and their efficacious pragmatism was demonstrated by the type and size of ships they built. The first success was the *fluyt, flute* in English and *felibotes* in Spanish, developed toward the end of the sixteenth century and improved over the next three or four decades. The fluyt was the result of a slow and gradual process that recognized and incorporated beneficial additions and modifications which the Dutch had learned from other nations and from their own coastal models of the Baltic trade and inland traffic. The Dutch excelled in designing bulk carriers of medium size. The fluyt was such a ship, a floating symbol of their practical expertise and flair for answering specific needs. It had a very large cargo space, a flat bottom, shallow draught, and full deck. Of its three masts, the foremast carried a single square sail, the mainmast held two square ones, the mizzen mast had a lateen sail, and a spritsail was rigged beneath the bowsprit. Its crew was small because its slow speed, ease in handling, and advanced use of pulleys and blocks reduced the need for physical labor. But a fluyt was defenseless. To answer the need for an effective warship, the Dutch shipbuilders adapted the basic fluyt design of the hull and characteristic stern, and added a larger canvas surface to increase speed. This martial version of the fluyt became known as a pinnace.[7]

During the seventeenth century, Dutch seamanship and ship design was acknowledged throughout Europe as superior. Holland did not appoint commanders on the basis of their social rank but promoted them according to demonstrated expertise. Expert sailors were readily available in Holland because that nation had always depended on the sea for economic prosperity; consequently, there was a long tradition of able men who had been taught their skill by fact, not theory. Because the types of ships the Dutch were building were cheaper to produce, they could dramatically increase the size of their fleets. Hence it was numerical superiority, quality of design, and nautical skill that enabled the Dutch to challenge Portuguese hegemony in the East Indies.

Each [Portuguese galleon] looks like a castle and is furnished with 80 or more bronze guns. The deck is so spacious, that the sailors often play ball. The rooms are numerous, spacious, and with plenty of headroom so that the galleons resemble comfortable houses rather than vessels. The ropes are handled for the greatest part with the aid of capstans. The planking is thick enough to resist gunshots. In short, these vessels would be unequalled if they were not such sluggish movers and could be better manned. The Dutch vessels which are handier to manoeuvre by the wind, overcome the Portuguese galleons very easily. The Dutch can take to flight when the wind is favourable to the enemy, and attack when the enemy is handicapped by low wind. To the Dutch any small wind is enough, while for the Portuguese vessels a half-gale is necessary for movement.[8]

THE European maritime nations directed their main effort to the East because they were bedazzled by the prospect of spices. Although the term *spices* once covered a bewildering variety of goods, by the fifteenth century the word referred to the same aromatic ingredients for seasoning and preserving food with which we are familiar today. The most important ones were pepper, cinnamon, nutmeg, and clove. They were highly prized because, being small in bulk but great in worth, they represented the ideal cargo. The most precious spice was the clove. The clove tree grew only on five small islands that represent the original Moluccas, or Spice Islands, in the eastern archipelago of Indonesia. Nutmeg came from the six islands of the Banda group, south of Ambon. It is therefore not surprising that "India" meant Indonesia to the Portuguese, whose sailing east was based on a desire to reach the Spice Islands and monopolize the production and trade of cloves and nutmeg, an endeavor that was feasible because the area where the spices came from was secluded and relatively small.

The earliest known European map that included Indonesia was Genoese and dates from 1457. The earliest chart based on Portuguese explorations in the archipelago is from 1510, and the earliest Portuguese settlement in Indonesia was on the coast of the Malay Peninsula, known at the time by the resounding Ptolemaic name of "the Golden Chersonese." The Portuguese Sequeira reached Malacca, the main city on the west coast of the peninsula, in 1508. Albuquerque captured the town in 1511 and made it Portugal's base for commercial and military operations in southeast Asia. Malacca remained Portuguese for 130 years. The Dutch captured it in 1641, and Malacca remained a Dutch colony until 1795.

Immediately after his conquest, Albuquerque sent a fleet of three ships, under the command of Antonio de Abreu, to look for the Spice Islands. He found them because several Javanese pilots showed him the way. Abreu stopped at Ambon and the Banda Islands (where he loaded a cargo of nutmeg) and returned to Malacca. One of his ships, commanded by Francesco Serrão, was wrecked in a storm, but the crew managed to reach Ambon and then made their way to Ternate, an island farther north of Ambon. Ternate grew clove trees on a narrow strip of coastal land and Serrão stayed on as an adviser to the sultan. His contact represents the first prolonged European one with the Moluccas.

The first Dutch voyage to the East Indies (1595–97) was intended to challenge the Portuguese monopoly of the spice trade that had lasted for nearly a century. The small Dutch fleet commanded by the incompetent and loutish Cornelis de Houtman never got to the Moluccas, though it did fulfill the sine qua non of maritime expansion by successfully returning to the home port. The fact that such a journey could even be contemplated was due to information gathered by the Moses of Dutch colonialism, Jan Huyghen van Linschoten (1562?–1611).[9] Having left home when barely seventeen, Linschoten worked with his brother in Lisbon and sailed in 1583 to Goa as a clerk in the retinue of the newly appointed primate of the East, the archbishop of Goa. Situated on the western coast of the Indian peninsula, between Bombay to the north and Mangalore to the south, Goa had been conquered by Albuquerque in 1510. It became the capital of *Asia Portuguesa* and when Linschoten lived there Goa was one of the largest cities in the world, with about a quarter million inhabitants.

Linschoten stayed in Goa for five years, from 1583 to 1588, but he never saw the East Indies. On the return voyage to Lisbon he was shipwrecked off the coast of Terceira, and was forced to remain in the Azores for two years, arriving in Lisbon in 1591. Having been away from Holland nearly thirteen years, Linschoten returned in the fall of 1592. Back in his hometown of Enkhuizen he wrote down his experiences, and completed his *Itinerario* quite rapidly. The book was published in three parts between 1595 and 1596 in Amsterdam, but a manuscript version of the first and, at the time, most important part went with Cornelis de Houtman on the first Dutch voyage to the East Indies in 1595. That *Reysgeschrift* was a collection of sailing directions (based on Portuguese rutters) to guide a navigator from Portugal to India. This information had not been available in written form to the maritime nations of northern Europe because it had been jealously guarded by the Portuguese government as a state secret. The complete *Itinerario* included a detailed description of Linschoten's own experiences during his thirteen years of service in Portugal, Spain, and Goa. In addition he furnished geographical descriptions, complete with the fauna and flora, of Africa, Asia, and the East and West Indies, based on various sources in Spanish and Portuguese, including firsthand information from individuals he had met. To complete his presentation, Linschoten reproduced maps and charts, again mostly based on Portuguese sources, and detailed illustrations of life in Goa. The *Itinerario* became something of a best-seller. It was translated into English and German in 1598, into Latin in 1599, and was published in French in 1610.

Linschoten's book was a treasure of practical information about *Asia Portuguesa*. Perhaps its most important advice was the recommendation that Dutch ships steer south after they rounded the Cape of Good Hope, and then sail across the Indian Ocean at about the latitude of the Australian continent, heading for the Sunda Strait between Java and Sumatra. This route purposely avoided Portuguese strongholds in India and Malacca but, more important, it also allowed the Dutch to sail to the East Indies year round. Staying in the southern latitudes of the Indian Ocean they could profit from the southeast trade winds, which they called *passaat* winds (winds that blew regularly all year long). In this fashion they outmaneuvered the Portuguese who were hobbled by their faith in the monsoon latitudes. They believed they could only sail during the northeast or winter monsoon, from October to April, and had to stay in port during the southwest monsoon, from May to September. Because the average duration of a voyage from Lisbon to Goa was between six and eight months, the Portuguese had to time their sailings for the approximately six-month period of the northeast monsoon. The trade-wind route of the Dutch remained the principal one for all shipping until the end of the sailing era. Coen, the fourth governor-general of the Dutch East Indies, exploited the advantage of sailing with the trades by establishing the city of Batavia on the northwest coast of Java in 1619. Later the capital of the Dutch East Indies, Batavia was to windward (the direction from which the wind blows) of Goa and Malacca.[10]

After the inauspicious beginning of Houtman's voyage, the growth of Holland's mercantile empire was swift and energetic. Dutch ports in several provinces sent fleets to the Indies on their own account. In 1598 a fleet under Van Neck and Warwijck reached the Spice Islands and returned with a valuable cargo. Between 1598 and 1600 Olivier van Noort became the first Dutchman to circumnavigate the globe, about twenty years after Drake. In 1600 the Dutch established their first stronghold in the Indies on the island of Ambon. The States General realized that the growing number of these independent companies was dissipating financial and political energy, and in 1602 the independents were persuaded to pool their resources and form the United East India Company, better known by its Dutch acronym VOC. The Company was granted the rights of monopoly to all commerce in Asia, and it brought the different managements into one presiding body, which was called the Assembly of Seventeen. The initial capital was six and a half million guilders.[11]

The Golden Age of Holland's colonial history was the seventeenth century. From the very beginning, the VOC subscribed to the truth of Sir Walter Raleigh's observation: "Whosoever commands the sea, commands the trade, whosoever commands the trade, commands the richesses of the world and consequently the world itself." Less than a year after it had been founded, the VOC owned and operated its own wharves. The number of ships and their tonnage increased dramatically, and the Dutch quickly surpassed the Portuguese and other rival nations. The Company's ships were better built, operated, and armed. The pinnace was developed specifically for the long voyages to Asia. By the end of the eighteenth century the pinnaces were built as large as 1,200 tons. They were both capacious cargo carriers and formidable warships. These maritime workhorses, known in England as East Indiamen, were then called *sphiegelschepen* (retour-ships) by the Dutch. *Spiegel*, which means *mirror* in Dutch, refers to the stern of a ship; during the seventeenth century it became elaborately carved, gilded, and decorated. The Dutch yachts (*jacht*) were also upgraded and enlarged until by the beginning of the seventeenth century they had become something like small warships that were swift and heavily armed. They were used in the Indies for patrols, convoy duty, and, finally, stayed in Indonesian waters as permanent war fleets.

During its existence of two centuries, the VOC outfitted 4,772 outward voyages and 3,359 homeward-bound fleets, a remarkable number. Not surprisingly, Amsterdam became the international center of cartography. The famous firm of mapmakers, Blaeu, was the official supplier to the VOC; its main office was about a two-minute walk from the East India House, the headquarters of the Company. The VOC paid millions to the state in convoy, license, and charter fees, and frequently supplied ships (fully manned and victualed) to the Dutch government during the many wars Holland had to fight, particularly during the seventeenth century.[12]

This great commercial enterprise was at first firm in its intentions of being only a trading company. This is evident from the policy of assigning mercantile ranks to the Company's officials. At Ambon, the vice governor had the title of "senior merchant," as did the military commander. The harbor master and the fiscal both held the rank of "merchant," while the secretary of police, the cashier, and the purveyor were "junior merchants." At sea, a "coopman" or "merchant" was the man who was really in charge, and could disagree with a captain's decisions when a ship's council was convened. In larger ships there was also a "chief merchant" and an "under merchant." In any case, a captain was not the totalitarian ruler on Dutch ships that he was on British ships. Business came first.

These purely commercial motives were soon perverted by the concomitant desire for monopoly. Monopolies may be legislated, but they can only be maintained by force, and the Dutch were soon in a position similar to the Portuguese. To hold on to their monopoly in the spice trade, they had to fight all comers and subject the local population to their will. To uphold their predominance all over Asia and the Orient, they had to settle permanently and continually extend their territories. The result was that by the end of the eighteenth century, the mercantile enterprise ceased to be private, and Holland became a colonial empire. But "the naval aggressiveness and commercial enterprise of the Dutch in the seventeenth century had worked a major revolution in the trade system of the Indian Ocean and adjacent waters. A great volume of trade deserted the northern half of the ocean for the southern. The Red Sea and the Persian Gulf gradually became commercial backwaters. . . . Similarly, the Malacca Strait lost much of its former importance and for a time was almost deserted by European shipping. Trade between south-east Asia and Europe went from Batavia to the Cape south of the equator all the way." One commentator came to the conclusion that the "Dutch were more deeply committed than the French or the English to sea-borne commerce as a means of livelihood." In fact, in both American and Asian waters, Dutch naval and economic strength taught the English and French a "mercantile imperialism which was to influence their policies of colonial settlement and trade for the next two hundred years."[13]

Like Portugal and Spain before, and England and France later, Holland succumbed to the cupidity that accompanies power and dominion. The inevitable historical entropy began to manifest itself toward the end of the seventeenth century, and the decline accelerated during the eighteenth. The drive for innovative changes in ship design and construction subsided into standardization, though the Dutch never succumbed to the mania for size that had hampered the Portuguese and Spanish fleets. Workmanship deteriorated and the technological innovations the Dutch had developed—such as wind-driven sawmills—were adopted by other nations and so no longer represented a competitive edge. The quality of Dutch ships worsened because shipwrights were no longer interested in foreign improvements and techniques, but were satisfied to entrench themselves in stubborn conservatism.

The Dutch repeated other Portuguese mistakes. At one time their renowned captains and fleet commanders had been chosen for their practical excellence demonstrated by actual duty at sea, but during the eighteenth century they were promoted on the basis of seniority. Like the Portuguese, the Dutch overextended themselves all around the globe. Their fleets were no longer sufficient for the large areas their diminishing numbers were asked to control. They often underestimated the enemy, but failures were not acknowledged and often falsified. There were instances when defeats turned into pinchbeck heroics by lying about the strength of the opponent. Dutch artillery, which had been the best in Europe, became smaller and less efficient. And, like the Portuguese, the Dutch began to find it harder and harder to muster superior crews, and were soon forced to resort to pressing into service the human refuse from their own cities and from abroad. Reminiscent of the erstwhile Portuguese government, the voc became extremely cost conscious, to the point of parsimony. One result was a general deterioration of its fleets and strongholds. In the last quarter of the eighteenth century, Stavorinus flatly stated that "the fortifications of Semarang are in the same state as all those of the Company which I had opportunities of seeing, to wit, most deplorably bad."[14]

Abuses were everywhere. One was caused by greed—the same offense that Linschoten had belabored the Portuguese for two centuries earlier. Greed was the reason that ships were overloaded with inordinate cargoes and a plethora of contraband shipped illegally for private profit. Honest enforcement of Company rules barely existed. It seems that everbody could be bought. Unauthorized trade was especially blatant at the Cape; retour-ships were never more overburdened than on the first leg of the return voyage from Batavia to South Africa. The planking of hulls would start buckling under excessive pressure and a ship would become incapable of riding out storms, and founder. It even happened that the decks were so tightly packed with goods that the crew could not man their battle stations in case of enemy attack.[15]

From governors down to common sailors, the greed was pervasive and democratic: all attended to "the main business, of well and speedily lining [their] purse[s]."[16] Unscrupulous skippers skimmed off their victuals to sell them "under the hand" and it was by no means uncommon for great binges in the captain's quarters to exhaust the ship's supply of spirits, even though alcohol was essential for the care of the sick.[17] It made sense that, in time of war, retour-fleets went by the north of Ireland and Scotland to avoid enemy ships in the Gulf of Biscay and the Channel; but even in time of peace the same route was taken because it provided a better opportunity to sell illegal cargo to foreign parties.

Although high officials such as governors could become wealthy from selling lucrative positions to local heads, the lower ranks were treated with great indifference by their employer. Speaking about Ambon, Stavorinus asserted that "how much soever justice may be administered here with severity towards the inferior classes, it is a lamentable circumstance, and as worthy of abhorrence as it is notorious, that the greatest and most shameful crimes of persons of high rank, or of favourites, remain unnoticed and unpunished."[18]

On either side of the equator self-interest reigned supreme. How money was squandered, in spite of the emergency of that time [late eighteenth century], may be illustrated with a few instances. Annually, spices, sugar and so on, to an amount of about 50.000 guilders used to be divided among the Directors and their friends. In The Hague, where meetings were occasionally held, a hotel existed the upkeep of which cost 16.000 guilders per annum. Each of the Boards had a special private yacht at the Director's disposition, an expensive luxury. Extravagances of this sort were even continued when the war with England threatened to bring ruin on the country and actually deprived the Company of all revenues, so that it became entirely dependent on the support of the State.[19]

No more than two decades later, the VOC was dissolved (1800), saddling the Dutch government with a debt of 134 million guilders.

Ironically, the VOC paid notoriously low wages and was a master at reducing its obligations. Among a host of dubious practices, the Company had a policy of stipulating how much money was worth. Normally, a *rijksdaalder* was worth two and a half guilders, but when an employee was paid in the Indies, the Company had reduced its face value to fl. 2.40, at the same time debiting the man's account for fl. 3.20. To make things worse, the VOC paid only half of its payroll in coin, the other half was in goods, and one can be sure that the items were carefully chosen to ensure that they would not diminish the Company's profit margin. It has been calculated that by the end of the seventeenth century, the VOC made a profit of 33½ percent on its minted coin. In the middle of the eighteenth century it was said that the VOC made a "permanent" profit of 140⅓ percent on its payroll in the Indies, while the employees suffered a loss of 39 percent. The Company's employees were charged for the most incredible reasons, charges that were directly subtracted from their pay. Among the more bizarre were the "hospital guastos," fees charged to a seaman for the number of days he was in the hospital at the Cape. When a man died on board, which was the rule rather than the exception, his next of kin were charged for the coffin and the cannon balls that were needed to sink the corpse to the bottom of the sea.[20]

A good example of the VOC's foolish cheeseparing also pertains to its ships, as though the Company had forgotten that these had been the instruments of its glory. Dutch cartography was once justly famous. By the end of the sixteenth century the general English word for a sea atlas was *waggoner*. The word was a corruption of the last name of Lucas Janszoon Waghenaer, who published a collection of sea charts of the North Sea and the Atlantic coasts of France and Spain in 1585 (*Spieghel der Zeevaerdt*). It was published in England as *The Mariner's Mirrour* in 1588 and remained the collection of charts most widely used by British seamen for over a century. But when Stavorinus was sailing for the VOC in the second half of the eighteenth century, the Company's sea charts were inexpedient. Nor could a conscientious captain go elsewhere for better ones because the voc, like the Portuguese, had a policy of secrecy concerning navigational matters. A captain received the requisite charts for his voyage in Amsterdam from the Company's headquarters and had to turn them back in Batavia. Whatever new information he acquired was transmitted to the voc's cartographers who were sworn to strict confidence. But the Company charts that Stavorinus was furnished with had coasts in the wrong place, so that a ship would steer unknowingly toward land instead of bearing away; islands were indicated in the wrong latitudes or not charted at all; bearings were inaccurate; and distances, unreliable. Stavorinus's criticism was perfectly justified.

It is really to be lamented, that so powerful a body as the East-India Company, whose prosperity so much depends upon the safe and prosperous voyages of their ships, should trouble themselves so little with the improvement of navigation in general, and the correction of their charts in particular. I could adduce many instances of their faultiness, both with respect to the Indies, and to the coast of Africa. Other nations pursue this object with indefatigable assiduity, especially the English, whose maps are, in general, infinitely preferable to ours.[21]

But later Stavorinus states an opinion that makes the voc far more ignominious.

This inaccuracy not only renders these charts useless, but likewise extremely dangerous; for instead of being, as they ought, the surest guide and dependence of the navigator, they mislead him, and become his bane. It is not impossible but that this may be purposely left so, and that it is an adopted opinion, that it is better to expose a few ships to the danger of shipwreck, than to correct errors, which might operate to render the navigation to the Spice Islands difficult and hazardous for other nations; for it cannot be pretended, that this notorious faultiness is unknown to the Company, since the commander of every vessel, on his return to Batavia, must deliver a journal of his voyage to a master-mapmaker, or hydrographer, specially appointed for that purpose.[22]

The main excuse for the abuses and venality was the trade monopoly the Dutch so zealously guarded and maintained. The monopoly ensured profits, but it also fostered greed, indolence, and mismanagement. Without the spur of competition and the inducement to excel, the monopoly of the Dutch turned against them. In the case of the spices they had fought so hard for, the Dutch engrossment with their sale produced huge surpluses, a superfluity they could not diminish for fear of lowering the price on the world market. Either the Company had superabundant stocks, sufficient to supply European demands for many years, or its avaricious policy of destroying the spice trees in order to prevent clandestine sales left it with scant supplies when natural disasters destroyed the few selected spots where the cloves and nutmegs were permitted to grow. There is perhaps no better image to illustrate that overreaching can cheat the very fortune that impelled it than the picture of the Dutch sacrificing their precious supplies of spices in order to maintain their trade dominion. A man was witness in the Spice Islands to a bonfire of nutmegs; each of the three heaps that were burned was "more than an ordinary church could hold." And back in Holland quantities of cloves, nutmegs, and cinnamon were burned on a small island in the province of Zeeland in amounts so large that the aroma seasoned the air for miles around.[23]

THE sea had been the means to reach the gold of conquest—which perforce became tired and counterfeit—yet the rich ultramarine was for many a most bitter blue. The odds for survival were very poor for the men who got Portugal, Spain, Holland, and England the riches that made them great nations. The hazards of a voyage under sail in the seventeenth or eighteenth century were not much better than they had been in the fifteenth.

In the fifteenth century the navigator had the use of an astrolabe and a quadrant (to measure the altitude of the sun and stars), though both were almost useless on a ship's heaving deck. In the sixteenth century, sighting a heavenly body became somewhat easier with the cross-staff, followed by its refinement, the back-staff, for sun sights. The sextant was not introduced until late in the eighteenth century. Even then, as great a sailor as Captain Cook made enormous errors in his position. The reason was that throughout these centuries, navigators had no way of calculating their longitude, i.e., their position in terms of east and west. Not until the chronometer was introduced in the nineteenth century was any kind of accuracy possible. Even latitude, that is, a ship's position north or south of the equator, was uncertain because its calculation depended on the clarity of the weather. Charts improved over the years, but Stavorinus's comments indicate that they left a lot to be desired. Until the nineteenth century, dead reckoning remained the primary means of navigation. Dutch captains called it "a blind and stupid pilot" because they were never certain of their course and distance. And dead reckoning depends for its calculations on the distances logged, and courses steered, since the last fixed position, with due allowance for currents, tidal systems, and leeway. And it was precisely those items that made dead reckoning such a hazard. Stavorinus provides a good example of this when he explains why the nagivation from Java eastward to Ambon was so dangerous.

The second cause of the danger and difficulty of the eastern navigation, are the currents, which set with so much violence between the islands and along the coasts of this archipelago, that if I had not experienced it myself, I should scarcely credit the account: in addition to this, they have no regular course, and sometimes run contrary to the wind, and at uncertain times. Add to these, as a third cause, the calms which prevail so much in these climates, and the dangers which surround navigators in this passage will be very manifest; for vessels are driven, in dead calm weather, by the violent currents upon unknown shoals and rocks, so that the most experienced seaman is unable, in such cases, to save the ship and cargo entrusted to him.[24]

Hence we may assume that, relatively speaking, the number of ships that were lost at sea did not diminish dramatically with the improvement of navigational equipment.

A sailing ship depends on the weather and the water for its progress, and a captain could be frustrated by the elements for a very long time and advance only a small distance. Nor was this difficulty restricted to an earlier age of sail. It took Stavorinus, in June 1768, eleven days just to get clear of the coast of Zeeland, forty days (from June 25 to August 4) to get through the Channel, and altogether five months to reach the Cape. It took him three days of tacking (i.e., working a vessel to windward by alternating course from starbord to port, while lowering and hoisting various sails) to round the Cape, and three days merely to enter the harbor of Macassar, advancing on one of those days no more than half a league. Bontekoe, after arriving at the equator, was prevented for three weeks from crossing it due to thunderstorms, squalls, and winds that kept changing direction.[25]

The actual time spent at sea was very long, and it did not get much less over the years. In 1620 it took Bontekoe five months to reach the Cape, and Stavorinus needed the same time a century and a half later. When Stavorinus left Holland in 1768, his ship was, "as usual," fitted out for a voyage of nine months. Yet at the end of the seventeenth century, the "legal" duration of a voyage to the Indies, according to an optimistic directive from the voc, was seven and a half months. In 1646 the Dutch East Indiaman *Nieu Delf* left Holland on 9 May, and did not arrive in Batavia until 12 July 1647, after a voyage of more than a year. The Indiamen from England fared little better; by 1800 it could take them up to nine months to make the journey from London to Calcutta.

The death rate of VOC personnel was very high: of every three people who went to the Indies, the likelihood was that only one would return to Holland. A crew's chances of survival on board ship were worse. Of the *Nieu Delf*'s crew of 322 men, only 152 were alive when the ship anchored in Batavia. The Dutch ship *Asia* was held "under the equinoctial line," like Bontekoe's, for nine days. During that short time, 62 people died. When Cornelis de Houtman left Holland for the first Dutch voyage to the Indies, he commanded altogether a crew of 249 men. When he returned, only 89 men were left, and 7 or 8 more died shortly thereafter. On Bontekoe's ill-fated journey, only 56 men from a crew of 206 survived. Chances did not greatly improve. When the British naval hero Anson returned home in 1744 (having left in 1740), 1,300 men had died from disease and only 4 from combat wounds. Modern research has estimated that the average rate of death on Portuguese ships during the sixteenth century was 50 percent of crew and passengers.[26]

As was true of colonial soldiers as well, most seamen died from disease. The most common illness was scurvy, a dread and usually fatal ailment that killed seamen from the sixteenth to the nineteenth century. Scurvy is caused by a severe lack of vitamin C, and is easily remedied by fresh fruit and vegetables, but these two dietary items were hard to find on board ships, except for short periods of time. Although the symptoms varied, most sources agree that the disease first manifested itself by lethargy, weariness, swelling limbs, swollen gums, and loss of teeth. Thereafter, men died from any number of symptoms which were due either to scurvy itself or to other infections which were easily contracted because of the patient's severe debility.

In addition to scurvy, the crew was also susceptible to what were called "raging feavers," afflictions that appeared to affect the brain, with the result that some men tried to commit suicide or jump overboard. There was also a very contagious "putrid feaver," that ravaged Stavorinus's crew on his voyage to the Indies in 1774.

The first symptoms of the fever, and which occurred some days before it actually came on, were a violent headache and pains in the stomach, debility, and loss of appetite. Some died during the first fit of the fever; others two or three days afterwards. A strong putrid smell was perceived even before they died, and many of the bodies emitted so dreadful a stench, in half an hour after the breath had left them, that they were forced to be instantaneously committed to the deep. Immediately after their death, and, in some cases, even before it, the bodies were blotched with black and blueish spots, especially upon the neck and breast, which indicated an entire corruption of the whole system.[27]

Stavorinus lost 42 men to this disease and scurvy in one month, and had 108 "confined by sickness." He also mentions other "distempers" such as "bilious fevers and spasmodic colics."[28]

When ships were unable to get the right wind to leave Holland's shores, they could be windbound for weeks or months. In that case it was the wet, cold weather, the fog and mists, that rendered the sailors unfit because they had no way to warm themselves or dry out their single change of clothing. Between the two tropics, heat would overwhelm a becalmed ship, and when no rain fell the men were tortured by thirst. Fresh water was always in short supply. Whatever amount had been stowed at the beginning of a voyage soon became scummy and putrid, and there are numerous accounts of men straining the drinking water between their teeth to keep from swallowing the worms and other vermin that were thriving in it. Even under the best of circumstances, the crew got no more than two pints per day, despite the brutally hard work they had to perform and the heavily salted food, which, according to one source, required an ostrich's stomach to digest.[29] When water supplies ran low and the ration was reduced to a pint, a cup, or even less, people would suck on lead bullets to get some saliva or drink their own urine, something that Bontekoe's crew was forced to do. It is indicative of the quality of the water that desperately ill men were given wine or beer to drink.

The quality of vittles was notorious too. Most perishable food, such as meat and fish, was salted, and other items, including peas and beans, were dried. There were no fresh vegetables, except for onions, though toward the end of the eighteenth century Dutch ships were supplied with sauerkraut (*zuurkool* in Dutch) and pickles. It was generally conceded that the food, even at the beginning of a journey, was so difficult to digest that normal people could not stomach it. To make things worse, the quality was often the worst imaginable because unscrupulous victualers would outfit a ship with provisions of the lowest grade, for instance, peas and beans that became *harder* when they were cooked, or meat that had been salted or pickled for years. Food stowed away in the ship's hold deteriorated rapidly. The holds were damp, dank, stinking, and very hot, offering ideal conditions for spoiling even the best of stores. The voc, as well as responsible captains such as Bontekoe and Stavorinus, tried its best to alleviate such conditions. As early as the end of the seventeenth century, the Company possessed the knowledge that salt water could be distilled and turned into fresh water. In fact, it tasted better than what was taken on board while still in harbor. But the crews were prejudiced against it and refused to use the distilling kettles.[30]

Every ship had quantities of wine, beer, and brandy-wine on board, spirits that were distributed for medicinal purposes. Sometimes beer and wine were heated. The two mixed could be served for breakfast as *bieren-broodspap* or "sugar-sops." Responsible captains tried to get fruit on board as often as possible, particularly lemons which they knew empirically to be a remedy for scurvy. Easier to keep were dried prunes. In general, victuals were of bad quality and in short supply, hence it is not surprising that a captain would try to get his crew fresh food whenever he could. One will read time and again of landfalls on islands to obtain fresh supplies and water. Another welcome addition to the diet was fish caught at sea.

Conditions were only aggravated by the total absence of personal hygiene. Men relieved themselves between decks, seldom washed (due to the lack of water), and were covered with vermin. Lice were known to have bitten holes in a man's body, and they could be so numerous that they had to be brushed off. The absence of hygiene was particularly lethal for the patients on the inevitable sick list. There were no doctors on board during the sixteenth and seventeenth centuries, only barbers or "surgeons." The latter were, more often than not, useless; Stavorinus notes "that after the surgeon fell ill, the number [of sick] decreased from day to day." The surgeon's favorite cure was bleeding. One ship's surgeon bled 400 patients in a single day. A wound in any of the limbs would cause gangrene; to prevent that, the limb was as quickly as possible amputated with a saw and the remaining stump was cauterized with boiling tar. The only anesthetic was liquor. It seems that in most cases it was not the perspicacity of the surgeon, but that of the captain, that prevented more casualties. Stavorinus kept his "sick-ward" clean and neat and aired.

I allowed no water to be made use of in cleaning out [the sick-ward], that the moisture might not contribute to encrease the contagion; and on the other hand, daily fumigations were made with juniper-berries and frankincense, likewise by burning of gunpowder, and pouring of vinegar on red-hot bullets. The cribs of the sick were sprinkled with vinegar, and the patients were directed to wash their hands and faces, and rinse their mouths with it, every morning. Their victuals consisted, one day, in mutton-broth, with lemonjuice [the ship had just left the Cape after a lay-over of several weeks]; the next, in rice-porridge; and the third, in bread and beer, with wine; and in the morning they had grouts, with Spanish wine.[31]

One should remember that measures such as these were practiced only by conscientious captains who were also strict and firm enough to carry them through. Similar solicitude and discipline were shown by Cook, with remarkably beneficial results, and by the great English captain John Hawkins, who, during the sixteenth century, fought hard for better sanitary conditions, contending that they were the secret of good crews and fleets. But not all captains felt concern or had the strength of character to maintain the necessary discipline among a recalcitrant and hostile crew.

After the Dutch fleets were regularly sailing between Holland and the Indies, the voc was forced to muster crews from the worst elements of society because they could no longer find able-bodied seamen who would work under conditions such as the ones I have described. Men were rounded up by recruiters called "soul merchants" (*zielenverkopers*) who would promise anything to anyone as long as they were able to enlist the man. Candidates were told to bring hammers with them because, once in the Indies, that was all they would need to chip the plentiful diamonds off almost any rock. As soon as a man had been accepted by the voc and been paid his advance, he would settle with the soul merchant who charged him for the food and shelter and equipment he had provided. Most of these charges were bogus and the prospective seaman was in debt to his benefactor for months or even years. But the soul merchant ran a risk as well. The odds that a man would live long enough to pay back his supposed debt were not very favorable. For instance, if a ship went down, the voc stopped paying all wages from the day the disaster happened. To insure that he got some cash at least, the soul merchant sold his souls to *ceelkopers* or "note buyers." These people, similar to insurance brokers, bought the sailors' contracts from the soul merchants for far less than they were nominally worth, and improved their own chances for profit by buying up as many souls as they could and distributing them among any number of departing ships.[32]

Taking everything into consideration, one can well imagine that it was difficult to get anyone to sign up. The result was that most crews had a large number of foreigners who generally came from the worst element of society. Many were criminals with little to lose and no sea experience whatsoever, men who were generally loathe to follow orders. Mutiny, either by entire crews or by single individuals, was far from uncommon. Fights, murder, drunkenness, and stealing were frequent. Order could only be maintained with the very real threat of brutal punishment. Fines were charged for swearing or drunkenness. Smoking a pipe, except before the main mast and with the consent of the captain, or carrying any kind of burning object without permission, was punished by being put in irons on reduced rations. Bontekoe's experience demonstrates how dangerous open fire could be. If a crew member stabbed another man, the culprit's right hand was fastened to the main mast with his own knife. After it was deemed he had stood long enough, he was allowed to free himself by pulling the right hand away from the mast while the knife was still in it.

A captain was authorized to punish insubordination and acts of mutiny by making the offender "walk the main yard" (*van de ra lopen*) also known as "to dance the main yard" (*van de ra dansen*). Most of the guilty party's clothes were removed, his hands and feet were tied and fastened to a rope that went through a pulley on the main yard. The man was thrown overboard, then hoisted up to the outer end (or yardarm) of the main yard and suddenly dropped. The lead weights at his feet would pull him down under and he would be hoisted up again in order to be ducked once more. After this had been done three times, the man was brought back on deck and was "booted" (*gelaarsd*). This meant he was lashed on his bare back with a thick rope or *dagge* between 200 and 500 times. If anyone physically assaulted a superior he was keelhauled. A rope, passing under the ship, was rigged from one yardarm of the main yard to the other. The man was weighed down, hoisted up to one yardarm, dropped into the sea, then hauled up, slowly at first so he could clear the keel, then faster, the entire width of the ship, and up to the other yardarm. This was done three times. A large sponge or rag was tied to one of his upper arms for him to bite on when under water, in order to keep him from swallowing large amounts of seawater, and his ears were stuffed with wool to prevent bleeding. If the weights were too light, a man was liable to smash his head against the bottom of the ship. *Keelhauling* is a Dutch word,[33] and the practice is said to have been invented by the Dutch. They did not officially discontinue the punishment until 1854. Other punishments for severe offenses were hanging or leaving a man on a deserted island. If someone had killed a fellow crew member he was tied to the corpse and tossed overboard. Being thrown overboard was also the punishment for the "brute sin" (*stomme zonde*) of homosexuality.

There were many varieties of punishments for a host of offenses, and their duration and severity were entirely up to the captain. Bontekoe seems to have been unusually kind and tractable, whereas Stavorinus adhered to the strictures mentioned. But abuses were common. One British captain in the eighteenth century hanged a young midshipman "because of muttering with a mutinous gleam in his eye." On the other hand, there were many celebrated cases of mutiny, when the crew murdered the officers without mercy or discrimination.[34]

Just as the principal hull design and the rigging of large ships did not change drastically after 1600, neither did the lot of seamen change much over three centuries. Excepting individual differences and with due regard for national peculiarities, the condition of the ships and the crews that manned them were generally the same for all navies. Anyone familiar with Melville's or Dana's nineteenth-century accounts knows that conditions in the U.S. Navy, or merchant marine, were hardly better. Most of the time one would have to agree with Linschoten who, toward the end of the sixteenth century, wrote "that onely by the grace and special favor of God, the Indian ships do performe their voiages, yet with great miserie, paine and labour, losse and hinderance."

PROMOTING Europe's overseas empires, be it manning fleets or finding colonizers, required propaganda. This need was especially felt by the Dutch and the English. In an earlier age, the impetus for Europe's seaborne explorations was already to a large extent inspired by literary works. "The popularity of travel books, and of references to remote lands in plays and allegories, was a striking feature of the literary life of the sixteenth century, and contributed greatly to the steady growth of interest and in exploration and discovery."[35] This crucial connection between the printed word and the manipulation of a nation's consciousness was recognized in England much earlier than in Holland. Richard Hakluyt (1552–1616) published what has been called "the very papers of empire" with *The Principall Navigations, Voiages, Traffiques and Discoveries of the English Nation (1582–1600)*. There is no doubt that "Hakluyt's *Voyages* are propaganda: they praise England, promote colonization, rally support for the growing naval forces, hail the achievements of the great captains, and at the same time reveal the weaknesses of England's great enemy, Spain."[36] That this national tuition was no secret at the time is evident from the poem "To the Virginian Voyage" by Michael Drayton (1563–1631); it ends with the stanza:

> The Voyage attend,
> Industrious *Hackluit,*
> Whose Reading shall inflame
> Men to seeke Fame,
> And much commend
> To after-Times thy Wit.

Such concerted effort was neither contemplated nor performed across the Channel. In Holland interest was stimulated by separate publications of experiences remembered and written down by various individuals.

They were printed for profit and, especially in the beginning, were offered to the public for both practical reasons and for the delectation of prospective readers. Frederik de Houtman summed up this dual benefit when he recommended his Malay dictionary and phrase book (published in 1603, the first of its kind in Europe) for use to "those who visit the Lands of the East-Indies," but he also voiced the hope that it would be "no less delightfull to all those who are curious Lovers of strangeness."

The flood of travel literature that was published in the seventeenth century began with the publication of Jan Huyghen van Linschoten's *Itinerario* in 1596. Linschoten's tone was one of excitement and curiosity; he stated that he left home at seventeen because he wanted to know "what the world had in it." Linschoten thought his literary efforts uncouth and unworthy and begged his readers' pardon for his "small skill, labor and uninstructed manner of writing." Linschoten and, later, Bontekoe claimed that they had to be persuaded to publish their work. In his foreword to the reader Bontekoe "begs to be excused" because "in the description of this his journey he had an eye more on truth than on elegance of saying." Both men emphasized the veracity of their narratives, to distinguish their work from such fanciful accounts as the one by the spurious Sir John Mandeville. Linschoten protested his lack of wit and warned his readers not to look in his book for "singular gallantries" because they would only find "natural and true descriptions." Bontekoe, too, is said not to have produced a description based on "hear-say (even as people say), no, but [it] comes from his own Experience, relating what wonders God shewed the author himself, like unto those of the ones who were with him."

Linschoten's *Itinerario* sold well, a success that was true of a considerable number of books that were published after his. The Dutch public's appetite was ravenous. During the seventeenth century, 461 books of travel were published, including translations and reprints. The greatest demand was for descriptions of journeys around the world or to the Indies; they represent 75 percent of the books printed. Eighty percent of those books were printed in Amsterdam, which indicates the importance Holland's capital had as both a commercial and an intellectual center. Of all those hundreds of books, Bontekoe's little volume—*Journalen van de Gedenckwaerdige Reijsen van Willem Ijsbrantsz. Bontekoe 1618–1625* (Journal or the memorable description of the East-Indian journey of Willem Ysbrantsz. Bontekoe of Hoorn)—was the most popular. It was reprinted thirty-eight times in the seventeenth century, and seventy times by 1800. It was translated into French, German, and English, and was even translated into Javanese and printed in Batavia in 1873 (second printing in 1883), and into Sundanese (printed in 1874).

The style of the Dutch accounts may at times not be as impressive as that of Hakluyt's narratives. Holland did not have refined courtiers like Raleigh. But in general, the tenor of the prose of both Dutch and British seamen is similar. These early authors allowed their extraordinary experiences to energize their narratives without having to resort to rhetoric. In effect this meant that realism was romance, that what was ordinary under these circumstances would elsewhere be received as remarkable, that fact could be like fiction, that sense could be discerning as well as sensual.

Honest Bontekoe was one of those brave mariners who faced the dangers of water, air, fire, and land, and lived to write about it. We know very little about his life. His full name, Willem Ysbrantsz. Bontekoe, indicates that he was the son of Ysbrants, who had been a seaman himself; the strange surname was added later. *Bontekoe* can be translated, in a contemporary spelling, as "Pyed Cow." The name derived from a depiction of such a multicolored ruminant on a stone bricked into the frontispiece of the house where the family lived.

Bontekoe was born in 1587 in Hoorn, once an important port in the province of Northern Holland. Hence he was born in the same year and in the same town as Jan Pietersz. Coen (1587–1629), perhaps the most famous, or infamous, governor-general of the Dutch East Indies. When Coen founded Batavia, the colonial capital, on the ruins of the small Javanese town of Jacatra in 1619, he wanted to call it New Hoorn, after his birthplace. And on his first journey to Java in 1607 with the rank of "junior merchant," he sailed on the ship *Nieu-Hoorn* (*New Hoorn*), and returned on it to Holland in 1611. This was the same ship that Bontekoe commanded on his first and fateful journey to the Indies. It left the Dutch island of Texel three days after Christmas in 1618, and exploded in November 1619 near Madagascar in the Indian Ocean. Bontekoe was only thirty-one when he was given command of the ship, while Coen, also at thirty-one, became the fourth governor-general of the Indies for his first term (from 1618 to 1623); his second term was from 1627 until his death in 1629. The two men were very different in temperament and character. Coen was decisive, bold, and ruthless. He had a vision of a Dutch-Asiatic trading empire that went far beyond what the VOC directors had in mind, and he applied himself to the realization of his dream with aggressive determination that left no room for compromise. Bontekoe, on the other hand, though an intrepid seaman, appears to have been rather mild-mannered and congenial, a relative rarity among seventeenth-century masters. It is clear from his journal that he sometimes persuaded his men with "sweet words" (*soete woorden*) and his crew often addressed him as "dear Skipper" (*lieve schipper*). It is true, however, that after his four years of combat duty off the coast of China, he became markedly tougher and sterner. He put a first mate in irons because he had smoked his pipe without permission—perhaps the memory of being blown up due to carelessness with fire had made him less sanguine—and he did the same to a minister who had quarreled with an assistant. Bontekoe's exchange with his fellow townsman and superior, Coen, at the end of his journey, is a model of understatement, but it leaves one wanting to know more about the conversation between these two unusual servants of the voc.

Bontekoe comes across as an endearing, honest, utterly unsophisticated man, without so much as a hint of self-importance. He was devoutly religious in a simple, straightforward fashion that nowhere betrays hypocrisy or unctuousness. I am sure that it is due to both his character and his style that his affecting tale became so famous. It is a style without pretensions, sober, direct, and with a seemingly natural inclination for revealing detail. Like so many other travel descriptions from that era, Bontekoe's prose has references to reality that have not been compromised by reflection or embellishment. In many ways, the style of these sixteenth- and seventeenth-century writers is remarkably similar to the "minimalist" style of recent American fiction, though the latter is arrived at with deliberate artifice.

Bontekoe's characteristic "voice" is important here because the events he experienced were not uncommon at the time, after all, and we have seen that hardship was the norm on board seventeenth-century sailing ships. But it is the manner in which he faced the extremity of danger, Hemingway's "grace under pressure," that makes the difference, and Bontekoe seems to have been equal to the task. For it should be remembered that his efforts were successful and that he did manage to reach the safe haven of Batavia despite the most incredible impediments. Because of the popularity of his tale, his name became part of general Dutch vocabulary; a *reis van Bontekoe* or a "Bontekoe journey" refers to a trip or enterprise that encounters uncommon bad luck and obstacles. The phrase has no connotation of failure; on the contrary, it implies that one surmounted the difficulties.

After he had survived his ordeal with the *Nieu-Hoorn,* Bontekoe took part in Coen's campaign to capture Macao. The attempt failed, but Coen had also ordered that the Dutch fleet terrorize the Chinese coast in order to force that nation to trade with the Dutch. "The 18 [August 1622] we were commanded with our eight sails, three ships and five yachts, to go to the river Chincheo [i.e., Ching-Cheu] and the coast of China, to see if we could move her to trade through fear of our enmity and violence." The disapproving and reluctant Bontekoe commanded a ship during this ignominious expedition between 1622 and 1625. He returned to Holland in 1625. For some time he lived quietly in Hoorn as a retired skipper, but he became famous in 1646 after his journal had been printed by Jan Jansz. Deutel in Hoorn. Within the same year, the authorized version was reprinted once, and three pirated editions also appeared. We know nothing about Bontekoe's life at this point, nor when he died or where he was buried. But posterity was less negligent than his own times, and he has been remembered ever since.

THE following translation represents just over half of the authoritative text established by G. J. Hoogewerff, published in 1952 (see n. 25). It describes the accident, the shipwreck, and the unfortunate journey to Batavia, including Coen's peremptory dismissal of so much suffering. I have kept Bontekoe's peculiarities such as his repetitions, odd capitalization, omission of personal pronouns, and other unorthodox usage. His style seems to be a mixture of biblical prose (particularly that of the Old Testament) and the manner of writing that is characteristic of a captain's logbook. Whenever I thought it necessary to provide supplementary words to clarify the sense, I have used square brackets; material in parentheses is Bontekoe's. The singular spellings of various nouns and terms were taken either from Sewel's *New Dictionary English and Dutch,* published in Amsterdam in 1691, or from the *Oxford English Dictionary.* I followed the same principles as in my translations of Rumphius (published in this series with the title *The Poison Tree*) and of Valentijn (in the present volume), in order to preserve the particular flavor of the original and its idiosyncratic but attractive style. Hence the reader will find words that were deliberately spelled according to seventeenth-century usage; I have avoided using words that were not current prior to 1700.

The 9th day that we had lain there [the island Sancte Maria, off Madagascar, now called Ile Ste. Marie], our people, as said, being fresh and healthy, we put our ship on the careen as much as we could, and cleaned the bottom with hard brushes and scrub brooms, and set sail; we ran South, to the latitude of 33 degrees, then turned East-ward again and set our course for the Strait of Sunda. And having come to the latitude of five and a half degrees, being the latitude of the aforesaid Strait of Sunda, being the 19. day of November 1619, so it happened that by the pumping of the brandy-wine the brand got into the brandy-wine;[37] because the steward's mate went in the after-noon (as was his wont) with his little vat into the hold, and would pump it full, so he could give out the next day morning to each fellow his half a quartern.[38] He took a candle along and jabbed the spike of the candlestick[39] in the bottom of the vat that lay one row higher than the vat he was pumping from. Having pumped his little vat well and full, he would be getting out the candlestick, that had the candle on it, and insomuch he had pushed it in rather well, he pulled it out with some force. There was a snaste[40] on the candle; that fell off and fell exactly in the bung of the vat he had pumped from. This caused the brandy-wine to catch on fire and it blew up immediately, and even out of the vat; the bottom burst out of the vat and the burning brandy-wine ran down below in the ship, where there were stone-coals.[41] Soon there were calls of: "fire! fire!" I was lying at the time on the upper deck and looked down through the iron grates. Hearing that noise I walked immediately down into the hold. Getting there saw no fire; asked: "where is the fire?" They said: "Skipper look there, in that vat." I stuck my arm in the vat and could feel no fire.

The steward's mate, who caused the fire, was from Hoorn, and was named Keelemeyn. He'd had two wooden cans with water with him; those he'd poured on it, whereby it seemed that the fire was out. But I called for water from up on deck, the which came immediately in leather buckets, and poured so long that we saw no more mention of fire. Got out of the hold; but about a half hour thereafter they began to call out again: "fire! fire!" whereby we all were much frightened. Went to the hold and saw that the fire had leapt up from below, because the vats were stacked three and four high, and the fire had gotten through the brandy-wine down into the stone-coals; went back to work again with leather buckets and poured so much water that it was to be marvelled at. But once again a new danger, because by throwing the water on the stone-coals it gave off such stinking, sulphury smoke, that one would stifle and choke in the hold from the oppression. I was mostly in the hold to cause some order and sometimes let other men come down into the hold for a change. I supposed that many already remained lying in the hold from choking, who could not find the hatches; I myself was often almost lost, sometimes put my head on the vats to get some air, turning my face to the hatch; finally walked out of there, went to the merchant Heyn Rol and said: "mate, it will be best that we throw the gun-powder overboard"; but the merchant Heyn Rol who could not resolve thereto, gave for an answer: "if we throw the powder overboard, we may put out the fire, and if thereafter we come to a fight with our enemy and we are then taken (having no powder), how are we then going to answer for it?"

The fire would not abate, and no one could endure it any longer in the hold because of the stinking smoke (as was told). We then chopped holes in the lower deck and poured mightily with water through them and through the hatches; but it was to no avail. We had put our long boat out a good three weeks ago and were towing it, and the shallop,[42] that was forward on the upper deck had also been put out because it was in our way while handling the water; and since there was great fright in the ship, as one can well imagine (for the fire and the water was before our eyes, and no deliverance from anyone on earth, because we were alone without seeing any land, ship, or ships), therefore much folk went over the side and crept stealthily with their heads below the chains,[43] so one would not see them and then let themselves drop into the water and so swam to the shallop and the longboat, climbed in them and hid themselves under the benches and decks till the time that they thought they had enough people in them.

The merchant, Heyn Rol, came by chance upon the gallery;[44] was amazed that there was so much folk in the longboat and shallop. The men called out to Heyn Rol and said that they wanted to cast off, and if he wanted to come along he could lower himself by means of the fall-rope.[45] Heyn Rol had himself persuaded and climbed down the fall-rope, and so came to be with them in the longboat. Heyn Rol, he said: "Men, let us wait until the skipper comes," but he had no command there, since when they had Heyn Rol inside, they cut the ropes and rowed away from the ship. And since I was busy with the men to order things so we could put out the fire, where possible, others from the crew came up to me and said with great astonishment: "Oh dear skipper, some advice! What shall we do? The shallop and the longboat are not with the ship and are rowing away!" I said to them: "If the shallop and the longboat are gone, then they left for such a reason that they won't come back." Then I walked hurriedly topside and saw that they were rowing away. The ship's sails were at that time gathered into the mast; the main sail was furled. I quickly called out to the men: "Pull down the sails! We will see if we can overtake them and run them down. May the this and that take them!" We made the sails ready and sailed at them. Coming upon them, at about three shiplengths they rowed across our bow, for they wanted not to be with us, but rowed against the wind, away from the ship. I then said: "Men, as you can see, our only succor (next to God) is with us ourselves. Let all lend a hand now (as much as you can) to put out the fire, and go immediately to the powder-room and throw the powder overboard, that the fire won't be getting into the powder." The which was done.

I went directly over the side with all the carpenters, with hollow chissels and augers to bore holes in the ship, with the design to let into the ship about a fadom and a half,[46] and so to put out the fire from below; but we could not get through the ship because there was so much iron work in the way. In sum, the need that was in the ship, I cannot well express; the crying and lamenting was great beyond measure. Then we bravely fell to pouring water again, whereby it seemed that the fire grew less, but a little time later the fire got into the oil; then all hope was lost: because the more water we poured the greater the fire seemed to become, that is how fast the fire ran through the oil. Because of this there came about such howling, lamenting and crying in the ship, that a man's hair would stand on end; yea, the closeness and oppression were so great that clammy sweat poured down people; yet were still busy with tossing water and throwing gunpowder overboard until the very end when the fire got into the powder. We had about 60 half vats of powder overboard, but still had about 300 within, wherewith we blew up, with all hands. The ship burst into a hundred thousand pieces; we were still 119 persons there when the ship blew.

When it happened I was standing near the mainsheet[47] topside and about 60 persons were standing right in front of the main mast where they were passing each other the [buckets of] water; and those were all together snatched away and smashed into a hodgepodge[48] that one did not know where there was a piece of them, as was true of all the others. And I, Willem Ysbrantsz. Bontekoe, skipper at the time, flew up in the air along with them; knowing nothing else but that I must die with them. I reached out my hands and arms to Heaven and called out: "There I go, o Lord! have mercy on this poor sinner!" And thought to have my end there; howbeit, I had all my wits while being blown up, and perceived a lightness in my heart that was still mixed with some jollity, so it seemed, and so came back down into the water, amidst the pieces and planks of the ship that was entirely shivered to pieces. Lying in the water, I found such new courage as if I had been a new man. Looking around, I beheld the main mast on one side of me and the fore-mast on the other; I climbed on the main mast and layed down on it and looked at what had been wrought, and said: "O God! how this fair ship has perished, like Sodom and Gomorrah."

And so lying there I saw not a living soul, where-ever I looked; and while I thus laid there thinking, so comes there a Young man bubbling up next to me, flinging with hands and feet, and got unto the knop of the prow[49] (that had floated up again) saying: "I am finished." I then looked around and said: "O God! is there somebody still alive?" This Young man was called Harmen van Kniphuysen, from Eyder.[50] I saw a yard float by the Young man, and since the main mast (whereon I was lying) was turning about again and again, so that I could not well remain on it, I said to him: "push that yard over to me, I will lie on it and haul me like that over to you, so we can sit together," the which he did, and so I came over to him. That otherwise I would not have been able to have gotten to him, was because I had been so sorely smitten when I was blown up. My back was much damaged, had also two holes in my head. And it got so bad that I thought: "o Lord! a little more and I'm dead." Yea, it seemed I was nearly dead.[51] We sat there next to each other, each with our arms around a timber. Stood up and looked out for the shallop and the longboat; finally perceived them, but [they] were so far away that we could hardly see if the prow or stem was toward us. The sun was on the water in order to go down. Then [I] said to my mate: "Harmen, it seems that our hope is lost here, because it is late, the sun is setting, the shallop and longboat are so far away that you can hardly see them; the ship is in pieces, and we can't take it much longer here (on the wreck); let us therefore pray to almighty God for a goodly deliverance." We did so and prayed God very earnestly to deliver us; the which we were; for when we looked up again, the shallop and the longboat were close to us, the which made us very glad. I called out immediately: "Save the skipper! save the skipper!" And they, hearing it, were very glad, and shouted: "The skipper is still alive, the skipper is still alive!" and thereupon rowed close to the wreck and stayed there like that with the shallop and longboat; dared not to come to us whereas they feared that a piece of the wreck would thrust through the shallop or the longboat.

The Young man, Harmen van Kniphuysen, had still enough spirit to leave the wreck and swim to the boat. He had sustained little injury when we were blown up, but I called out: "Wouldst yee have me, you have to get me, for I've been so smitten that I cannot swim." Then the trumpeter jumped out of the longboat, with a lead line (that they still had) and brought the end over to me. I fastened it around my waist and they hauled me to the boat, and thus came (the Lord be praised!) in the boat. Being in the longboat [I] came aft, with Heyn Rol, Willem van Galen and the under-steersman, named Meyndert Krijnsz. of Hoorn, who all marvelled greatly that I was still alive. [Earlier] I had a little Cabin[52] made in the back of the boat, that could hold a couple of men, athwart the boat; I crawled in it and thought: I should consider something; for I guessed not to live for long, because of the blow on my back and the two holes in my head; but yet I said to Heyn Rol and the others: "Stay tonight near the wreck; tomorrow, when it's day, we'll salvage some victuals, and possibly find a compass to find the land." For there was in the shallop and longboat neither compass, chart, nor cross-staff, nor none or little food and nothing to drink; with such haste had they sailed from the ship. [They] said too, that the upper-steersman, Jan Piet of Hoorn, had taken the compasses from the bitakle;[53] seemed he already was afeared that they would leave the ship, the which happened after all.

Now while I was lying there in that hole or cabin, the merchant had the men lay out the oars and set them to rowing, like he thought to find land when it was day. But when day came, we were deprived of the wreck and also of land. Were very sorrowful; came and looked aft in the hole, where I lay, if I were still alive, and seeing that I still lived, said: "Oh dear skipper! What shall we do? We have lost the wreck and we see no land; have neither food nor drink, neither staff, nor chart, nor compass! What advice do you have for us?" Whereupon I said: "Men, you should have listened to me when I said last night: that you should stay near the wreck, that we would get victuals, for the meat and bacon and cheese was floating around my legs, so that I could hardly get through it." They said: "Dear skipper, come out of there." I said: "I am so weak, that I can hardly move;[54] if you want me out of here, you will have to help me." Then they came and helped me out of there, and I sat down, looked over the men, and they rowed. I asked directly: "Men, what food do you have in the boat?" and they brought out about 7 or 8 pounds of bread for everybody: we had two empty little vats, and put that bread in it. I further said: "Men, take in the oars, it must come otherwise, for you'll get weary, and we have no food to give out. Put in the oars." Then they said: "What shall we do?" But I said: "Take off your shirts and make sails from them." They said: "We have no sail-thread." I said: "Take the fenders[55] of the boat and pick them apart and twist it into sail-thread, and plait the rest into sheets and gores."[56] Whereupon everyone took off his shirt and they were pieced together into sails, and they in the shallop did the same. Then counted our people and found there were 46 in the longboat and 26 in the shallop; which makes 72 people in all.

There was a blue ruf-coat[57] and a pillow in the boat; those were given me. I put on the ruf-coat and put the pillow on my head, because I (as told) had two holes in my head. We did have the surgeon with us in the boat, but he had no medicines; yet chewed some bread and laid the mouthful[58] on the wounds, wherewith I (through God's mercy) was healed. I proposed to take off my shirt as well, but they would not have it; still took care to keep me alive. We let it [the boat] drift all day; were in the mean while busy with making sails. They were done by evening, set them, and began to sail. This was on the 20th day of November 1619. We began to set our course by the stars, because we had a fair idea where the stars belonged to come up and go down; and so set our course by night.

It was so cold at night that the men's teeth chattered, and by day so hot, that one would perish from thirst; for the sun was mostly above our heads.

On the 21, 22 and 23 ditto we devised a cross-staff for measuring altitude; fashioned a quadrant on the deck and with a staff drew a cross in it.[59] We had the joiner Teunis Sybrantsz. of Hoorn with us; who had a pair of compasses. He also had some partial knowledge of how to draw a staff, so that we together made and formed a cross-staff, wherewith we shot [the sun]. I also cut a chart on the back of the board and put the Island of Sumatra therein, with the Island of Java, with the Strait of Sunda that goes between both islands. On the same day that we lost the ship, at midday, I had measured altitude by the sun, and found [ourselves] five and a half degrees Southern-latitude from the Equinoctial line, and on the chart this position was about 90 miles from land.[60] I also cut a compass in it; then measured off all the days with the pair of compasses by guessing, and set the course 70 miles next or above the hole, so that, when we found land, to know better where we would have to go. Thus we sailed according to the shooting with our staff and the measuring [with the pair of compasses].

Of the 7 or 8 pounds of bread I gave each man his portion[61] every day for as long as it would last; but was almost gone. Each one got during the day a little piece as big as the joint of a finger. We had nothing to drink; therefore, when it rained, we took our sails down and stretched them out athwart the boat, and so caught the water on the sails and gathered it into our two little vats; and when they were full we put them out of the way until it was a dry day when it didn't rain. I cut off the toe of a shoe and every one came to the little vat and drew the little toe full and drank it down, and went back to his place where he had been sitting. And although we were in such dire need, the men said: "Skipper, you take as much as you want for it won't help us anyway." When I saw their courtesy, I wanted no more than they. Thus sailing with shallop and longboat, and because the boat sailed faster than the shallop, and since there was no one in the shallop who knew navigation, those who were in the shallop begged (when they came close to us) if they could come over into the boat; saying: "Dear skipper, let us come over, so we can be with one another"; fearing they would stray away from us. But those in the boat were against it and said: "Skipper, if we take them in, then we'll all be done for, cause the boat cannot carry everybody." Therefore had to cut them off again from the boat.

The misery was great among us; we had no more bread and could not see any land. I kept on persuading the men that we were close to land, that they be of good courage; but they murmured among themselves against it and said to each other: "The skipper can say that we sail toward land, but perhaps we sail away from land." One day (when it appeared that we could no longer endure without food) God almighty caused gulls to come flying over the boat, as if they wanted to be caught, because they almost flew into our hands and let themselves be grabbed. We plucked their feathers and cut them to pieces; gave every one something; ate them raw like that and it tasted me as well as any food I ever ate; yea, tasted so sweet as if I had stuck honey in my mouth and throat. Had we only had more; was just or barely enough that we could live, and not more.

And since no land came forth, we were made so weak, that the men resolved (when those in the shallop begged us again to be allowed to come over) to take them in; because there was no result with land; feared that we should have to die from thirst and hunger, and that if we had to die, we resolved rather to die with and among each other. Thereupon took in the people from the shallop into the boat and took all the oars from the shallop, along with sails; set them in the boat as well. We thus had in the boat a sprit-sail, fore-sail, main-sail and mizzen. We then had also about 30 oars, the which we laid across the benches, like a deck. The boat was so ample that the people under the oars could sit down right well; put therefore one half of them beneath the oars and the other half above the oars; could thus stow the men right well. We were then with 72 people in the boat; looked at each other with sad eyes, having neither to eat nor drink. There was no bread left, nor did the gulls come again, and it would not rain.

When it was again most apparent that we would not keep our lives, there came (through the Lord's mercy) unawares bursting up from the sea a party of flying fishes, being as big as a big smelt, in the manner of a school of sparrows,[62] and flew into the boat. Then there was a scrambling! Each one did his best to get something. We distributed them and ate them raw, and tasted like honey; but it could help but little. Yet it fortified more or less and did as much (with God) that no one died,the which was to wonder at because the men were beginning to drink salt water already, heedless of my warning. I said to them: "Men, drink no salt water, because it will not quench your thirst; you will get looseness of the bowels and die from it." Others chewed on gun-bullets and musquet-bullets; others drank their own water. I drank my own water for as long as it was good; because afterward it became unfit to be drunk.

Our straits became greater and worse all the while, and the men began to look at one another so desperately, suspiciously and cruelly, that it appeared they almost would take hold of each other for food; yea, spoke about this among themselves and thought it good to eat the boys first; when they would be finished [with them] they'd cast [lots] to see who they'd take then; by which I was much moved in spirit and out of great need I prayed to God almighty, that His Fatherly commiseration would not let it get to that, and would not let us be tempted beyond [our] power, knowing of what we were made. I cannot rightly say how fearful I was of that proposal, the more so since (so I deemed) I did see some who would have made a beginning of killing the boys; but I spoke to them firmly (with God's help) and prayed for the boys and said: "Men, let us not do this. God will bring relief, because we cannot be far from land, as determined by our daily measuring and shooting." They gave for an answer: "You have said that a long time and we get no land; yes, [are] perhaps sailing away from land"; being greatly discontented. They allowed me a time of three days, when, if we in that time had not come to land, [they'd] eat the boys. Verily a desperate design! Prayed about it to God with ardent zeal, that he would cast his merciful eyes on us and lead us to land within that time, so that we would not commit horrors before his eyes.

And so time passed and the need was so great that we could not endure it any longer. We thought often: were we on land that we could eat but grass, the which is need indeed. I exhorted the men with as many comforting speeches as I could think of at that time. Said that they should be of good courage; that the Lord would provide; but was myself fainthearted; would comfort another and was in need to be comforted myself. Endured and suffered so much with one another that we became so weary and tired that we hardly had strength to stand up. Heyn Rol, the merchant, was so far gone, that where he sat there sat he; could not come any farther. I still had enough spirit that I could come from the back to the front of the boat. Drifted like that at God's mercy until the 2 December 1619, being the 13 day that we lost the ship; there was a gray sky with rain and calms; made the sails loose and stretched them across the boat and crawled all of us under the sails and gathered our little vats full with water. The men had few clothes, because they had left so hastily, and their shirts had been made into sails, as was told before;

most of them had on nothing more than a linen pair of drawers, the upper body naked. And so [we] crawled (to create warmth) all together under the sails, and I was at the tiller at the time and my guess was that [we were] close to land. Hoped it would clear, while I was at the tiller, but stayed just as foggy without it wanting to clear. I got so cold from the moky[63] air and rain, that I could no longer take it at the tiller. Called therefore one of the quarter-masters and said: "Come and relieve me at the helm, because I can no longer endure it." Then came the quarter-master and relieved me; I crawled also amidst the men, to get warm again.

The quarter-master had not been at the helm for an hour or it began to clear already, and looks out and sees land immediately. He called out with great joy: "Men come out, the land lies directly before us! Land! Land!" You should have seen how quickly we were out from under those sails! Set the sails again and sailed toward the land; came to the land that same day. The Lord almighty be believed and praised, who heard our prayers and supplications, because we said a prayer in the morning and in the evening, with ardent devotion unto God, and also sang a psalm before and after the prayer, because we still had some prayer books with us. Most of the time I was the reader in this but afterward, when the reader came in our boat from the shallop, he did it himself.[64]

Now coming near to the land, the sea ran so high onto the land that we dared not land; but found along the inside of the island (because an island it was) a little bay; there we dropped the grapple into the sea, and had another small grapple, the which we put on land so that the boat was moored and jumped (the best we could) to a man on land and everyone went his way to forage. But as soon as I came onto land, I fell to my knees and kissed the earth from joy and thanked God for his grace and mercy, that he had not tempted us, and that he had given an answer to this matter; because this day was the last, whereafter the men had resolved to take hold of the boys and eat them. Here it appeared that the Lord is the best Steersman, who led us and steered us that we would get to land, as was told.

On this island we found many coco-nuts,[65] but could not (the which we sought) get fresh water; but we sustained ourselves with the sap from the young coco-nuts, the which is a goodly drink. And we ate from the old nuts (whose kernel was hard), but a little too much and imprudently, because all of us became very sick the same night, with such miserable pain and stabs in the body and belly, that it seemed we had to burst. Crawled together in the sand. Each one complained more than the other, and from behind was brought forth the purgation, thereby we immediately felt much eased; were the next day fresh and lively again and walked almost round about the island. We found no people there, but did see signs that people had been there. But otherwise there was nothing else here to eat but coco-nuts. Our men said to me that they had seen there a snake, at least a fadom long, but I did not see it myself.

This island lies about 14 or 15 miles from the land of Sumatra. We got as many coco-nuts as we could stow into the boat, for victuals, the old cocoes to eat and the young ones to drink from. In the evening set sail again away from the island to the land of Sumatra; got sight of it the next day. Came up to it, ran along it until the nuts were gone again. Then they wanted to go ashore again; sailed close along the breakers[66] of the land, but found no opportunity for landing because the sea was running so powerfully.

Then we resolved that 4 or 5 men should jump overboard and see if they could swim to the land through the breakers, and then walk along the shore to see if they couldn't see an opening anywhere to get the boat into. The which came to pass. Jumped overboard, got through the breakers onto the land and walked along the shore, and we also sailed with the boat along the shore.

At last they found a river. Then they took their drawers off and waved with them that we should come there. Seeing that we sailed immediately at it. Coming up to it there was a sea-bank right at the mouth of the river whereon the sea poured so mightily that I said: "Men, I am not running in there unless all of you consent to it, because if the boat turns over, you cannot blame me for it." And asked them row by row what they had to say to it. Gave for an answer: yea, and that they would venture it. Then I said: "I venture my life with yours." I immediately gave the order that on either side aft they'd put out an oar and put two men on each oar. I was at the helm, to keep the boat straight into the sea. Then we ran the boat into the breakers. The first sea that came bounced the boat a good half-full with water. I called out: "Men, bail out, bail out!" And they bailed out with hats, with shoes and with empty little vats that we had in the boat; and got most of the water out. Then came the second sea; that one threw the boat almost full of water up to the benches, which made the boat lay so badly as if she wanted to sink. And I called out already: "Men hold straight, hold straight, bail out, bail out, or we all are undone!"—We still held it straight into the sea and bailed out the water as much we could.

Then came the third sea and that one fell short so that we took in little water from that one; and there was immediately calm water. So got through it with God's help. We tasted of the water and it was clearly fresh, whereover we altogether rejoyced and put the boat on shore on the right side of the river.

Coming on land, it was covered with tall grass; looking upon it, we saw little beans lying in the grass, as if they were little beans from Eyder. Then every one began to search and eat, I myself did my best, thinking: I shall see that I get my part too, and our men walked a little [distance] to the corner. Found there fire with some tobacco lying [next to it], by which we were much gladdened. It seemed that there had been people from that land, who had made a fire and after having drunk tobacco[67] had forgotten some tobacco, or had left it on purpose. We had two axes in the boat, with them we chopped trees down and branches off, and made a fire in as much as 5 or 6 places. Our people went to stand or sit around them in [groups] of ten or twelve, and drank tobacco. When it was evening, we made some lusty fires and put a watch in three places, from fear of the inhabitants of the land, because it was a dark moon.

Now that same night we got very sick from the beans we had eaten, that it was as if we should burst from the pain and the stabs in the belly (as we had experienced with the coco-nuts before). And whilst each one lamented, there came the inhabitants of the land, and thought to beat us all to death right there; even as you will hear hereafter. Our watchmen we had set out were just becoming aware [of it]; they came up to us and said: "Men, what shall we do? There they come!" We had no arms but two axes and also a rusty sword, and were sick besides (as was told) from the beans. Resolved however that we would not let us be beaten to death like that; took therefore fire-brands in hand and marched against them in the dark; the sparks of fire flew over the land, the which was terrible to behold in the dark. Nor did they know if we had arms with us or not. They fled from us, behind the forest, and we returned to our fires; yet stayed that entire night standing or sitting by the fire with fear and worry; but the merchant Heyn Rol and I got into the boat because we did not trust it on land.

In the morning, when it was day and the sun came up, three inhabitants came walking out of the woods and onto the beach. We sent three of our mates to them, who could speak some Malay because they had been in East-India before that time, so they had partly learned the language. And when those came to them, the three inhabitants asked them what kind of folks we were. And they said: "We are Hollanders and have lost our ship by the misfortune of fire, and have come here to exchange for some refreshments,[68] if you have them." They answered, that they had hens and rice, the which we were very desirous of. Then they came to us, near the boat and asked if we had arms. We gave for an answer; "yea, enough guns, muskets, powder and bullets." I had the sails hauled over the boat, so that they could not see what was in the boat. Then they brought us rice, that was cooked, with some hens. We asked of each other what money we had with us, and brought it together. The one brought forth 5, the other 6, this one 12, this one [brought forth] less, the other more [Spanish] reals, so that altogether we had about 80 reals, and with that money we paid for the hens and rice the which they had brought.[69] Having these, I said to the men: "Now men, sit with each other, and let us now for the first time eat our bellies full and see how it will be after that." The which we did. After finishing the meal, we considered what to do now, how to provide us better with what we were in need of. And since we were not very sure, we asked them how this land was called, but couldn't understand [them] very well; could otherwise understand nothing else but that it was Sumatra. They pointed their hands down, that Java lay there and mentioned Jan Coen, that he was our Chief there on Java; the which was true, because Jan Pietersz. Coen of Hoorn was at that time General, so that we then were partly sure and certain that we were to windward of Java; because we had no compass, had always been unsettled in mind whether [the] things [we had fashioned] were doing right, and were now somewhat more satisfied in this matter.

But since we were in need of more victuals, so we could undertake our journey again, we resolved that I with four mates would sail in a little prawe[70] up the river to the village, that was upstream a piece, with the money that we had left, to buy victuals there, as much as we could get. The which I did, and went up there.

Coming into the village we bought rice and the hens and sent it to the boat to Heyn Rol, the merchant, giving the order that each would get his share, that they should not wrangle, and I with the four mates had 2 to 3 hens with some rice cooked in the village; went and sat together and ate as much as we desired. There was drink too, that they draw from trees, the which was so strong that one could right well get drunk from it.[71] Drank of that all around, together, when we had eaten. While we ate, the inhabitants of the village sat all around us and looked at us, as if they wanted to look the bites out of our mouths.

After the meal I bought a buffle[72] for five and a half reals and paid them; but the buffle being paid for, we could not get a hold of him due to his great wildness; wasted much time with this, and since it was getting late, I wanted to go back to the boat with the four mates; would, so I thought, get the buffle the next day. The before mentioned four mates begged me about this, if I would allow, that they'd stay there for the night, importing that during the night, when the beast be sitting, they would get it. Although I dissuaded them to do this, so I consented in the long run, because of their long urging. I took my leave, and said or wished each other a good night.

Coming to the shore of the river, where the prawe was, there stood a multitude of inhabitants and jabbered vehemently with each other. It seemed that one wanted that I would go and the others didn't. I grabbed one or two (out of the multitude) by the arm and drove them to the prawe, to take off as if I was still master, [whereas] I was but half a servant. They looked as dreadful as boggle-boes,[73] but they let themselves be told, and two went with me into the prawe. The one went to sit in the back, the other in front, each with a little paddle in their hand, and shoved off. They each had a kris at their side, being a weapon or poniard, with a damaskeened blade.[74]

When we had gone for a while, the one in back came up to me, because I sat in the middle of the prawe, and pointed that he wanted money. I felt in my pocket, got a quarter out and gave it to him. He stood there and looked at it, and knew not what he would do; but he took it at last and wound it in his cloth, that he had around his waist. The one in front, seeing that his mate had gotten something, also came up to me and showed me that he also wanted something. And I seeing this got another quarter out of my pocket, and gave it to him. He stood there and also looked at it; it seemed that he was in doubt if he should take the money or lay hold of me, the which they could have done right easily, because I had no weapon and they had (as was told) each a kris at their side.

There I sat like a sheep between two wolves, with a thousand fears. God knows how I felt. Went like that down the stream (for there was a strong current). About halfway (to the boat), they started to shout and parliament; it appeared from all the signs that they wanted to cut my throat. I, upon seeing this, was so oppressed, that my heart shivered and trembled in my body from fear; turned to God therefore and prayed to him for mercy, and that he would give me understanding, so as I would know what was the best thing to do in this situation. And it seemed as if I was told inwardly that I should sing, the which I did, though I was so sorely oppressed; and sang that it resounded among the trees and forest, because both sides of the river were overgrown with tall trees. And when they saw and heard that I began to sing like that, they began to laugh and gape, so one could see down their throats, so that it seemed that they thought I was no danger to them; but at heart I felt far differently than I trust they were thinking.

There I experienced indeed, that a man can still sing when afraid and oppressed; and therewith we got so far that I saw the boat. Then I stood upright and waved to the people (who were standing by the boat). They, perceiving me, came to me immediately, along the shore of the river, and I pointed to those two who had brought me, that they should steer the prawe to the land, the which they did, and showed them that they should walk in front, because I was thinking: so you can never run me through from behind. And so we came to our people.

Having escaped that peril and dire straits (through God's mercy), and coming upon the boat, the two inhabitants asked where our people were. We said: under those little tents; because our people had made little tents from leaves, where they crawled in. They also asked where I and Heyn Rol, the merchant, slept; said: in the boat beneath the sail. Then they left again for their village. Then I told Heyn Rol and the other folks, how I had fared, and that I had bought a buffle in the village, the which we could not get a hold of that evening; that the four mates, who I had taken along, had prayed me, if they could stay there for the night, that they'd catch it when the beast was lying down and bring [it] on board, the which I had consented to after long urging, on condition that tomorrow morning they had to come on board in time with the beast.

Having told this, and whatever more had befallen us, we went and laid us down together to sleep for that night. In the morning, when it was day, yea when the sun had risen a great deal already, we perceived neither men nor beast. Then we began to despair, that things could not be well with the four mates, and after yet another while of waiting we saw two of the inhabitants come along, who were driving a beast before them and toward us. Having come to us and after I saw the beast, [I] said that it was not the same beast I had bought and paid for. Our steward could understand them somewhat; he asked why they had not brought the same beast that I had bought, and also where our people were (to wit those four men, who had gone with me to the village). Gave in answer, that they could not get a hold of the beast, and that our people were coming with yet another beast; so that we were partially satisfied. And whilst this beast, that these two blackamoors had brought, was jumping and rearing up violently, I said to Willem van Galen, the sergeant: "Take the axe in hand and hack that beast in its heels, so that he cannot run away from us; because we cannot suffer to lose anything." The which he did; took hold of the axe and chopped it in its heels that it fell down.

Then those two blackamoors began to yell and scream wondrously, and at that screaming some 2 to 300 men (who knows) came walking out of the forest and thought to cut us off from the boat and beat us all to death; but we became aware of them in time through three of our mates, who had lighted a small fire at some distance away from us, and those came running up and said: that they were coming.

I stepped a little ways out of the wood and saw there about 40 coming out of the forest; said to our men: "Hold fast, we are not in danger of those people, because we are also strong with men." But they sallied out so strong and it lasted so long, that it seemed there'd be no end to it, with shields and swords, and [they] looked like boggle-boes, wherefrom I began to yell with dismay: "Men, each one do his best to get to the boat, because if they cut us off from the boat then we will be undone."

Then we began to run, all of us, to the boat, those who couldn't get to the boat, chose the river and swam therein. They pursued us to the boat, and when we got into the boat it was not ready to put away from shore with such great haste, because the sails had been hauled across the boat to form a tent. They were right on our heels near the boat, while we climbed in it, and they stabbed our men with hassagays[75] in the body (when they were climbing over the side) that their guts were coming out of their body. We defended ourselves with our two axes as best we could and our rusty sword profited as well, because in the back stood a large fellow of a man (being a baker) who defended himself courageously with it.

We had put out a grapple aft, and a grapple in the sea. Having come to about where the mast was, I called to the baker: "Cut the rope, cut off the grapple-rope!" and he hacked, he hacked, but it wouldn't come loose. Seeing this, I got to the back, took the rope, and laid it on the prow; then I said: "now hack," and he hacked it off at once. Then there were some of our men standing in the front of the boat by the grapple-rope and pulled the boat out to sea. The blackamoors walked after us into the water, but since it was steep there they lost the ground immediately; had to leave our boat therefore, and we fished our people out, the ones swimming in the river, and hauled them into the boat. With that, when our folk was in the boat, God almighty gave us a wind that came with a burst directly from land, the which had up till then been blowing from the sea. Verily a remarkable sign of God's merciful hand. We set our sails and sailed straight way out of the inlet, into the tall breakers, and got over the bank now (where we had endured such peril when coming in, as was told) and little water got into the boat.

The blackamoors or inhabitants of this land thought we would not get out of there and they went to the point of the land and thought to take care of us there and smite us to death; but it seemed that this did not please God, because the boat was built high and sturdy at the bow, and jumped up into that sea; and so with God's help got out of that inlet. Once outside the baker (who had defended himself so well aft with the sword) became entirely blue about his head, because he had been wounded in the belly right above his navel, by which the wound was surrounded by a blueness, and which I cut out in order to stop the poison from going any further, but to no avail, howbeit he died before our eyes. Being dead we put him overboard and let him drift. Then we counted our people and found that we had lost 16 men, to wit eleven who they had smitten dead and the baker, who we had put overboard, also the four mates who had stayed in the village; about whom we were altogether much grieved, lamenting them, yet we thanked the Lord, that all of us had not perished there.

I for my part will maintain that those four mates who stayed in the village were the salvation, next to God, of my life, because if they had also wanted to go to the boat, when I went, so they (to wit the blackamoors) would have beaten all five of us to death, so I firmly believe; because when I stood on the shore of the river with all those people, they wrangled (as said) among each other about my sailing away, but I persuaded them and proved to them, that I was coming to them the next day with all the men. Then it appeared that they thought: let us not start something [now], then we shall hold and kill them with the least danger. Had thought that I would not desert those four mates, had enough pledge and surety therein, but it didn't succeed. But it is a lamentable thing, that we had to leave those mates there; but supposed that they had already smitten them dead.

We set our course and sailed before the wind along the coast; still had eight hens with a little rice in the boat and that for the 56 persons, we were still strong then. Plainly too little for so many people. We gave each his share of this. That being gone we said to each other that it was best that we chose land again, had already great hunger and at sea there was nothing, at the time, for us to get and live from. Turned back to land therefore, saw a bay, and sailed in it. On land we saw many people standing together, and we walked up to them, but they did not await us, but walked away from us. Could not get any victuals there; then found fresh water; drank as much of it as we could, and got our two little vats full with that water, and sailed around the cliffs. There we found small oysters and winkles; each one gathered his pockets full with them. At the place where we had lost our people I had bought about a hat full of pepper, the which came in right well with eating those oysters, because it glowed pleasantly in the stomach.

Then sailed out of the bay again, to continue our journey. Some distance away from land, a great storm began to blow, so that we had to take in all our sails; those we then hauled over the boat, and crawled altogether under the sails, and let us drift at God's mercy until about two hours before day came; then it eased off and became good weather again; then came out and hoisted our sails. Then we got a head wind and sailed away from the shore. It seemed that God wanted to free us of greater misfortune, for had we not gotten this storm and this contrary wind, we would have sailed along the shore and perhaps have run in at the watering place on Sumatra that was close by, where our people were wont to land; and those [there] were now the bitter enemies of the Hollanders, because shortly before this time many Hollanders had been beaten to death there, who had come there to get water. And when it was day we saw three islands lie straight ahead; resolved to sail to them, supposed no people to be there, but did hope to get something there for our sustenance; got there the selfsame day. We found directly some fresh water there, and there grew as well tall reeds, as thick as a man's leg. Those we chopped down with our axes. These reeds are called bambouses.[76] We pierced the knuckles with a stick, except for the lowest knuckle; we poured water in and put stoppers in them, and this wise we got at least a load of fresh water into the boat. Found there palm-trees too, which up in their tops are so tender, as if reed-pith, those we chopped down as well, and took the top parts that were good for victuals. The men walked throughout the island and through the woods, but found nothing else that was worth anything.

Once I walked away from our people, and seeing a mountain (being the highest of the island), went up it and looked all around, being very sad and troubled in spirit, on account of it (so it seemed to me) being up to me to find the way, and because I had never been in the East-Indies, nor had any steering-instruments, especially no compass (as was told), so I knew not what else to do but to rely on the Lord, for I was often at my wits end, and then as well. And so fell down onto my knees and prayed to the Lord, begging him whilst he had saved me up till now and kept me under his merciful wings and had delivered [me] from fire and water, from hunger and thirst, and from evil people, that it would further please his fatherly goodness to preserve me and open to me the eyes of understanding, so to find the right way for us to come to our Nation and Friends again. Yea, with great sighs I prayed: "O Lord, show us the way and lead me; but if in your wisdom you consider it good and the best not to bring me safely to our Nation, then please let (if it is thine Divine will) some of our men come aright, so that people may know how it went with us and the ship." And having thus spoken with God, I stood up, in order to go down again, and as before looked all about, to all quarters, and behold: I saw to my right that the clouds were floating away from land, whereby it became clear at the horizon, and e'en now saw two high blue mountains, and it immediately came to mind that in Hoorn I had heard Willem Cornelisz. Schouten[77] say (who had been 2 or 3 times to East-India) that there were on the corner of Java two high blue mountains; and we had come by Sumatra, the which was on the left, and these I saw on the right, and between there was a passage where I could see no land, and I knew that the Strait of Sunda runs between Java and Sumatra, and I therefore fancied with surety that we were [going] the right way, and so walked joyfully down the mountain again and went to the merchant and told him, that I had seen such two mountains. When I was telling him this, the clouds had drifted back over them again, that one could not see them again. Told him also what I had heard Willem Cornelisz. Schouten say, as well as what conjecture I made from that, to wit: that I surely believed that we were right before the Strait of Sunda. Then the merchant said: "Well Skipper, if you are so full of spirit, then let us call the men together and betake ourselves thereto, because your conjecture and reason have foundation according to my judgment."

We then called the men together and they carried the water in the bambouses and the tops of the palm-trees which we had gathered as victuals to the boat, and cast off; got a good wind, set the course for going straight into the passage; [steered] at night by the stars. Around midnight saw a fire that at first we took to be a ship; held it to be a carrack;[78] but coming up on it, it was a small island that lies in the Strait of Sunda and is called Right-in-the-Way, and passed that little island. And awhile later we saw yet another fire at the other side, to wit starboard, passed this on by as well, [I] thought them all to be good signs of fishermen. In the morning, with day rising, it becalmed; were then on the inside of the island Java. We had a man climb up the mast, who saw and called out: "I see ships lying there!" Counted up to 23. Then we almost jumped up from joy. Presently we put the oars out and rowed over to [them], because it was (as told) becalmed.

Had we not found these ships there, where we were rowing toward, we would have sailed to Bantam, where we would have fallen into a trap, because they were there at war with our nation, which was also a remarkable preserving of us by God. Thanked the Lord for it and for his kindness.

These were all Dutch ships; he who commanded them was from Alckmaer, called Frederick Houtman. He was standing at the time on the gallery and was looking at us through a prospective glass or spectacles,[79] amazed at our wondrous sails, not knowing who it was. Sent out his longboat, the which rowed to meet us in order to see what kind of folk we were. Coming together, they saw us, and knew each other immediately, since we had sailed with them from Tessel and had gotten away from one another beyond the Channel in the Spanish Sea.[80] The merchant and I got into their boat and went to Houtman's ship, called the Maid of Dordrecht. Commander Houtman called us aft into the Masters cabin, bade us welcome, had a table spread for us to eat with him. But when I saw the bread and other food, my heart beat wildly in my body, and tears of joy streamed down my cheeks, so that I could not eat. Our other men, coming on board, were directly divided among the ships.

Houtman ordered a yacht presently, that would take me with the merchant to Batavia. And after we had told him everything about our situation, of our adversity and what had befallen us, we stepped into the yacht and sailed away. Came before the city of Batavia in the morning. People of our acquaintance in the ships had already provided us with Indian clothes so that we were attired already before we came into the city.

We went into the city; came before the Hall where the General Jan Pietersz. Coen of Hoorn had his residence. We asked the halbardeers if they would ask: if we might come before the General, had to speak with him. They walked away, came back, were allowed in, and came before him. He knew not of our arrival, but making ourselves known, bade us welcome. Then it all had to come out, and I said: "Lord General, we sailed at such a time from Tessel on the ship New-Hoorn, and at such a time, having come somewhere about Strait Sunda, at such a latitude, we had the misfortune that our ship caught fire and blew up." And we told him everything bit by bit, how and wherefore it had happened, how many of the crew we had lost, and that I myself had been blown up with the ship, but had been saved through God's grace along with a Young man; and had been protected till the present, the Lord be praised. Upon hearing this the General said: "What does it matter; that is a great misfortune." He asked after all the circumstances and we told him all, even as it had happened. And he said again; "What does it matter; that is a great misfortune." At last he said: "Boy, bring me the golden beaker here." He had Spanish wine poured into it and said: "Good luck skipper, I drink to you! You like to think that your life was lost, and that it has been given back to you again by God almighty; stay and eat at my table, because I mean to depart for Bantam, to the ships, to bring some order. Stay here until I send for you, or until I come back again." Then he drank to the merchant as well; had yet other discourses. He finally left, and we stayed there and ate at his table, for the time of eight days. Then he sent for us again, before Bantam, in the ship the Maid of Dordrecht, whereon he had been before, and he sent for me first and said "Skipper Bontekoe, you may provisionally, until further orders, go to the ship the Berger-Boat and there be the master of it as you've done before." I said: "I thank my Lord General for that favor."

NOTES

1   The literature on European maritime history is enormous. I make, therefore, no attempt to be comprehensive. The following studies are all commendable and give ample source material and I cite additional works when they are relevant.

The history of sailing vessels is traced in Björn Landström, *The Ship* (London: Allen and Unwin, 1961). The entire period of discovery discussed in this chapter is covered in Boies Penrose, *Travel and Discovery in the Renaissance, 1420–1620* (Cambridge: Harvard University Press, 1955). The succession of naval powers can be studied in C. R. Boxer, *The Portuguese Seaborne Empire, 1415–1825* (New York: Knopf, 1970); J. H. Parry, *The Spanish Seaborne Empire* (New York: Knopf, 1979); C. R. Boxer, *The Dutch Seaborne Empire, 1600–1800* (New York: Knopf, 1965). The development of European maritime expertise is presented by J. H. Parry in two works: *The Age of Reconnaissance* (1963; reprint, Berkeley: University of California Press, 1981) and *The Discovery of the Sea* (1974; reprint, Berkeley: University of California Press, 1981). The subject and period were presented comprehensively in a recent work: G. V. Scammell, *The World Encompassed: The First European Maritime Empires c. 800–1650* (London: Methuen, 1981). See also Peter Padfield, *Tide of Empires: Decisive Naval Campaigns in the Rise of the West* (London: Routledge and Kegan Paul, 1979), vol. 1, *1481–1654*, esp. 152–80 for Holland.

2 For Chêng Ho, see Joseph Needham, *Science and Civilization in China* (Cambridge: Cambridge University Press, 1971), vol. 4, *Physics and Physical Technology*, part 2: *Civil Engineering and Nautics*.

3 Parry, *Discovery*, 33.

4 The best study of naval artillery is Carlo M. Cipolla, *Guns, Sails and Empires: Technological Innovation and the Early Phases of European Expansion 1400–1700* (1965; reprint, New York: Minerva Press, n.d.).

5 Quoted in ibid., 116.

6 Parry, *Discovery*, 238.

7 A good study of Holland's expertise in naval design is Richard W. Unger, *Dutch Shipbuilding before 1800* (Assen: Van Gorcum, 1978), esp. 1–62. It has an extensive bibliography.

8 This comment by a seventeenth-century Portuguese was quoted by Cipolla, *Guns, Sails and Empire*, 88–89.

9 The basic, modern edition of Linschoten's work is the one published by the Linschoten Vereeniging (Linschoten Society), the Dutch equivalent of England's Hakluyt Society: Jan Huyghen van Linschoten, *Itinerario. Voyage ofte Schipvaert van Jan Huyghen Van Linschoten naer Oost ofte Portugaels Indien*, ed. H. Kern, 5 vols. (The Hague: Martinus Nijhoff, 1910–39). In English there is Charles McKew Parr, *Jan van Linschoten: The Dutch Marco Polo* (New York: Thomas Y. Crowell, 1964).

10 The history of the Far East is also the history of the Indian and Pacific oceans. For the first see G. A. Ballard, *Rulers of the Indian Ocean* (Boston: Houghton Mifflin, 1928); for the latter see O. H. K. Spate, *The Pacific Since Magellan* (Minneapolis: University of Minnesota Press), vol. 1, *The Spanish Lake* (1979), and vol. 2, *Monopolists and Freebooters* (1983).

11 For the Dutch presence in Asia see Kristof Glamann, *Dutch-Asiatic Trade 1620–1740* (The Hague: Martinus Nijhoff, 1981). Additional information is available in *Dutch Capitalism and World Capitalism*, ed. Maurice Aymard (Cambridge: Cambridge University Press, 1982), esp. 93–145, 215–33. See also *Islam and the Trade of Asia*, ed. D. S. Richards (Pittsburgh: University of Pennsylvania Press, 1970). For a study, in English, of the heyday of Dutch colonialism in Java, including Coen's career, see George Masselman, *The Cradle of Colonialism* (New Haven: Yale University Press, 1963). It has an extensive bibliography. Statistical information on the VOC can be obtained from *Dutch-Asiatic Shipping in the Seventeenth and Eighteenth Centuries, 1595–1795*, ed. F. S. Gaastra, J. R. Bruijn, and I. Schöffer (The Hague: Martinus Nijhoff, 1981) vols. 2 and 3. Still the best survey of Indonesia's colonial history is Bernard H. M. Vlekke, *Nusantara: A History of the East Indian Archipelago*

(Cambridge: Harvard University Press, 1945). A short history of how the Dutch established their authority in the Indies is E. B. Kielstra, *De Vestiging van het Nederlandsche Gezag in den Indischen Archipel* (Haarlem: De Erven F. Bohn, 1920). Pertaining primarily to the sixteenth century, somewhat chauvinistic in tone, but containing many, though often undocumented, contemporary quotes is W. J. van Balen, *Nederlands Voorhoede* (Amsterdam: N. V. Amsterdamsche Boek-en Courantenmaatschappij, 1941). Holland's surprisingly innovative role in military science, including that in technology, is discussed in William H. McNeill, *The Pursuit of Power: Technology, Armed Force, and Society since A.D. 1000* (Chicago: University of Chicago Press, 1982). The standard history of the colonial Dutch in Indonesia is *Geschiedenis van Nederlandsch Indië*, ed. F. W. Stapel et al., 5 vols. (Amsterdam: Joost van den Vondel, 1938–40).

12 See F. W. Stapel, *De Vereenigde Oostindische Compagnie in de Groote Oorlogen der XVIIde Eeuw* (Groningen: J. B. Wolters, 1932); and T. H. Milo, *De invloed van de zeemacht op de geschiedenis der Vereenigde Oost-Indische Compagnie* (The Hague: Martinus Nijhoff, 1946).

13 Parry, *Reconnaissance*, 200, 186, 189.

14 J. S. Stavorinus, *Voyages to the East Indies*, trans. S. H. Wilcocke, 3 vols. (1793, 1797; London, 1798; reprint, London: Dawsons of Pall Mall, 1969), 2:143. Johan Splinter Stavorinus (1739–88), a postmaster in the Dutch navy, made several journeys as captain for the VOC to the Company's possessions in Africa and Asia between 1768 and 1778. His accounts of those travels, which contain a great deal of important information, were published in 1793 and 1797, after his death. They were quickly translated into French and English. The English translation by Wilcocke is very good, and improves on the original by rectifying inaccuracies and errors.

15 J. de Hullu, *Op de schepen der Oost-Indische Compagnie*, ed. J. R. Bruijn and J. Lucassen (Groningen: Wolters-Noordhoff, 1980), 76. This edition prints five important articles by the Dutch historian de Hullu about the life of ordinary personnel on the VOC's ships. The articles were originally published in journals between 1913 and 1914. Despite de Hullu's sometimes antique style, these are important pieces, based primarily on archival material.

16 Stavorinus, *Voyages*, 1:146.

17 de Hullu, *Op de schepen*, 115.

18 Stavorinus, *Voyages*, 2:385.

19 E. S. De Klerck, *History of the Netherlands East Indies*, 2 vols. (1938; reprint, Amsterdam: B. M. Israël, 1975), 1:433.

20 de Hullu, *Op de schepen*, 66–67, 78.

21 Stavorinus, *Voyages*, 2:112.

22 Ibid., 168–69.

23 Ibid., 416–17.

24 Ibid., 430–31.

25 The best edition of Bontekoe's work is *Journalen van de Gedenckwaerdige Reijsen van Willem Ijsbrantsz. Bontekoe 1618–1625*, ed. G. J. Hoogewerff (The Hague: Martinus Nijhoff, 1952), 15. All references are to this edition and it is from here that I gathered the subsequent biographical material. This is also the text I used for my translation (26–52).

26 Parr, *Jan van Linschoten*, 77.

27 Stavorinus, *Voyages*, 2:97–98.

28 Ibid., 1:13.

29 de Hullu, *Op de schepen*, 83.

30 Ibid., 88.

31 Stavorinus, *Voyages*, 2 : 7, 104.

32 de Hullu, *Op de schepen*, 50–54.

33 A number of English words pertaining to the sea and seafaring are of Dutch origin. Some others are: *lee* (from *lij*); *deck*; *yawl (jol)*; *yacht (jacht)*; *lighter (lichter)*; *buoy (boei)*; *sloop (sloep)*; *buss (buis)*; *jib*, both the noun for a sail and the verb for working such a sail (from *gijpen*); *luff* or *loof (loef)*; *boom*, a beam or pole (*boom*); *caboose*, in the original sense of a cook's cabin on board ship (*kombuis*); a *rover*, or pirate, from the same word in Dutch for a robber; *filibuster (vrijbuiter)*; a *school* or *scull* of fish (from the Dutch: *school vissen*); *pillotage* (from *peillood*), to *swab* [a deck] from *zwabberen*; *ballast (ballasten)*; *kink*, i.e., a twist in a rope *(kink)*; *skipper (schipper)*, and so on.

34 For mutiny and punishments aboard ships, see J. R. Bruijn and E. S. van Eyck van Heslinga, *Muiterij. Oproer en berechting op de schepen van de VOC* (Haarlem: De Boer Maritiem, 1980); and H. Hoogenberk, *De rechtsvoorschriften voor de vaart op Oost-Indië 1595–1620* (Utrecht: Kemink en Zoon, n.d.). The latter is a legal study based on archive material. See also de Hullu, *Op de schepen*, 98–113.

35 Parry, *Reconnaissance*, 34.

36 From the introduction by Blacker to *The Portable Hakluyt's Voyages*, ed. Irwin R. Blacker (New York: Viking Press, 1965), 3. For the various ramifications of Hakluyt's work see George Bruner Parks, *Richard Hakluyt and the English Voyages* (New York: American Geographical Society, 1928).

37 *Brandy-wine*, or *brandy*, is a Dutch word. It derives from *brandewijn* which literally means "burned wine." I have kept the original sequence where Bontekoe repeats the word *brand* because in older English usage the latter could also mean "something that causes fire."

38 Sewel (*New Dictionary English and Dutch*) gives *quartern* for the Dutch *mutsje*; it seems to have been a quarter of a pint.

39 In the original, *steker*. This was, as Hoogewerff points out, a candleholder that ended in a sharp point (Bontekoe, *Journalen*, 26n.). Thus it could be jabbed into wood and be used in places where there was no level area. Accidents due to careless handling of candles were unfortunately very common. A French ship, the *St. Jean Baptiste*, was set on fire in the late eighteenth century in the same way: a candle set a cask of brandy on fire when its level was checked in the hold. John Hawkins had particularly bad luck with accidents due to fire; he had to fight large fires on the *Daintie*, the *Jesus of Lubeck*, and the *Roebucke*, and his ship the *Primrose* burned up entirely after a sailor dropped a candle.

40 *Snaste*, like the original *dief*, refers to the burning or burnt part of a candlewick that should have been snuffed.

41 Sewel has *stone-coals* for *smitskoolen*; i.e., mineral coal as distinguished from charcoal.

42 *Longboat* for *groote boot* and *shallop* for *sloep*. The longboat was the largest boat carried on board a full-rigged ship, and was principally used as a lifeboat; Sewel gives *shallop* for *sloep*, and the word is used in the sense of a dinghy, a small vessel employed for communicating between ships or for landing on shore. The English *shallop* derives from the Dutch word.

43 *Chains*, later called *chainwales* or even *channels*, were wooden projections outside the ship's side, a little behind the mast, where the shrouds were fastened. In this manner the shrouds (the ropes that support the mast) could be spread wider and made more secure to give better support.

44 A *gallery* was a walk built out from the captain's cabin and extended beyond the stern.

45 *Fall-rope* for *val-reep* (Sewel).

46 *Fadom* in Sewel for *vaem*. From the Old English word *faedm* which is identical to

Dutch *vaem* or *vadem;* it is a measurement equal to six feet, presumably the length across the outstretched arms of a man. It is equal to about 1.80 meters.

47 The "mainsheet" is as close as I could come to the original *groote hals.* A sheet is a line or rope attached to a sail, and in Dutch a *hals* was one of the ropes tied to the lower corners of sails to keep them stiff and frontward when there was a good wind. It is difficult to say which line was intended, although a groote hals was usually attached to the mainsail.

48 *Hodgepodge* for *hutspot.* The latter is a Dutch name for a mixture of meat, vegetables, and potatoes, stewed together. In Dutch, as in English, it can also mean a mess of something. The original form in English is *hotch-pot* and though it may first have been a French word, it came into English from Dutch.

49 I do not quite know what is meant by the "knop van de steven." *Steven* means prow, the old name for the pointed stem, or beak, of a ship. Evidently, the *knop* (a word used in English as well) must be some kind of protuberance.

50 *Eyder* or Eider, is a river and a district in Schleswig-Holstein, west of Kiel, in the narrow stretch of land between Denmark and northern Germany. This is the same place where the beans come from that are mentioned on p. 39.

51 I use "I was nearly dead" for the troublesome phrase "dat my hooren en sien vergingh." In modern Dutch this is said in reaction to a great deal of noise, which does not seem to apply here; it could be taken literally, so that Bontekoe is saying here that he is losing his hearing and sight (*horen* and *zien*); in southern Holland it can also mean that one cannot tolerate a person. But there was an older usage which meant that a person was nearly dead, and this is most likely what Bontekoe intended.

52 *Cabin* in Sewel for *roef.*

53 *Bitakle* is the spelling in Sewel for *bittacle,* now commonly known as *binnacle.* This was a wooden stand that held the mariner's compass and was situated near the helm. Bontekoe has the expressive phrase *nacht-huys* or *night-house,* probably because there was a light in it to illuminate the compass for the helmsman.

54 *Weak* for *lam* and *move* for *reppen.*

55 *Fenders* for *willen;* a *wil* is a *stootkussen* in Dutch, something that prevents the ship from banging against, say, a pier. The word *fender* is first recorded in the *Oxford English Dictionary* in 1626, hence reasonably close to Bontekoe's time.

56 "Plait . . . into sheets and gores" for "van de rest leght plattingh tot schooten en geerden." *Plattingh,* according to Hoogewerff, refers to strips made from thread to serve as ropes; they were flat and not twisted into round rope, hence I used *plaited. Schoot* referred to a rope that held one of the lower corners of the gaff-sail (*gaffel* in Dutch) and mainsail to keep the sails tight. *Gore* for *geer,* that is angles cut slopewise at one or both ends of pieces of canvas to widen and increase the depth of a sail. *Gore* came into English from the Dutch *ghere* or *gheere.*

57 *Ruf-coat* in Sewel for *bolkvanger.* The latter is a rare word in Dutch; *bolk* is a heavy gust of rain; *vanger* from the verb *vangen* is "to catch," hence a coat of course material to protect against rough weather. In other words a pea jacket, though this word did not enter the language until after 1700. *Pea jacket* comes from Dutch: *pea* is a variation of *pee,* the English spelling of the Dutch word *pij* that referred to a coarse woolen cloth that was sold in England as early as the fourteenth century. The word for a pea jacket in Dutch is *pijjekker.*

58 The noun *mouthful* in Sewel for *kaauw,* as in "a Mouthful of chewed victuals."

59 A *cross-staff* could be made easily. Usually constructed of boxwood, it consisted of a square-sectioned piece of wood about three feet long, the staff, which was graduated in degrees of altitude. A "cross" or transversary, could slide across the staff; it was a rectangular piece of wood with a square hole in it that fitted snugly on the staff at right angles. One end

of the staff was held to the observer's eye and the upper and lower edges of the cross were made to coincide with the observed body and the horizon beneath it. The point where the cross cut the scale on the staff gave a reading in degrees and minutes of altitude. By Bontekoe's day, the staff was fitted with three or four crosses, intended to measure different altitudes that were read off the corresponding side of the staff. The Dutch used cross-staffs into the nineteenth century. The quadrant Bontekoe refers to is most likely the simple instrument for measuring altitude known as the "seaman's quadrant," which could be easily made by the navigator himself. It was a quarter circle of wood (or brass), with a plumb line suspended over the center of a circle of which the quadrant formed a part. One radial edge had two pins or sights by means of which the heavenly body could be sighted. Two observers were necessary: one to bring the observed object into the line of the two pins and another to note the position where the plumb line crossed the arc of the circle. A navigator is said "to shoot" a heavenly body, that is take an altitude of it. This is the verb Bontekoe uses and it is kept in the translation.

In the only other English translation of Bontekoe's journal, *graed-boogh* was translated as *sextant*. The sextant, however, was a more sophisticated instrument and was not developed until the second half of the eighteenth century. See Willem Ysbrantsz. Bontekoe, *Memorable Description of the East Indian Voyage 1618–1625*, trans. and ed. C. B. Bodde-Hodgkinson and Pieter Geyl (London: Routledge and Sons, 1929), 47. I did not use this translation because, though adequate, it has a number of similar errors, and the tone is wrong: Bontekoe's prose is made to sound more genteel than it was, and the man too forceful.

60   In Bontekoe's day a Dutch mile was about three English miles.

61   *Portion* for the original *rantsoen* which is normally translated as *ration*. The latter word, however, did not come into English until after 1700.

62   I kept the original "school of sparrows" because of the colorful designation. Although no longer usual, except for a group of fishes, *school* was once also used in English for a flock or company of animals, including birds.

63   *Moky* for *doockighe* is misty, foggy, or thick.

64   *Reader* for *voorlezer;* he was the representative of the church on board Dutch ships. Later he became known as the *ziekentrooster* who was defined in Stavorinus (1 : 515) as "a person not in orders, who officiates as chaplain on board of ships, reading prayers, and attending the sick when at the point of death." Today probably better known as a lay reader.

65   *Coco-nut* is most likely an Iberian term for "a grinning face, grin, or grimace," referring to the facelike appearance of the base of the shell. Linschoten has *cocus,* and *cocoes* was one common plural. The word was often confused with *cocoa,* hence from about 1620 the British merchants in London often used *coquer-nuts,* from the Dutch term *koker-noot,* which refers to the same fruit.

66.   *Breakers* for *barning,* i.e., *branding*. The latter is an old word in Dutch for *surf,* yet Sewel gives only "a Burning" for *branding*. He also does not list *surf,* and for *breaker* he gives a Dutch definition that only refers to someone who breaks something. *Breakers* in the sense of waves breaking over rocks or shoals is also fairly late usage, later than Bontekoe, for the *Oxford English Dictionary* lists its earliest date of usage as being 1684. *Surf* in that same sense is of even later usage, and its other meaning as the swell of the sea that breaks on a shallow shore is, like *breakers,* from the late seventeenth century. It was most often used in connection with the coast of India, but Skeat argues that it related to an earlier word, *suffe,* whch can be found in Hakluyt, and connects it with an even earlier, Middle English word, *sough*. Hence *suff* or *suffe* would have been chronologically more correct for *branding,* but it was not an ordinary word. It is a rather peculiar condition, and one wonders what the common English word was, prior to the middle of the sixteenth century.

67   I kept *drunk tobacco* for "smoked tobacco" because this peculiar expression was in the original Dutch (*toeback ghedroncken*), was common in the seventeenth century, and was still used in Malay (*minum*) in the Indies in this century. "To drink tobacco" was also used in that sense in English, for instance in Hakluyt, or by Ben Jonson in *Every Man in His Humour* (3:2): "The most divine tobacco that ever I drunk."

68   *Refreshment* for *ververschinghe* in the old sense of fresh supplies or provisions.

69   *Reals, rejaelen* in the original, were small silver Spanish coins. Around this time in England each one was worth about sixpence, and three and a half stivers (*stuivers*) in Dutch money. There were double and quadruple reals, but in the colonies the real of eight, better known as a "piece of eight," was the most common denomination.

70   *Prawe* an old spelling for the common vessel of the Malay Archipelago, *prauw* in Dutch, *proa* in Portuguese, from the Malay *perahu*.

71   The liquor which was tapped from trees could be either the sap from the Arenga palm, known in English as *sagwire* (from the Portuguese *sagueira*), or palm wine from the palmyra or from the coco-palm (known as *toddy* in English).

72   *Buffle* for *Buffel*, a common spelling in the sixteenth and seventeenth centuries. Bontekoe is most likely referring to the gray water buffalo (*Bos bubalus*), *karbouw* in Dutch, from the Malay *kerbau*.

73   *Boggle-boes,* in Sewel, for *bullemannen*. The singular, *boggle-bo,* is the same as a boggle, the older English term for a phantom, a goblin, a spectre. It was usually thought to be black and to have something of human attributes. Toward the middle of the eighteenth century a boggle-bo was defined as a "bugbear to fright Children, a scare crow."

74   The *kris* (or *creese* in an older English spelling) is the ubiquitous Indonesian dagger that used to have a very important role in Indonesian social life. The kris (from Malay *keris*) often had a wavy, double-edged blade. It used to be true that most blades were *damaskeened* (*damascened* in modern spelling), that is, ornamented with a watered pattern. Bontekoe calls it *met vlammen*, i.e., literally "with flames." Most of the damascened patterns look like flames, and these patterns, as well as the metals used to achieve them, were called *pamor*. Pamor had religious and mystical ramifications, as did just about everything else associated with forging and owning a kris.

75   *Hassagays* for *hesegeyjen* (in modern spelling *assegai*). This refers to a short spear or lance with an iron point. A native Berber word, adopted in Arabic, it came into Dutch and English via the Portuguese who used the word specifically for the light spears used by African warriors.

76   *Bambouses* for *bamboesen*. The modern spelling of "bamboo" first came into English via Dutch, most likely through Linschoten's work. The original word is the Malay *bambu*, although some experts have argued this.

77   *Willem Cornelisz. Schouten* (?–1625) was also from Hoorn. He was a famed navigator and accompanied Jacob Le Maire (1585–1616), another Dutch captain, on the expedition between 1615 and 1617 to discover a new way from the Atlantic to the Pacific Ocean. During their circumnavigation, they sailed south of the Magellan Strait, and discovered a strait (now named after Le Maire) between Patagonia and Staten Island. They were the first Europeans to sight Cape Horn. It is Bontekoe who informs us about the death of his friend Schouten in the last pages of his journal that relates his voyage to China (in Hoogewerff's edition, pp. 192–93); Schouten died in the Bay of Antongil on the east coast of Madagascar in the spring of 1625. The account of Schouten and Le Maire's voyage can be found in *De Ontdekkingsreis van Jacob Le Maire en Willem Cornelisz. Schouten in de jaren 1615–1617*, ed. W. A. Engelbrecht and P. J. van Herwerden, 2 vols. (The Hague: Martinus Nijhoff, 1945).

78 The *carrack* (Bontekoe has *kraeck*) was a medium-sized trading vessel of both northern and southern Europe from the fourteenth through the seventeenth century. It had a combination of square and lateen rig, with high fore and aft castles. Carracks were built up to a tonnage of about 1,200. Almost all the ships used for Spain's and Portugal's colonial voyages during the sixteenth and early seventeenth centuries were carracks.

79 *Prospective glass or spectacles* for *kijcker of bril.* Instruments such as the telescope (called "glasses" into the nineteenth century) were extremely rare during the first quarter of the seventeenth century. According to Hoogewerff, Bontekoe's mention is the first in the journals of Dutch navigators (p. 51). It is fitting that Frederick de Houtman should have one; this remarkable man was not only a linguist, mariner, and later governor of Ambon, he was also the astronomer who wrote the first European description of the stars in the tropical heavens.

80 Tessel (or Texel) is the first of a series of islands off Holland's northern coast that curves along the coast of the provinces Friesland and Groningen. Tessel was the rendezvous point for all fleets departing to the Indies. The "Spanish Sea" or "Mare Hispanicum" was the old name for the Bay of Biscay.

François Valentijn

NO serious consideration of Dutch colonial literature can ignore François Valentijn (1666–1727), author of a panoramic description of what he called the Old and New East-Indies (*Oud en Nieuw Oost-Indiën*), a tome that Henry Yule called a "continent of a work."[1] The importance of Valentijn's effort is scholarly as well as literary, but his is an achievement that has been tarnished by controversy. His life was not as interesting as those of the mavericks who produced the best of colonial letters, but his forceful personality stung his critics to question his integrity.

Valentijn was born in the spring of 1666 in Dordrecht, a medium-sized town south of Rotterdam that claims to be the oldest urban settlement in Holland.[2] Dort, as its name is often abbreviated, is remembered as the birthplace of Cornelis and Jan de Witt, two great statesmen of the latter half of the seventeenth century, and the painters Albert Cuyp and Nicolaes Maes, and as the site in 1618–19 of the famous religious congress, the Synod of Dort, that decided a prevailing religious dispute in favor of orthodox Calvinism in a manner that was anything but Christian. A charge of moral hypocrisy similar to that charged of the synod has been leveled at Valentijn.

Valentijn's mother was the daughter of a Protestant minister and his father was vice principal ("conrector") of Dordrecht's Latin School, where Valentijn received his preliminary education. Given this background, it is not surprising that Valentijn also became a minister. After studying theology and philosophy at the universities of Leyden and Utrecht, Valentijn passed his qualifying exams when just eighteen and left Holland at the age of nineteen to become a preacher in the Indies. There is little doubt that he went to the tropics to improve his position in life. His parents were anything but wealthy, and the only resource he had was his intellect. He had no alternative but fending for himself and, by his own admission, he did so with a sobriety and shrewdness that left no room for sentiment. The assessment that Valentijn was never young is surely correct and he mentions with pride that, when barely nineteen, people thought he was in his late twenties because he "was so old by nature" (*Uit,* 41).

Although Valentijn spent the greater part of his life in Dordrecht, it was the first eight years he lived in the tropics that made his fortune. Altogether Valentijn spent nearly sixteen years in the Indies, during two separate stays: the first was from December 1685 to December 1694, and the second, from January 1706 to August 1714. But it was not his vocation that enriched him. He notes that he had to be satisfied with a salary of one hundred guilders a month during his tenure on the island of Ambon (*Uit,* 71). It was, therefore, imperative that he find a more expeditious way to wealth, and the solution was to marry money. During his first sojourn in the tropics he deliberately looked for a likely prospect and found her in the person of Cornelia Snaats, the widow of his "friend and protector," Henrik Leydekker. There is no doubt that he made the right choice, for within two years after he married, Valentijn was able to leave the Indies and return to Holland with his daughter, Maria, and his four stepchildren. He had no employment for the next ten years, and according to his own disingenuous testimony, he returned to the Indies for a second time only because of the "great urging" of "several mighty Lords," and not at all for lack of money (*Priangan,* 1:271).

After a difficult journey, Valentijn was back in Java in January 1706. Exhausted from the rigors of that voyage, he petitioned the colonial government—i.e., the VOC or Dutch East India Company—to allow him to stay in Java for a year. His final destination was the island of Ambon where he had been stationed before, but this time he had been promised that he would not have to make "sea visitations" to the neighboring islands. However, in June of that same year, the government ordered him to act as an army chaplain during a military campaign in eastern Java. Valentijn protested vehemently, arguing that such an assignment had nothing to do with his initial appointment in Ambon. But because the ecclesiastical authorities were subordinate to the temporal power of the VOC, Valentijn had no recourse but obeying. He was back in Batavia after four months, but was unable to leave for Ambon until February of the next year. He worked in Ambon for five years, but in May 1712 he was forced to return to the colonial capital of Batavia to defend himself against accusations pertaining to clerical matters and to his Malay translation of the Bible. He always boasted of having many friends in high places, but there is evidence that he also had quite a few enemies. At that time his most powerful opponent was the reigning governor-general Van Riebeeck[3] who sided with the church officials against Valentijn. Though the charges were dropped, Valentijn had not ingratiated himself with either secular or religious administration. Knowing that Valentijn was pathologically afraid of the sea, the colonial government ordered him to accept a position on Ternate, a remote island at a great distance north of Ambon and east of Celebes. Valentijn refused categorically, and his insubordination resulted in his dismissal, but at the same time the government refused to let him return to Holland. After the death of Van Riebeeck in November 1713, he was finally allowed to book passage back to the Netherlands, and Valentijn and his family arrived back home after another grueling journey on 1 August 1714.

He settled once again in Dordrecht and spent the remaining thirteen years of his life writing *Oud en Nieuw Oost-Indiën,* playing music, and participating in the European rage of that time: collecting and displaying exotic curiosities such as shells, molluscs, and coral. Valentijn obviously had sufficient means because he never again looked for regular employment and he devoted most of his time, from about 1714 to 1724, to writing his magnum opus. He was very fortunate in having time to write. As great a man as Rumphius had to write a large part of his classic herbal in his spare time. Valentijn enjoyed the cooperation of a long list of retired officials who, as he proudly stated in the preface to the first part of the third volume, supplied him with "sundry very neat and genuine Papers." What is more, the fact that his work was printed at all, and prior to his death as well, was extraordinary. The VOC had a strict policy of not allowing its former employees to publish anything that pertained to the colonies and their administration, although the execution of this policy was erratic and based on personal motives. For instance, Van Riebeeck did not allow Valentijn to ship two "of his best" crates of personal effects home (3. 1.104). In a seeming contradiction, Valentijn was granted permission to print his book, which became a commercial success as well. The five "books" of *Oud en Nieuw Oost-Indiën*, printed in eight volumes, were published between 1724 and 1726. The author had the rare opportunity to correct the galley proofs, and the entire work appeared eight months before his death in August 1727.

By comparison, the six volumes of Rumphius's *Ambonese Herbal* were not published until almost half a century after its author's death in 1702, and if one counts the "Auctuarium" or "Addition" as volume seven, the entire herbal was not in print until 1755. Rumphius never earned any money from his labors, but Valentijn had 650 "subscribers" for his work, an impressive number for his day and age.

DESPITE the good fortune of its principal, Valentijn's life has little to recommend itself to posterity, and it is his work that has assured the perpetuity of his name. *Oud en Nieuw Oost-Indiën* is Valentijn's entire investment in the shares of fame. Its dividends did indeed sustain his reputation but they have also diminished him. The reason for this paradox is that Valentijn is ever present in his work, disdaining anonymity or objectivity. Clearly in love with himself and his enterprise, the author of *Oud en Nieuw Oost-Indiën* is not overly fastidious in recommending himself to his readers. Cocksure and pugnacious, Valentijn and his work cannot be distinguished from one another. This partisan olio of historical fact and fancy lacks any resemblance to design or speculative scheme. Its utter disregard for narrative or geographical consequence, for chronology, or for the importance of the circumstantial processes concerning human events, has been the despair of scholars. And yet Valentijn's rambling work, totally unacquainted with method, refuses to absent itself from any historical examination of what used to be called "the East" or, for that matter, from Dutch colonial literature. There are good reasons for this.

Valentijn's historical importance is easily accounted for and depends primarily on the same prolixity that to more sanguine temperaments might seem superfluous excess. One can deduce this from a breakdown of the nearly 5,000 pages of *Oud en Nieuw Oost-Indiën*. Volume 1 includes descriptions of the "six Moluccas," by which Valentijn means the islands Djilolo, Ternate, Tidore, Batjan, Makjan, and Motir, as well as northern and eastern Celebes and adjacent islands. The second volume presents the government of Ambon and the other islands under its jurisdiction such as Ceram, Buru, Nusa-Laut, Oma, as well as geographical descriptions and "worldly histories" of these islands. Both parts of the third volume provide a clerical history and a description of the religious administration of Ambon and its neighboring islands, in addition to a "neat treatment" of the flora and fauna of the same, followed by a description of Banda, Timor, Celebes, Borneo, Bali, Tonkin China, Cambodia, and Siam. The first part of volume 4 describes "Great Djava" and the lives of the governors-general from Pieter Both, who held that post from 1610 to 1614, to Mattheus de Haan, who was governor-general from 1725 to 1729. This is followed by an account of the founding of the colonial capital of Batavia. Part two returns to the description of Java, then meanders to a presentation of the Dutch settlement (or "comptoir" as Valentijn puts it) in Surat (India), followed by the "Lives of the Great Moguls," as well as "an account of the affairs" of China, a description of Formosa or "Tayouan," and finishes with narrations of Valentijn's four voyages between Holland and the Indies. Part one of the fifth and final volume inexplicably describes Coromandel and other regions of India, as well as Persia, Malacca, and Ceylon, while the volume's second part describes Malabar, Japan, the Cape of Good Hope, and Mauritius. The title page of the entire work announces that what follows is all "neat Descriptions," augmented with "very neat Maps" and adorned with "very many neat Prints."

Even from this brief description one can deduce that there was little ordering behind this jumble. A closer look only makes it worse. Sumatra is dealt with between descriptions of Malacca and Ceylon; Celebes can be found in volume 1 and in the second part of volume 3; what used to be called Indochina is sandwiched between Bali and Java; India is discussed in three volumes, and the culminating descriptions of Valentijn's own sea voyages come at the end of the fourth book, and not the final, fifth one. Valentijn's account of Java is very sketchy, Sumatra gets a mere forty-six pages, while Borneo receives an even skimpier seventeen. Valentijn's maps are disasters (*Priangan* 4:715−16), and his illustrations are considered suspect as well. A famous one, depicting a mermaid, was, according to a British writer, copied from one of the "phantasmagoria" of the Amsterdam author and publisher Louis Renard.[4] Valentijn manifestly believed in mermaids and mermen (or "Sea-People") and became quite nasty when he spoke of that "Stiff-Necked World that do not believe this, as they also do not believe that there are Cities like Rome, Constantinopel or Alcairo in the World" (3. 1.331). He himself attests to having seen one of the sea-people, with a "gray Polish Cap" on its head on the high seas, between St. Helena and Ascension Island, on 1 May 1714 (*Uit,* 181).

When one considers the objectivity so dear to our academic historians and the related question of professional ethics, Valentijn fares no better than when his organizing skills are examined. It would seem that the greater part of *Oud en Nieuw Oost-Indiën* is not original. The descriptions of his own journeys—which contain some of his best writing—are obviously based on his own experience, but Valentijn had firsthand knowledge of only Ambon, Banda (plus some small islands in that same region), Java, and the Cape of Good Hope. When this list is compared with the contents, it becomes clear that a great amount of information was gathered elsewhere.

François Valentijn was an intellectual magpie in every sense of the word: I have mentioned his loquacity already; he also pilfered other people's work without scruple and hoarded the loot for his own purposes.

One should remember, however, that magpies were once also considered the cleverest and most musical of birds, two attributes that apply to Valentijn as well. This "letter-thief" as one critic dismissed him[5] cited his sources only if they were generally known or when he could flatter one of his patrons (*Priangan* 1:271). He occasionally mentioned an author's name in the text, but only in an offhand manner, as if it were a piece of debris that the verbal avalanche happened to have carried along. Although plagiarism and falsification are not historically evil, the modern community of scholars finds such blatant pilfering indecent.

Valentijn's most repugnant larceny was his purloining of Rumphius's work. The colonial historian De Haan, Valentijn's most devastating critic, documented the minister's intellectual embezzlement most persuasively. The case is particularly damning because of the kind of man Valentijn's older contemporary was. Rumphius (1628?–1702) was the greatest naturalist of the East Indies. He arrived in Java in June 1653 and never again left the tropics. He was employed by the VOC, first as a soldier, then as an engineer, and finally as an official, attaining the highest position he could possibly hope for, that of senior merchant, in 1662. His illustrious reputation is based on his monumental herbal of tropical plants that was published in seven volumes betwen 1741 and 1755. He was also the author of the *Ambonese Curiosity Chamber,* a work describing tropical shellfish, shells, minerals, and stones, which was published in 1705, three years after his death. He furthermore wrote an account of an earthquake (the only work of his to be printed during his lifetime, in 1675), a history of Ambon, a lexicon of the Malay language (up to the letter *P*), three books describing the "land-, air-, and sea animals of these islands" and a report on Ambonese agriculture and fortifications. Rumphius's character was cruelly tested during the final third of his life. His first wife and a child died during an earthquake in 1674, and he outlived his second wife as well. In 1667 he was denied the promotion he eminently deserved, and the next year, after fifteen years of service, he was refused a leave of absence, which he wanted to have time to devote to his studies. In 1687 a fire destroyed half of the indispensable illustrations that had been completed for his herbal, and in the fall of 1690, the herbal's first six completed "books" (out of a final total of twelve) were lost at sea. But the worst affliction he had to endure was blindness. This man, who loved to roam the island of Ambon in search of plants from the most insignificant to the most imposing, and who then described them with an extraordinary delicacy and a joy in their excellence, lost his sight at the age of forty and was blind for the remaining thirty years of his life. Rumphius bore his sorrows with a spiritual valor that is a revelation to even the best of us. And it is not only his genius and his soul, but also his modesty and decency that, because one cannot help comparing them, diminishes Valentijn.

Rumphius lived half a century on Ambon, from 1653 to his death in 1702. Valentijn served as a minister on Ambon for a total of twelve years, and there is no doubt that he knew Rumphius during his first sojourn— during the time from April 1686 to July 1687, and from May 1688 to May 1694—a stay disrupted only by his ten months' tour of duty on the neighboring island of Banda, an assignment Valentijn wholly detested. During his first few months in Ambon, Rumphius was one of his instructors in Malay (*Uit*, 71). In his detailed description of the city of Ambon, Valentijn notes very carefully that Rumphius's burial plot (*graf-thuin*) was on Macassar Street (2:125).[6] Elsewhere, Valentijn announces that, in 1710, his stepson Gerard Leydekker married the widow of Paulus Augustus Rumphius, the only son of "Georgius Everhardus Rumphius, that famed blind Gentleman who wrote the *Ambonese Curiosity Chamber*," and that his youngest stepson, Bartholomeus, married in 1711 Adriana Augustina Rumphius, who was the eldest daughter of Gerard's wife (and Rumphius's granddaughter) (*Uit*, 160). In the third volume of *Oud en Nieuw Oost-Indiën*, Rumphius is called the author's "Bosom-friend," and in the process of describing the island Manipa, Valentijn tells his readers that he is adding "a neat little Map . . . which Rumphius (a Man, whose neat annotations about this land of Amboina we have often made use of) did draw very handsomely" (2:32). At another place Valentijn declines to elaborate on a descriptive list of Ambonese stones "because that has already been done at length by Mr. Rumphius in his *Ambonese Curiosity Chamber*, and we refer the Reader to the same" (2:138).[7]

It would be inaccurate to maintain that Rumphius was never mentioned by Valentijn, though I detect a note of vainglory in these references that is in character with the disposition of their author. No more does it seem accidental that the only work by Rumphius that is mentioned by title is also the only work that was printed by the time Valentijn was writing. The first volume of Rumphius's unrivaled herbal did not appear until fifteen years later. But nowhere, to my knowledge, does Valentijn ever specifically denote the provenance of large segments of his description of Ambon and things Ambonese, constituting that which he should have been most familiar with and for which he was most fulsomely praised. Most of it comes from Rumphius, and what he "reworked" or simply took from his mentor is a great deal. It includes the material (now lost) of Rumphius's three "books" on "land-, air-, and sea animals,"[8] the physical description of Ambon,[9] Rumphius's history of Ambon and his description of Banda,[10] even information from the herbal, which was still awaiting the voc's permission to be printed. It is likely that Valentijn pirated Rumphius's Malay dictionary as well (*Priangan* 1 : 276). As one can see, this is a most thorough plunder of Rumphius's intellectual treasure house.

These unacknowledged borrowings are only a sampling, but they do not augur well for Valentijn's veracity. There are more instances; for example, his description of Batavia (a city he knew well) was also someone else's work (*Priangan* 1 : 271). And even when he mentions an authority he makes no attempt at an approximate reference. It has also been shown that in "reworking" his pilfered booty, Valentijn was sometimes amazingly lax in his adaptations.[11] Nevertheless, like the mischievous magpie, Valentijn dissimulated well enough to fool portions of his audience for nearly two centuries. It has been said in his defense that such practices were common during the seventeenth and eighteenth centuries. That may be true to some extent, but it would not do to pronounce all his peers equally guilty. A careful reading of *Ambonese Herbal,* for instance, immediately reveals Rumphius's scrupulous references to his sources, even if his data are not as precise as modern standards demand.[12] And it is not enough to argue that in Valentijn's day there had never been a "scientific method." Scholars of the history of science undoubtedly know of any number of dedicated and scrupulously objective men. One example of someone who also wrote a treatise of an exotic subject is Bernardino de Sahagún (1499–1590). This Franciscan friar wrote a monumental ethnographic work in twelve books, *Historia General de las Cosas de la Nueva España,* about the religion, customs, and natural history of the Aztecs and the Valley of Mexico. Besides using numerous works and ancient codices, most of which are now lost, Sahagún used a large number of what anthropologists call "informants." A recognized authority praised the Spanish monk's diligence and care, saying that Sahagún chose "the best informants, carefully selected for their science and probity" and, after many other stages in his investigation, "passed all the information thus gathered through various sieves," concluding that Sahagún "followed the most rigorous and exacting of scientific anthropological methods."[13] I am arguing that an excuse of intellectual innocence does not temper the judgment on Valentijn.

And yet Valentijn's incondite work has had a remarkable staying power. Even modern scholarship has found function and merit in this cheerfully amorphous work.[14] The reason for this has its own ironic logic: Valentijn's very faults are responsible for his measure of immortality. The undeniable fact that he was not a "serious investigator" but a "collector who preferred quantity to quality"[15] prevented this otherwise vain cleric from constructing a theoretical work that posterity would have scorned.

What he did produce is a work that is full of fine phrases and wellnigh devoid of ideas, but his bold colonization of facts made *Oud en Nieuw Oost-Indiën* a wealthy repository of material that benefits even his most hostile critics.[16] There remains, however, the curious fact that a critique of this work often reverts to moral judgment; Valentijn has only himself to blame for that.

Valentijn's panoramic picture of the Indies is a staunchly personal one, and he never lets his readers forget this. While learning a great deal of information, the reader is also forced to become well acquainted with the author. Even if this personal manner contributes much to the charm of *Oud en Nieuw Oost-Indiën,* the smug, complacent tone also seems to invite rebuke. Valentijn's resolute chauvinism—in terms both of his nation and his religion—grates many a postcolonial nerve. He announces in his preface that he performed his vast labor

in order to exalt the Dutch Nation not only above all the Ancients who have ever been to the East, but to exalt them above all Europeans, especially in the light of their Supremacy in those Lands, and the many Kingdoms they enjoy there, and to show that these Successors of the Ancient Batavians have not degenerated from their renowned Fore-Fathers, indeed, far from it; although some have thought I intended to do a great Ill Service to mine own Nation with this my Writing. On the contrary, I have avoided this by design wherever I could, and passed it by discreetly so as not to soil a Work that is otherwise fundamentally good, with this or that singular passion.

It would be interesting to know what kind of criticism he was trying to forestall. That his conscience perhaps was bothering him can be deduced from the few phrases from the same preface that intimate a great deal more than Valentijn probably intended. Noting that the work of a certain "Mr. Outhof" seemed so much like his own, Valentijn confesses that "one could think, with some justice, that in this I had served myself with his Worship's thoughts." He is eager to submit that this was not the case, yet feels compelled to mention it because "I feared that for some Learned minds this could have stained my reputation, as if I merely sought to make a fine show with another's feathers, wherefore to remove this appearance, I judged it fit to add this brief warning." But posterity demurred and discovered that the magpie's disclaimer turned out to be only the truth.

Valentijn's self-congratulatory tone is particularly repellent if one compares him to Rumphius. The latter wrote in the preface to his herbal that it was "not produced by a learned *Medicus, Physicus,* or those who profess such arts, but merely by a lover of the natural science, who ascribes to himself a modest knowledge of the botanical arts."[17] Valentijn, on the other hand, "is certain that all People of learning and observation will have to confess that they never saw the likes of this compilation on the East Indies, besides the fact that it will contain a large quantity of things that one has never read in others and, what is more, in such a neat order." We know that no one has ever agreed with him on the last pronouncement, yet *neat* was Valentijn's favorite word. It is prominently displayed in the complete title of *Oud en Nieuw Oost-Indiën*, and it reoccurs throughout the work like a mocking echo. As if afraid that his readers will not agree with him, Valentijn, like an academic hustler trying to sell intellectual snake oil, keeps insisting on the virtue of his work with suspicious doggedness:

And one will meet here with several choice and rare Writs never dug up by other writers, and a multitude of very neat lists of Viceroys, Governors, Administrators, and the foremost Servants of the Honorable Company which I dredged up with great effort; about the which many will be amazed as to how I knew to lay my hands on them, and being that I had to collect them from many diverse Countries, which cost me more trouble than one will be wont to believe about digging up all of this out of darkness and forgetfulness.

Such blatant lack of humility belies the creed of the Dutch cleric, but it seems to me that Valentijn went to the Indies not to serve his Creator but to improve his lot, and that his choice of profession was at that time not unusual for someone who wanted to exploit his intellectual gifts. It is true, nonetheless, that unless one was stationed in a colonial city, the life of a Protestant minister was far from easy. For one thing, there was a distinction made between ministers who could only preach in Dutch and those who could also do so in Malay. Though it was the language of the conqueror, Dutch was not used as a political tool for at least three centuries of the Dutch colonial presence in the Indies. In order to spread the Gospel, the Dutch had to give in to reality and concede that Malay, the lingua franca of the archipelago, was far more important.[18] Always the opportunist, Valentijn complied most likely because there was a financial reward. It would seem that he was quite diligent, for he tells us that he learned enough Malay in three months to allow him to preach in that language.[19] His instructors were Rumphius and De Ruyter (*Uit*, 71). Fluency was very important because the duties of such a "Malay preacher" were many and varied. He had to give a sermon in Malay every Sunday, teach the local population the Protestant doctrine in Malay, and examine them on their progress. He also had to oversee the education of several children of native aristocrats who lived in the minister's house and performed household chores in exchange for room and board. But the worst part of the man's duties, particularly for Valentijn, was the twice yearly inspection tour of some fifty outposts on any number of islands that fell under the jurisdiction of Ambon. During such a trip he had to preach a sermon in every village, examine the populace in the Catechism, the Ten Commandments, and the Articles of Faith, baptize newborn infants, correct written work, listen to grievances, and, if the cases were not too serious, pass judgment on petitioners.[20]

Valentijn always preferred Batavia, the capital of the colonial Indies, but he had to make do with Ambon, the island that was the original destination of the Dutch when they wanted to establish a monopoly in the spice trade. Even so, he remonstrated vehemently when he was forced to exchange the relative comforts of Ambon for the perils of an inspection trip or for the austere and lonely existence on a small island such as Banda, where he was stationed for ten months in 1687 and 1688. For one thing, there were no wealthy matrimonial candidates in places like that. But raising objections mattered little. The Church had a subordinate position in the colonies and had to answer to the VOC because the Company subsidized its activities.[21] The VOC had the right to fire recalcitrant clergy and to send them back to the Netherlands; hence, as a political force, the Dutch Reformed Church was far less influential than the Roman Catholic Church was in, for instance, South America. A good example of their lack of influence can be seen in an attempt by the Protestant clergy to outlaw all other religions. They were rebuked by Governor-General Joan Maetsuycker (1606–78), a man who held that post for a quarter of a century (the normal tenure was five years). Maetsuycker was suspected of being a Catholic, but the Protestant VOC employed him because he was the best legal mind they could find. Valentijn, the champion of Calvinism, had no love for Maetsuycker, and called him a "Jesuit" and a "sly and consummate fox" in his "life" of the governor-general (4. 1. 297–306). Aside from personal reasons, Valentijn may have disliked him because of the governor-general's resolute opposition to the power of the Church. "When the Consistory of Batavia pointed out to Governor-General Maetsuycker that the Law of Moses forbade the tolerance of non-Christian religions, he simply answered: 'The laws of the old Jewish republics have no force in the territory of the Dutch East India Company.'"[22]

In practical terms, the Church's subservient position meant that when Valentijn incurred the displeasure of his ecclesiastical superiors, he also had to contend with the supreme authority of the VOC. And the Am-

bonese Church Council was far from pleased with Valentijn's performance. They called him lazy, lax in his duties, pathologically afraid of the
sea, and too much preoccupied with the search for a rich wife (*Priangan*
1:272–73). It was said that he had little time for the local Christians,
that he refused to visit "the island Haruko" because of his fear of the sea,
that he exploited the native "disciples" in his house, and that, in general,
he would do anything for money with little regard for his "honor or reputation." The reports from his religious superiors paint the picture of a
shameless materialist consumed by greed, a hypocrite who would slander
anyone not useful to him and flatter his superiors if it suited his purposes.
In short, he was a man who would do anything to enrich himself or to
further his career.

More evidence for these accusations can be determined from Valentijn's
involvement in a controversy concerning the Malay translation of the
Bible. At the time of Valentijn's first sojourn in Ambon there was still no
Malay translation of the entire Bible.[23] Some years later, the competent
linguist and Protestant minister in Batavia, Melchior Leijdecker (1645–
1701), began a translation in a kind of Malay that was based on the language used in authentic Malay texts. Leijdecker started the task in 1691
and was almost finished at the time of his death. A colleague completed
the translation that year, 1701, but it was put aside by the ecclesiastical
authorities for more than two decades. This unfortunate delay was due
mostly to a controversy about what kind of Malay would be the most
useful. Should it be the local variety spoken in a bewildering plurality of
regions—which would necessitate a Babylonian confusion of "legitimate" translations—or should it be the written form of Malay that was
comprehensible to the educated elite all over the archipelago? The first
kind, the obviously unduly restricted local usage, was called "low Malay,"
and the second, based on written Malay and closest to the lingua franca
that was used throughout the region, was known as "high Malay." Leijdecker's translation had been in "high Malay"; Valentijn's predilection
was for "low Malay."[24]

According to Valentijn's own statement, he began a translation of the
Bible in "low Malay" in 1689 and finished it in 1693 (3. 1.180). The
Church Council in Batavia, prejudiced against Valentijn, wrote in its report that no one believed him, openly stating in a letter of 27 September
1700 that Valentijn had most likely used someone else's work because he
was too busy taking care of the affairs of the rich widow who was to become his wife (*Priangan* 1:275–76). When Valentijn came to Batavia to
lobby for the acceptance of his text, the Church Council deliberated, and
decided in favor of Leijdecker. The historian De Haan has proved that it

is inconceivable that Valentijn could have completed the task in such a short time; it is also highly suspicious that he never showed his manuscript to anyone at this time, not even when he was arguing with the authorities about his "superior translation" (*Priangan* 1 : 276–77). After he returned to the Netherlands, Valentijn published a small volume in 1698 entitled *Deure der Waarhyd, enz.* (The doors of truth), wherein he sharply criticized the proponents of "high Malay"—which meant the Church Council in Batavia—all the time referring to his own translation, without ever citing a single example from it.

Valentijn maintained that he returned to the Indies for the second time solely to promote his Bible translation, a statement that no one ever believed. In 1706 he presented the Council in Batavia with a manuscript and asked them to compare it to Leijdecker's work. The final verdict ruled against him because of the uneven quality of the Malay and the suspicion of fraud that Valentijn was never able to remove. Valentijn's "surreptitious and illegal version that could endure neither test nor trial" was never heard from again and the manuscript was never found (*Priangan* 1 : 278).

Various experts have demonstrated that Valentijn's Bible translation was most likely the work of others. One candidate was his colleague Simon de Larges who died in 1677. His widow gave the manuscript of her husband's translation to another minister who died in 1687, coincidentally in Valentijn's house in Ambon. Valentijn was this man's executor and De Larges's manuscript was never found among his papers.[25] More damning was the opinion of his superiors in Ambon who felt that Valentijn never became fluent in Malay. Among some of the reasons they gave for their judgment was that their colleague was always too busy with private matters; second, that he had *memorized* his first sermon in Malay (Valentijn asserted in *Oud en Nieuw Oost-Indiën* that he was "competent" in the language); and, finally, that until 1693 he read his prepared sermons and was not able to extemporize (*Priangan* 1 : 276). It is possible that most of his work in Malay was done by his wife, Cornelia. The future Mrs. Valentijn was a noted linguist by the time she was thirteen.[26] He probably also used Rumphius's knowledge of Malay. He states in *Oud en Nieuw Oost-Indiën* that Rumphius was his instructor in Malay when he first came to Ambon in 1686, and there is the suspicion that he used the older man's Malay dictionary, which Rumphius had to leave unfinished when he was struck blind in 1670.

The enterprising cleric may also have availed himself of the work of yet another remarkable man of the seventeenth century, which was itself probably the most notable era of Dutch colonialism in Indonesia. Herbert de Jager (1636?–94) was known to his contemporaries as the finest scholar of oriental languages.[27] He was a farmer's son from Zwammer-dam, a small town east of Leyden. In 1657 he went to the university at Leyden as a scholarship student in theology with the intention (as had Valentijn) of becoming a minister. Encouraged by strong recommenda-tions from his professors, De Jager petitioned the VOC in the spring of 1658 to subsidize his further studies. His request was granted. Toward the end of this period, in the fall of 1661, De Jager asked his benefactors to be excused from getting a degree in theology because of a "defect in his voice" and because he no longer had "the least inclination to study The-ology." Instead he wanted to spend one more year at the university to study science and oriental languages. The decision was again in his favor, and De Jager completed his work at the university in September 1662, specializing in oriental languages and, at the request of the VOC, in math-ematics (*Studium Mathesios*) with the express purpose of becoming an expert in fortifications.[28] That year De Jager left for the Indies with in-structions to establish a Latin School in Batavia that was meant to allevi-ate the need for sending the children of Europeans back to their home-land for schooling.

When he left the Netherlands in the employ of the VOC, De Jager's rank was that of a junior merchant (*onderkoopman*) with a salary of forty guilders a month. This was very little for someone with a university edu-cation. It was only four guilders more than a *ziekentrooster* or "Com-forter of the Sick,"[29] and fifty guilders less than a minister who was on his way to the Indies for the first time.[30] Valentijn was precisely that in 1685 when he arrived in Java at the age of twenty. His starting salary, as he in-forms us, was eighty guilders, and he received a twenty-five percent raise after three months because of his "zeal and the so quickly acquired ability in the [Malay] language" (*Uit,* 71). We now know that his vaunted flu-ency was bogus, but the young Valentijn made one and a half times more than De Jager who had scruples about becoming a clergyman, who was at least seven years older, and who was a linguist of genius whose achieve-ments had been praised by the university faculty at Leyden.

Being a man of many talents, De Jager was immediately put to work in the VOC's Secretariat in Batavia. Less than two years later he was ordered to accompany the new Dutch overseer of the VOC's territory in Persia. He lived mostly in Isfahan (far to the south of Teheran) which was the capital of that country at the time. At this point De Jager's abilities worked against him. Because of his fluent Persian and intimate knowledge of Persian soci-ety, his superiors would not allow him to leave. After five years in Isfahan the commissioner refused to let him return to Java, and De Jager remained for the next ten years in Coromandel, a coastal region in southeastern

India. While in Coromandel, De Jager mastered the Tamil and Telugu languages, and studied Sanskrit. When he was finally able to go back to Java in 1680, the erstwhile temporary appointment had turned into a fifteen-year tour of duty. For the next three years he taught Arabic and Malay to ministers in Batavia, and in 1682 he was both officially and publicly praised for his "perfect knowledge of the Malay language."[31] His linguistic Midas touch persisted. Despite ill health and a frail constitution, De Jager was appointed staff member of the new commissioner to Persia, again as the result of "his expert knowledge of Persian." He did not get back to Java until April 1687. By that time De Jager was past fifty, suffered from asthma and other respiratory ailments, and still possessed few worldly goods. Very little is known about the last seven years of his life, but official records mention that he suffered from memory lapses and periods of insanity, that he was declared *non compos mentis,* and that he died penniless in Batavia on 6 January 1694. A man who knew De Jager all his life provided this melancholy epitaph: "His learning was the cause that he died in poverty in Batavia; he left a treasure of learned notes, howbeit all neglected because almost no one among us [in Batavia] was curious about them" (*Priangan* 1:221). These "notes," as well as De Jager's books, were finally shipped to the Netherlands and were received by the VOC in Amsterdam in August 1695,[32] but they subsequently vanished without a trace.

Although Valentijn's remark that "the famous Mr. De Jager had a thorough knowledge of more than twenty (mostly Oriental) languages" (3. 1.207) is probably an overstatement, it is accurate to say that De Jager knew at least eight—Dutch, French, German, Arabic, Malay, Persian, Tamil, and Telugu—and most likely had more than a rudimentary knowledge of Sanskrit and Javanese. The remarkable range of De Jager's learning can be ascertained from a letter to Rumphius (with whom he corresponded in German) wherein he conveys his opinion that as much as "three-quarters" of Old Javanese is derivative from Tamil and Sanskrit.[33] Besides his genius for languages, De Jager was also a renowned botanist. In a letter from Coromandel in 1680, his superiors declare that when they wanted to know which local herbs and medicines were safe to use, they preferred to ask De Jager and not their professional expert because the former "had studied the matter and has thoroughly searched and inspected the lands hereabouts and can give us greater and more complete satisfaction about the like than our Surgeon can."[34] De Jager corresponded with Rumphius between 1683 and 1689 about tropical botany. Rumphius referred several times to De Jager in his *Ambonese Herbal* and did so with obvious respect for this "learned botanist."[35]

The colonial historian De Haan alleges that Valentijn stole from this extraordinary but unfortunate intellectual. Valentijn mentions De Jager by name in *Oud en Nieuw Oost-Indiën* (5. 1.220, 249, 269–70), and there can be little doubt that Valentijn had met him or, at the very least, knew about him. The European communities were never very large and rather incestuous as well. Valentijn knew Rumphius personally and the "blind seer of Ambon" maintained contact with De Jager; De Jager's aunt was also living in Ambon at the time of Valentijn's first tour of duty.

Most of De Jager's manuscripts disappeared, even though after his death his books and papers were catalogued by Melchior Leijdecker, the same minister whose Malay translation of the Bible caused so much difficulty for Valentijn. The items were auctioned 24 May 1694, and less than a week later Valentijn arrived in Batavia on his way back to the Netherlands. It is unlikely that the sorry death of so eminent a man would have passed unnoticed, particularly when the man's concerns and expertise held special interest to someone in Valentijn's position. Yet in *Oud en Nieuw Oost-Indiën* Valentijn clearly states that De Jager left again for Persia in 1693, that he had not returned from there when Valentijn was in Batavia (May 1694), and that De Jager died in Persia in 1696 (5.1.270, 249). One would have to agree with De Haan that this must have been "a deliberate lie" (*Priangan* 1 : 223–24) in order to give the impression that Valentijn could never have derived his purported expertise from De Jager's work. Such expertise would, for instance, include De Jager's intimate knowledge of Persia and Coromandel, two regions Valentijn described in detail in the first part of the fifth volume, while a disclosure of possible sources would also undermine Valentijn's boast (in his preface) that he knew "those Eastern languages, especially the Malay language, and the Arabian letter whereof they make use . . . down to their very foundations."

VALENTIJN succeeded in cheating oblivion, but he did so by undermining the creed he had been ordained to cherish and uphold, and appears to have had no difficulty in exchanging moral courage for the promise of fame. The testimony of his own contemporaries, as well as that of subsequent scholars, makes it clear that nothing is further from the truth than that the Reverend François Valentijn led a scrupulous, honorable, and pious life, as the Dutch critic Busken Huet still believed toward the end of the nineteenth century (*Uit*, 35). The magpie's dissembling can still offend and his loquacious sanctimoniousness was better suited for pulpit than print.

If one asks me why I was moved to write this Work, then I would have to say that it was done only to preserve some honor in the World of learning, to show that, though I did not have permanent Employment, I used my time diligently, and to answer to that duty that is upon me and everyone else, to wit, to employ the talent God gave me to my utmost ability in the service and the use of the community, wherefore I, though being one of the least among the Members of this my native city, reckoned myself obliged to apply everything within me to the advancement of my Nation, to the luster of the Honorable Company of the East, and, to a certain consequence therefrom, also to the honor of Dordrecht; insomuch as it is not a dishonor for that City to have natives who know how to bring the Netherlands, that small nation that seems as if risen from mud, firmly and forcefully into its own light of day.

In a statement like this, Valentijn's false modesty is barely restrained by the obligations of good taste because he is clearly convinced that he has indeed increased the reputation of his country by his own example. He is not pretending here, either, for he was always eager to worship at his own altar. Busken Huet is quite correct, therefore, when he asserts that if *Oud en Nieuw Oost-Indiën* has any consistency at all, it comes from the constancy of the author's personality, and that in this respect the Dutch minister resembles the French courtier Saint-Simon (*Uit,* 23–24).

Though the duc de Saint-Simon (1675–1755) can be said to have been Valentijn's contemporary, their lives have little in common, although their writings do. The French duke became famous for his voluminous memoirs of the French royal court, particularly of Louis XIV at Versailles. Because Saint-Simon included even the most private details of French royal and aristocratic life, his work was not published in its entirety until the second half of the nineteenth century. Like Valentijn's, Saint-Simon's work is an overwhelming mass of observations that has no other form than the insensible perspective of the observer. If it suited his purpose, neither author failed to catalogue, in Bagehot's phrase, even the "scum of events." Such unrelieved attention to detail can be tedious. Both writers had the bureaucrat's love for inventory. Valentijn spent hundreds of pages copying the minutes of the Church Councils, while Saint-Simon never tired of cataloguing the genealogies of even the most forgettable courtier. Both men were pedants and of meddling dispositions. Their opinions were adamantine and not subject to change. In fact, both Valentijn and Saint-Simon gave the impression of having never been young, as if they, as was said of the younger Pitt, had never grown but were cast.

The enormous panoramas that both Valentijn and Saint-Simon produced are necessarily of uneven quality. Yet in reading them one must be alert because even in the most torpid passages one will suddenly discover a fine phrase or a fascinating description. In the midst of a dreary inventory (albeit historically useful) of buildings in the city of Ambon, Valentijn suddenly interrupts his description of what was once the hospital, in order to digress:

It is also very meet for the Judges to lean from those upper windows when somebody is to be executed because, directly across, on the other side of the road, is a stone scaffold with a sound gallows and several posts: I said a sound gallows, because from the foregoing one I once saw a rogue hung who, it so happened, was strung up three times. Having also climbed up to that gallows, which was very frail and made of wood, the hangman, when he pushed [the victim] off the ladder, came tumbling down along with the criminal, the gallows, and everything else. This could have been troublesome if a troop of soldiers, who in such cases are always posted in a circle around the scaffold, hadn't closed ranks as well as they did. The executioner, a stout fellow and not easily left at a loss, at first untied the criminal at the command of the Fiscal,[36] then brought him back onto the scaffold and hung him from one of the posts thereabouts. But because the rope broke, the man came down a second time. With that he supposed himself to be free, and the fellow didn't know what to make of it; yet, in pursuance of his sentence, he had to hang until dead, whereupon the hangman strung him up for the third time so firmly that he remained an inhabitant of the air. (2.130).

Both Valentijn and Saint-Simon will delight us with descriptions of customs and behavior that are quaint because antiquated. Although Proust admired Saint-Simon's obsession with what might be called a sociology of everyday life as lived by the French ruling class, Valentijn has somewhat of an edge because his exotic material does not become tedious as quickly. His own century relished striking and unusual detail because it still believed that reality could be fanciful; today, beyond their anthropological value, such incidents of travel still have worth in their ability to beguile us with a nostalgia for what we would like to believe was a more puerile age. Here are some culinary details.

One of the common and foremost Dishes for the Ambonese Table is the head of a Pig with its mouth stretched open, wherein they stick a Lemon and adorn it further with Bonga Raya (a kind of large, fair, bright-red flower) and which they usually place before the most esteemed person at the table. The remainder of that pig they cook or roast on bamboo skewers, sprinkling it with water and its own fat. They sometimes chop a part of it into small pieces and stew it with ritsjens (a kind of red fruit, much hotter than Pepper, called in this land Achai or Spanish Pepper) as well as with garlick, pepper, cloves, salt, ginger, or Lanquas (wellnigh a root, like ginger),[37] making it so tart to the taste that it be a good tongue that can endure one and the other.

If they eat fish at a meal, then the head of the fish is the part that one places before a King or whoever is the most distinguished person there. Therefore, and most fitting for such a dish, it is also called Kapala Ikan, that is, the head of the fish. And of that head the King, or other Person of repute, commonly gives the right and left side to two Orang Tuha Tuhas, being the oldest or joint Rulers of the village, and the rest he gives to this one or that one of his friends, keeping for himself as much as is needful for him. (2:157)

Or, "an egg that holds a chick is for the King or for the foremost Person present at the table, and they eat it as if it is the finest dainty that one can offer them" (2:159).

Occult lore is furnished:

The people from Ambon also believe that if a woman dies while pregnant or during childbirth, she is changed into a Pontianak, by which they mean a spirit, a ghost, or a devil with very long hair, that flies now here and now there, and that she, using the trees as a resting place, becomes entangled in one of them. Indeed, one can hear her there cry out for her child, and hear the child wail for her. She also roams about the villages like a bat, looking for her husband. Now in order to prevent such a woman to turn into a Pontianak they are wont to do the following.

Before she is buried and while laying out such a woman, they place in each armpit a chicken egg so that, according to Ambonese thinking she won't fly away and be prevented from it because she, feeling the eggs in her armpits, imagines that she has her child under her arms and is afraid to drop it if she began to fly, which causes her to remain in the same place where she is.

They also put as much wadding or cotton between the nails of the hands and feet as they can, and then stick under each nail a pin, up to its head. They then take some charcoal and Bobori (otherwise Borri Borri or Indian Saffron) the which, having rubbed and mixed them together, they use to make a cross with in the hollow of the feet. They then take a Kuso, or long grass still in seed, and make of it a knot, crosswise, for each ear, tie the legs together at the calves or midway with a little string, and put her into the coffin like that.

The third day after burial she arises from the dead (according to the way they think) at night, around midnight, smells her big toe and says: I have died. Thereafter she gets up, goes to the house where she died, remains there for an hour or two, and then returns to the grave without having found anyone awake; thereafter one hears from her no more. (2:144–45)

Peculiar remedies are given.

There is here in this Land yet another inconvenience, consisting of a shrinking of the Privy parts, that is often deadly, and is fraught with a great danger to life if one does not take care of it at once. The natives call it Tateruga, that is, in Portuguese, the Turtle. They use as a remedy the privy member of a Cayman or Crocodile, and the one of the turtle, and they dry both of these, rub it on a stone with water and Lolan wood,[38] and give it unto the Sufferer for two or three days, and smear it also on his Loins and stomach, and thereafter give it to him to drink with sweet Arak,[39] whereby he becomes fully restored. (2:253)

A realistic detail can correct our historical perspective by reminding us of the hazards inherent in seventeenth-century colonial existence.

A short time before that a sentry had been hauled away from his post on Japara's mountain by a tiger during the night, and while holding him it had jumped through a Loop-hole on top of the mountain to down below, a most fearful height; wherefore the Javanese governor brought out several thousand Javanese with spears to surround that mountain and that tiger, by means of having those men gradually approach one another while holding their spears together and raised high. And, though not without first losing several Javanese, it happened in the end that they caught him on their spears after some terrible roaring and leaps into the air. They found the corpse down below, though headless, and the head a little further, but completely sucked empty. And such cases happen here more often. (Uit, 68)

Both Valentijn and the duc de Saint-Simon were blessed with an exceptional power of observation. This assured their work a measure of longevity, if only as repositories of otherwise ephemeral facts. But their talent is the flip side of their vanity, because they were blithefully certain that what they saw mattered, precisely because *they* had chosen to see it. And because they were primarily interested in themselves, we also learn a great deal about them as individuals. Even De Haan has to admit that in Valentijn's case such intimate personal details add up to the most interesting aspect of his work.

Valentijn tells us several times (Uit, 42–43, 87; 4. 2.97) that he became easily seasick, though he does not inform us that he was afraid of the open water and, as was said about him in Ambon, would return to land even if "there was so much as a little movement of the water" (*Priangan* 1 : 272). This surely was a serious handicap in an archipelago of over thirteen thousand islands in the age of sail, when it took nearly three years for Valentijn to make his two round trips between Holland and the Indies. His vanity does not prevent him from reporting that the only cooking he liked was that of his motherland (*Uit*, 62; 2 : 158), although he was by no means the only Dutch colonial who felt that way. His dislike for native food was partly due to the prevalence of coconut oil. "Everything we do with butter, they do with Coconut-Oil, and they fry their fish, meat, and everything else in it, and the which one can hardly (if the oil is fresh) distinguish from butter, although I couldn't endure this oil and tasted it immediately, which is one reason why all their food was distasteful to me" (2 : 159).

One must also agree with De Haan, however, that it would sometimes have been better if Valentijn had not revealed so much about himself because, being blind to his own failings, he unwittingly recommends himself as the archetypal imperialist who does not have the slightest interest in or sympathy for the people he subjugates. In a self-serving description about his alleged intimate relationship with Governor-General Camphuis, Valentijn trips over his own prejudices. Having held a high position for the voc in Japan, Camphuis was fond of things Japanese. Every Thursday he invited people to a Japanese dinner, and Valentijn was once so honored.

I was exceptionally dumbfounded because I saw nothing else but some cups with a little cooked Rice, and various nasty Japanese composts with an odor that bothered me. Besides, one had to shovel the food into one's mouth with two long, round Chinese sticks in the Japanese fashion, which I also didn't like; but I had a small stroke of fortune because my neighbor, who didn't have the sticks, quietly (although I did notice it) robbed me of the same, wherefore I was necessitated to make shift with a spoon that was lying there as well; and I must confess that in all my days I have never been at a meal where the food was less to my liking, and so had to make shift with dry rice at the Governor General's table, while everybody else said they'd never had such dainty victuals; but one must know that I've never been a lover of all that sharp, hot, odd looking and even stranger tasting and smelling Indies food." (4. 1.322; cf., *Uit*, 62)

He hated cabbage while still living in Holland, but after the scarce provisions on board ship, he learned to like it at the Cape of Good Hope (*Uit*, 55). That he couldn't stomach fish, due to an illness in Batavia, is made known to us in two brief but telling entries in the description of his last journey home. They show the cleric's appalling lack of sensitivity for his fellowmen and a corresponding outrageous egotism.

The 28th [April 1714] I became violently ill from eating an onion—that had been lying all that time next to the stockfish (whereas I can't stand any fish at all). One of our crew also died today. . . . At 50 degrees and 37 minutes we lost Jacob Croonenburg [between 3 and 6 June 1714], a soldier, who had served us up till then as our baker, and whereby we lost a lot; therefore, because I cannot stand any fish, and the provision of victuals was gradually decreasing, I had to make do with biscuits. (*Uit*, 181, 185)

But due to this same subjectivity one also discovers some surprising contradictions that make Valentijn more complex than the one-sided bigot he sometimes appears to have been.

Brom's curt dismissal, for instance, is hardly warranted. He feels that Valentijn "didn't have an eye for the landscape, no ear for the music, no heart for the people in the East."[40] But in reading the story about King Pelimao (included below), one is struck by Valentijn's sympathy for the Alfuran king, if not by his admiration for the man's natural dignity. Despite several instances when Valentijn sounds like the stock imperialist, there are enough passages to indicate that he had some compassion for the plight of the native population. This is the only aspect of Valentijn's work about which De Haan has something positive to say (*Priangan* 4:730). Valentijn's sane interpretation of religious tolerance, relative to the native population, is equally unanticipated. This is again clear from the story of King Pelimao, but it can also be found in the following remark, wherein he upbraids a European for mocking native superstition; this he finds wrong because he is "of the opinion that, no matter how blind he [the pagan] may be, one should not mock anyone's religion, nor pain him with reproach, because those are not the means to have him mend his ways, but they are the means to embitter him even more" (*Uit*, 102). In another context the minister is not fooled when the Ambonese Christians participate in a superstitious ritual. Their protestations to the contrary are dismissed by Valentijn because he is convinced "that there's still quite a lot of the old leaven" in their Christianity (2:143).

Valentijn alleges to have possessed physical courage. There is cause to believe this because it would suit the general forthright, if not blustering, tone of his work. Though it could have been a case of courage born from desperation, Valentijn maintains that on one of his enforced tours of the islands around Ambon, a storm came up and threatened to shipwreck both him and the native crew. The latter were about to jump overboard when Valentijn drew his "Broadsword" and threatened to "cut them to pieces." Due to that naked steel they weathered the storm and managed to get to the nearest island (*Uit*, 75). In another well-told tale, Valentijn is his own hero defending house and inhabitants against "a black," that is "native," criminal. Upon hearing noises downstairs, he alerts his wife and goes down the stairs, in one hand "a candlestick with a single burning candle and in the other a naked kris, or a flamed dagger." After he cleverly surprises the thief who was hiding in a "large tutombo or box, very nicely like a snake" he hands him over to the *ratelwacht*, an official described by Sewal as "a Watch-man who, walking the rounds at night, rattles and cryes every half hour what time of the night it is (somewhat like the Bell-man at London)."[41] The next day the miscreant is punished, "and the flies were chased from his body in such a way that I have never perceived him since" (*Uit*, 100).

Valentijn's love for music is more startling. Even his hostile superiors in Ambon conceded that he had a fine voice (*Priangan* 1:276). He enjoyed making music with similarly inclined colonials (*Uit*, 44–45, 64–65), and in his description of Ambon he seems well informed about native instruments, musicians, and their manner of singing (2:164–65). Music also inspired one of the most charming passages in *Oud en Nieuw Oost-Indiën*.

Just as a body, toward evening, can discover a rare recreation and a great refreshment by sitting or strolling under the pale moon, so too is it one of the finest diversions here in Batavia that at about nine, ten, or eleven o'clock, at high water, there are now and then some boats, with all kinds of Musical instruments (foremost the wind-instruments) and musicians, that draw nigh very softly through the canals. And they commit a most handsome Musick (that echoes gloriously between the houses, and that is sometimes joined by voices), and are closely followed by another boat with young Company. I have laid listening to it for half the night, incapable of being satiated, and I have heard such perfect concerts that were masterly performed by some slaves on a hand-Viol, viol di gamba, harp, cither, or guitar, that it could not have been bettered by any concert in the Fatherland. Nor can one imagine a more delightful city in the world for strolling, since one discovers that along the canals are not only all kinds and many fragrant flower-trees, but also (the which one finds nowhere else) that they are green throughout the entire year. (4. 2.365–66)

As with Saint-Simon, but even more astonishing in the often dour Dutch minister, one is amazed to discover a natural sense of humor. Both the French and the Dutch writer had an eye for the absurd, which is probably why they both loved gossip and were masters of anecdotal prose. Valentijn constantly interrupts himself to tell a good story, even if it has nothing to do with the matter at hand. The story, included here, of the fiscal and the shoemaker comes in the midst of a report on how sumptuously the Dutch lived in Batavia. Valentijn, of all people, feels that they should be admonished for living as they do, particularly by those "who have the duty to prevent others from doing such. I have been told a story to this effect, that I can't pass up and will add here, insomuch as I knew that Sir Fiscal very well, to whom all this is said to have happened, and find the case too quaint not to share it with the reader" (4. 1.363). And there is an incident on the island of St. Jago[42] when a Portuguese steals the hat and wig of the ship's assistant (*Uit*, 45); and a scene aboard ship when the steward, Faro, tries to hang on to a large pot of suet on a tossing and bucking ship. He falls down and can't get up because he keeps slipping on the suet while being blown about by the wind; it is a scene of slapstick worthy of Chaplin (*Uit*, 116). There are many amusing stories scattered throughout *Oud en Nieuw Oost-Indiën*, and the story of the shoemaker and the fiscal is a good example. It reads like a *fabliau*, similar to the Miller's or the Reeve's story in Chaucer's *Canterbury Tales*.[43] There is also his wry concluding remark about the sometimes incredibly quick marriages that were contracted in the colonies. "I once saw such a sudden marriage in Batavia, involving a certain Bayle, but I must confess that the spark of love must have kindled wondrously fast among the lovers on that occasion because there was but one day between the two. Albeit that both were very good marriages because there was no time to get to know one another's nature and behavior" (*Uit*, 59). And I cannot help thinking that his observation about the teeth of the Ambonese is a dig at his compatriots. He tells us that some things the Ambonese do would "misbecome" the Dutch, such as their "long nails [which they] redden with Lack (which is otherwise called Alcanna by the Arabs)," but this is not true about their "white and clean teeth, which is very common among them, and they despise many Europeans who have teeth that are yellow or covered with a blue growth, and in this they undoubtedly surpass us" (2:165).

Valentijn's sense of humor, his predilection for the absurd and the dramatic, his dry wit, and his love for striking detail are all aspects that make for a good writer of prose.[44] And it is true that if the historical value of Valentijn's work would vanish, one would still have to praise him as one of the finest writers of seventeenth-century Dutch prose. His descriptions of people and society are written in a style that has, in Johnson's phrase, "an inartificial majesty." It is only Valentijn's mania for being inclusive, like Saint-Simon's, that waylays the reader's attention. Valentijn's Dutch is robust, with vigorous turns of phrase and an unusually expressive vocabulary. Most commentators have noticed his stubborn refusal—he even scorned words like *governor* and *admiral*—to use a diction that was based on foreign loanwords. This was not pedantry on his part. The Company's official documents were replete with them and, to give one example, Herbert de Jager's official correspondence often reads like a bad French translation of Dutch.[45] Valentijn's practice might have been another manifestation of his conservatism, but in this case it is a commendable one. His expressive idiom is lost in English, but the related aptitude for conveying vivid detail, such as calling a lunar eclipse a "Moon-Swoon" (2:146), can be appreciated in translation. Noting that the Ambonese get to be very old, Valentijn refers to a man who "was so old that his entire back-bone was calcined and so bare that one could see every joint like those of a Japanese cane" (2:181). The Portuguese governor of St. Jago is described by Valentijn as living in a most sorry state; the wooden floor of his official residence was "dangerously illustrious" (*Uit*, 46), where the second word, *doorluchtig*, can also mean *transparent*. The governor had a priest with him who was dressed in a "long, black, and rather ancient coat, and who also had a broad-brimmed hat on his bald head (a glorious Umbrello if he wanted to go outside)." On the same island the commander of the guard presented a paltry sartorial impression. When the Dutch ship's officers came to pay their respect he was desperately trying to get an old red coat over a yellow shirt. The coat seemed either "not to have been made for him, or wasn't used by him for a long time, and, though he looked already quite skinny, yet he had to labor mightily to screw himself into it" (*Uit*, 49).

FOR centuries Valentijn's *Oud en Nieuw Oost-Indiën* was used as the most comprehensive and authoritative source about the Dutch colonial empire, but its literary qualities were not appreciated until the late nineteenth century. Even a modern and feared critic such as E. du Perron admitted that Valentijn was "a remarkably fine storyteller in prose."[46] But whether one reads him as a historical source, as a thesaurus of strange lore and exotic detail, or for his literary abilities, one cannot escape the man himself. His narrow historical perspective and shameless narcissism, his brazen pilfering and lack of charity, as well as the immodesty of his claims for himself, his nation, his religion, and the VOC, make it impossible to forgive him, but one has to accept Valentijn warts and all.

This is one of the hardest truths about people to acknowledge, especially in the case of this exasperating Dutch braggart, but one cannot ig-

nore it. Maria Dermoût (1888–1962) understood this better than anyone. One of the finest colonial writers, she ransacked *Oud en Nieuw
Oost-Indiën* for the lore and legend she needed for her extraordinary fic-
tions.[47] Hers was a form of larceny too, for all creative writers are magpies to some extent. There is, however, a difference between retrieving
facts in order to resurrect them with the flesh of fiction, and Valentijn's
embezzlement of scientific funds which he passed off as his own coin. One
would suppose that to a woman who felt a deep affection for Rumphius,
whose work she considered to be "a revelation," and whose exemplary
life embodied love and caritas to her, a man like Valentijn could only be
anathema. And yet she understood the contradictions and was able to accommodate all of Valentijn in her appreciation.

We're living in Ambon and I was given Valentijn as a present: three fat volumes in
yellow paper dust jackets printed with black old-fashioned letters and curlicues,
Old and New Indies [*sic*]. I read it a lot, especially the *Description of the Moluccas* and *Moluccan Affairs* [*sic*], and put it away because he irritates me so much;
he is so conceited, so hypocritical, stole so much from Rumphius; and yet I pick it
up again because he paid attention so well and because he could tell a story.[48]

THE ENSIGN

They also believe that, if they fall into the hands of the Judge because they have
perpetrated something and are tortured, they can endure all pain as long as the
hair on their head is left, but if it is shaven off then all the hidden force has flown
away with it.

There was a clear example of this in the year 1704 concerning the King of Amet
who, having committed a murder in order to partake of flesh to his heart's content, and having been caught for this, and having been tortured, wouldn't admit
to the least little thing, but finally did so when they cut off his hair; the same we
shall report now at greater length.

Several years ago I saw a native Ensign who had murdered his wife most cleverly. But it was found out because of an old woman who saw that he had cut her
[his wife's] throat, had caught the blood in a tub, and, with the help of a slave, had
brought the corpse to the beach in the thick of night and put it into a vessel, and
had thrown it into the sea along with some stones.

As soon as day broke he asked all and sundry if they had not seen his wife, and made a great noise saying that she had gone to the beach, that is, to ease herself (as if they don't have closets for that), and had there surely been devoured by a cayman.

This dragged on like that for a while until this old woman, who was troubled at first whether she should concern herself with it because he was a very vengeful man, acquainted the Fiscal with the matter, and he caused him [Ensign] and his slave to be taken prisoner. The slave was the first to confess, saying that his master had commanded him and that he had merely obeyed. This was presented to him [the master], but he laughed at it, asking if one should or could believe the witness of a slave against his master, and if this continued then a slave would always be the master of his master's life. It was put to him that a certain woman had seen it, but he remained stiff in his purpose and denied everything. Thereupon they began to torture him; but he screamed above all the violence, that they were doing this to him without right or reason, torturing him because of a matter whereof his own slave and a hostile woman neighbor had accused him, and demanded in the midst of the torment that he'd be shown the *corpus delicti*, or the dead body (because the woman did not know what he had done with it). This could not be done, and they were at a loss about this matter, even as far as that the Governor was already speaking of setting him free.

My predecessor, at the time one of the Members of the Council of Justice, knowing what trust the native has in his hair, said to Lord De Haas: My Lord, I know of another means that we should try first before we let him go free, and I assure Your Worship that he would not be wanting to get rid of his hair so quickly, and will confess to it if he has done it.

Lord De Haas laughed at this and said that such a sturdy fellow, who had been able to endure the worst, and even newly discovered ways, of torture, would only mock them. But at the urging of my predecessor it was approved by the Council, and a shew was made as if they were beginning with it. He saw the Surgeon stand ready with some large shears, and asked, when he was brought in, what this meant, and what that Barber was going to do. He was told that the man had come to cut his hair, so that they could torture him for once without his hair. He begged to be spared from this and confessed everything. And he was also executed in my presence; his right hand was chopped off and, because of the regard they had for his glorious deeds in the service of the Honorable Company in Java, he was very mercifully beheaded. (2:143–44)

KING PELIMAO;
AND THE KING OF ULAT

Pelimao, an Alfuran[49] King from the great Island of Ceram, inland in the Mountains behind Sepa,[50] wasn't really under the authority of the Honorable Company but could, at best, only be regarded as its ally, and was therefore the supreme Prince of his region. And so this Prince, having perceived that several of his subjects had fallen away from him and had become Christians in order to be protected from his righteous anger and had placed themselves under the power of the Honorable Company, and did so rather to be delivered from the levy he demanded of them than from a true desire for Christendom; and he, expecting that his other subjects could easily follow this hurtfull example, and make him shortly a King without a people if he didn't devise a means against this or an exemplary punishment regarding the same, thought it good upon mature deliberation to punish the first of those deserters he could lay hold of in such a way that all his other subjects would surely give warning of this and would dread to do the like.

And during a certain expedition, he succeeded to lay hands on some of those fellows and, be they schoolmasters or other Folks, nor making a distinction between men and women, he punished and treated them with uncommon cruelty. The Masters he tied to stakes, cut off their privy parts, while with others also the hands, feet, noses and ears, and threw these to the dogs. With the Women he cut off their breasts, branding some with fiery hot irons almost anywhere on and in their bodies in such an abominable fashion that many of his newly converted subjects who were threatened with the same punishment, fearing they too might at some time be exposed to such punishment, would first turn renegade and return to their former Lord unless, according to their request, they were protected by the Lord Governor not with a few soldiers (even as afterward happened, but in vain, and the which could have been done so easily at the time), but absolutely if they were to be exposed to the fury of this King who could attack them whenever he wished. For surely, if one wanted these people to come over to Christendom and count them as subjects, one ought at least to protect them or, if one did not want to do that, then refuse them and not accept them, nor withdraw them from their lawful Prince.

Though some reverted, others, on the contrary, fled to Victoria Castle[51] and acquainted the Governor with what had been perpetrated on their fellow Believers at Pelimao's command. The Lord Governor De Vicq, seeing full well that he had made a mistake when he left those people so exposed to the fury of that Prince, and aware that he would not fail to take his revenge, discovered from some informers that Philip du Pree, the Secretary of the Native Court,[52] was a bosom friend of this King. He had often given him lodging in Ambon and had also made merry with him in his main village, and could easily deliver this King to him because they had lived like brothers and had called each other nothing but Sudara, that is to say brother. It was approved in council to ask this of Du Pree, with the assurance that he would be performing a great service to the Company, wherefore he accepted to carry out this villainy (because was this at bottom anything else if one deals with one's bosom friend so treacherously, as this Du Pree did?).

Howbeit, to give this piece of work a semblance of validity, Du Pree went trading in a Shallop,[53] laden with some Goods that had been obtained from Ceram, in order to exchange Rice, Silk Petola Cloths,[54] brass Basins, and all sorts of ordinary blue and brown Basta,[55] and Salampun,[56] Sagu,[57] Slaves, Gold, Linggoa Planks,[58] Tutombos[59] from Ceram, Mats, Cacatuwas,[60] Luris,[61] Birds of Paradise, and other items, for other goods, derived from Amboina. They also gave him, if it were to be necessary, some soldiers to take along who, when they came near the shore, were to hide themselves below in the Shallop. But what really prompted him to do this was the promise of a certain benefaction if he came to deliver him [Pelimao] safe and sound, and they kept the undertaking very quiet and secret.

And so he departed, assured of the Governor's favor and hopeful of a good result, and when he came to that land, nigh unto the King's village, he came to anchor, and the first thing he did was to set out up the mountain, coming where Pelimao lived, and where he was indeed greeted by him as a bosom friend, as had happened so often in former times. After he had been well entertained for some time, Du Pree desired this King (as he had done more often) to come visit him in his Shallop, so that he would be given the opportunity to answer to some degree to the courtesy he had enjoyed there for so long already, and have him partake equally well in return of Spanish Wine, Sack, and above all Brandy-wine (that he desired so eagerly). The King, thinking no evil of such a great and old friend, accompanied him with a small retinue down the mountain to his Shallop, and went on board the same. But Du Pree, seeing that he kept some people with him, found a means of sending these landwards again, while he began to make merry with the King.

In the meanwhile he made the King and the few people he still had with him in a short time so drunk from that excessive drinking of Brandy-wine that they did not know themselves anymore. He then had him fettered, hoisted sail, weighed anchor, and sailed away to the Castle. The King, who meanwhile had become sober and discovered his hands and feet heavily bound and chained, stood up straight with amazement. And seeing directly what they had in mind for him and for what reason he was treated like this, could nonetheless not constrain himself from reviling this Du Pree as the most treacherous villain on earth, asking him over and over again in a most bitter fashion how he could be such a great traitor unto a bosom friend who had never done him wrong and who had always shown him nothing but good feeling, swearing that, if he got loose, he would avenge himself upon him in such a way, no matter how many guards surrounded him, that others would never again treat their friends so ignominiously.

And thereafter he remained silent, and would not give answer to him or to others, except for saying that he who was a King, and not subject to anyone, would not deign to answer such a traitor.

In the meanwhile they came to anchor before the Castle and acquainted the

Governor with the news that the undertaking had succeeded very well, and that that King was in chains on board ship. He was brought on Land and into a narrow prison, where they examined him about what had happened before, not only asking him if he had charged his people to do the like, but they were even foolish enough to ask him also why he had done such, as if this Prince had been wondrously amiss. But he gave them answer so remarkable for a Heathen and Alfur, as I ever would have expected of an intelligent European.

Far from him to be even astonished by the violence done to him, or take the trouble to disguise the matter wherewith he had been charged, or deny it. On the contrary, he used such powerful reasons before his judges that those who heard them were roused to set him free again.

I am, he said, a King free-born, who is not subject to you nor any other; and therefore not beholden to give you any reason for what I do and not do insofar as my subjects are concerned. If I had insulted you with something in your Nation, I would have declared myself guilty and found grounds why you have taken me prisoner in such a treacherous manner and by such a great villain as is Du Pree; but now I find myself entirely without any fault about having transgressed in anything.

The punishment I used in regard to my renegade subjects is a matter which I should not nor will answer to you for, inasmuch I, as their King and Souverain, did so since I had that power over them, and only employed such to frighten others from a like revolt.

He said this to be a right that no one in the world could call in question, and that he was not subject to anyone and, even if he had done wrong, he did not owe anyone apology for it, nay, that he now, though so unlawfully imprisoned and placed before a judge he noways considered to be in authority over him, he never left off being the same King as he had been before. And that he, as King of his subjects, had dealt fitly with them the way all Princes, and even the Honorable Company herself, would have dealt with renegade subjects, and be empowered to do so without given account of her actions to anyone.

But who has given you, he said to the Governor, the power to protect those subjects who had become unfaithful to me, without me ever having wronged you? As for the Religion which they feigned to have passed over to, I no more needed to suffer it in my Nation, since they had never known it and since I did not want to have it introduced, than you would have given a place to my Heathen Faith. Nor did my subjects become Christians for any other reason than to escape the yearly levy they owe me. And so, who has given you the right to defend such rebels against their lawful King? Wouldst you not have been right, if I had protected such rebels against you, to declare War on me because of such unjust protection that goes against all right and reason? . . .

They also demanded of him how he had dared use such cruelties against subjects of the Honorable Company, and who were now Christians. And he answered: Concerning your Religion, it has no purpose in my Nation, where I have as much to say as you in yours, and I need not give you a reason why I will not tolerate it in my Nation. Would it be acceptable to you if I made your Christian subjects mine against your will, and make them Heathens so they'd be discharged of your Christian Laws and Charges? You would have judged me to have sorely abused you, and so I judge you to have done unto me.

As for the cruelties, why art you so cruel to hang a thief who has stolen something? Is it not because he has transgressed your Laws and hast sinned against you, and to make others afraid of doing like evil? As little right as I have now to ask of you a reason for your just deeds, so have you as little right to inquire after my reason for my lawful action. You may do this in your Nation and Realm, but I may not do the same in my own Realm and Nation and onto my own subjects, and should give you a reason for it. Every Prince punishes his people as he sees fit and considers best for his Realm, or as the Laws of his Nation imply. Thus you punish your villains and rebels in your fashion without having to answer for it to anyone, and I have punished mine as I saw fit, and I am not obliged nor desirous to account to you for it.

And so the answer to everything that they asked him came down to his saying that he was not their subject, and that they could well look upon a King who had done them no wrong and who had nothing to do with any of their questions. But he did call for vengeance for the injustice they had done him, and that, however it would go with him, those who were his own would not leave off to wreak this injustice on both Du Pree and them; that he not feared any of them in the least, while he did not scruple to die directly, and that he would give them clear proof of this in his further behavior.

Since this matter was dealt with in the form of a trial, they would be at a loss about it if they really got to the bottom of it, and even many of the Magistrates themselves (as some of them told me of their own accord) were of the opinion that that man had truly not done anything to us, and had done nothing to his people that we ourselves would not have done to ours if they had rebelled against us. But he would no more answer to anything, and ate so little of the victuals they gave him that in the end, out of spite starving himself before the trial had been accomplished, he came to die. They supposed at first that he had poisoned himself; but upon opening him, and having not found any signs of poison, they saw that his stomach was empty, and that nothing but a starvation of himself had been the cause of his death. He was dragged by his legs down the street to the gallows, and also hung from them. Those of his retinue that had come with him, and had been used as witnesses against him, and not being guilty of this misdeed, were sent back to their Nation.

The Governor was glad that the man's death had delivered him of the same, thereby enabling him not to have to listen to his bitter reproaches any longer.

I have this story from divers people who had known him, but who also often doubted its truthfulness, not able to believe that there could lodge in such a barbarous man so much intelligence for him to express himself so forcefully. But afterward, I took it down as I tell it here, from the mouth of a very able Judge, who dealt himself with him several times on this topick in Malayo which he spoke reasonably well. And he declared to me that he [Pelimao] had said all this boldly and forcefully before all of them, not only once but several times, and with the conviction and gravity as would have done the best of Dutchmen. Wherefore many of those Judges were of the opinion that it would have been better if they had sent that King back to his Nation again since they could not see that he had really trespassed against us or be subject to us. But that Governor understood differently, not willing to admit that he had done wrong, though he did not have a leg to stand on. This happens more often in the Indies, although it does not serve the Honorable Company at all.

Now if an Alfur, and a wild Mountain king at that, had the intellect to give such an answer to the Governor and the Native Court in Amboina in the Year 1678 (when this did happen), then how much more reason is there to believe that among the Ambonese, who daily converse with our Nation, there might be even greater and sharper intellects that are capable of providing even greater proof of judgment and knowledge, the which we could demonstrate at some length if it did not get us too far from our chosen track.

The Ambonese are also of a vengeful nature, to such an extent even that they transmit their hatred for this or that man who has sorely offended them to their children as a kind of inheritance. There has been a sad example of this around that same time in the person of a King of Ulat, on Honimoa.[62] He had a bitter grudge against one of his kin that had proceeded from a Law-suit against his Father, nay his grandfather, and he had promised that, no matter what the cost, he would avenge it at one time or another.

One day, having understood that four of his enemy's children, being girls, accompanied by a female slave, had gone to one of their estates thereabouts by the Sea or the beach, he called several of his people, and commanded them to bring him the heads of those four children and the slave. But they refused this as being a deed which they judged they should not do, whereupon he reviled them for being cowards, women, or men who were not worthy to wear breeches but that they should wear a woman's habit instead, and threatened that he would throw a black dog into their houses. This is the most bitter infamy one can fling in the face of a married Ambonese, because this does mean that, while they are women, and therefore not able to lie with their wives, he would throw a black dog into their houses so that that beast could get those women with child. His subjects, not able to endure the latter reproach, would rather dare the worst and decided therefore to go at it with their seven people, including a slave.

Four of them cut off each of the heads of the four children, while the slave took away the head of the female slave, and two stood guard. And thus having done everything to their satisfaction, they carried the heads home in sacks and surrendered them to their King. And he thought to have devised this neatly, in as much as somebody who would find the trunks of those bodies there, would think that the Papuas[63] had done this, no matter what kind of thoughts the children's Father might have. Nay, that King would even have dared to say to his [i.e., the father's] face that this was his just punishment from God, on account of the wrong that had been done unto him [i.e., the King] and his forefathers.

And so this remained hidden for some time; but folks from a neighboring estate who had seen it full well, finally made it known to the Father of those Children, and he to the Chief of Honimoa, the Son of the Lord Governor De Vicq. The latter quietly seized first the accomplices who had committed the deed, and after that the King as well who had commanded them to do so, and sent them together to the Castle, where they were examined.

The guilty ones confessed to the misdeed immediately, but said that they had done this on the King's order, and then only after intolerable reproaches and threats, and that, therefore, he had to answer for it in their stead. But they readily demonstrated to them that they, being Christians, knew full well that God's law forbids the killing of any body, and even more so such innocent children, and that they were obliged to obey God more than their King. And when they examined Him himself, what kind of thing this was, he said to know nothing about anything. But when they pressed him hard, and everything was demonstrated clearly, he admitted the fact that he had charged them to avenge him for the aforesaid reasons.

And they were therefore sentenced, those four, and the slave as well, to be broken upon the wheel while alive, he to be beheaded, and the two others to be whipped, branded, and put in chains for the rest of their lives. The King, who was to be executed first, came to the Scaffold neatly dressed in white (being here commonly the garb of those who are condemned to death), made a grave speech to the judges, thanking them for the mercy they had shown him, and thereafter said unto his own: Men, I go ahead of you. If I was the first to have sinned by charging you with this, so shall I also be the first to suffer for it, hoping that God will have mercy on me and on you. Though he (as will appear) did not think to die, since there had been those who had persuaded him that he would get a pardon. And his own, hearing him say this, answered: yes, Lord King, we hope to follow you soon.

Continually thinking about his pardon, the King looked around a hundred times, if he could not see someone arrive with it. But, not perceiving anyone, the Prayer was finally said for him, and when he had come to the Our Father, he prayed along with that, but would not come to the end since he kept on starting at the beginning over and over again, until he was finally ordered to finish, the which he did, though all the time looking around to see if his Pardon would come. But not seeing anybody, he perceived himself to have been misled, disposed himself to die, and was beheaded, even getting, at the request of the King of Nusanivel,[64] a coffin. The other five were broken on the wheel, calling out nothing else but: Pati Cara, o, Pati Cara, o Minom Kita Orang Punja Darah; that is to say: o Pati Cara, o Pati Cara, drink our blood: because he had betrayed them. (2:176–80)

THE FISCAL AND THE SHOEMAKER

It happened that a certain Fiscal, after seeing a Shoemaker's wife who seemed reasonable to him and after he had conceived of the notion to make himself agreeable to this woman, that that Fiscal had the boldness and rashness, when her husband was gone, to come to her on an evening in Sailor's clothes, and withal disclosed himself to her in every way as to who he was, with the request that he might come to her now and then.

The woman, who was honest of mind but also very afraid of that man, knowing what power he had, deemed it best to grant him good words at first, saying that she could not suddenly declare herself upon such a matter. And she did this expressly in order to consult first with her husband about it and together find a means to be rid of him in a way they would consider best in order not to be wooed any longer. And so she desired of him that he would go presently, because her husband was about to come home, but allowed him to return the next day toward evening.

As soon as her husband came home she told him about the entire affair and he, much troubled by it, said that she had done well to set a time for him to come again, adding that he would leave around that same time; but that she should warn him as soon as the Fiscal had come into his house again so that he could thoroughly avenge himself on that man.

And what they had agreed upon between the two of them they also carried out, and as soon as that Gentleman came to her, once again in his Sailor's clothes, she had her husband warned of this.

Upon hearing this, the Shoemaker came home very quickly, and, taking hold of a goodly strap, entered very quietly and suddenly. He stood there as if amazed to find a Sailor with his wife, then first railed and reviled him soundly and thereafter put the strap to him so harshly that that poor Fiscal, who wasn't all that strong, thought to remain dead under the Shoemaker's hands, as that strap wasn't an ordinary but a doubly solid one. And that strap did get to the Fiscal so well all over him that he, no longer able to endure the strokes, said softly and as if in confidence, to the Shoemaker that he wasn't a Sailor as he had presumed, but the Fiscal.

The Shoemaker having heard this and understanding full well who he was referring to, began to hit him again very hard, saying with great difficulty, you varlet, thou wouldst mention to my face the name of such a virtuous and honest man, whom I know very well, in order to cover your filthy and godless designs on my wife and thereby hope to escape my hands, but I will teach you better manners nor neglect to inform that good Gentleman of this.

After he had used him so roughly that he felt it was enough, and seeing that more than a little blood ran down his face, and that he had been hit quite well, he let him walk away, though not without calling after him, you cur, take care never to come here again or I will harry you even better. But the Fiscal, without any desire to listen anymore to him, ran as hard as he could to his house, looking back every now and then to see if that Shoemaker with his strap was not following him.

But the nicest part of all this came when the Shoemaker went to the Fiscal the next day around nine o'clock before the noon, and asked one of the boys if he could speak with his Lord. The boys said that his Lordship wasn't feeling too well, but when the Shoemaker pressed more closely and said that he had to speak to their Lord about a matter of consequence, they went to announce him. Their Lord, not knowing what to say, thought it better (no matter how indisposed he was) to hear him out. And so he came to him, his entire face covered with plasters and cloths (under pretense, as his boys said, that he was suffering from St. Anthonies Fire in his face),[65] and as soon as the Shoemaker saw him he said that the night before a Sailor had been in his house who had accosted his wife and who he had lustily trounced, but who had been impudent enough to say that he was the Fiscal (to wit, he, with whom he was now speaking). He briefly added that, knowing full well how much wrong the varlet was doing to that Gentleman, he had trounced him even harder for a second time. But when that one finally escaped, he, the Shoemaker, had thought it needful to acquaint him with this immediately, so he could have this rascal searched out and have the opportunity to punish him.

The Fiscal, who thought he was going mad, and who already had been caught once, said, fellow, if you have nothing else to tell me then be off at once or I will know what to do with you. But the Shoemaker, who didn't get too close to him now, knowing full well that a dog is very bold in his own yard, said before he left, to be sure Sir Fiscal, yet I had to tell you that that varlet used your name so you would know about it, whereupon the Fiscal said again, get yourself going fellow, I know all about it already. Whereupon the Shoemaker greeted him politely and went his way, smirking all the while. But before he got home almost half of Batavia already knew what had happened between him and the Fiscal, wherefore that Gentleman durst not show himself for a long time, and when he did appear, he could not escape the numerous scoffing jests that his good acquaintances passed among them about the effect on him of the strap and the smart strength of that leather. But he never again came into the house of the mischievous Shoemaker, who had so fiercely beaten love out of his body that he feared his soul would have soon followed after. (4.1.363–64)

NOTES

1   Henry Yule and A. C. Burnell, *Hobson-Jobson: being a Glossary of Anglo-Indian colloquial words and phrases, and of kindred terms; etymological, historical, geographical and discursive* (1886), 2d. ed. (1902; reprint, New Delhi: Munshiram Manoharlal Ltd, 1979), 575.

2   Biographical information is based primarily on two secondary sources, as well as on Valentijn's own information. They are G. P. Rouffaer and W. C. Muller, "Valentijn (François)" in *Encyclopaedie van Nederlandsch-Indië*, ed. D. G. Stibbe, 2d. ed. in 4 vols. and 3 supplements (The Hague: Nijhoff, 1917–32), 4:501–8, hereafter cited as "Valentijn," *Encyclopaedie*; F. de Haan. *Priangan. De Preanger-Regentschappen onder het Nederlandsch Bestuur tot 1811,* 4 vols. (Batavia: Bataviaasch Genootschap van Kunsten en Wetenschappen, 1910–12), 1:270–80, hereafter cited as *Priangan,* with volume and page number. Valentijn's own work was used in two different editions. François Valentijn, *Oud en Nieuw Oost-Indiën, vervattende Een Naaukeurige en Uitvoerige Verhandelinge van Nederlands Mogentheyd in die Gewesten . . . beschreven, en met veele zeer nette daar toe vereyschte Kaarten opgeheldert,* 5 books in 8 vols. (Dordrecht and Amsterdam, 1724–26), hereafter cited in the text by volume, part (if one exists), and page number. For Valentijn's description of his own four voyages I used a separate edition, although Valentijn included it in part 2 of vol. 4; *Van en Naar Indië. Valentijns 1ste en 2de Uit- en Thuisreis, vooraf-gegaan door Busken Huets Litterarisch-Critische Studie over François Valentijn,* ed. A. W. Stellwagen ('s-Gravenhage: Stemberg, 1881), cited in the text as *Uit* and page number. It should be noted that when I refer to Huet's essay on Valentijn, I am citing from Stellwagen's edition which is preceded by Huet's study.

3   Abraham van Riebeeck (1653–1713), was born at the Cape of Good Hope, the son of J. van Riebeeck, the founder of the Cape colony. He studied law at Leyden University and after graduating went to the Indies in 1677, with the rank of junior merchant. He advanced rapidly and was finally appointed as governor-general in March 1708, the post that he held until his death in November 1713. During his tenure the important tin mines on the island of Banka, off the east coast of Sumatra, were discovered. Van Riebeeck was forced to order armed intervention in local conflicts, such as those between the principalities of Bone and Goa in Celebes, and between the islands Ternate and Tidore in the Moluccas. He also presided over the establishment of the first coffee plantations that were developed around Batavia. Van Riebeeck was an indefatigable explorer and led several expeditions into the still unknown interiors of Bantam, Cheribon, and Preanger (all Javanese regions). He even traveled to the wild southern coast. He ordered a road constructed down to that coast, and it was on this southern journey that he died (in 1713 at the age of sixty). Valentijn called his opponent a bitter man with a "surly" or "testy" (*gemelijk*) character.

4   S. Peter Dance, *The Art of Natural History: Animal Illustrators and Their Work* (Woodstock: Overlook Press, 1978), 47–50.

5   Gerard Brom, *Java in onze kunst* (Rotterdam: Brusse N.V., 1931), 11.

6   The most celebrated colonial author, Multatuli, says that he lived in Valentijn's house in the city of Ambon, when Multatuli was stationed there as assistant resident during the first half of 1852. Multatuli, *Volledig Werk,* ed. Garmt Stuiveling, 15 vols. (Amsterdam: Van Oorschot, 1973–83), 2:297.

7   Other mentions of Rumphius are in *Oost-Indiën* 3.2.3; 4.2.322–23.

8   M. J. Sirks, *Indisch Natuuronderzoek* (Amsterdam: Amsterdamsche Boek- en Steendrukkerij, 1915), 47–48. See also G. P. Rouffaer and W. C. Muller, "Eerste Proeve van een Rumphius-Bibliographie," in *Rumphius Gedenkboek 1702–1902,* ed. M. Greshoff (Haarlem: Koloniaal Museum, 1902), 167.

9 "Valentijn," *Encyclopaedie*, 504.

10 F. de Haan, "Rumphius en Valentijn als Geschiedschrijvers van Ambon," in Greshoff, *Rumphius Gedenkboek 1702–1902*, 212.

11 Ibid., 20–21.

12 See my translation of and annotations for a selection of texts by Rumphius: E. M. Beekman, *The Poison Tree: Selected Writings of Rumphius on the Natural History of the Indies* (Amherst: University of Massachusetts Press, 1981).

13 The appraisal is by Wigberto Jiménez Moreno and is quoted in Laurette Séjourné, *Burning Water: Thought and Religion in Ancient Mexico* (1956; reprint, Berkeley: Shambhala, 1976), 17–18.

14 Valentijn's account of Ceylon was translated fairly recently into English, purely for its historical value: *François Valentijn's Description of Ceylon*, ed. and trans. Sinnappah Arasaratnam, Hakluyt Society, 2d ser., vol. 149 (London, 1978). Valentijn's historical significance is discussed in a review of the above volume by J. van Goor, "Boekbesprekingen," *Bijdragen tot de Taal-, Land- en Volkenkunde* 137 (1981): 365–66.

15 De Haan, "Rumphius en Valentijn," 21.

16 A good example would be De Haan, who quotes and refers to Valentijn throughout the four volumes of *Priangan*, despite his serious reservations about Valentijn's reliability. The British translator of Stavorinus's travel books quotes Valentijn repeatedly, stating at one point: "The inestimable work of Valentyn, to which the reader is so frequently referred, is scarce even in Holland; it consists of five large folio volumes, containing upwards of 1000 copper plates [*sic*]. The translator is in possession of a copy, which he procured at much pains and expense; and would his limits allow of it, he would be more copious in his extracts from it, as it is a treasure locked up in a chest, of which few have the key, no translation having ever been made of it." J. S. Stavorinus, *Voyages to the East Indies*, trans. S. H. Wilcocke, 3 vols. (1793, 1979; London, 1798; reprint, London: Dawsons of Pall Mall, 1969), 2:354. For information on Johan Splinter Stavorinus, see note 14 to the chapter on Bontekoe, above.

In the nineteenth century an American ethnologist referred to Valentijn as the expert on Ternate and Buru (!). See Albert S. Bickmore, *Travels in the East Indian Archipelago* (New York: Appleton, 1869), 240, 270, and further.

Arasaratnam (*Valentijn's Description of Ceylon*) mentions two other (hard-to-find) translations of Valentijn's work (19). There is a translation of his description of the island of Banda in *Early Voyages to Terra Australis, now called Australia*, ed. R. H. Major, Hakluyt Society, 1st ser., no. 25 (London, 1859), 75–76; and a translation of *Description of the Cape of Good Hope, with the matters concerning it*, ed. P. Serton et al, Van Riebeeck Society, 2d ser., no. 2 (Cape Town, 1971).

17 Beekman, *Poison Tree*, 17.

18 J. W. de Vries, "Het Nederlands in Indonesië: I. Historische achtergronden," *Neerlandica Extra Muros* 41 (Autumn 1983): 50–52.

19 In *Uit* he states that he arrived in Ambon on 1 May 1686 (p. 69) and that he preached a sermon in Malay on 3 August of the same year (p. 71).

20 H. J. de Graaf, *De geschiedenis van Ambon en de Zuid-Molukken* (Franeker: Wever, 1977), 179–82.

21 J. L. Swellengrebel, *In Leijdeckers Voetspoor. Anderhalve Eeuw Bijbelvertaling en Taalkunde in de Indonesische Talen*, 2 vols. Proceedings of the Royal Institute for Linguistics, Geography, and Ethnography, 68 and 82 ('s-Gravenhage: Nijhof, 1974), 1:8.

22 Quoted by B. H. M. Vlekke, *Nusantara: A History of the East Indian Archipelago* (Cambridge: Harvard University Press, 1945), 132.

23 Swellengrebel, *In Leijdeckers*, 1:11–13.

24   Ibid., 13–20; De Vries, "Het Nederlands in Indonesië," 51.

25   Swellengrebel, *In Leijdeckers,* 1 : 15; "Valentijn," *Encyclopaedie,* 503.

26   "Valentijn," *Encyclopaedie,* 503.

27   My remarks about De Jager are primarily based on two articles from the nineteenth century. P. A. Leupe, "Herbert de Jager," *Bijdragen tot de Taal-, Land- en Volkenkunde* 4 (1862): 17–22; and P. A. Leupe, "Herbert de Jager," *Bijdragen tot de Taal-, Land- en Volkenkunde* 3 (1869): 67–97. Other important information is in De Haan, *Priangan* 1 : 220–24. See also the article on "De Jager" in *Encyclopaedie van Nederlandsch-Indië* 2 : 177–78.

28   Leupe, "De Jager" (1862), 20.

29   See Stavorinus, *Voyages to the East Indies* 1 : 515.

30   Leupe, "De Jager" (1869), 69–70.

31   "De Jager," *Encyclopaedie* 2 : 177.

32   Leupe, "De Jager" (1869), 85.

33   "De Jager," *Encyclopaedie* 2 : 178.

34   Leupe, "De Jager" (1869), 85.

35   For these letters, see Rouffaer and Muller, "Eerste Proeve van een Rumphius-Bibliographie," 189–90; Rumphius's reference to De Jager as a "learned botanist," is in Georgius Everhardus Rumphius, *Het Amboinsche Kruid-boek,* 6 vols. (Amsterdam, 1741–50), 5 : 442; see also 1 : 50; 2 : 48, 254; 5 : 23, 25, 64, 116, 183.

36   A *fiscal* was sixth in importance below the governor of a province. He was a magistrate who guarded against offenses against the revenue (*fiscus* in Latin). Stavorinus (*Voyages to the East Indies* 2 : 380) states that a fiscal's duty was "to take care that the property of the Company be not injured; he has likewise a concluding vote in the council of polity." Perhaps one could envision the fiscal as a kind of public prosecutor (see also 2 : 383).

37   *Lanquas* or *langkuwas* is *Alpinia galanga,* a herb with a long stem and clusters of flowers. The white variety is used for cooking. The rhizome and seeds of the red were used for medicinal purposes. At another place Valentijn says that *lanquas* is "green ginger" (2 : 158).

38   *Lolan wood* is probably a reference to the shrub *Caesalpina Sappan* L., elsewhere known as *sappan* or *sepang* (*sapang*). Its leaves were used as a medicine.

39   *Arak, arack,* or *arrack,* derived from the Arabic *arak,* meaning the "perspiration" of the date palm, generally referred to any native distilled hard liquor. In the Indies it was often a distillate made from molasses, but it was also made from rice, and from the sap of the areca palm. Stavorinus (*Voyages to the East Indies* 2 : 391–92) remarks that heavy drinking was normal on Ambon: "in the afternoon, more strong liquor is drunk, either arrack or geneva [i.e., jenever], than at Batavia, or in the west of India . . . ten or twelve drams is not an uncommon whet in a morning at Amboyna."

40   Brom, *Java,* 11.

41   W. Sewel, *A New Dictionary of English and Dutch* (Amsterdam, 1691), 283.

42   St. Jago Island, the largest of the Cape Verde Islands, is known in Portuguese as São Thiago. It had a very unhealthy climate, high volcanic mountains in the interior, but also, so important at that time, many perennial streams of fresh water.

43   Two other examples are the hilarious tale of how a "surgeon" revenges the theft by the "Quarter-master" of several bottles of his "Clove Comfits" (*Uit,* 80–82); and the story of how Governor-General Maetsuycker discomfited his wife because she had allowed one of his shirts to be made with only one sleeve. The story is definitely intended to put Maetsuycker in a bad light, which it does, but it is also a fine tale (4.1.303–4).

44   A fine example of a dramatic story is the one Valentijn narrates about a *seur,* a peculiar

term which Valentijn translates as *bookkeeper*. The man existed—see *Priangan* 1 : 22—and his strange and violent behavior reads like a modern tale of the absurd (*Uit*, 105–20).

45 See the letters Leupe prints ("De Jager" [1869], 76–79). The French- or Latin-derived words are too numerous to be listed, but one of the letters includes such usage as "geraeckte ik ook bij occasie," "mijn defentie jegens," "gunstigh approbatie . . . heeft gelieven to be-nificeren," "collatie van deze chargie . . . approbatie gelieven to confirmeren," "in de con-duite van de hoofdbesoignes naer de prudence ende de circumspectie," "en nederigheyt te ambriëren indien dezelve nogh niet gesuppleert is," "het favorabel expreseren," "de pa-trocinie . . . te distitueren," and "respectueuse memorie." For constrast, let me just mention a few of Valentijn's Dutch expressions or words: "het grimmelt van allerlei menschen" (2 : 130); "dat er nog al iets van den ouden suurdeegsem in zit" (2 : 143); "doch ik geloove niet, dat zij hunne vingeren daar blauw aan telden" (*Uit*, 100); or "bloedvriend" for kin (2 : 179). See also Huet (*Uit*, 30–31).

46 E. du Perron, *De Muze van Jan Companjie. Overzichtelijke Verzameling van Neder-lands-Oost Indiese Belletrie uit de Companjiestijd (1600–1780)* (Bandoeng: Nix and Co., 1939), 93.

47 Johan van der Woude, *Maria Dermoût. De vrouw en de schrijfster* ('s-Gravenhage and Rotterdam: Nijgh en Van Ditmar, 1973), 71, 100–101, 111–12.

48 Maria Dermoût, *Verzameld Werk* (Amsterdam: Querido, 1974), 448. There are, for instance, a number of details from Valentijn in her finest fiction, *De tien duizend dingen*. The "Professor" in that novel travels with a complete set of Valentijn and Rumphius (*Ver-zameld Werk*, 258). That novel was published in the present series as *The Ten Thousand Things* (Amherst: University of Massachusetts Press, 1983). Dermoût's stories that are en-tirely based on Valentijn's information are "Koning Baaboe en de veertig jongelingen," "De boom des levens," and "De goede slang" (*Verzameld Werk*, 89–107, 447–58). The edition of Valentijn mentioned by Dermoût is a truncated one from the nineteenth century. *Oud en Nieuw Oost-Indiën* was never reprinted in its entirety, and only two abbreviated versions exist. Dermoût's edition is the three-volume *François Valentijns Oud en Nieuw Oost-Indiën*, ed. S. Keyzer ('s-Gravenhage, 1856–58); this was reprinted in Amsterdam in 1862 and was for some time a kind of Baedeker for colonial officials because the text restricted itself to descriptions of colonial Indonesia. The only other "edition" of Valentijn is the ex-cerpt of his travels edited by Stellwagen (see n. 2).

49 *Alfuran* was a general term for the pagan peoples who lived in the mountainous inte-rior of Ceram and Buru. The word itself probably derived from a language once spoken in northern Halmahera; *halefuru* meant *wild terrain* or *jungle*. Over the years it came to mean *bushman* or *aborigine* and was used for *pagans*, i.e., anyone who was neither Christian nor Muslim. Stavorinus quotes Rumphius's description of them from a rare document that is now lost. "I met with the following account of them, in the description of Amboyna com-posed by Rumphius, which, having been prohibited by the government at Batavia, has never been printed, but of which a manuscript copy is preserved in the secretary's office at Am-boyna." He then quotes Rumphius:

[The Alfurans] are large, strong, and savage people, in general taller than the inhabitants of the sea-shores; they go mostly naked, both men and women, and only wear a thick bandage around their waist, which is called *chiaaca*, and is made of the milky bark of a tree. . . . They are sharp-sighted, and so nimble in running, that they can run down and kill a wild hog, at its utmost speed. An ancient, but most detestable and criminal custom prevails among them, agreeable to which, no one is allowed to take a wife, before he can shew a head of an enemy which he has cut off. . . . They are not to be broken of this horrid custom; and it is the only objection they make to embracing the Christian religion, that they must then abandon it; for no one attains a higher degree of fame and respect, than he who has brought in the most heads. (*Voyages to the East Indies* 2:357–61)

50   *Ceram* is the largest island of the Moluccas. In Valentijn's time it was a rough and wild place, populated by Alfurans in the interior and by the colonial Dutch and other people living in small settlements on the coast. *Sepa* was a small town on Ceram's southern coast between the Bay of Elpaputih and Teluti Bay.

51   *Victoria Castle* was a stronghold on the shore, intended to protect the city of Ambon from attack. It was built by the Portuguese and taken over by the Dutch after they expelled their rivals. Stavorinus described the fort, then called New Victoria because it was rebuilt after the earthquake in 1755, as follows: "It stands close to the waterside, a little to the west of the mouth of Way Nitu, and exactly opposite to the road, where ships commonly lie at anchor." He goes on to give a very detailed account of the structure, but finally judges it to be inadequate because of "the lowness of its site, by which, in my opinion, it would not be able to make any long or effectual resistance, if the enemy were once landed, and could get their artillery on shore, so as to erect batteries on the surrounding heights" (*Voyages to the East Indies*, 2:401–8).

52   I translated *Landraad* as *Native Court* after J. S. Furnivall, *Netherlands India, a Study of Plural Economy* (1944; reprint, Amsterdam: B. M. Israel, 1976), 36.

53   *Shallop* for *Chaloep*. This was a large, undecked, heavy boat, with one or more masts, carrying fore-and-aft or lug sails, and sometimes armed with guns.

54   *Petola* refers to an expensive kind of cloth, brightly colored with a distinctive design.

55   I am not sure what is meant by *Basta*, but Valentijn may be referring to *basuta* (*kain basuta*), a silk fabric from Surat, a town and district near Bombay, India.

56   *Salampun* puzzles me, too. Perhaps it is a variation of *selampuri*, a cotton fabric or chintz, which was at the time a common trade item. Or it may refer to *selampai*, a word that translates as *handkerchief* or *scarf*.

57   *Sagu,* or *sago*, was the staple food of the Moluccas, particularly on Ambon, Ceram, and Buru. The sago tree is a palm; the most common variety used to obtain the food is the *Metroxylon Rumphii*, named after Rumphius, who taught the inhabitants how to obtain the mealy pith from the tree which is then processed into the farinaceous meal known as sago meal.

58   *Linggoa* is the name of the lingo tree (*Pterocarpus Indicus*), which was found throughout the archipelago. It was a very desirable tree because of its durable wood.

59   *Tutombos* are boxes.

60   *Cacatuwas* is a variant spelling of cockatoos.

61   *Luris* are commonly known as lories, a small, brightly colored kind of parrot.

62   *Honimoa* was the older name for an island commonly known as Saparua. It is one of the Uliaser islands that are east of Ambon and south of western Ceram.

63   *Papuas* was a general term denoting the coastal people of New Guinea and adjacent islands. Like *Alfuran,* it was used in speaking of a large number of different ethnic groups as well as pirates who were not necessarily born in that region. As a general term, *Papua* became synonymous with cruel, barbaric and ferocious people who roamed the seas for booty and killed anyone if it suited their purposes. There are quite a few accounts attesting to the fear these people inspired. The word itself, *papua* or *pepuah,* means "frizzled" hair, and *negeri pepuah,* the name for New Guinea, meant "the land of men with frizzled hair."

64   *Nusanivel* (also, at times, *Noussanivel*) was the name of the southernmost district on Leitimor, which is the lower one of the two peninsulae that together form the island of Am-

bon. The term *king* is a hyperbole. Every village—or *negree* as the Dutch term *negorij* is translated in Stavorinus—had its chief, and some of these chiefs might call themselves *rajah*. The rajah of Nusanivel, for instance, had control of three villages that constituted his "realm," when Stavorinus was in Ambon. Nevertheless, at one time, he adopted the title of "king of ten thousand swords" (*Voyage to the East Indies* 2 : 364).

65   *St. Anthonies Fire* was the old and popular name for the disease called *erysipelas*. It manifested itself by a high fever and an inflammation of the skin that gave it a deep red color, hence it was sometimes called "the rose" or "the sacred fire." It was once believed that if a person who was suffering from this disease prayed to Saint Anthony, he would be cured by this patron of swineherds.

Franz Wilhelm Junghuhn

FRANZ WILHELM JUNGHUHN
(1809–64) was one of those nineteenth-century romantic spirits who combined a passionate thirst for knowledge with a profound feeling for nature. Essentially a loner, he did not fit comfortably in what was then established German society and, like other recalcitrant men of genius, found in the tropics the chance to realize his potential.[1]

To please his father, Junghuhn studied medicine in Halle and Berlin, although his passion for botany was already evident in his earliest publication (1830), a scientific article, in Latin, on mycology. When he returned home to Mansfeld an der Wippra in 1830, he tried to commit suicide in a fit of depression. His father considered the attempt's failure as proof of his son's incompetence.

While still a student, he entered Prussian military service as a "surgeon" in 1831; that year he also fought a duel in Berlin. His opponent, a fellow student, was unscathed and Junghuhn himself received only a minor wound, but it was strictly illegal for Prussian officers to duel and at the end of 1831 he was arrested and sentenced to ten years in prison. On the first day of 1832, Junghuhn found himself incarcerated in Fort Ehrenbreitstein. To realize his desperate wish for freedom, he successfully feigned madness and managed to escape. He walked from Coblenz—a city on the Rhine below Bonn—to Toulon in southern France, where he joined the French Foreign Legion.[2] After six months of duty in North Africa he was declared unfit to serve in a hot climate and was repatriated to France. When he reached Paris, Junghuhn applied to the German authorities for clemency and found out that it had been granted already, just before he escaped from jail. Down and out in Paris, he managed to locate the famous but reclusive botanist Persoon, who told Junghuhn that there were opportunities awaiting adventurous people in the Dutch East Indies. Junghuhn managed to get to Holland, and, after passing the requisite exams, was hired as a health officer third class in the Dutch colonial army. He arrived in Batavia in October 1835 and spent most of the next thirteen years traveling for scientific purposes in Java and Sumatra, paying only the most cursory attention to the job for which he had been hired.

Due to his enlightened superior, Dr. E. A. Fritze, Junghuhn was able to devote most of his time to the study of nature. He tried to become a member of the prestigious Commission for Natural Sciences but failed at first, although the same commission employed him the following year to investigate the Batak region of Sumatra.[3] After two years he returned to Java in 1842 and in 1847 published his observations. In 1845 he finally received an honorable discharge from the army and was appointed a member of the Commission for Natural Sciences.

Junghuhn's remarkable health began to suffer from the rigors of almost perpetual traveling in the tropics. He spent a great deal of time climbing in the Javanese mountains, explored working volcanoes such as the Merapi, Slamat, Tangkuban Prahu, and Galunggung, and journeyed to regions where no European had ever been. His published reports reveal him as an ideal observer—a man gifted with a great deal of patience, self-control, devotion to knowledge, and a passion for nature that he never compromised. The unremitting heat and attendant difficulties of traveling in the tropics, when he often spent months alone in uncharted territories, sapped his strength and forced him to apply for a European leave. He "longed" as he wrote "for snow and ice." He left Java in 1848, but typically for him, he did not travel by the accustomed sea route. He went overland and reached Leyden in the same year.[4] The initial furlough of three years was expanded to seven, a period that he mostly spent in Leyden, writing, or in traveling around Europe. During this European sojourn Junghuhn married (in 1850), made Alexander von Humboldt's acquaintance (they later corresponded when Junghuhn returned to the tropics), and wrote his most important texts.

One of these represents his main scientific work: the four volumes of *Java, zijne gedaante, zijn plantentooi en inwendige bouw* (Java: Its configuration, flora, and interior structure) (1850–53; 2d ed. 1853–54).[5] It provides a detailed geological and botanical description of the island, amply displaying Junghuhn's talents as a botanist, geologist, volcanologist, geographer, and climatologist. Its most notable contribution was a greatly detailed scientific description of Java's mountains and volcanoes, in which he considered them in geographical order from west to east. In 1854 an album of plates was added, comprising eleven "picturesque views" drawn by Junghuhn himself which, in their provocative mixture of sharp detail and grandiose perspective, still appeal to the modern eye. Junghuhn was the first scientist in the Indies to use the new technique of photography to record what he saw, even devising a timer to take his own portrait.[6]

The other important work from this period was his controversial book *Licht-en Schaduwbeelden uit de Binnenlanden van Java* (Images of light and shadow from Java's interior), which he published under a pseudonym in 1854. Not until 1864 did it appear with his own name on the title page. *Licht-en Schaduwbeelden* presents a narrative of various travels in Java, most of them the same ones he had described more objectively in the four volumes of *Java*. The prose is vivid and lyrical and presents a fine example of a kind of travel literature that is not devoid of scientific aspirations. This was not, however, the reason the book became a cause célèbre. Interspersed with the descriptive narrations are romantic discussions on the nature of religion by four brothers called "Day," "Night," "Dawn," and "Dusk." The tone is sharply critical of Christianity while it pleads at the same time for a pantheistic deism to be primarily represented by "Nature." *Licht-en Schaduwbeelden* was published in Holland, even though it provoked the controversy Junghuhn had anticipated, but the German version was banned in both Germany and Austria because the authorities felt that the book contained a "slanderous degradation of Christianity." This was by no means a singular venture into controversy. Several of the great naturalists of the eighteenth and nineteenth centuries were either critical of or indifferent to orthodox religion. Alexander von Humboldt considered Christianity merely a myth beyond his comprehension and never wasted his time on theological quarrels. Yet he practically sanctified the scientific method when he elevated "induction and reasoning" to assume the "severer aspect" of the "philosophy of Nature."[7] Surprisingly though, few of these naturalists became intractable atheists. As the translated text indicates, Junghuhn would have very much approved of the dictum of the American naturalist John Bartram that "through this telescope, I see God in his glory."[8] Like many of his peers, Junghuhn subscribed to Pope's pronouncement that he was "slave to no sect, who takes no private road, / But looks through nature up to Nature's God" (*Essay on Man*).

The pantheistic harmony both Junghuhn and Humboldt felt to be present in nature was shared by Wordsworth who, in turn, appeared to have been inspired by the work of John Bartram (1699–1777) and his son William (1739–1823). In 1764 John Bartram wrote to Benjamin Rush that he had "queried whether there is not a portion of universal intellect diffused in all life & self motion adequate to its particular organization." It seems that for all these naturalists the direct experience of nature led them away from established religion. John Bartram, for example, hoped that a more diligent pursuit of botanical studies "will lead you into the knowledge of more certain truths than all the pretended Revelations of our Mistery mongers & their inspirations."[9]

In 1851 Junghuhn published his catalogue of the plants he had discovered in Java and Sumatra: *Enumeratio plantarum, quas in insulis Java et Sumatra, detexit Fr. Junghuhn.*[10] While still alive he received the highest honor a botanist can hope for, that of having a plant named after him, which, as the Englishman Peter Collinson wrote to Linnaeus, is to be granted "a species of eternity."[11] Among several, there was *Festuca nubila Junghuhniensis*, a rugged species of grass he found over 8,000 feet above sea level on the slopes of Mount Merbabu in Java, and a large club-moss, *Dacryduüm Junghuhnii*, he discovered in Sumatra.

In 1855 Junghuhn returned to Java with the rank of inspector and was charged with the task of establishing the cultivation of the cinchona tree. This occupied him until his death in 1864. Ironically, Junghuhn primarily became known as the man who made quinine production possible in the Dutch East Indies, whereas his far more impressive achievements as a naturalist were known to only a few. His place as a pioneering naturalist is ensured now and, like Rumphius, Junghuhn's scientific merit is considered to parallel his literary abilities. One finds in his work an awed yet measured appreciation of what in many ways was still pristine tropical nature. All his writing is suffused with a pragmatic lyricism which admirably conveys the grandeur of the tropics without falling prey to sentimental excess.

AFTER his death Junghuhn was rightly celebrated as the "Humboldt of Java." This epitaph referred to Alexander von Humboldt (1769–1859), the most widely admired naturalist of his age.[12] It is said that when Humboldt lived in Paris during the Empire, Napoleon was jealous of the Prussian scientist and diplomat because he was rumored to be as famous as the French emperor.

Humboldt's fame began when he traveled to South America, accompanied by Aimé Bonpland, between 1799 and 1804. In June 1802 he climbed Mount Chimborazo in Ecuador, then considered the highest peak in the world. This feat established his popular renown which was to last for the next half century.

The scientific data and theories emanating from his South American travels were published at Humboldt's own expense in a monumental work entitled *Voyage de Humboldt et Bonpland 1799–1804,* which finally comprised thirty volumes and was printed in Paris between 1805 and 1836. Junghuhn could not have consulted this enormous series; it was so costly to produce that it ruined its author financially; Humboldt was not even able to keep a complete set for himself. Individual volumes were published separately, however, and they proved to be quite influential as well as popular. One of these was *Voyage aux régions équinoxiales du nouveau continent fait dans les années 1799 à 1804 par Alexandre de Humboldt et Aimé Bonpland* (Paris, 1814–19). It was translated into English as *Personal Narrative of Travels to the Equinoxial Regions of the New Continent during the Years 1799–1804* and was published in London in 1825. This work influenced Darwin's decision to make his own momentous journey on the *Beagle* between 1831 and 1836. Humboldt's *Personal Narrative* was one of the few books Darwin took with him and he refers frequently to Humboldt throughout the notebooks which form the basis of his work *The Voyage of the Beagle* (1839; 2d, rev. ed. 1845). Darwin notes that because "the force of impressions generally depends on preconceived ideas, I may add, that mine were taken from the vivid descriptions in the Personal Narrative of Humboldt, which far exceed in merit anything else which I have read."[13] At one point he wrote to England that "formerly I admired Humboldt, I now almost adore him; he alone gives any notion of the feelings which are raised in the mind on entering the Tropics."[14] As if to affirm their intellectual kinship, Humboldt has numerous references to Darwin in the great work of his old age, *Kosmos* (*Cosmos*) (1845–62).

Junghuhn's work may also be said to have found its inspiration in Humboldt, though his style is closer to Darwin's limpid English prose. For one thing, Junghuhn avoided Humboldt's prolixity while displaying an equally impressive range of accomplishments. Like Darwin's *Voyage of the Beagle,* Junghuhn's *Licht-en Schaduwbeelden* echoed the innovative form of *Personal Narrative,* where Humboldt mingles impressions of tropical nature with scientific observations but eschews a more personal and romantic narration. Junghuhn's work also resembles Humboldt's *Ansichten der Natur* (1808; published in English as *Views of Nature* in 1850) which offered a series of tableaux describing exotic aspects of tropical nature, augmented with "illustrations" based on scientific data. But Junghuhn was more successful than Humboldt in perfecting a prose style that, though dependent upon reason and objective data, could still convey the excitement and splendor of tropical nature. As Humboldt wrote in his introduction to *Cosmos:* "descriptions of nature ought not to be deficient in a tone of life-like truthfulness, while the mere enumeration of a series of general results is productive of a no less wearying impression than the elaborate accumulation of the individual data of observation."[15] Both Humboldt and Junghuhn wanted to avoid the romantic excess available in nature descriptions by Chateaubriand or Bernardin de Saint-Pierre, but they did not want to relinquish the quickening of the creative powers that a contemplation of tropical nature will provoke.

Junghuhn's pantheism may also have found its source in Humboldt, though neither writer ever divorced emotional fervor from scientific observation. In his introduction to *Cosmos*, Humboldt explained his intentions in terms reminiscent of Junghuhn: "Nature considered *rationally*, that is to say, submitted to the process of thought, is a unity in diversity of phenomena; a harmony, blending together all created things, however dissimilar in form and attributes; one great whole animated by the breath of life."[16] Junghuhn was as astonished as Humboldt by "the universal profusion of life" experienced firsthand, and was also moved by what Humboldt described as "this mysterious reaction of the sensuous on the ideal [which] gives to the study of nature, when considered from a higher point of view, a peculiar charm which has not hitherto been sufficiently recognized."[17]

Humboldt and Junghuhn were both enthusiastic mountain climbers possessed with a desire to observe and explain the nature of volcanoes. Humboldt recorded careful observations of the volcanoes in the Andes, and Junghuhn, in the second volume of his main work, *Java,* presented a "history of the volcanoes of western and middle Java." Junghuhn's love for mountains became legendary; it was said that when he was dying he asked his physician to open the windows which looked out on Java's famous volcano Tangkuban Prahu, remarking that he wanted "to bid farewell" to his "beloved mountains" and "breathe once more the pure mountain air."[18] In *Java,* Junghuhn adopted Humboldt's innovation of printing cross sections "of the vertical profile of a country . . . showing at a glance the relative extension of high-lying and low-lying districts" in addition to comparative elevations of mountain peaks, ridges, and passes.[19] Not surprisingly, it was Junghuhn's work on Java's volcanoes that led Humboldt to praise him in the fourth volume of *Cosmos*. Quoting often and at length from both *Java* and Junghuhn's book on Sumatra, Humboldt based considerable portions of his section concerning "true volcanoes" on *Java,* praising its author as a "learned, bold, untiringly active naturalist." And Humboldt relied entirely on Junghuhn for his discussion of the "volcanic island-world" between "the parallels of 10° south and 14° north," recommending him not only for his firsthand descriptions of the major volcanoes, but also for his discussion of sedimentary formations, for his contributions of "the first example of the fossil Flora of a purely tropical region," and for having provided proof of the "ribbed formation" (*gerippter Gestaltung*) of the Javanese volcanoes. In general he commended Junghuhn for his "admirable observations upon the structure of the volcanoes, the geography of plants, and the psychometric conditions of moisture" in the Malay archipelago.[20]

Junghuhn was as fascinated by climatological studies as Humboldt, who turned it into a significant scientific endeavor. He was similarly attracted to Humboldt's cherished notion of a "geography of plants." Humboldt published this theory as a separate *Essai sur la géographie des plantes* in 1805—dedicating the German edition, published in the same year, to Goethe, the author of *The Metamorphosis of Plants* (1790)—and developed it at length in *Views of Nature* and *Cosmos*. Generally speaking, it accounted for the change in flora as a result of climactic variations. The mapping of this "geography" fittingly combined Humboldt's desire for rational investigation with the enjoyment of contemplating nature because "the impression produced upon the mind by the physiognomy of the vegetation, depends upon the local distribution, the number, and the luxuriance of growth of the vegetable forms predominating in the general mass." Thus "descriptive botany [when] no longer confined to the narrow circle of the determination of genera and species, leads the observer who traverses distant lands and lofty mountains to the study of the geographical distribution of plants over the earth's surface, according to distance from the equator and vertical elevation above the sea."[21] In the first volume of *Java*, Junghuhn mapped such a "geography" of Java's plants in both scientific terms and descriptions, which are still unsurpassed in their accuracy and eloquence. Taken as a whole, Junghuhn's work complies with what Humboldt felt was the "main purpose" of his expedition to South America: an attempt "to find out how the forces of nature interreact upon one another and how the geographic environment influences plant and animal life. In other words, I must find out about the unity of nature."[22]

From 1855 until his death in 1864, Junghuhn was officially charged with the cultivation of cinchona trees in the Dutch East Indies. This task made him a controversial figure in scientific circles but also accounts for his being popularly credited as the man who made quinine available in the Indies. Again one wonders if Humboldt provided the stimulus. Among many other accomplishments of his South American journey was Humboldt's study of the natural environment of the tree that produced the "fever bark" (*Cinchona condaminea*) in the upper Amazon region in Peru. He published a treatise on the "Quina Tree" in 1807, wrote about it in *Views of Nature* and again, extensively, in *Plantes équinoxiales* (1805–17). Both Britain and Holland dispatched botanists to the regions described by Humboldt in order to bring back specimens for regional cultivation in their colonies. By the turn of the century, the Dutch had established a monopoly on the manufacture of quinine from their extensive forests in Java. It had been Junghuhn who correctly designated the mountains above Bandung in western Java as the best geographical location for the cultivation of these trees. He was severely criticized for his method of planting and for favoring one kind (*Cinchona Pahudiana*) above all others, but his work laid the foundation for a business enterprise that in the first three decades of this century showed a net profit of over four and a half millon dollars.[23]

THOUGH he spent twice as many years in the tropics as Humboldt and Darwin together, and endured great hardships and dangers, Junghuhn never appeared to have lost the sense of awe Humboldt felt compelled to reiterate in his old age.

It is clear that for these three great naturalists of the nineteenth century Aldous Huxley's criticism, that "the Wordsworthian who exports his pantheistic worship of Nature to the tropics is liable to have his religious convictions somewhat rudely shattered," is not applicable. Not one of them felt that "the life of those vast masses of swarming vegetation is alien to the human spirit and hostile to it."[24] Darwin, in fact, reserved his negative feelings for barren wastelands such as Patagonia where hardly a shrub distinguished the landscape. Junghuhn lived in the tropics for more than two decades and the subsequent translation shows that his devoted respect never diminished. Humboldt's enthusiasm is easily documented, and Darwin recorded his state of mind as follows: "the elegance of the grasses, the novelty of parasitical plants, the beauty of the flowers, the glossy green of the foliage, but above all the luxuriance of the vegetation, filled me with admiration."[25]

Similar sentiments were recorded by William Bartram. Despite experiencing considerable hardships and very real dangers in East Florida, which he recorded in his famous *Travels* (1791), Bartram observed in a manner remarkably like Junghuhn's final paean to Nature (see pp. 120–22 below):

How harmonious and soothing is this native sylvan music now at still evening! inexpressibly tender are the responsive cooings of the innocent dove, in the fragrant Zanthoxilon groves, and the variable and tuneful warblings of the nonparel; with the more sprightly and elevated strains of the blue linnet and golden icterus;

this is indeed harmony even amidst the incessant croakings of the frogs; the shades of silent night are made more chearful, with the shrill voice of the whip-poor-will and active mock-bird. My situation high and airy, a brisk and cool breeze steadily and incessantly passing over the clear waters of the lake, and fluttering over me through the surrounding groves, wings its way to the moonlight savannas, while I repose on my sweet and healthy couch of the soft Tillandsi ulnea-adscites, and the latter gloomy and still hours of night passed rapidly away as it were in a moment.[26]

One wonders if Humboldt, Junghuhn, and Darwin read William Bartram's *Travels,* for they share affinities of style and conception. It is likely, because Bartram's *Travels* enjoyed some international success. After its initial appearance in Philadelphia in 1791, it appeared in London in 1792, and was reprinted the next year. A German translation was published in Berlin in 1793, and a Dutch version was printed in Haarlem in 1794, and again in 1795 and 1797. A French edition appeared in 1799, with a second edition in 1801. Furthermore, Bartram's marvelous descriptions of the Okefinokee Swamp were quite literally an inspiration for Wordsworth, Coleridge, and Chateaubriand. The book would have been of more than passing interest to Humboldt, Junghuhn, and Darwin.

Junghuhn was, like Humboldt, a Romantic. This is not only a reference to his temperament but also to his selfless dedication of his cultivated intellect to a grand purpose. As Alexander von Humboldt wrote to his brother Wilhelm in 1822: "we live in a century where nothing stays in its place." The great advances Romanticism inspired in the nineteenth century were no longer based on academic speculation but derived from examining things at the source. In Germany one can point to the work of the brothers Grimm in folklore and philology, or to Humboldt's grandiose attempt to encompass all of nature based on his own observations; there was Darwin's adventure on board *The Beagle* followed by his laborious research which preceded the theory of evolution; in Finland, Elias Lönnrot collected traditional songs, lyrics, and magic formulae from country folk before they were irretrievably lost, and thus fashioned Finland's epic, the *Kalevala;* and in the United States, Audubon ("the American woodsman") displayed all the birds and quadrupeds within one single "palpable vision of the New World."

An infectious optimism energized these enormous nineteenth-century endeavors—an optimism alien to the scrupulous specialism of our present day. Its most fitting metaphor can probably be found in Humboldt's *Cosmos,* whose very title announced a belief in the harmonious order of the physical world, and which seriously intended to embrace "everything we know today of the phenomena in the celestial spaces and of life on earth, from the stars in the nebulae to the geography of mosses on granitic rocks, *and in a book which stimulates by its lively language the imagination.*"[27] Mere hyperbole was never intended, and Junghuhn could have said with Humboldt that "I have tried to be truthful in my description, scientifically true without going into the arid region of knowledge." Men like Junghuhn expanded a cramped vision while preserving the requisite awe for the grandeur of nature. He was read with admiration and approval by Humboldt and Schopenhauer, and translated in *Harper's Magazine* for the edification of an American audience as early as 1853.[28]

Junghuhn called scientific instruments such as the sextant, thermometer, compass, microscope, magnetometer, and eudiometer his "symbols of faith," while at the same time he confessed to belonging "to the high, vaulted church with its roof strewn with stars."[29] It is this responsible yet sympathetic veneration for the forces of nature one wishes to have restored.

THE following translation provides incidents of travel from 1846 and 1847, when Junghuhn made what was probably his longest sustained journey, traversing Java from west to east.[30] This selection, which ends with a description of a tropical night, was chosen to provide readers unacquainted with the tropics with a firsthand account of a diurnal round in those regions. The same experiences were used by Junghuhn in his main work, *Java,* but in a more sober fashion. One should note that Junghuhn's correlations between environmental facts and the flora and fauna of Java are clearly reminiscent of Humboldt's "geography of plants," while they also hint at Darwinism, although *On the Origin of Species* was not published until late 1859, less than five years before Junghuhn's death.

We continued our journey through a vast, relatively flat, mountainous terrain which toward the south gradually descended. It was crisscrossed with canyons or gorges at considerable distance from each other, at their bottom foaming streams coursing to the sea. In the top layer of soil between these canyons were sometimes gently sloping depressions and small valleys or grooves in the shape of troughs, covered primarily with woods. The rest of the surface was covered with the almost glistening white, grayish-green *alang-alang*[31] and *glagah*[32] grass, with only a few scattered trees. These groves of trees, reminiscent of islands in this waving sea of grass, gave the entire region the appearance of a park, with lilac-blue *bungur* flowers (*Adambea glabra*) or the yellow flowers of the *sempur tree* (*Colbertia obovata*) flashing prettily through the green of these little oases.

A large number of deer (*Cervus russa*) enlivened the region. Whole groups of them sprang through the grass to hide from the increasing heat of the sun deep inside these little groves. And the wild boars (*Sus vittatus*) who never fall victim here to the island people, were even tamer and only reluctantly left the few puddles which had not yet dried up in our path. Grunting all the time, they got out of our way. We often saw peacocks fly from one shrub to another or sit on the ground with their beautiful plumage shining in the sun, apparently dining on termites. Besides *glagah* reed, there also grew amidst the *alang-alang* some other kind, to wit, *manja* grass. From its curved ears very large, pear-shaped nests were suspended, floating some three to four feet off the ground. The only opening was at the bottom. They were the work of a tiny bird, called *manuk manja*, which lives from the seeds of this kind of grass. It protects its young from small vermin, especially from attacks by ants, by suspending its artfully woven nest from a thread. Small flights of these pretty birds (*Ploceus barbatus*) swept over the carpet of grass.

From within the groves we heard the cooing of turtledoves, accompanied from time to time by the hoarse crowing of a wild cock. And because their existence is so closely tied to that of ruminants, there was no lack of tigers here either; such abundant numbers of deer and *kidangs* (Javanese deer), rhinos and wild boars are usually not found in the dense primordial jungle. And it happened sometimes that when we approached one of those *glagah* stands, as big and tall as a Javanese house, our horses would stop and, trembling and shaking in every limb, refuse to go on. Their fine sense of smell had detected a tiger which could well be hidden quite close to us. They prefer such *glagah* stands and, in typical feline fashion, do not betray their presence during the day, no matter how close you pass by their lair.

Because around noon the heat in these *alang* fields often reaches a temperature as high as 90 degrees, we refreshed ourselves, from lack of water, by chewing on the green fruit of the little *malaka* tree (*Emblica officinalis*),[33] because they were within easy reach. If one looked up through the pinnated foliage of these little trees, it seemed as if a thin veil had been stretched between our eyes and the clear blue sky, thereby affording us with a most enchanting sight.

When we descended further and were nearing the coast, the scenery around us gradually changed. The *malaka* trees and groves became less frequent, and the south wind coming off the sea was now more noticeable while bringing us some greatly appreciated coolness. Soon we saw in front and below us a strip of palm trees. Between their grayish trunks, often burned black from fire, glimmered the distant ocean blue. These palm trees rose above the grass-covered ground at some distance from each other and stretched out by the thousands to our left and right. Each trunk rose up straight as a pillar, and was adorned only at the top by a crown of leaves. Practically all of them were fan or *gebang* palms (*Corypha gebanga*), with amazingly large dry leaves continually rustling in the wind. We frequently startled large hornbills (*Buceros plicatus*)[34] sitting high up in the palms, who then flew to another part of the forest all the while huffing and puffing with that peculiar sound typical of these birds.

We didn't go directly down to the coast via this narrow but miles-long strip of fan-palms, but proceeded at an angle westward where a somewhat higher region, or flat mountain terrain, jutted into the sea in the form of a cape (*udjung*). There, near caves filled with birds' nests, had to be the village of Gnarak[35] which was our destination for that night. The somber forest of tall trees casts its shadow in this part of the country up to the very edge of the coastline, and presents a sharp contrast with both the withered *alang* fields without any shade, as well as with the fan-palms which spread out on this side of it. From a distance one could already discern a totally different quality of the land due to the drastically different physiognomy of organic nature.

Perhaps nothing is more appropriate to demonstrate to a traveler in what manner all of creation is harmoniously linked than to make a journey from the high country—the volcanic interior of a tropical land—across terraces of sandstone and other Neptunian mountain varieties,[36] down to the coast. The difference in elevation above sea level causes a difference in climate (a varying average temperature), while various original elements of the soil give shape to different forms of life for every distinct level on an ascending scale. Different plants mean different animals who feed on them. Here an arid layer of sandstone containing much silica (quartz) and covered with a meager crust of cracked clay; while over there might be a chalk cliff rich in carbon dioxide and easily soluble in water; or a fertile soil enriched by a river and disintegrated felstone from lava rivers and banks of trachyte.[37] And again, over there figs and other tall trees providing much shade and fruit for countless birds, monkeys, and squirrels who, in turn, are hunted by the wild cats; while here one finds an abundance of grass that provides food for deer as well as for wild boars who live on the sweet and extensive root system of the *alang-alang* grass. Then there are tigers who prey on the boars, and peacocks who not only feed on fruits but also like to peck around in the remnants of animals who fell victim to the tigers in order to find worms, especially intestinal worms.[38] We can see, therefore, that one single cause—the original mineral and chemical composition of the rock surface or its increasing or diminishing elevation above sea level—can affect a thousand other ones that—be they the character of the soil (weathering), climate (higher or lower temperature), *alang* grass, tigers, or peacocks—are merely links in *one* chain. Nor can one say that even one link, no matter how insignificant it may appear (such as the intestinal worm, for instance) is either useless or entirely devoid of significance.

Around noon we reached Gnarak and took possession of the empty little bamboo house (*pasanggrahan*)[39] which was built a short distance from the village toward the coast. Behind us beat the surf and around us the shady fruit trees extended their crowns until they formed a unified whole with the foliant arches of the nearby primordial forest. We dismissed the coolies, paid them, along with an additional reward, and refreshed ourselves with a bath and a cup of coffee along with some rice cakes brought to us by the *mandor* (supervisor) of the caves where the birds' nests were. After we entrusted our boys with the care of our other needs, we were on our way to the coast. On the floor of the forest we were now walking on we saw a multitude of hermit crabs (*Pagurus* varieties) of all shapes and sizes; they had forced their hindquarters into single seashells and were now dragging these along with them.

After we had been occupied for several minutes with clearing a path through the brush we suddenly found ourselves at an edge where, right in front of us, a steep wall several hundred feet high dropped precipitously down to the sea. What was presented to our eyes may well be called impressive. Far and away the blue, mirroring surface of the sea, which appeared to be calm, spread out before us into infinity. Far beneath us high waves were chasing each other restlessly and battered with such crashing force against the cliff, that the rock we were standing on to watch this grandiose spectacle shook from it. Our eyes followed the coast westward where the surf, crashing into the beach, formed a line as white as snow and which extended for a distance measureless to the eye, as the border between land and sea. Over the entire coast hovered a strange, fine mist which was apparently formed from the miniscule particles of seawater beaten into foam. Even the tropical afternoon sun was unable to dissolve it. Because of this completely still saline mist, all distant prospects of the beach were not clearly visible, so that it seemed we were looking through a thin veil. The green of the forest that surrounded us looked down from the top of the cliff onto this white foam of the raging sea; not only did it reach over the edge but it hung far below it as if the space it required on dry land was insufficient for its luxuriant growth. Down even the steepest cliffs rooted various shrubs and *pandan* trunks with their fruit, shining among the masses of leaves, the size of a man's head and a bright vermillion red.

When we stretched out on the ground, leaned out over the ridge, and looked diagonally below us, we could see above the seething and foaming water the entrance to the cave where the tiny swallows, *manuk walet* (*Hirundo esculenta*) built their edible nests.[40] Each cresting wave slammed thundering into the cave so that the water was higher than the entrance which at such times was out of sight. But a few moments later the wave was mightily blown back again by the counter pressure of the air in the cave which had been compressed in too small a space. A column of spray spewed hissing and horizontally over the surf and once again the swarms of little swallows appeared who knew just how to gauge the moment between the receding and advancing waves to shoot rapidly into the cave while others flew out again at the same time. For a long time we were spellbound by this admirable spectacle, but we didn't envy the men from Gnarak who had to collect the nests. Three times a year they climb down ladders, when the sea is very calm, and crawl into the cave to pluck from the rocks the birds' nests the Chinese pay so much for. Most of them are found on the ceiling of the cave which rises beyond the height of the entrance. And thus man pursues these birds even in places where they feel safe from rapacious animals and secure from any other enemy.

Toward evening we occupied ourselves with getting our collections in order, which had been enriched with many a rare plant, shellfish, and insect. The air in our bamboo dwelling had dropped from 87 to 82 degrees, but it didn't seem to drop any further. This considerably high temperature which reigns here practically unchanged year-in year-out accompanied by a great deal of moisture, brought to this region such a wealth of flora and fauna that someone from a northern climate can hardly imagine it. No matter where our eyes wandered—be it the air, the water, the earth, or even the smallest crack visible to the naked eye—everywhere we encountered the manifold indications of life.

We could not occupy the room we had chosen for the night until we chased a colony of colossal frogs (*kòdok*) away. They kept returning, however, to renew their challenge to our right to it, and could do so because they handily cleared the four-foot-high ladder which went up to the door of the *pasanggrahan* which had been built on stilts. From the nook came the peeping of bats (*lalai*) who hung there resting during the day in the shape of large black clumps. Along the walls and the ceiling (only the middle room had one) wandered numerous *tjitjaks* (*Hemidactylus fraenatus*, or small lizards of a gray color).[41] They are the most wonderful animals with an agility that entertained us splendidly. They were busily catching the flies and mosquitoes which constantly buzzed by our ears. In the cracks of the house lodged scorpions (*Buthus cyaneus*) and our boys caught several of them. Far less pleasant than the quiet scorpions and the equally silent and useful *tjitjaks* were the *tokés* (*Platydactylus guttatus*) or lizards the length of one's foot and repellent because of their brown and yellow spotted skin. They announced their presence in a loud voice and called out to us, always ten times in a row, "gek-koh, ghék-koh" more and more drawn out and sometimes from three different places at once, which did not presage a restful sleep.

After we had finished our work for the day we sat down in the pleasant shade of the *alun-alun*[42] of the neighboring village which was separated from our little house by just one stand of fruit trees. There we hoped to divert ourselves with the quiet contemplation of our surroundings. Our boys had placed a bamboo bench for us under the *waringin* tree. Some of them were sitting on the ground and played quite familiarly with the village children or amused themselves with their chatter. Others remained in the *pasanggrahan*. The small open space of the *alun-alun* was enclosed by the forest on all sides. In the immediate vicinity of the square this meant fruit trees or trees which had been planted there. Between their trunks we could see the brown huts of the natives. Above the bright green of the enormous banana leaves, which in many places reached the nook of the small houses, one could see the dark leafy vault of the *manggis* trees (*Garcinia mangostana*),[43] or *Mangifera indica* with its golden apples.[44] Yonder stood a *rambutan* tree (*Nephilium lappaceum*) with its branches so laden with the reddish fruits that they bent down to the roof of the nearby house, while over here one saw the fruits of the *nangka* tree[45] (*Artocarpus integrifolia*) which reach the dimension of a grapefruit, or the large serrated leaves of the breadfruit tree (*A. incisa*),[46] and in yet another place the kapok tree (*Gossampinus alba*)[47] spread its horizontal branches. Many other cultivated trees stood between those already mentioned and their combined foliage formed a leafy roof for the entire village. Above this roof rose the straight, thin trunks of the countless cocos and *pinang* palms[48] with leafy plumes adorning their tops. High above the foliage roof the wind rustled through the tops of the palm trees still shining in bright sunlight, while the shadow of the shade trees covered the entire *alun-alun* already.

At only a slight distance from the houses and their adjacent storage sheds for rice (*lumbungs*), the fruit trees of the village reached with their branches into the primordial forest and were so much entangled that one could no longer discern a line of demarcation. Helped by our Javanese boys we collected within a few hours blossoming and fruit-bearing branches from more than fifty different kinds of trees, and even so we had not exhausted half the wealth of varieties there. *Tjempaka*[49] and *manglit* trees (*Michelia* and *Uvaria* types and other *Anonaceans*), as well as *kiara* trees of the *Ficcus* variety with their crowns quite dense and wide, were the most numerous in this region, although one can find just as many *Myrtaceans* and *Rubiaceans*. A few *karet* or *kolelèt* trees (*Ficcus elastica*)[50] whose white sap, when exposed to the air, hardens rapidly to form the well-known India rubber, extended so far beyond the other trees that even from the *alun-alun* we could easily see their tops. Many gray monkeys or *monjets* (*Cercopithecus cynomolgus*) swung from the branches of these trees.[51] One saw them even in the immediate vicinity of the village because they like to munch on bananas and other sweet fruits. There was also a great number of various birds who swooped around at great speed or betrayed their presence in the trees only by their voices or pecking. In this manner we sat there absorbed in contemplating this immense wealth of nature, and it awoke many a slumbering thought in our souls.

While we talked the turtledoves gradually ceased cooing; most huts of the Javanese have some in cages suspended from long poles. The Javanese have a greater love for the peaceful cooing of their doves (*manuk gegugur*) which evokes calm and tranquillity, than the European has for the warbling of his canary or the song of the nightingale.[52]

Evening fell. Only a few *bajings* (squirrels—*Sciurus platani*) could be seen scurrying up trees while the last beam of sunlight vanished over the tops of the palms. *Kalongs,* hanging from a large *djambu* tree (*Djambosa*),[53] began to stir while flights of little green parrots (*Psittacus vernalis*) flew over and dashed with incredible screeching around the branches of a tall *balungdang* tree (*Stravidium excelsum*) which stood to our left. They'd settle on branches, hurry away again, return once more, fly around the tree—in short, they were constantly in motion and seemed to have so much to tell each other that the piercing screams of these little busybodies affected our eardrums. This particular tree was their resting place for the night, and they returned to it every evening. Even smaller birds—the so-called rice thieves (*burung glatik* or *Fringilla oryzivora*)[54]—had settled in great flocks on the *waringin* tree next to us. Soon they stopped their warbling and bedded down for the night.

This was the time, however, when the *kalongs* began their nocturnal journeys.[55] All day long we saw them hanging motionlessly from their tree and, from a distance, had thought that they were large black fruit. Pear shaped, as if suspended from thin stems, they hung by the hundreds from the defoliated branches. But these apparent fruits were in reality the bodies of so-called flying foxes (*Pteropus edulis*), gigantic bats the size of a cat. Hanging upside down, they are hooked to a branch by their hind legs and produce a softly peeping scream when, for instance, one animal bites another or tries to take its place. They returned every morning to this same tree, their daily resting place, to bask in the full sun which beats down on their meager, hairy bodies. Not a single leaf offers any shade because their excrement provides the soil with such an abundance of natural fertilizer that a tree rooted there soon withers and dies. Even at a considerable distance the unpleasant odor of ammonia betrays the nature of this strange fruit hanging from the withered branches.

While turtledoves ceased their song, the monkeys quietly withdrew among the branches, and the parrots and rice birds returned to their resting places, the setting sun was for the *kalongs* the signal to begin their nightly journeys; one saw them leave the tree one after another and float ponderously through the night on the measured beats of their wing membranes. Though keeping a considerable distance, they flew behind one another, yet they still formed a communal flight which at a height of approximately 100 feet above the forest, moved inland in one and the same direction. From a different region in the east came a second flight of *kalongs*, flying slightly higher than ours, which crossed them at an angle. But similar to the drawers in a cabinet which are pushed in different directions, both flights glided right above each other without disturbing the other's path. And so the large black bodies of animals belonging to separate flights pursued their own course in a direct line to the same destination without paying the slightest attention to each other. They represented undoubtedly diverse populations from different *kalong* states who knew exactly in what part of the forest the tree grew where they wished to have their nocturnal dinner, notwithstanding the fact that such a tree was often several miles from the point of departure. On several previous occasions I had seen swarms of these animals around such a tree in the evenings—usually a *ganitri* tree (*Elaeocarpus angustifolius*)—which bears the fruit they like the most.[56] They will circle such a tree all the time screaming and quacking, and deny each other access to the fruit.

The gathering dusk also caused a refreshing coolness. The temperature had now dropped to 80 degrees. From a tall tree (*Uvaria odorata*) somewhere in the village came the fragrant scent of *kenanga* flowers[57] which, when the coolness increased, spread throughout the wooded area. One sometimes saw the little flying squirrel (*bilok; Pteromys sagitta*) gliding from one cocos palm to another, and the Javanese began barricading the chicken coops under their houses. Not only were small predators similar to martens and weasels (*Herpestes javanicus; Lisang gracilis; Musangs*)[58] prowling around, but even the iguanas (lizards resembling crocodiles)[59] emerged from the bosom of the waters in order to pay an unwelcome visit to the village's chicken coops.

Trying to keep the large predators such as panthers and tigers away from their houses, our villagers started fires at various locations and posted guards armed with lances and *tong-tongs*[60] who had to sound the alarm as soon as danger was afoot. To be sure, an ugly screeching could be heard from all sides which, as the Javanese claim, means that the tigers have left their lairs. This screaming of the peacocks now came from several places in the forest.

Not only were all other birds still, but no other sound could be heard. Only the buzzing of the mosquitoes (*tjamok*) increased and became more pervasive. And it seemed to us that in the damp and hot forest region this buzzing invariably indicated the approaching night which comes so suddenly and swiftly that it never fails to make a profound impression on a newcomer to the tropics. Scarcely half an hour had passed since the sun had set, and yet various objects in both village and forest could no longer be distinguished and were totally enveloped in the veil of darkness.

Now thousands of invisible musicians began to play their instruments—such as auditory organs, tracheae, air cells, and whir-holes. All of them appeared to have waited for darkness to reach a certain level in order suddenly, as if by prearranged signal, to ring out their polyphonous concert. Suddenly every leaf had found a voice—if not the entire forest. The air trilled, the leaves chirped, the trees hummed, countless insect choirs buzzed and sang. We were able to distinguish the most varied tones, from the highest falsetto to the lowest bass. Some sounds resembled a vibrating violin string, others imitated the shrill, quivering way children sing. Countless multitudes of living lights, as if tiny flickering stars, doled through the canopy of leaves where within a certain radius around themselves they cast a bright illumination. This was the phosphor light of various kinds of small beetles which illuminated the entire show from the damp ground up to the highest point of the leaves which extended over it like a roof.

We vividly recalled our northern homeland where twilight lasts such a long time and where everything slowly comes to rest when the silence of night increases. How different it was here. Almost at once profound darkness follows bright daylight; when the torch of day is extinguished nature's silence also stops and the nocturnal, never-ending concert of buzzing, chirping, whistling, screeching, and whirring insect choirs commences. Millions of *Diptera,* especially mosquitoes and daddy longlegs (*Tipulidae*), as well as night moths, termites, tree crickets, katydids, true cicadas, *Phasmidae, Manteida,* and other *Hemiptera,* especially countless *Coleoptera* (beetles) which during the day were hidden either in the foliage of trees or in other hiding places, were now flying and whirring about, producing sounds which dissolved into one earsplitting, chirping buzz, joined by the voices of lizards and frogs which accompanied it with either a clear sound from the trees or with muffled tones from puddles.

And it happened sometimes that the loud screeching and whirring slightly decreased or stopped entirely. But as if a conductor had suddenly given the sign, the whole choir of hundreds of thousands of musicians again began to raise their shrill treble voices which were so loud that they went right through you. The big cicadas (*Tosena* varieties and others) who live in the top of trees were the loudest. Our boys knew how to lure them down from their high abode by means of a candle which they put in the thickest foliage, catching them in their nets along with hundreds of other insects.[61]

From several holes in the ground poured forth such an astounding mass of winged termites (*rajap* or *Termes fatalis*) that we had to cover our mouths so that we wouldn't eat them uncooked. After pan-frying them, these termites present for the Javanese (including the upper classes) a tasty side dish with their rice. They were also an easy catch for the fluttering, insect-devouring bats. We also saw several nightjars[62] fly in ever tighter circles above the *alun-alun,* where the bodies of the fastest ones were sometimes visible against the lighter sky.

As the majority of birds had done in the morning and remainder of the day, thus, in similar fashion, the countless hordes of insects celebrated their brief existence during the evening and first half of the night. If a choir of cicadas with their loud, piercing voices joined in with the general concert, they did so suddenly and all at the same time; and just as abruptly all of them would fall silent again. Yet they would keep the beat so precisely that we, due to the darkness surrounding us, had to believe that they could hear each other—although they lack auditory organs—or had some other way of communicating. And just as we had been able to do with the frogs, we could also distinguish a large number of different types among the cicadas, mostly depending on whether the sound was higher or lower, though it always had a noticeable beat.

For a long time we remained under our tree, listening to the voices of the night. Many thousands of animals were moving about whose mode of living we did not know, and perhaps would never know. Through the leaves of the *waringin* trees we saw high above our heads the twinkling stars—light from strange and distant heavenly bodies about which we knew even less. We thought of our feeble powers, the feeble powers of man, the short span of man's life, and we succumbed to a profound melancholy when we beheld the inexhaustible wealth of nature which, be it up there above us in the world of stars or down here below in the realm of plants and animals, is completely impenetrable.

The sun of science will attempt to illumine her depths, but she will never be fathomed. Yet from this impenetrable depth we are met by a soft and comforting glimmer. From the infinite variety which seems to drown us, emerges One fundamental principle, One general truth: each animal delights according to his nature, and it has therefore been appointed in such a way that it is *capable* of delight—one in the light of day, the other in the depth of night, one in sunlight, the other in shadow. All these thousands of forms gifted with life rejoice in the delight of their lives; they *enjoy,* and the fundamental cause of nature which is revealed in such laws must therefore be a kind, benevolent, and loving one, and one completely aware of the destiny it strives for. . . .

and there arose the image of that faith:* the soft moon who instills fancies. And when she cast her first beams over the foliage of the trees and illuminated a small portion of the *alun-alun,* our souls were filled with the comforting feeling which, as if it had been quickened by that very beam, rose up to join the cause which had engendered it. "For there must indeed be *one* bond which links all these millions of living creatures; One all-knowing soul, One God must be beyond all this! Verily, in the brilliance of the sun, in the twilight of the stars, in the soft radiance of the moon, in the wondrous harmony which embraces all that nature nourishes—in our very soul lies Thine revelation!—All knowing! Thine world is beautiful to behold."

The buzzing of the insects had largely silenced, only the tapping sound of the sated woodpeckers on their branches was to be heard in the increasing silence of the forest. And around midnight, without a word but enraptured by admiration for the greatness of nature, our spirits rife with thoughts, we wended our way in silence to our camp.

The next day. Since the *lurah*[63] of the village was absent—along with most of his subjects he was at a wedding in a nearby village—it was only thanks to the inter-

---

*The broken sentence, followed by the run-on fragment, was in the original.

vention of the *djuragan mandor* of the birds' nests that we managed to find coolies to allow us to continue our journey. These coolies were the men who gathered the nests and who were presently without work. But they would perform the coolie labor only on the condition that they received far higher wages. And even then they would probably have refused if they didn't have a greater need for money than their countrymen because they were addicted to smoking *afium* or opium. We were obliged to pay them in advance so they could lay in a fresh supply of *madat.*[64]

The entire day we traveled along the coast and came upon only one small village where we had breakfast. We continued our journey until, around four in the afternoon, we were forced to stop from fatigue and needed to look for a suitable place to bivouac, near flowing water. Another half day's journey in a westerly direction should bring us to a large village near the coast which we wanted to reach early the next afternoon in order to set out for the high country in the interior.

We made camp for the night on the east side of a cape, *Tandjung-Gnodos,* where a nearby stream of crystalline purity emptied into the sea. This region was exceedingly wild. Primordial forests of astonishing dimensions reached from the mountains down to the coast, where the trees even bathed their sloping branches in the waves. Only in a few places, primarily in the back of small lagoons, could one find a diminutive sandy beach that was not as yet overgrown. No matter where we looked, neither near nor far, was there any sign of human industry.

Quickly we made our preparations to set up camp. Our boys and coolies cut branches from the nearby trees, built huts and made fires while I, along with two Javanese, went further to the west in order to learn more about what surrounded us. The cape or projecting spit of land (*tandjung* or *udjung* in Malay) was the end of a descending ridge and formed a flat plateau which rose perhaps some fifteen to twenty-five feet above the beach of adjacent bays. Many of such low *udjungs* reached a ways into the sea between small bays with lower contours. All of them were covered with forest trees.

When we reached the other side of the cape and emerged from the forest, our eyes were met by a curious scene. Enclosed between this and the next cape in the shape of a half moon, was a beach, totally barren and sloping very gently upward to a distance of around 500 to 700 feet from the sea, where it stopped and turned into hills of sand. Inland from these hills began the forest again and continued without interruption deep into the ever higher mountains. This barren and flat beach was perhaps the distance one can cover in three-quarters of an hour. High above our heads circled birds of prey (*Falco* or *Haliaëtos* variety),[65] while on the beach we saw hundreds of bones and the immense shells of turtles, partly bleached, partly still a darker color, strewn about as if on a battle field.

It was a savage scene. Spurred on by amazement and curiosity we climbed down and walked among the skeletons on that barren strand. We noticed immediately the tracks of many tigers and smaller animals. The prints were quite clear, especially closer to the shore where the sand was smoother and firmer than further inland. To our right, in the direction of the hills and where the coast sloped up gently and evenly, the sand gradually loosened up and was much drier. Here we found it in many places turned up, uneven, forming several heaps divided by trenchlike slopes, so that it appeared that animals of various kinds had fought a fierce battle with each other.

The entire surface of the beach was littered with the bones and shells of turtles. From where we stood we counted dozens of shells still intact so that we could easily surmise that if we took the entire beach into consideration, there had to be hundreds of them. The majority were on that part of the beach which was furthest away from the sea, at the foot of the hills. What surprised us the most was that they were all turned over on their backs. These were the shells of the giant turtle (*Chelonia mydas* or, somewhat rarer, *Chelonia imbricata*) which, proportionately in height and width, measured a length from three to five feet. Some had been there for a long time and were completely bleached smooth from the sun and rain. Others were of a darker color and still had strips of dried flesh inside. We even found several which had been recently killed and were lying on the sand with their plastron torn apart and surounded with smashed and stinking intestines. In several places we saw long, straight tracks—paths, as it were, of about three to four feet wide and consisting of two evenly spaced grooves. It looked like a heavy body had been dragged between them. These tracks began at the edge of the beach and ran through the skeletons straight to the foot of the hills. The two Javanese seemed to know what it meant because they had followed the tracks and called out happily to us from the hills where we saw them busily digging in the sand: "*tampat telor, telor*" ("a nest with eggs").

Those hills were really sand dunes at the very edge of the mountains. Over this dry, clear sand crept here and there the long tendrils of the *daon katang* (*Convolvuli*) adorned with reddish-blue flowers on thin stems.[66] In other places the sand was either barren or sparsely grown with a prickly, creeping variety of grass called *djukut lari lari* (*Spinifex squarrosus*). But from the crests of the dunes looked down not only *babakoan* (*Tournefortia argentea*)[67] and other small trees, but also the rich foliage of *Pandanaceans*. In one particular place at the foot of these hills, we found a nest buried quite shallowly in the sand, containing more than a hundred round eggs. They were a pale color, as large as a small apple, and had a soft shell like parchment.

It was now clear that the long paths were the tracks of giant turtles who, after emerging from the depths of the ocean, had crawled here some 500 to 700 feet in order to lay their eggs in the sand at the foot of the dunes, leaving the hatching to the basking rays of the sun. Had they been attacked during their short journey on land which they attempted only a few times per year?

We decided to spend the evening there so we could watch whatever took place. We took as many eggs as we could handle and returned to the camp. The forest that grew on the coast of the cape was totally different from the forest on the dunes. It consisted almost entirely of *kibunaga* trees (*Calophyllum inophyllum*)[68] with their lively green and shiny foliage that formed a dense shade-canopy some thirty to forty feet off the ground. The thousands of white flowers which adorn these trees embalmed the air with a most fragrant scent. Many of the older trunks had divided at a short distance from the ground into colossal branches which spread out on all sides and touched the ground from the weight of the leaves. The Javanese had prepared their own beds as well as ours on such horizontal branches about seven to eight feet off the ground. They did this by cutting off twigs which they then laid next to each other across the main branches and covered with more twigs and leaves. Down among the trees they started fires, because several of our Javanese had noticed crocodiles or *buaja* (*Crocodilus biporcatus*) at the mouth of the stream, who, as is well known, leave their watery domain at night to prowl around the beach. These animals are even more dangerous than tigers because they have a hard armor that covers their entire body.

We had such a seat prepared, high above the ground and safe from danger, in a *kibunaga* tree located at the edge of the forest and next to the boneyard. After we had finished our meal, mostly tasty turtle eggs, we climbed around six o'clock in the tree. The other Javanese had been ordered to come running with lit torches at the sound of the first shot.

We lay in wait. Evening fell. First we saw one, and then several other turtles leave their watery domain. As soon as they were on dry land and only small waves from the surf still touched them, they stretched their long necks and looked up, turned a bit to the side, cast a cautious glance around, and then began to crawl rather rapidly and in a straight line across the beach, without stopping. That is to say, they pushed themselves forward with their paddle-shaped feet and hurried the shortest distance to the foot of the hills. Because it was gradually getting darker we could see only about a quarter of the beach, lengthwise, but so far as we could still make out objects, we saw four of such heavy bodies drag themselves across the sand. No other noise but the muffled sound of the surf. Suddenly we heard something splash below us. It was much longer than a turtle and far more agile. A crocodile, at least fifteen feet long and hunting for prey, was now also waddling to the foot of the hills. Without a sound and with baited breath we waited for the tragedy to unfold.

In the distance a turtle crawled back and disappeared into the sea. Not long thereafter and in the immediate vicinity of where we were hidden, a similar dark body turned seaward from the hills. But it was not even halfway when suddenly from the neighboring wood a horde of animals appeared. At first there wasn't a sound to be heard, but the moment they reached the turtle they let loose with a brief, snorting howl, quickly surrounded the animal and attacked ferociously. We estimated that there were about thirty of them. They grabbed their victim by the head and neck, by its limbs shaped like fins, by the tail and hindquarters, and began to tear and rip pieces out of it, turned it around in a circle and indicated when they barked spasmodically their keen yet hoarse snorting that they were possessed by a most gruesome voracity or thirst for blood. They went at it like lunatics and were apparently not aware that the crocodile—silently, with a light and soft tread like a *tjitjak* catching flies on a wall—was crawling closer and closer on his stomach. Suddenly he rushed forward like an arrow, and had already pulverized two or three of the whining dogs between his fearsome jaws before the others realized it and suddenly dashed away from each other.

They were *adjaks* (*Canis rutilans*),[69] the so-called wild dogs who live in packs, are smaller than wolves but more savage and voracious. The turtle wasn't dead yet but had suffered too much to be able to escape. The crocodile returned to the sea with what was probably a good catch.

The *adjaks* once again threw themselves from every direction on their prey, attacked it with a concerted effort and were apparently ripping the shells apart. I aimed my rifle and was about to pull the trigger when one of the Javanese put his hand on my arm and whispered something. His keen eye had spotted a shape emerging from the dark forest. It stood there, stopped, ranged its terrible eyes over the scene, crouched down low and fell suddenly among the dogs with an astonishing leap. A horrifying rattling roar came from deep in its throat. The *adjaks* scattered in frenzied panic. Now howling in a less grunting but more whistling manner, they ran quickly back into the forest and the tyrant of the jungle, the royal tiger, slammed his claw into the shell of the animal lying in front of him as if to indicate his victory.

A second, but smaller, tiger—perhaps a panther—also stole nearer. The first turned around grunting and spitting. I aimed, pulled the trigger, and the shot reverberated in the silent evening and echoed in the mountains. For this one time the battle between giant turtles, crocodiles, wild dogs, and tigers had come to an end.

We fired another shot, but it was already too dark under the canopy of leaves to aim properly, although we could still make out the outlines of objects on the bright, barren beach. We had missed or, at least, had not wounded anything lethally. Both tigers had fled. We could have fired two more shots from our rifles but considered it more prudent to reload. We were just climbing out of the tree when the Javanese from our bivouac came running up to us shouting loudly and lit up the entire scene with the burning pieces of split wood they had brought along. Near the turtle we found a dead *adjak*. And though the turtle had not yet expired it had suffered terribly, and the Javanese finished it off with their *gòlòks*.[70]

Because this kind of turtle cannot retract head or feet under its shell it becomes, despite the enormous size and solidity of this means of protection, an easy prey to predators who are much smaller, provided they attack in large numbers. This also explains somewhat why there were such a large number of skeletons and shells in the savage arena where the animals had been destroying each other. The remnants of flesh and intestines left behind by the wild dogs, tigers, panthers, and crocodiles are devoured the next morning by sea eagles and other birds of prey. One always sees several hovering high up in the air, circling this particular spot.

We were amazed to see that the giant turtle had already been overturned and was lying with its partially torn plastron turned up. We couldn't decide, however, if this was the tiger's doing or whether the combined force of the wild dogs had managed this earlier. The Javanese insisted on the latter. We tied the ropes from our *pikolans*[71] around the turtle and fastened them to three bamboo stakes. The turtle was so heavy that six coolies, three on each side, needed all their strength to lift this load.

Back in the bivouac the animal was butchered. Not only did it provide us with good meat—and in such quantity that it would have fed five times more people than there were in our party—but also with an enormous number of young small eggs, the size of a hazelnut, or slightly larger. These eggs consisted almost entirely of yolk, and were made into a soup which provided us with a good meal.[72]

THE following passage translates the final pages of *Licht-en Schaduwbeelden*. It evokes Junghuhn's profound rapport with tropical nature and shows that there need be no conflict between facts and feeling but that, on the contrary, they can enhance one another.

Before I was about to entrust myself to the arms of Morpheus, a vague but urgent yearning drove me back in the open air in order to have one final look at nature decked out in her nocturnal finery and then take such to bed with me as stuff for dreams. But since it wasn't advisable to wander around unarmed in such a wilderness and at such an hour, I took one of my hunting rifles and left camp.

Thousands of conflicting thoughts crossed my mind when I stepped softly and unnoticed under the trees with the intention of reaching the shore of the lake.[73] The Javanese who had arrived with the resident[74] had thrown their bamboo torches (*obor*) into the watch fires which in several places were still burning near our huts. Their bright light gradually diminished, however, and one could only rarely distinguish the outline of human figures moving as dark shadows back and forth in front of the fires. The hands of those who were supposed to tend the fires were tired and the majority of the Javanese had retired to their huts. Others slept next to the heaps of charcoal which were dying out, the dull glow no longer able to illuminate the high ceiling of the forest. Only a few of the nearest tree trunks were still visible in the reddish light. But these also vanished into the darkness behind them when I came out of the forest and stepped onto the shore of the lake.

Not a cloud was in the sky and the full moon, with a radiant nimbus and surrounded by thousands of flickering stars, looked down on me from her great height; but she also looked just as clearly up at me from the watery depths.

I watched and listened. The forest was silent. The surface of the lake was smooth as a mirror and rarely did the image of the moon ripple and pull itself into slanting stripes of light when the splashing ducks from the other, densely overgrown, shore had caused a slight swell in the lake. Their chattering, which is exactly like that of tame European ducks, was practically the only noise to disturb the nocturnal silence every once in a while. Not a sound came from the huts, which were now completely out of sight behind the trees. From both the right and left tall *kimérak* trees arched over the shore. Next to the edge of their crowns they were still brightly lit by the moon, but beneath this canopy one looked into the dark, secret heart of the forest which was cast back just as somberly by the nearest strip of water from the lake. Only more proximate tree trunks stood out as brightly lit pillars against this dark edge of woods. The center of the lake peacefully mirrored the entire heaven of stars. One thought after the other crowded within my soul.

The rhinos lie quietly in their swampy blinds and the wild bulls are equally at rest; perhaps a few might silently graze on a small knoll of grass between the trees. Tigers seldom come down this far because one rarely finds wild boars, deer, or hinds here. Here is nothing but forest; grass and meadows are not found very often. The *kalongs* from the lowlands are not seen at this elevation, nor will a nightjar let the beat of its wings disturb this nocturnal peace where even the buzz of insects or the chirping song of a cicada are seldom heard. Only a lone firefly blinks on and off by the shore.

The black monkeys (*lutung*) do not stir in the crowns of leaves but sit quietly on branches. Tiny squirrels have hidden in their nests or in a crack of an old tree trunk, and all the birds are asleep. Perhaps a wild cat (*Felis minuta*) with its shiny eyes steals cautiously along moss-covered branches to catch an unwitting bird in its nest, or a *Paradoxus musanga* slinks just as silently and warily on the ground to pilfer a wild hen or partridge. But all the other animals have retired. Also the waterhens and cormorants (*Plotus*) sit motionlessly in the tall, reedy grass on the shore or on a fallen tree which hangs over the water. Nor do the fish in the lake stir, and neither do the small crabs or shells make any noise, and all of creation is still.

But despite this silence, life continues—in the water, in the air, and on the earth. It beats secretly in a million pulses which soon, when the borrowed brilliance which still radiates from the lunar disk retreats before the true light of the sun, will move anew and replenish the drama with a teeming host of the most varied of forms.

Nature, thou art splendid, be it night or day, and thou speaketh a tongue only he can comprehend who, like that often misunderstood and more often abused man, can ask with pious simplicity: "he who created the ear, wouldst he not hear? And he who created the eye, wouldst he not see?"

And so in solitude and deep in thought, I sat on the shore of the lake whose mirror was not disturbed by even a wavelet or smallest wrinkle. Not a leaf stirred, nor the slightest breeze lapped my face. I might have fancied to be in a lost, desolated nature if my own heart did not beat in my chest, or if my mind did not tell me that beneath, next, and above me, life slumbered on, ready to awake at the first crack of dawn, or if the borrowed light of the moon had not proclaimed that where there is light—in the entire vast universe—there must be warmth, movement, must be life!

A horrible scream resounded in the dead of night. An awful complaint came from the trees, sufficiently woeful to scare anyone who is a stranger to the Javanese mountain forests. Because it was too dark to see anything clearly, it seemed that the screaming came at first from below, then from between the trees, while later it seemed to come from up high, until it seemed to come from every direction. One could have easily imagined it to be a muffled groan for help, the last sigh of someone dying, or the crying of a young child. And so it happened that earlier travelers had the strangest notions of what caused such screams. On the island of Ceylon it is even said to be a devil's ghost—a spooky, devilish bird. But I was already acquainted with it and soon I saw what screamed so, after it came closer to the open, moonlit shore of the lake. There I saw it glide with spread wing membranes, stiff and immobile like a paper dragon, from tree to tree and at such an angle that when it left the top of one tree it arrived halfway up the trunk of another and had to climb quite rapidly back up again. It was the so-called flying lemur (*Galeopithecus variegatus*),[75] quite a harmless animal that delights in itself at night and flies around in the forest looking for fruits. But be its cry ever so hideous to a human ear because it evokes memories of human misery and misfortune, for other *Galeopithecae* the very same call is lovely and reassuring, because the familiar voice tells them that they are not alone, that others of their kind are present, and that they would find them if only they would follow the lure of the voice.

Soon this was the only sound I heard in the ever more silent forest. It was no longer ominous to me. With every fiber of my being I experienced the delight which the contemplation of nature affords, and it appeared to me as if I felt the kinship, the sympathy, which links all living creatures.

The moon was already waning. I got up from the rock I had been sitting on and bid the moon and the stars, the lake and the ducks, the forest with its millions of flowers, buds and fruits, the *Galeopithecae* and all other animals which, each in its fashion, delight and rejoice in their own being—I bid them all a good night!

Wondrous, inexhaustible nature, quickened by God's breath, until the morrow: I bid thee a good night!

NOTES

1 Biographical material comes from the following sources: *Gedenkboek Franz Junghuhn 1809–1909* (Memorial volume Franz Junghuhn) (The Hague: Martinus Nijhoff, 1910); *De onuitputtelijke natuur* (Inexhaustible Nature), ed. R. Nieuwenhuys and F. Jaquet (Amsterdam: Van Oorschot, 1966); C. W. Wormser, *Frans Junghuhn* (Deventer: W. Van Hoeve, n.d.); Paul van't Veer, *Geen blad voor de mond. Vijf radicalen uit de negentiende eeuw* (Calling a spade a spade: Five radicals from the nineteenth century) (Amsterdam: Arbeiderspers, 1958).

2 Junghuhn wrote an account of these early adventures entitled "Meine Flucht nach Afrika. Beschrieben von Franz Junghuhn." This was not published until 1909 as an addition to a biography: *Franz Junghuhn. Biographische Beiträge zur 100. Wiederkehr seines Geburtstages* (Franz Junghuhn. Biographical contributions to the one hundredth return of his birthday), ed. Max C. P. Schmidt (Leipzig, 1909).

3 These travels through the Batak region of Sumatra may be compared to van der Tuuk's experiences there, which have been translated in the next chapter in this volume. Junghuhn's account was published as *Die Battaländer auf Sumatra. Im Auftrage Sr. Excellenz des General-Gouverneurs von Niederländisch-Indien Hrn. P. Merkus in den Jahren 1840 und 1841, untersucht und beschrieben von Franz Junghuhn* (The Batak Lands of Sumatra: Explored and described by Franz Junghuhn as commissioned by His Excellency P. Merkus, Governor-General of the Dutch East Indies), 2 vols. (Berlin, 1847). It should be mentioned that more often than not Junghuhn wrote his work in German first and then either translated it himself into Dutch or had someone else do it. See the comment by W. C. Muller in "Junghuhn's geschriften," in *Gedenkboek Franz Junghuhn 1809–1909*, 324–26.

4 Junghuhn's account of his journey back to Europe was first published in a journal and then printed in the same year as a book: *Terugreis van Java naar Europa, met de zoogenaamde Engelsche overlandpost in de maanden September en October 1848* (Return voyage from Java to Europe with the so-called Overlandpost in the months of September and October 1848) (Zalt-Bommel, 1851).

5 Junghuhn's chef d'oeuvre was afflicted with an epidemic of printing mistakes. To be on the safe side I cited the title of the second printing; one may say the work was published between 1850 and 1854, undergoing a most confusing number of transformations, which were not Junghuhn's responsibility. Frans Junghuhn, *Java, zijne gedaante, zijn plantentooi en inwendige bouw*, 4 vols. ('s-Gravenhage: C. W. Mieling, 1853–54).

6 These plates, plus a generous selection of his photographs, were reproduced in a recent anthology of Junghuhn's writings: *Java's onuitputtelijke natuur, Reisverhalen, tekeningen en fotografieën van Franz Wilhelm Junghuhn* (Java's inexhaustible nature: travel tales, drawings and photographs by Franz Wilhelm Junghuhn), ed. Rob Nieuwenhuys and Frits Jaquet (Alphen aan den Rijn: A. W. Sijthoff, 1980).

7 From the introduction to Alexander von Humboldt, *Kosmos. Entwurf einer physischen Weltbeschreibung* in *Gesammelte Werke von Alexander von Humboldt*, 12 vols. (Stuttgart:

Cotta, 1889), 1:4–5. English quoted from the contemporary translation: *Cosmos: A Sketch of a Physical Description of the Universe,* trans. E. C. Otté, 5 vols. (London: George Bell, 1888), 1:2.

8 Ernest Earnest, *John and William Bartram: Botanists and Explorers* (Philadelphia: University of Pennsylvania Press, 1940), 140.

9 Ibid., 139.

10 Junghuhn is mentioned with approbation in a specialized study on beach and littoral flora from the turn of the century: A. F. W. Schimper, *Die indo-malayische Strandflora* (Jena: Verlag von Gustav Fischer, 1891). The first volume of *Java,* in the German translation published in 1852, is one of Schimper's sources, and he refers to it as a "classic work about Java" (31). Schimper also mentions a subalpine variety of casuarina on Java called *Casuarina Junghuhniana* (29) and a Javanese species of the huge genus of *Euphorbia,* better known in English as the spurge plants, called *Junghuhnia glabra* (113).

11 Joseph Kastner, *A Species of Eternity* (New York: Knopf, 1977), 318.

12 Although this remarkable man is now nearly forgotten, his achievements were considerable. Humboldt made pioneering studies of volcanoes and earthquakes, indicating the presence of "faults" in the earth that conduct "seismic waves." He almost single-handedly created the science of climatology (now better known as meteorology) and was the first to describe such well-known items as the influence of cold and warm ocean currents (one was named after him) on the land climate, and the influence of climate on the flora and fauna of a region. "Isothermal lines" and "isodynamic lines" are his formulations and he was the first to make use of graphs for scientific purposes. His "geography of plants" was of inestimable value. Humboldt also "laid the foundation of modern physical geography." See L. Kellner, *Alexander von Humboldt* (London: Oxford University Press, 1963), 231–34. The basic biography is still Karl Bruhns, *Alexander von Humboldt. Eine wissenschaftliche Biographie,* 3 vols. (Leipzig, 1872). Yet he was not universally admired. When the English translation of *Vues des Cordillères et monuments des peuples indigénes de l'Amérique* (1810) was published in 1814, it provoked a scathing attack in *The Quarterly Review* of July 1816 (440–68). "We know of no two travelers, ancient or modern, who have traversed so many leagues of foolscap as Doctor Clarke and the Baron de Humboldt." I single this out because it is indicative of the kind of recalcitrance Humboldt was up against. In *Vues des Cordillères* Humboldt recorded another of his contributions to knowledge: the civilization of the Mexican Indians. The British reviewer attacked him fiercely for this because it was supposed that such "rude people, like the Mexicans, without any written language, either symbolical or alphabetical, without any system of numeration [*sic!*], could have much progress." The reviewer found Humboldt's interest in these civilizations misplaced because "the Mexicans may have advanced, but, we believe, not a great way beyond the village children, the landlady, or the Bosjesmans." The latter refers to the Bushmen of southern Africa. Humboldt was the first to treat the great cultures of the Aztecs, Incas, and Maya with respect, at a time when it was not yet fashionable to do so. It must have given him a keen sense of satisfaction when in his old age he could refer in *Cosmos* to the work of another enlightened traveler, the American John L. Stephens, who in 1841 published in New York his *Incidents of Travel in Central America, Chiapas and Yucatan* (augmented in 1843 by his *Incidents of Travel in Yucatan*), which provided eloquent testimony for the great civilizations of that region.

13 Charles Darwin, *The Voyage of the Beagle* (1839; reprinted in The Natural History Library, Garden City, N.Y.: Doubleday, 1962), 500.

14 Darwin's letter is quoted by Alan Moorehead, *Darwin and the Beagle* (Harmondsworth: Penguin Books, 1971), 43. This volume is also of interest for its copious illustrations.

15 *Cosmos,* 1:ix.

16   Ibid., 1:2–3.

17   *Views of Nature*, trans. E. C. Otté and Henry G. Bohn (London: Bohn, 1850), 210, 219.

18   Wormser, *Frans Junghuhn*, 43.

19   Humboldt's "cross sections" are described in Kellner, *Alexander von Humboldt*, 91, and can most easily be sampled in Douglas Botting, *Humboldt and the Cosmos* (New York: Harper and Row, 1973), 61, 208, where a graphic representation of the various plants on Mount Chimborazo is provided. Botting's book is primarily valuable for its copious illustrations.

20 Humboldt included Junghuhn's work in *Kosmos,* vol. 4, sect. 2 on "eigentlicher Vulkane" ("volcanoes proper"), subsection d. Humboldt called Junghuhn a "kenntnisvollen, kühnen und unermüdet thätigen Naturforscher [knowledgeable, bold, and indefatigably active naturalist]." The original can be found in the edition cited: *Gesammelte Werke,* 2:233–40, 189–90; in the English translation, *Cosmos,* 5:22, 297–308.

21   *Cosmos,* 1:42 and x.

22   Humboldt's description of his "main purpose" is from a letter to Freiesleben in 1799. Quoted by Botting, *Humboldt,* 65.

23   The tree with its febrifugal bark was named by Linnaeus after a certain Spanish countess de Chinchón (he misspelled her name) who was the wife of the Spanish viceroy of Peru in the early seventeenth century. She was cured of malaria by an Indian who gave her an extract from the bark to drink. Hence quinine came to be known as "Countess Powder." Its name was changed to "Jesuit's Powder" when the Jesuits traded in the bark that they obtained from Catholic missionaries in South America. Until 1850 the bark was stripped from the trees after they were felled. No one heeded the warnings of the Jesuits to replace them with new saplings, and this exploitation severely depleted the number of cinchona trees. This is what encouraged the British and Dutch to attempt to grow them in their colonies. Only the Dutch were successful, particularly with the variety *Cinchona ledgeriana.* By the 1930s the Dutch plantations in Java produced some 20 million pounds of cinchona bark per year, having for all practical purposes a virtual monopoly. As *Fortune* put it: "the Dutch monopoly of cinchona, the tightest crop monopoly in the world . . . is not only a monopoly but a very powerful and very profitable monopoly." See the article "Cinchona—Quinine to You" in *Fortune* 9, no. 2 (February 1934): 76–86. That article requires the Dutch for their careful methods and belabors them for their business practices. Junghuhn is not mentioned. Humboldt's research was performed in the original, and most famous, spot where the trees grew naturally: the Quina woods in the mountains around the town of Loxa in Peru. He provides climatological and geographical details which may well have influnced Junghuhn in his choice of the mountain region above Bandung. See Humboldt's *Views of Nature,* 280–81, 390–92, 422–23.

24   Aldous Huxley's remarks from "Wordsworth in the Tropics," in *Collected Essays* (New York: Harper and Row, 1958), 1–2.

25   Darwin's impression of the tropics from *Voyage of Beagle,* 12.

26   *The Travels of William Bartram,* ed. Francis Harper (New Haven: Yale University Press, 1958), 97–98. The *Zanthoxilon* is the Hercules' club or toothache tree; *nonparel* is the bird called painted bunting; *golden icterus* probably refers to the Baltimore oriole; *Tillandsi ulnea-adscites* is Spanish moss.

27   Humboldt's remarks about *Cosmos* from a letter to Varnhagen in 1834, see Kellner, *Alexander von Humboldt,* 200–202 (italics added).

28   *Harper's* printed Junghuhn's account of tiger fights in Solo under the title "Royal Amusements in Java," *Harper's Magazine* 8, no. 47 (April 1854): 635–37. Its author is billed as "Franz Junghuhn, a Dutch traveler, who has written a very valuable treatise on the

internal state of Java from personal observation." The translator is not mentioned, although the translation is good. I find this an uncommonly swift transposition, because the original Dutch edition of *Java*, where this account can be found in the third volume, was published between 1850 and 1854, and the German edition—which is more likely to be the source—was published between 1852 and 1854. The only other possible source I know of is a publication of ten "sketches" in *The Journal of the Dutch East Indies* in 1845. The tenth "sketch" contains the same material and is of some interest because it almost caused Junghuhn to be dismissed from his job. This was because he made a number of unflattering descriptions and remarks about the native aristocracy, jibes that were preserved in the American translation. See "Schetsen; ontworpen op eene reis over Java, voor topographische en natuurkundige navorschingen, aan het einde van het jaar 1844," in *Tijdschrift voor Nederlandsch Indië* (1845).

29   For Junghuhn's "church" see Wormser, *Frans Junghuhn*, 221 and for the "symbols of his faith," see Nieuwenhuys in his introduction to *De onuitputtelijke natuur*, 5.

30   The present translation is based on portions from the original edition of *Licht-en Schaduwbeelden uit de Binnenlanden van Java* (Images of light and shadow from Java's interior) published under the pseudonym of "Dag" ("Day") in Leyden in 1854. The specific passages can be found on pp. 243–74 (without the conversations about religion) and on pp. 415–22, which represents the fine coda of the book.

31   *Alang-alang* (*Imperata arundinacea*) is the most common grass of the Indies. Usually two feet high, it can grow up to four feet. Its narrow leaves are stiff and long, and it has a plume of silky, silver-white hairs. Extremely resilient, *alang-alang* is the bane of farmers.

32   *Glagah* reed (*Saccharum spontaneum*) is a tall grass resembling sugar cane. It is often found with *alang-alang* in arid soil, for example, on the slopes of a volcano after the lava flow has destroyed everything. Its long sharp leaves make it very difficult to pass through.

33   *Malaka* tree has a different Latin nomenclature in *The Encyclopedia of the Dutch East Indies*: i.e., *Phyllanthus emblica*. It can grow up to sixty-five feet tall. Its wood is used to make charcoal or is turned into axe handles, while its bark is used to color bamboo products. The pale yellow and sour fruits are eaten either raw or as preserves.

34   *Hornbills* are grotesque birds distinguished by their enormous bill surmounted by a hornlike casque. Their flight is noisy and they have, as Junghuhn notes, strange, croaking voices. Junghuhn was probably referring to the largest species, which is also found in Java: *Buceros rhinoceros*. This bird can grow up to four feet, has black and white plumage, and a red or yellow beak. There is also an *Aceros plicatus*, which is the Papuan hornbill.

35   *Gnarak* is an anagram of the first word in the name of a district as well as a mountain on Java's south coast: *Karang Bolong*. This is the place where the legendary birds' nests were gathered, also described by Rumphius in *The Poison Tree* (Amherst: University of Massachusetts Press, 1981), 232–40.

36   *Neptunian mountain varieties* refer to a theory of A. G. Werner (1749–1817) which argued that mountains had an aqueous origin. This was the prevailing theory of the eighteenth century. It was Humboldt's extensive travels in the Andes that convinced him to refute that theory. His exploration and geological data persuaded him, and subsequent generations of scientists, that such origins were volcanic, a theory also referred to as Plutonism. Darwin's explorations of South American mountain ranges and Junghuhn's work in Java only confirmed Humboldt's views. Goethe, however, refused to substitute the more "modern," that is more disjunctive, theory of Plutonism for his favorite Neptunism because the latter was more orderly and was, as it were, more "classical."

37   *Felstone* is compact feldspar occurring in amorphous rock masses. *Trachyte* is a light-colored rock.

38   Junghuhn's note for the relationship between tigers and peacocks reads: "Every Java-

nese knows that, in the wild, tigers and peacocks are inseparable, though few are capable of providing an explanation. It is known that the tiger prefers the hot lowlands, as does the peacock. On Java, however, there is a chain of mountains which, at 9,000 feet above sea level, forms a plateau covered with excellent grass and is therefore inhabited by a multitude of deer—in fact, too many of them. Notwithstanding the colder climate at this elevation, one will also often find the royal tiger here, because he can find easy and abundant prey, and one will always see peacocks fly from one stand of trees to another."

39 *Pasanggrahan* does not refer to just any house made of bamboo but to a building specifically erected for the use of traveling officials. Private parties could also use it. In Java before 1882 these buildings had to be built and maintained by the populace.

40 *Manuk walet*. There is here again a discrepancy between Junghuhn's and more modern terminology. This happens frequently. These remarkable little birds are called *burung walet* on Java, while the kind Junghuhn describes has the Latin nomenclature of *Collocalia fuciphaga*. These are dark brown with a brown-gray belly and they fashion their nests exclusively with their saliva. The latter is as tough as rubber and as elastic as chewing gum. Highly prized by the Chinese, these nests have in fact neither taste nor odor and have a consistency resembling tough aspic.

41 The *tjitjak* (*Hemidactylus fraenatus*) was considered an oracle animal that knew the future and hidden (i.e., supernatural) things, and was thought to possess wisdom. In Bali this lizard is dedicated to Sarasvati, the goddess of scholarship and booklearning. Van der Tuuk (who is covered in the next chapter) notes in his *Kawi-Balinese-Dutch Dictionary* (3:82) that when a *tjitjak* made its smacking noise just when someone had finished saying something, the Balinese would say "trusan Sarasvati" or "may the goddess Sarasvati make it come to pass."

42 An *alun-alun* or central square is to be found in most villages on Java. It is a large square field of grass, often surrounded by *waringin* trees. One or two of these holy trees usually grow in the center. Around this square one finds the houses of the notables, native royalty, regents, or district heads. Even in the larger cities the *alun-alun* is used for festivities. If there is a mosque, it is usually located on the western side of the *alun-alun*.

43 *Manggis* trees (*Garcinia mangostana*) are probably indigenous to the Indonesian archipelago, and are variously called *manggis* in Javanese, *manggistan* in Malay, and *manggu* in Sundanese. It is a common, very popular tree, famed for its fruit, which has a delicious white pulp, hidden by a red, leathery skin that is used in native medicine as an astringent.

44 *Mangifera indica*, commonly known as the *manga* tree, is ubiquitous in the tropics. Its fruit is egg shaped, usually yellow with an orange pulp.

45 *Nangka* tree (*Antocarpus integrifolia*) is a fairly large tree much sought after for its wood and fruit. In English it is usually called "Jack tree." It provides a hard yellow wood, which is often used for furniture, tools, and in construction. The native population is particularly fond of its large fruit, and they also use its sap as a kind of glue.

46 The *breadfruit tree* (*Artocarpus communis*) is a large (forty to sixty feet high) tree with glossy leaves and fairly large green fruit containing a white fibrous pulp. It is said to be indigenous to the Indies. Captain James Cook recommended this fruit after he saw it in the Pacific, which resulted in the famous voyage of H. M. S. *Bounty* under the command of Captain Bligh to obtain it. It is particularly popular in the Pacific islands and the West Indies.

47 *Kapok trees* were once extensively cultivated in Java for their silky material or down, called *kapok*. Junghuhn is referring to a specific genus. Kapok is not a textile fiber, hence it never competed with the cotton industry. But it was popular for its naturally moisture-proof and buoyant qualities, and therefore was used in life preservers and the like, and, because of

its elasticity, was used as stuffing in mattresses. In English it is also known as *silk cotton.*

48   The *pinang palm* (*Areca catechu* L.) produces the important betel nuts, an ingredient in *sirih* chewing. This used to be a habit in the Dutch East Indies as common as smoking, and is reminiscent of chewing tobacco. A betel chaw consists of a piece of the *pinang* nut, a piece of *gambir,* and a little chalk made from seashells, all wrapped in the fragrant but bitter leaves of the betel or *sirih* plant. This package can be chewed for about fifteen minutes. The sap from the *sirih* leaves stains the teeth and mouth a bright orange red.

49   The *tjempaka* tree (*Michelia champaca*) is a tall tree planted in Java mostly for its fragrant, beautiful flowers of a yellowish-red color. Although it has good wood it is seldom cut down because its flowers are so valued. Women wear the *tjempaka* flowers in their hair, and the blossoms are also used to perfume a heavy oil which is used on hair.

50   The *karet* or *kolelèt* tree (*Ficus elastica*) is the tall ficus tree that produces the sap that rubber is made from. The *kiara* trees and a host of other varieties belong to this same Ficus family, which is spread all over the Malay archipelago. One other member is the *Ficus benjamina,* better known as the holy *waringin* tree.

51   *Monjet* monkeys are better known in English as Macaque monkeys, belonging to the genus *Macaca.* They are distinguishable by their long snouts and they live in troops and feed mostly on fruits and insects. The Javanese often keep them as pets.

52   The love the Javanese have for turtledoves, or *perkutut* as they are called in Javanese, exists to the present. It is still believed that their cooing predicts the future. A contemporary Javanese psychologist described a loner as a person who wants to be left alone "because he is busy listening to his *perkutut.*" See Niels Mulder, *Mysticism and Everyday Life in Contemporary Java* (Singapore: Singapore University Press, 1978), 44.

53   The *djambu* tree is probably indigenous to Ambon but is cultivated all over Java for its red and white fruits.

54   *Rice thieves* (*Padda oryzivora*) are little birds called *glatik* in Javanese. They are very common and a great nuisance to rice farmers. The *glatik* is about the size of our sparrow and has a red beak, white "cheeks," black tail, and a grayish-purple underbelly. They come by the hundreds to a field when the rice is ripe, and the farmer defends himself with an elaborate system of strings which he stretches over his entire rice field and which all lead to a bamboo hut at the edge. From these strings hang bamboo slats, dry leaves, dolls, or bits of cloth. When the farmer pulls at the strings in his guard house, the whole field suddenly seems to come alive and the birds are scared away. The *glatik* is a relative of the North American bobolink.

55   The *kalong* or flying fox (*Pteropus vampyrus*) is a bat about a foot long, with a wingspread of five feet.

56   I corrected *genitri* to *ganitri* to conform to the Sundanese name of this tree as well as its Latin nomenclature which is *Elaeocarpus ganitrus,* while Junghuhn has *Elaeocarpus augustifolius.* The *ganitri* tree is rather large and produces fruit the size of cherries. In Java the pits are used to make prayer beads or necklaces.

57   The *kenanga* tree (usually *Canangium odoratum*) is a very tall tree renowned throughout the Malay archipelago and Micronesia for the extraordinary scent of its flowers. These blossoms are used to scent linen closets, or as hair adornments or religious offerings.

58   The *Herpestes javanicus* is the Javanese mongoose. The *Lingsang* (which Junghuhn spells incorrectly as *lisang*) is another small predator. It has yellowish-white fur with large dark spots and stripes, and a tail with dark rings. It feeds primarily on birds. Lingsangs resemble the genets. The *Musang* or *luwak* in Javanese (*Paradoxus hermaphroditus*) is a small mammal that feeds on fruits and small animals. It is usually gray or brown gray with dark spots and several black stripes on its back. A nocturnal predator, it preys on chickens,

for instance, but it is also fond of the cherries of the coffee plant—hence its other name, *coffee rat*. All three—the *musang*, the Javanese mongoose, and the *lingsang*—are members of the *Viverridae* family of civets.

59 The fact that Junghuhn indicates that the "iguanas" prey on chickens means that he is speaking of the genus *Varanus* which contains one species incorrectly called *iguana* (*Iguanidae*). The latter have a ridge on their back and are herbivorous. The true *Varanus*, such as Junghuhn mentions here, is carnivorous or insectivorous.

60 *Tong-tongs* are wooden blocks which are beaten to sound an alarm.

61 Humboldt was also impressed by the nocturnal clamor of tropical nights. He describes such a night on the banks of the Orinoco.

> After eleven o'clock, such a noise began in the contiguous forest, that for the remainder of the night all sleep was impossible. The wild cries of animals rung through the woods. Among the many voices which resounded together, the Indians could only recognize those which, after short pauses, were heard singly. There was the monotonous, plaintive cry of the Aluates (howling monkeys), the whining, flute-like notes of the small sapajous, the grunting murmur of the striped nocturnal ape (*Nyctipithecus trivirgatus*, which I was the first to describe), the fitful roar of the great tiger, the Cuguar or maneless American lion, the peccary, the sloth, and a host of parrots, parraquas (*Ortalides*), and other pheasant-like birds. Whenever the tigers approached the edge of the forest, our dog, who before barked incessantly, came howling to seek protection under the hammocks. Sometimes the cry of the tiger resounded from the branches of a tree, and was then always accompanied by the plaintive piping tones of the apes, who were endeavouring to escape the unwonted pursuit. (*Views of Nature*, 199)

Darwin records a similar impression of the presence of tropical insects in a Brazilian forest.

> Nature, in these climes, chooses her vocalists from more humble performers than in Europe. A small frog, of the genus Hyla, sits on a blade of grass about an inch above the surface of the water and sends forth a pleasing chirp: when several are together they sing in harmony on different notes. . . . Various cicadae and crickets, at the same time, keep up a ceaseless shrill cry, but which, softened by the distance, is not unpleasant. Every evening after dark this great concert commenced; and often have I sat listening to it, until my attention has been drawn away by some curious passing insect. (*Voyage of the Beagle*, 29)

62 I used *nightjar* as a translation for Junghuhn's *Kaprimulgus* because it is the closest to the bird he intends. The nightjar or goatsucker is, in Linnaeus's terminology, *Caprimulgus europaeus*, because on ancient authority it was believed that these birds did indeed suck the teats of goats. The birds have a soft plumage and can therefore fly noiselessly. This is necessary because, like owls, the nightjar hunts insects at night and catches them on the wing, as Junghuhn describes in this translation. In the United States a related *caprimulgus* is the nighthawk, and both bear some resemblance to a related genus, *Antrostomus*, which includes the whip-poor-will.

63 *Lurah* generally means in Java someone appointed over others, hence a chief or head.

64 *Madat*. In a note Junghuhn states that *madat* is the name for the opium extract which is as thick as molasses. It is used to soak tobacco leaves, which are subsequently smoked.

65 *Falco* or *Haliaëtos* variety refers to birds of prey. The former belongs to the true falcons; the latter probably indicates sea eagles.

66 *Daon katang* is a creeper of the genus *Convolvuli*. The particular variety Junghuhn refers to is *Ipomoea pes caprae* or *Ipomoea biloba*, which thrives particularly well on sandy beaches. The name Junghuhn gives refers normally only to the plant used as a medicine by the native population.

67   *Tournefortia argentea,* in Sundanese properly spelled *babakoan,* is a relatively small tree with a curved trunk, growing primarily on the coast, especially on coral beaches. In Ambon the leaves of this tree, which taste like parsley, are eaten raw as a legume.

68   *Calophyllum inophyllum* is a tree that grows near beaches. Its trunk is disproportionately thick and its branches start low, near the base of the tree. It has lovely white flowers which are used by the native doctor or *dukun* for medicinal purposes. The pits of the fruits produce a greasy, green oil, which is used as a native medicine against skin diseases. This substance was known in British India as "Indian laurelnut oil."

69   *Adjaks* (*Canis javanicus* or *Canis rutilans*) is the only true wild dog in the Indies. It has a short, sharply pointed head, is rust colored, and has a black tail.

70   *Gòlòks* are short heavy types of sabers used by the Javanese as both axe and machete.

71   A *pikolan* is both a measure of weight and a manner of transport: it represents what a man can carry from both ends of a yoke.

72   One of Junghuhn's most celebrated passages, this slaughter of the gigantic turtles was paraphrased by Schopenhauer in *The World as Will and Idea.* The disproportionate suffering these turtles had to endure in order to propagate their kind shows, according to Schopenhauer, "the objectification of the will to live." The passage can be found in chapter 28 of the *Ergänzungen* to the second volume of *Die Welt als Wille und Vorstellung,* first published in 1818, and again in 1844 with fifty supplementary chapters. The latter is the edition which includes the passage on Junghuhn.

73   The lake of this coda is, according to Nieuwenhuys, Telega Patengan, a mountain lake on the western slope of the Gunung Patuha in western Java. Junghuhn visited it in 1837 with Fritze and made a colored lithograph of the spot for his *Album of Plates.*

74   A *resident* was the highest administrator of one of the thirty-six regions that comprised the former Dutch colonial Indies.

75   This same *flying lemur* or *Galeopithecus* was used by Darwin in his theory of evolution as an example of a transitional animal.

> Now look at the Galeopithecus or so-called flying lemur, which formerly was ranked among the bats, but is now believed to belong to the Insectivora. An extremely wide flank-membrane stretches from the corners of the jaw to the tail, and includes the limbs with the elongated fingers. This flank-membrane is furnished with an extensor muscle. Although no graduated links of structure, fitted for gliding through the air, now connect the Galeopithecus with the other Insectivora, yet there is no difficulty in supposing that such links formerly existed, and that each was developed in the same manner as with the less perfectly gliding squirrels; each grade of structure having been useful to its possessor. Nor can I see any insuperable difficulty in further believing that the membrane connected fingers and fore-arm of the Galeopithecus might have been greatly lengthened by natural selection; and this, as far as the organs of flight are concerned, would have converted the animal into a bat. (*The Origin of Species* [1859; reprint, New York: Collier Books, 1962], 174)

Herman Neubronner van der Tuuk

HERMAN NEUBRONNER VAN DER TUUK (1824–94) is another example of a man whose exceptional talents and abrasive personality were given sanction in the tropics. Like Junghuhn, van der Tuuk used existing institutions to pursue his real interests. And, again like Junghuhn, van der Tuuk was a freethinker who even in his youth was militantly opposed to Christianity. Despite an uncompromising attitude toward society, van der Tuuk, like Junghuhn and Rumphius, left a life's work of remarkable proportion, which is still acknowledged as fundamental and, in some ways, is still unsurpassed. His industry was as amazing as that of Rumphius and Junghuhn, but his personality was far more bilious and his written pronouncements had a vitriolic brilliance that could have made him the Voltaire of the Indies. Instead, he painstakingly labored to establish primary sources for the linguistic study of Indonesian languages.[1]

VAN DER TUUK was born in 1824 in Malacca when it was still a Dutch possession.[2] His father was from Groningen and became a high official in the colonial judiciary. His mother was of mixed blood and came from a family that had lived for generations on the Malay peninsula. He spent his childhood in Java, in the city of Surabaya, and only went to Holland when he began his formal education. When he was sixteen, van der Tuuk was admitted as a law student at the University of Groningen because his father wished him to pursue that profession. But his surrender to authority did not last long and soon he became completely absorbed in the study of languages. Besides the enviable gift of quickly comprehending the unique character of a language, van der Tuuk had a photographic memory that allowed him, for instance, to learn a dictionary by heart within days. Apparently he learned Portuguese first as a somewhat romantic gesture to the memory of his mother, a woman he later supplied with fictitious Portuguese aristocratic forebears (he even claimed that she descended from Albuquerque).[3] He next learned English and became enthralled by Shakespeare, an admiration that lasted throughout his life. It exemplifies van der Tuuk's passionate temperament as well as his exemplary thoroughness that, in order to perfect his knowledge of English, he devoted time to the study of Anglo-Saxon. Having mastered both the tongue of *Beowulf* and Shakespeare's idiom, he was perplexed when, during a stay in London, he discovered that no one understood his peculiar English.

While still in Groningen he began to study Arabic, and continued to do so after transferring to the University of Leyden, in either late 1845 or early 1846. His law studies were neglected and in 1846 he abandoned law entirely. In Leyden he added the formal study of Sanskrit to his curriculum, so we can be sure that when he departed for the Indies he knew—besides the mandatory Latin and Greek—Portuguese, English, Arabic, and Sanskrit. One must remember that the study of these languages (except for Greek and Latin) was still an unorthodox novelty. Shakespeare's work had only recently been admitted to Dutch cultural life, while oriental languages were considered an elective and not a formal course of study.

The lack of a law degree as well as family pressures forced van der Tuuk to apply for a position with the Bible Society (*Nederlands Bijbelgenootschap*) as their representative in the Batak region of Sumatra. Supported by several of his professors, his application was favorably received and he was appointed to the position in 1847 and remained in the employ of the Bible Society until 1873. This partnership was one of those ironies of circumstances that occurred more often in nineteenth-century society than they do today; it was ironic because van der Tuuk was vehemently opposed to Christianity, to missionary work, to the promulgation of the Holy Writ in native societies, and to any kind of authority, especially a moral one. He once wrote that an afterlife "can only be found in the mind of an onanist" (172). Yet he was employed by the Bible Society for over a quarter of a century and translated the Gospels as well as Acts and Exodus into the Toba-Batak language. He was only able to pursue his study of native languages because the fruits of his labor were to be applied to missionary work. A brutally honest man, van der Tuuk did not hide his increasingly bitter denunciation of Christianity. An extreme individualist and arrogant nonconformist, van der Tuuk made it plain to the society that his only "mission" in life was the pursuit of knowledge, particularly the science of linguistics as applied to Indonesian languages.

Many of his letters to the society made no bones about his disgust for Christianity, Calvinism, Holland, Dutch society, and colonial government. One has to admire the enlightened tolerance of the religious association who supported him for such a long time, put up with his recalcitrant opinions, and remained appreciative of his intellectual genius.

Van der Tuuk's ideal was freedom of thought; the pursuit of this fundamental right energized many a social rebel of the nineteenth century. His demand for this freedom was a logical extension of the atheism that he confessed to in the following excerpt from a letter he wrote on his way to the Indies in 1849.

What is existence? It was granted to us without our permission and we are supposed to be thankful for it and may not throw it away without His permission. But this relationship between man and God is merely a contract. God pleases you to be bored in this world without inquiring if you really want to, and, once you're stuck with this present, you also get the following conditions: heaven or hell. That contract should be null and void because one of the parties concerned didn't give his permission. And what is left of man is nothing but a machine, even if you begin with a hypothesis such as christianity. We are taught—and most people believe it—that life is a present, but one should always add that it is a present with conditions attached to it and without the consent of the recipient. It's nice how the Muhammadans noticed this, for instance, in an image which you might know as well: "life is a rope that God uses to fetter man; he who wants to live right has to adjust his steps to the direction in which He pulls the rope." Oh well, we're here after all, and that's why we should make ourselves as comfortable as possible and not pay any attention to conditions a sound mind would never acknowledge and which are only binding for believers. (39–40)

Almost as soon as he arrived in the Indies, van der Tuuk fell seriously ill, and the illness was accompanied by what seems to have been a mental breakdown. It is clear that, despite his astonishing energy and will power, van der Tuuk was subject to profound depressions which he quaintly attributed to "having too much blood." Yet even when in a hospital, he continued his studies, often at night, and produced a paper on the "Centralization of the Malay Language" which one contemporary expert characterized as "one of the corner stones of the study of native languages" (45). During this difficult time van der Tuuk wrote two letters to the Bible Society which were of such a rancorous nature that, had they been sent in the business world, would have resulted in his swift dismissal. But the society let the letters pass and attributed their fury to mental indisposition. Although the following description could equally serve to characterize the style of Multatuli, Voltaire, or Swift, van der Tuuk defended his kind of writing in a passage from one of these letters, announcing a standard he would never compromise.

Forgive me for these sentences. Perhaps this pen has drawn some bile from the ink. Forgive me for writing to you the way I would write to a close friend, that is to say: without violating my individuality and, therefore, without forcing my language into what for me would be a constricting corset. . . . My language must from necessity be tough, harsh, and unpleasant because it is *mine*; if you were to change it you would obscure a system by destroying one of its components. However, I could not part before I had made you feel that I've thought about my kind of writing which, I hope, you will be as proud of as I am. This was the reason I bored you for a moment. You may punish me by sending me an academician! (49–51)

Van der Tuuk was first sent to a region that was still a frontier. Northern Sumatra was divided into Atjeh (or Achin), the northernmost portion, and the Batak lands to the south. These territories were difficult to reach and explore because of their mountainous terrain and generally inhospitable landscape.

Both Atjeh and Batak peoples were bellicose, the first being the more martial. Ruled by powerful sultans, Atjeh had been known for centuries as a fabled and exotic land where gold was to be found. Converted to Islam in the ninth century, the kings of Atjeh pursued a militant Muhammadanism that tried to force conversion on neighboring peoples; at the same time the rulers vigorously resisted European influence not only for political reasons but also as an article of faith. Atjeh had been constantly at war with the Portuguese on the Malay peninsula, and it fought the Dutch successors from the seventeenth until the first decade of the twentieth century.

Atjeh tried to extend Islam's influence to the Batak people, an endeavor that resulted in frequent altercations between the two nations. The Achinese considered the Bataks inferior and treated them scornfully, an attitude that may have contributed to the moderate success of the Christian mission in the Batak lands. But the Bataks were not easily assimilated either and viable Dutch influence in the region dates only from the beginning of the nineteenth century; the independent Batak states were not truly annexed until the first decade of the present one.

The Toba highlands comprised the most important settlement of the Batak region. At their center was Toba Lake, a large body of water some 3,000 feet above sea level. Van der Tuuk was the first European to reach the shores of this magnificent lake which had national as well as religious importance for the Bataks;[4] they considered it to be the dwelling place of the gods and of the forces that controlled the world. The Toba-Bataks were the most numerous group of Bataks, and at the time van der Tuuk first encountered them they had succumbed to neither Islam nor Christianity. For that matter, the entire region could scarcely be considered responsive to Dutch authority, so van der Tuuk was living in what was essentially a rather precarious outpost of European civilization.

For various reasons van der Tuuk did not take up permanent residence in Barus until 1852. Barus was the capital of the residence Tapanuli (which included the Batak lands) on the western coast of Sumatra. It had been subjected to repeated assaults from the Achinese until about a decade before van der Tuuk's arrival. Once settled, van der Tuuk devoted himself entirely to mastering the various Batak languages. He did so in a manner that, at the time, was completely unorthodox, if not unbecoming to a European.

First he sought to make the acquaintance of a learned man from the region. This *guru* taught him the language and the lore and lived in van der Tuuk's house as an equal. After he became more familiar with the language, van der Tuuk would talk to anyone for any length of time, providing the person was not European. As a result, his aplomb and sincerity became known among the native population and people were persuaded to come and visit him. A person might stay for days while van der Tuuk conversed with him in his native tongue, asked him to write down whatever he knew of his own culture, or recorded his informant's oral reports. Always polite and friendly—although a scourge to his own kind—van der Tuuk had no trouble identifying with the local population, and he was trusted and praised by them in kind.

In 1853 van der Tuuk made a journey to Toba Lake high up in the mountains of the Batak region. It was an extraordinary accomplishment for a lone European, as will be evident in the following description given in a letter to Professor Van Gilse, secretary of the Bible Society, dated 23 July 1853.

My long silence is due to a journey to the lake and a brief indisposition caused by the bad food I was obliged to ingest. During that journey I was twice in danger of being eaten alive.

After I descended into the valley of Bakkara[5] near the lake in order to pay a visit to the King of all Bataks—Si Singa Mangaradja[6]—that particular highness, even though he had me fetched, became so suspicious of me (due to intrigues of a Batak who does some trading here) that I, surrounded by thousands of Bataks from every district and all armed with spears, became the subject of much debate that would have ended with my being consumed as a spy of the Dutch government, if two of my companions had not threatened His Holiness with war. Resistance on our part was impossible because we were only thirteen, and had no more than two rifles and two pistols among us. At the moment when several of these lip-smacking gentlemen were discussing our tastiest parts, a Malay horse trader (who had much interest in saving my life) advised me to sidle up with my pistols to H.H. and, if any of his worshippers made the slightest move, to grab him by the scruff of his neck and put a barrel in front of his holy nose. I noticed that my move toned him down a bit—at least for the moment.

The reasons for his suspicions were not unfounded. For thirty years a Malay zealot had ransacked the entire Bakkara valley. The houses had not been rebuilt yet and because His Holiness was too poor to buy wood (which came from a great distance) he and his worshippers had to make do with shacks that were only fit for goats. Furthermore, my escort, thinking they were doing me a favor, spread the rumor that I was not a Dutchman but the son of the holy king the zealot had murdered. That son was abducted by Si Pokki[7] (that is the name the Toba-Bataks gave the aforementioned conquerer; his title was undoubtedly *fakih* which the Malay in the north pronounce as *pokki*) and was the legitimate heir to the throne because the Si Singa Mangaradja who is now ruler is a younger son. In order to pass muster as that prince, or Radja Lumbung as he is called, my escort had circulated the story that after the Dutch had killed Si Pokki in the Rau region,[8] they had captured the Batak prince and sent him to the other side (that is: to Holland) in order to raise him. The superstitious Bataks swallowed such a story, of course, despite the fact that many things, especially my appearance, should have told them that somebody was making a fool of them.[9] And if that agitator (who knew perfectly well what a European looked like) hadn't intervened, we would have abandoned our plans to reach the east coast. Although I paid no attention to these fairy tales and during the entire journey of over a month have always presented myself as a Dutchman, the Bataks thought that my explanations were due to my fear of not being well received by my "younger brother" who, quite rightly, was afraid that I was going to push him aside.

Things were further complicated by a runaway slave from Atjeh (a Batak) who, several months before my arrival, had people from all the fortresses[10] in the "treeless Toba region" (*Toba na sae*)[11] pay him tribute by proclaiming that he was Si Takki Torop, the travel companion of Si Marimbulu bosi, who is a hero of Batak stories which tell of his wanderings down here on earth as immortality incarnate, and who always has his arrival announced by one of his servants (who also enjoys the prerogative of immortality). Only later did I find out that it was precisely my firm denials which made some of the assembled mass choose my side against His Holiness, indicating that my small retinue and my explanations were proof that my intentions were innocent. But Opput so hahuaon [i.e., the Singa Mangaradja's own name] remained hostile to me; even when I took my leave he would not accept any of the presents I had intended for him. This romantic story is the reason that I saw very little of the lake. It has no particular name—*tao* means "lake," and it is simply called after districts which border it, such as Tao Bakkara, Tao Silalahi.

Surrounded by steep rocks the Bakkara valley is situated, as I was told, on the southeastern shore of the lake and, it seemed to me, stretches from west to east.[12] From this valley one can see the eastern side of the island Samosir[13] while the other shore with its tall mountains was clearly visible, and judging by the smoke is just as densely populated as the entire *Toba na sae* region. Unfortunately, I could see only a piece of the lake from the Bakkara valley, and am therefore unable to report anything about its shape or length, and so forth. Because Bakkara lies in something resembling a bowl it was rather hot there even though the rocks we had to climb down couldn't be more than a hundred feet high. On the northwestern side of the valley is Pollung. It was so cold there that I needed my blanket at night, while my travel companions kept warm in Batak fashion by rolling in a mat three at a time, something that would make everybody suffocate here in Barus. I won't relate to you the stories I heard about the lake and about the rivers that empty into it, because I know from experience that the distrust of the people makes them lie on purpose. Two swift but shallow rivers course through the valley to the lake. They cascade from high cliffs. I was told that not a single one of the rivers that empties into the lake is navigable.

The trip back from Bakkara was more of a flight. We hurried to get outside His Holiness's territory and only then did I notice that I had been brought to the lake the long way around, while they pretended all the time that a shorter route was impossible. Now I realize that from Barus the lake can be reached in three days. During that journey I was surprised by the size of the population which lives in numerous confederative little states.

The second time I was in danger of being eaten alive was during the trip back, in the vicinity of Dolok Sanggul,[14] half a day's traveling west of Bakkara. I have to thank my life to the long conferences the robber held with his cohorts which allowed me to remain half an hour ahead of him. In this case it concerned a small Chinese box which the greedy Bataks thought was full of gold.[15] The treachery of the robber, who was the chief of Si Borboron, got him on war footing with my host in Dolok Sanggul. I completed the return journey in three days, after roaming around from the end of February to the beginning of April. The unfortunate end of the journey has made me more careful and has discouraged me for the moment from making any more trips like this.

In the district *Aèk na uli*, a distinguished Batak chief let me read a *pustaha*[16] which contained a creation story. We can safely assume therefore that there are still stories and chronicles in the Batak region. One of these days I hope to come into possession of a *pustaha* which contains the founding of the state Nai Pospos.[17] It's a pity that the Bataks know full well what they have there, and with incredible impudence ask for a gift if they loan you a book. When I asked that chief to loan me the *pustaha* I referred to, he demanded a European dog the size of a calf, a dozen bottles of gin, ten Spanish piastres, and three *padang rusaks* (which are a kind of wrap made in Atjeh) with the result that I had to abandon the idea of copying it. Bataks known in the Silidung region[18] confirmed for me what Burton[19] had already mentioned about the presence of Batak law books. I will, therefore, make a journey to the Silindung region as soon as I know whether they will let me have such a law book for a moment so I can copy it in a *sopo*;[20] I might as well forget about taking it with me. As far as important items of Batak literature are concerned, we have to look to the future.

I am now convinced that translating the Bible into Toba-Batak is easier than preparing a dictionary of a language that has so many different speech types. There is no need to worry about this when translating the Bible but a dictionary cannot do without such scholarship. I understand, therefore, that publishing a dictionary of Toba-Batak should come after the Bible translation, and I therefore propose to the Executive Committee to occupy myself primarily with the language itself while at the same time translating Zahn's Bible stories[21] for practice. I could start on the real translations back in Holland, and could finish them rather quickly if I had completed the linguistic aspect of my work over here. The Executive Committee can only profit from this proposal because, when I am working on such a translation in Holland, I would need no more than half the salary I presently enjoy. Don't think however that my Batak dictionary can ever be called complete because as long as it is so dangerous for a European to travel through this region no one will ever be able to collect everything that is required for such a work. One is dealing here with a language that is spoken by a most peculiar people. Countless words are either untranslatable or can only be described. But with a translation of the Bible one need not worry about such problems. All one needs to do is use the spoken language and refrain from being too literal. I hope you will consider my proposal. When I am in the process of finishing my grammar and dictionary I will try to get a copy to you. Not only will it give someone an idea of my work, but perhaps it can also serve as a kind of insurance if my texts and I meet with some disaster on the way back to Holland.

One might as well forget about staying among the Bataks who are independent of the colonial government. Everywhere I tried, I was refused because the Bataks see me only as a wolf in sheep's clothing who will swallow them whole. The Muhammadans among the Bataks only encourage that image since they would love to get rid of me because I feel obliged to expose quite a lot of extortion. The disdainful way the Muhammadan treats the Batak is incredible, and the way a person who's addicted to gambling is turned into a slave would make your hair stand on end. The government around here is nothing to speak of. They have twenty-five men in a place which can be overrun at any moment by a handful of men from Atjeh. It is afraid to properly punish the extortion practices of the chiefs because an uprising would require a larger force. To uphold the law here in a manner befitting a civilized nation would cost too much, of course. The forced cultivation of pepper hasn't made friends for our government, and its inability to compete with the Chinese in the salt and linen trade has made [the Bataks] curse the day when they invited us to come.

Our only ally up north is the Radja-muda[22] of Tarumun who, for two hundred guilders a month, has taken it upon himself to warn the government of the slightest move of the Achinese. But his support is not all that strong because the Achinese hate him for his Dutch manners and dress. Not long ago the rumor was making the rounds that, during a pilgrimage to Mecca, a son of the king of Atjeh had asked the Sjarif[23] to support them against us. At the same time some twenty fanatic friends of Atjeh came to ask the civil authority to allow them to live in Tappus. So don't be surprised if you hear one of these days that we have been murdered. (58–64)

THE following are some of the notes van der Tuuk made during his trip to Toba Lake. He may have intended them for an official report, but he never wrote one. It was not until Nieuwenhuys transcribed them in 1962 that they became public knowledge.

The festivities started the next morning around half past eight when two forked sticks were put in the ground with a rice pounder between them. From this improvised rack they hung four *ugungs* [gongs] tuned at different pitches by means of a wax called *puli*. Then they put a wide board next to this rack to be used by the four men who play the *ugungs* as well as those who play the *odaps* [drums]. On the other side of the rack they spread a large mat for the guests and the man who played the *sarune* [a kind of oboe]. The water buffalo had already been wrestled down and, with its legs tied together, lay anchored by one of its horns in the ground. The host of the banquet, with a fine vestment thrown over his shoulders, held up *santi santi* [sacrificial rice] in his hand which he dedicated to the protective spirit or *mortua sombaon*.[24] He begged the god's mercy for himself, his kin, and his guests. During the prayer his children, all richly attired, offered us *sirih*.[25] He then asked me to dance with him, but when I explained my ineptitude in that art, he took my teacher as a substitute. When the dance was finished they killed the water buffalo, then divided and prepared it. After the meal he apologized for it in typical Batak fashion, saying that I should not blame him if my stomach was not sated. Because I did not know the Batak way of saying thanks with its incomprehensible number of verses, I had my teacher answer for me, and I presented my host with some bullets and two packs of tobacco. The feast ended with mutual congratulations.

Around noon we left our host and took the road to Arbaan. The next morning we left Arbaan and continued our journey to Parbotihan,[26] where we arrived around half past two in the afternoon. The horse trader who had been my travel companion left me the next day and went east to Matiti. I was not allowed to go with him because, it was said, if I did it would cost me my life. The Bataks who live further east were supposed to be thinking that I was Si Pokki—a name used here to indicate the Padris—and would avenge the insults they had suffered from Tuanku Rao[27] who had managed to get all the way to the lake, and, in the Bakkara region, had laid hands on the king of all Bataks, Si Singa Mangaradja. The horse trader was supposed to prepare the chiefs of Matiti and of districts further east before I arrived.

During his absence I stayed in Parbotihan and made several sidetrips which were of considerable use to me. For instance, I climbed Mount Siala and could vaguely see the sea to the west. The view from this mountain was overwhelming. I also visited a cave southwest of Parbotihan where the natives collect their *sirih* chalk by torchlight. A trip to Aèk Godang, half an hour south of Parbotihan, presented me with a view of one of the largest grave monuments of the Bataks. It is a monumental stone coffin, beautifully carved and edged with red, white, and black.[28] It represents a creature with the body of a horse but with head and trunk of an elephant. Below the sculpture's head is a human image. The lid of the coffin was the footrest of a sculpture of a male, richly attired and leaning with his back against a pillow. Behind him was another, but smaller, sculpture that had been placed at the back of the coffin. The seams of the lid had been sealed with chalk. They had erected a structure over this monument, open to all sides, while from the roof over the sculpture hung the jawbones of cows, buffalos, and pigs which had been eaten during the funeral feast of the deceased.

The radja of Aèk Godang possesses an enormous *pustaha* which makes the one in the Royal Institute[29] pale by comparison. Because it dealt mainly with magic I did not pay much attention to it. To buy it was simply out of the question. I stayed nine days in Parbotihan and, despite the miserable food, would have stayed longer because almost every day I learned something new.

The people who live in Marbun freely confess to being cannibals and swear that there's no better meat than human flesh. The tastiest part, they claim, are the palms of the hands and the soles of the feet. Even the children in Parbotihan have tasted it several times. I was amazed how much hospitality these people showed me. They trusted me so much that they let me speak to the women, and not even the children ran away. The cannibalism[30] cannot be used as a measuring stick for the character of these people; it appears that it is simply a very old custom. I frequently talked to them about this barbaric habit but they didn't see anything unnatural about it. One of them, with a straight face, told me about his experience when he was butchering a human being.

This particular fellow wanted to know how we got there. When I drew the islands of Great Britain and Ireland over against Holland he asked me why we were so afraid of the British. I asked him where he'd heard such infamous lies and got the reply that several Malay traders had assured him of that. Such a thing did not fail to grieve me but, I said to myself, isn't it our own fault? So rarely do we speak intimately with the native population that even a Malay, who is more often in contact with us, has to hear everything he knows about us from people who are against us. We have the inhabitants of Padang to thank for the stories of Holland's submissive attitude to England.[31] The so-called *sinjos* [Eurasians] pretend to be British, while they are also the ones who speak with the natives about other things besides business and governmental affairs. Most Dutchmen here are bureaucrats and only speak to the native population when they have some dealings with them.

That same chief complained to me about the ill treatment several of his subjects had suffered at the hands of government overseers. He told me that if there is a complaint against a Batak he is immediately tied up before he has been proven guilty; that their benzoin[32] is repeatedly taken from them; that they are forced to perform coolie labor; that the Chinese are always in the right, and when a Chinese or rich Malay is in the wrong he gets off with a slap on the wrist while a poor Batak or Malay gets it in the neck. All these things happen, I was told, without the knowledge of the civil authorities because the Bataks generally do not dare complain.

I was at a loss to give him a satisfactory explanation for the fact that, though in good faith, the government makes the distinction between a so-called respectable person and the common man. It is unfortunately all too true that whatever the chiefs want will now happen more easily than when they were not subject to our government. The government takes a position as if it were still in Holland: it regards a well-to-do native as a civilized person. To some extent this is due to the fear that the chiefs might foment an uprising. This may be true in Java, but it's not true here where a native only clings to his chief insofar as he is upheld by a European. There are a number of them around here who make a bad impression in the independent regions. People are quite right, for instance, to laugh at the way we administer justice. Because there is no prison we put a criminal, after administering some "a posteriori," in the block, a punishment that does not prevent him from stealing again. When our government wasn't established yet, the jealousy among the chiefs guaranteed that the comman man was not suppressed, but now they are hand in glove with each other against a government of infidels, and they are intent on hoodwinking it.

There is, furthermore, an additional plague the common man has to deal with—that is the Chinese who are, as it were, our pigtail after we establish our authority somewhere. The Chinese want to make everyone dependent on them by lending the chiefs—who are often big gamblers—money, and in this manner they cut many a complaint short that has been lodged against them and which the chiefs are obliged to report to the government. You can imagine that I did not like to hear such complaints because, in the end, I was forced to offer myself as the means for the wronged Batak to obtain justice. This is sometimes very difficult, especially when one is dealing with touchy bureaucrats, which is fortunately not the case here. I try as much as possible not to get involved with such things, but I cannot escape them because these simple people see in every European a person vested with power, no matter how much he may argue to the contrary. I fear that this will get me into some difficulty because already many a Chinese or Malay who has the opportunity to oppress the mountain people harbors a grudge against me, and I would therefore rather be in a place where our government wasn't established yet.

During my journey I often had the occasion to notice the influence of the British; no wonder, because the name of Singapore and other places has reached even these parts. In these mountain districts one finds many a trader from the Malay district of Rau (which we subdued) who are known as the most enterprising inhabitants of this island, where you will find them everywhere. These Malay always like to trade with Singapore but, according to them, they are forcibly hindered by the (Dutch) government, while they constantly complain about the insufferable statute labor,[33] and maintain that this work the people have to perform harms the small businessman. How badly the Bataks of this region think of us was proven to me once by a Batak who wanted to examine the ivory knob on my walking stick. When one of his comrades tried to dissuade him because I would resent it, he exclaimed: "Well now. I'd like to see him resent it up here. Down there they've got a lot to say, but here the tables are turned. Down there they're quickly on their high horses but here they will have to rein in a bit." (67–71)

THE nearly six years (1851–57) van der Tuuk spent among the Bataks were fruitful. He had to work, however, under adverse circumstances that either were of a local nature, typical of the tropics (such as the fact that paper simply disintegrated in a short time), or were due to the constant pressure from the Bible Society to devote all his energy to material that would be used to spread the gospel. His letters to the society became in-

creasingly belligerent and he took his employers to task for being ignorant of conditions in Sumatra. He felt generally the same way about the
Dutch government in Holland, saying that it had no notion what quotidian life in the colonies entailed, while he constantly berated the sorry
specimens The Hague sent over as rulers.

Van der Tuuk was incensed by the practice of statute labor; it required
a small farmer to raise crops for the Dutch colonial government above
and beyond his own needs and what he owed his chief. Van der Tuuk was
bothered by it morally and practically: even a politician should be able
to see, he contended, that the system would only serve to pit the native
population against Dutch rule.

Two other complaints constantly occur in his writings. Van der Tuuk
failed to understand why the Dutch seldom bothered to get to know the
native population more intimately. They always maintained a distance, he
felt, and, consequently, suffered from a profound ignorance of local custom and lore. For the most part, according to van der Tuuk, this was due
to a lack of linguistic skills. At best, an official of the Dutch government
knew some Malay, a variety more commonly known as *pasar* Malay or
what was needed to buy food in the local market. Van der Tuuk branded
this "Malay gibberish." But officials seldom knew any of the languages of
the people they were responsible for. And since, ironically, most knowledge about the numerous languages of the Malay archipelago came from
missionary efforts, no one but a rare scholar would know the literature
and mores of a particular region. But missionaries only learned a language
in order to translate the Bible, and this case of putting the cart before the
horse infuriated van der Tuuk. He failed to see the sense of translating items
unknown to the Bataks (such as wine, camels, or an altar) or the reason he
should persist in a foolish enterprise that encountered only disgust when
the Bataks read the translated Bible. He confessed to being tongue-tied
when he tried to explain such concepts as "Abraham's bosom" (96). In a
letter to a colleague from 1867, van der Tuuk formulated the problem in
the following manner.

Everything that up till now has been done for native languages I consider useless.
Nor will it ever get better as long as one does not study the languages for their
own sake. One cannot advance in any occupation if one doesn't love the work. If
one learns a language only for the purpose of translating the Bible one is no more
than a wretch, and that's why I've more contempt for myself than for somebody
else. I understand that it was a cruel fate that steered me into the arms of the Bible
Society. Professor Juynboll[34] persuaded me, but I am sorrier that family consid-
erations persuaded me all the more. In the Indies the job of Bible translator is

anything but an honor because you are always confused with being a missionary, that is to say some fellow who escaped his grocery store. . . . I don't have to tell you that I'm anything but flattered when I'm called *pious* and, in fact, consider it a curse word. (131–32)

Van der Tuuk constantly besieged the society with sound but unwelcome advice. He noted, for instance, that Islamic proselytizers were much more successful in their missionary goals than the Protestants because they first learned all they could about a population in order to sway them to their cause and, even then, only with an eye to the second generation. By comparison, the Protestant desire for instant conversion was unrealistic. Islam was also unwittingly aided by the Dutch government whose officials were so ignorant of the people they lived among that the Malay teachers were able to make a better impression by presenting their language in Arabic script and instilling Islamic notions. Because the Dutch supervisors knew nothing about the literature or the language, they failed to censor educational materials, and Islam was free to lay a firm foundation in the schools on which future conversions could be built.

But next to counsel that was of direct interest to the society, van der Tuuk also offered advice about other things, advice that was not always welcome. He told the society that the Bataks thought it peculiar that he didn't "keep" a woman, and proceeded to tell his employers that for Europeans, sexual life in the tropics was a constant problem that was only aggravated by governmental rules and regulations. Because van der Tuuk was not a prude (which made him a rarity in nineteenth-century society) he confessed his belief that sex was a necessary part of life. He declared, in fact, that in hotter climates the "animal needs" of a man increased, and that he who wanted to be an exception to the general rule of keeping a mistress would be "brought to an early grave due to unavoidable depression" (93). Colonial administrators and military men below the rank of captain were badly paid; van der Tuuk noted that only few men of high rank could afford to marry and that, therefore, the keeping of a native mistress (euphemistically called a *njai*, the Balinese word for "housekeeper")[35] was a "necessary evil" (93). Though it was reprehensible for a missionary even to contemplate a thing like that, such a man, van der Tuuk argued, would nevertheless suffer from forced celibacy, and he would also be the laughingstock of the bewildered Bataks. He further noticed that statute labor had an "immoral effect" on the Batak population because in districts where the forced labor was exacted the male population fled to districts where it was not and, consequently, produced a surplus of males there and a corresponding lack of women. The result was a "most flagrant immorality. In Atjeh, pederasty is publicly tolerated, as it is here in Barus, while the consumption of opium increases, and therefore it [i.e., statute labor] hinders any kind of progress" (95).

Despite deplorable conditions and much official resistance, van der. Tuuk did pioneering work for the study of Indonesian languages. One reason for his success was that he went into the field and worked with native people in a patient and respectful manner that displayed genuine interest. Years later, in Bali, he entirely submerged himself in native society, but the necessity for what is now common practice among linguists and anthropologists already was evident to van der Tuuk in the middle of the nineteenth century. He collected folktales, local lore, treatises on religion, funerals, and magic, as well as love songs, laments, and prayers, including one that pleaded for an erection (66). His vitriolic sense of humor made him send the society copies of Batak tales that were replete with ribaldry and sexual jokes.

After he returned to Holland in 1857, van der Tuuk produced a Batak grammar, dictionary, and reader, with a separate volume of notes that included a number of folktales. A modern linguist, P. Voorhoeve, judged van der Tuuk's work in the Batak languages to be "astonishing," and wondered how "this genius arrived at such a wellnigh complete understanding of Batak texts despite the scanty data concerning the Batak language that were available in [van der Tuuk's] student days. After his work, all these older data lost their importance." Van der Tuuk was the first to use a script for transcribing Batak, an ortography he designed himself, which was based on "the phonetic order of the Sanskrit alphabet." Even today, van der Tuuk's work on several Batak languages remains "the only printed source" and has as yet "not become superfluous." "The main work in the field of Batak grammar was likewise done by van der Tuuk."[36]

During his stay in Holland from 1857 to 1868, van der Tuuk was constantly involved in controversies with leaders in the Dutch academic world. His invaluable practical experience and intellectual gifts (he reports that he learned Tagalog, the language of the Philippines, in six weeks for purposes of comparative philology) made him a formidable opponent for more conventional scholars.[37] Van der Tuuk relied on personal observations and denounced the prevalent scholarship that put its faith entirely in books; at the same time he defended the native population against what he considered hypocritical defamation by the pillars of Dutch society. In 1866, for example, he defended the practice of cannibalism:

It is true that they still eat people in the Batak region, but that doesn't mean that the population has sunk below the level of animals. Would you put the christians below the animals even though they did put people on the rack, quartered them, burned witches, etc. etc.? I hope you're too good a christian to assert such a thing. Cannibalism in the Batak region isn't a hobby—I have known Bataks who abhor human flesh—but is a form of punishment for spies—for that same reason there were two occasions when I myself almost wound up in some Batak stomachs—and for erotic gentlemen who take too many liberties with someone else's wife. It is undoubtedly barbaric to punish criminals in that manner, but it is even more barbaric when followers of a religion of love burn people who think differently during a time when that pathetically childish religion still had no notion of modern theology. (125–26)

In the summer of 1868 van der Tuuk returned to the Indies, again as a representative of the Bible Society, but this time he was stationed in Bali. He remained there until his death in 1894.

He traveled with a companion, an arrangement that did not suit his temperament at all. "If you ever want to travel with someone, make sure that you do not take a married man as a traveling companion, because such a fellow is quite a nuisance with his yapping about letters from his wife, etc. Everywhere we stopped, Jäger sent a telegram, and if all married people are like him then marriage must be a terrible curse because it seems to get on your nerves" (140).

It was impossible for him to sail directly to Bali due to uprisings and epidemics, and van der Tuuk did not arrive at his destination until April 1870. During his enforced stay on Java he accepted a government assignment to study the language spoken in the Lampong district in southern Sumatra.[38] He traveled through the region for about a year. Van der Tuuk accepted the assignment, no doubt, because of his natural curiosity about languages, but also because he wanted to escape European society: "I yearn to live among the natives in order to escape our so-called civilization (138). . . . I would rather associate with natives stinking of fish than with nicely dressed hypocrites" (108). Back in Java in September 1869, van der Tuuk was still unable to travel to Bali. Java did not impress him, he preferred Sumatra, and, later, Bali. This in itself was a fairly uncommon position because Java was considered the most prized and civilized among the islands of the Indies.

The heat is terrible here when there's no rain, because they have a west or rain monsoon. What a difference with the climate of Sumatra's west coast where you are never bothered by the heat. Should one blame the climate for the fact that the Javanese, although more civilized than the Bataks and Niassers,[39] live so abominably, or is despotism the culprit? You can't imagine worse hovels than these Javanese houses, and I'm particularly aware of it because I know the solid houses of Sumatra's people. The civilization of the Javanese is entirely on the surface; he has a refined language, dresses tastefully, knows many delights to waste his money on, but he lives like a rat in a sewer. How some people can point to the condition of the Javanese as proof that the culture system works,[40] is a mystery to me, although I don't dare to conclude either that he is so miserable because of that system or because of the despotism which is a time honored tradition here. One can compare Java to France under "the grand Louis": you encounter a superficial civilization but it is no more than a veneer to cover a great deal of misery and immorality. (152)

That there was also a sensitive aspect of his personality may be surmised from the following letter written to the Bible Society on 24 May 1869, which dates it from time he was traveling through the Lampong district.

At the same time your letter arrived I received news from Java that Engelmann had died.[41] I hope that his passing away which, according to your letter, depresses you a great deal, will move you less than it does me who sits here sighing about it in loneliness, without anyone to talk to and overwhelmed with things to do.

Engelmann's death is a great loss to science because he was one of the few who cherished science for its own sake. Our friend died suddenly in Batavia. They found a bowl with blood on the table so that it seems likely that he choked on his own blood. Poor man. His life was full of cares already when he was still a student, and when he was finally able to devote himself heart and soul to what he loved, he went the way of all flesh. May the earth rest lightly on him. In moments like these one feels sadness and distress.

I live here in an open building, right across the river Seputik,[42] surrounded by forest. My home is a house without a front or back door, and my two servants and I live in the central room which divides the two miserable holes. In that central room burns a tube made of banana leaves filled with melted resin which is supposed to keep the royal tiger at bay who slinks around here making his hiccuping sound. I am writing this under the light of a small petroleum lamp, all the while smoking like a chimney to keep the insects away who swarm all around you in the wet monsoon. To catch a mosquito in one piece should be quite a feat because under the loose planks of the floor a heap of rubbish burns that is supposed to keep these fellows away from the sleeping quarters. They're enough of a bother in the dark, but, according to my servant, to catch one now is impossible. Ergo: patience until half past five in the morning, because the man who brings this to Tarabanggi along with a package for Sukadana leaves around six. The mosquitos are quite small here and won't impress you; you can catch more in Telokbetong. I

live here completely surrounded by Lampongs and learn a great deal. My stay is important to the Bible Society because I have learned here to be completely alone. In Bali too I intend to banish myself from the company of those Indo-Europeans who do nothing but play cards—a society that demands a great deal of your time but gives no pleasure in return. It seems likely that they will extend my time here, but if they don't, I'll gladly leave this land of forests, crocodiles, swamps, and royal tigers. I don't want to stay here because there is barely any literature to speak of, with the result that I have to collect everything from the mouths of the native people. I am sorry now that I accepted the government's assignment. In one corner of the envelope is a recently caught dwarf-mosquito and in the other one a collection of other pests. I have added a stink moth, which can easily be recognized by its legs and larger size. I am sending this as an open letter to the resident, with the request to catch a couple of large mosquitos for you because Telokbetong teems with them. Hoping that the mosquitos will cheer you up, I remain. . . .
(145)

In April 1870 van der Tuuk finally arrived in Bali. The area was already famous for its climate and mountains, and he found a beautiful island that had been subjugated only recently. Even though Bali is today a touristic cliché, it had little significant contact with Europeans until the beginning of the nineteenth century. Military campaigns began in the 1840s and the Dutch had to repeat them for the next sixty years. These campaigns were intended to ensure fealty, but armed intervention was also frequently necessary to stop internecine warfare between local regions. Resistance was fierce, however. For instance, once a Balinese radja was convinced that he was fighting a losing battle, he would not negotiate for surrender but instead gather his close kin and most loyal followers (including women and children) around him and lead them into a final attack (*puputan*) until everyone was killed. It should be mentioned that the Dutch interfered very little with the local rights of the aristocracy although, as van der Tuuk repeatedly complained, their treatment of the common man was extremely harsh.

Bali was also unusual in that its population was predominantly Hindu. Neither Islam nor Christianity ever gained a foothold. Besides its uprisings, Bali had also an infamous reputation for frequent epidemics of cholera and smallpox. But for a man of van der Tuuk's temperament, the island's refined civilization and intelligent population made it worthwhile despite inevitable dangers.

Van der Tuuk settled down in the northern part of Bali, in the small village of Baratan, a few miles from Pabean-Bulèlèng, the harbor of Bali's capital, Singaradja. He had a simple house built of bamboo and wood, and lived like a Balinese. His behavior was certainly eccentric at that time, particularly because he made it quite clear that visitors such as government officials were not welcome and that he preferred native life to European society. A high official in the colonial administration once found him wearing only a sarong, sitting on a bamboo bench (or *balé-balé*) eating Edam cheese. When he saw the man approach, van der Tuuk yelled at him: "I'm not at home."[43]

Soon he was unable to tolerate socks and shoes. He spoke the language like a native and even bathed outside like the Balinese—something no European would ever consider—under the *pantjuran,* a kind of bamboo pipe that brought water from a natural source. Van der Tuuk became known among the Balinese as *Gusti Dertik* ("Sir van der Tuuk") who was, as one radja put it, "the one man on Bali who knows and understands Balinese." Respected and revered, the Balinese often consulted him on matters of law, health, and education.

Van der Tuuk lived like this for nearly a quarter of a century, surrounded, as he wrote, by "dogs (4), monkeys (3), chickens (didn't count them) and other trifles which appear to constitute the heart of existence (I also keep ten ducks)" (164). One should add to this list his *njai,* several servants, and two Arabic donkeys. Van der Tuuk was convinced that these donkeys were the perfect beasts of burden for Bali's mountainous terrain, and he irritated the colonial government by constantly demanding subsidies to raise donkeys for the public good (219).

His house was an indescribable mess, poorly furnished, without European comforts, and totally neglected in favor of his linguistic work. Manuscripts, old texts, books, and pages from his growing dictionary on Kawi lay everywhere on planks, tables, crates, even on the floor. Yet van der Tuuk knew his own chaos well enough to retrieve a relevant sheet of paper within minutes. What he was working on was a large Kawi-Balinese-Dutch dictionary. *Kawi* was another name for Old Javanese, and van der Tuuk had proved that Balinese contained a great number of Kawi words. In fact, the Balinese knew Kawi better than the Javanese, though theirs was only a formal knowledge demanded by religious texts and literary conventions. The way van der Tuuk could record Kawi words along with their meaning was to listen to Balinese priests, copy countless Balinese manuscripts, and compare similar words in various original sources. Van der Tuuk was using comparative philology to establish a dictionary of a practically unknown language, while at the same time hoping to produce a better understanding of Balinese. It was an immense task and he never finished it. The dictionary was published after his death between 1897 and 1912 in four large tomes totaling 3,622 pages.

As he had done before in Sumatra, van der Tuuk attacked the obdurate colonial system as well as missionary efforts during his years in Bali. His antireligious sentiments became more strident, and in June 1873 he resigned from the Bible Society and entered government service. That the latter proved galling as well can be surmised from the following passage, although it also indicates his reasons for switching employers.

Why, you might ask, am I in Batavia? Just imagine, they had me come all the way from Bali in order to give exams in Javanese and Malay. Science misused for practical reasons! I, who was totally immersed in Kawi and Balinese, must leave home and dogs in order to examine some plodders in languages which do not interest me at all. You know that I'm presently in the government's stable, and I regret it now. But what could I do? My disgust for that idiot from Nazareth increased every day. And no wonder, if every day you've got to see those brokers of blessedness who believe that a religion which started with adultery and ended in suicide is so wonderful. The babbling of Jehova Junior made me so sick that I considered myself a man who makes coffins [i.e., his Bible translations], one who receives orders for things he doesn't want to use. (170–71)

In Bali, van der Tuuk saw once again the futility of the Protestant mission. The following letter was sent to the Bible Society in July 1870.

The two missionaries here were sent by the Utrecht Mission. They lack technical training since in Utrecht they were only acquainted with Malay gibberish. Although they speak Balinese—they've been here about four years—I can tell that it won't be easy for them to write anything that is understandable in Balinese. They should have come here only after a dictionary and grammar had been published. On top of that, they live in the European quarter and seldom speak with a Balinese. What's worse, they are both married to European women. I built my house in a secluded spot and made up my mind to have as little as possible to do with Europeans, otherwise I don't see how I can learn the language properly. Everything depends on the way one relates to the Native population, and it's a pity that in Holland they don't prevent the missionaries from marrying European women. The early preachers of islam were much better; they married Native women and it was their children who spread the new faith. The illusions Holland entertains about preaching the gospel is ridiculous to someone who knows the Native people well. Up till now such missions have led to few satisfactory results. The people in Europe do not understand the relationship between the Native and the European, which is why they are foolish enough to send off missionaries who are not suited for the job at all. The missionaries here say that the religion of the Balinese is in decline, but they forget that this does not necessarily mean that the people are ready to embrace christianity. Islam has particularly made progress on the coast by means of opium, which is a sad state of affairs.

I have been rather successful with my studies. I hope to learn the language within two years because it seems quite simple up till now. As far as my life is concerned, it isn't very pleasant because conversation is totally lacking, but I'll bear it if I can see progress in my work. One shouldn't come to the Indies as a student of languages and hope to have some fun, because one is totally isolated. Most Europeans haven't the slightest interest in such studies, while the well-paid bureaucrats think you're crazy if you're possessed by the need to learn languages and are content with a small income. The same thing is true in Holland where the businessman turns up his nose at those "dead languages." (155–56)

VAN DER TUUK discovered that the Balinese, though quite tolerant, resisted foreign influences.

People [in Holland] simply won't understand that someone raised in another religion judges a new dogma just as harshly as the bigoted christian. They should hear in Holland what an Arab has to say about christianity. But if he says so to a missionary, the man usually gets very angry, and the Arab stops talking from politeness. Islam has also had a hard time on Bali. The Balinese are so proud that they call becoming a Muhammadan "to jump down" and changing one's religion "*njaluk*" which is to say "to put on other clothes." A Balinese is not a fantatic but he is very attached to his religion. And this is no surprise because it permeates his thinking. If he renounces his religion he also parts with his literature, and that is something that for the moment is inconceivable. (165)

A Balinese was baptized here a little while ago. I don't know if one should rejoice. The pagan Balinese were *not* upset about it, but wrote it off by declaring that the man was crazy. They are very tolerant of people with different persuasions. One usually ascribes tolerance to indifference, but this is not the case with the Balinese at all. They are proud of their old religion and consider people who think differently some kind of lunatics who humiliate themselves when they make the change. One can learn from this that tolerance doesn't always mean being lukewarm. Both christianity and islam have little hope of success here. (168)

Because he lived among the people, van der Tuuk knew all too well the faults of the colonial regime and the quiet despair the common Balinese suffered at the hands of their own aristocracy. He noted the frequent practice of the Dutch government to tacitly condone local oppression without defending the rights of the common people. "Not so long ago an old man was whipped with thorny branches because he had bought some goods from a Chinese in the name of his overlord. When his body was covered with welts they tied him up and left him in the sun for eleven to twelve hours!" (159). Nothing was done about it and the victim could never lodge a complaint with the colonial authorities because they would only believe the man's social superior. Van der Tuuk was quite correct when he predicted that "this land will cost us many an expedition because at some point the dam will burst" (162).

When one reads van der Tuuk, one thinks inevitably of Multatuli, Holland's most famous author and critic of colonial policies during the nineteenth century.[44] It is clear that van der Tuuk had read Multatuli's work, but it is also clear that he had some pertinent reservations about it. For instance, he attacked Multatuli's posturing, a trait that does indeed detract from the main purpose of the work at times.

What's Multatuli doing these days? Has another volume of his *Ideën* [Ideas] appeared yet? It's a pity he repeats himself so often. His conceit harms him more than he thinks. He wants us to learn his work by heart! This becomes quite clear from his notes. We read him for the clever way he writes but not because we can learn any new ideas from him. He wants to replace Christ, but a Jesus II would be too much for our time; we already got more than enough with No. I. Jehova and Co. are bankrupt and ruined a lot of people. Whether Jesus II, Multatuli, or anybody else who wants to don the prophet's robe, will be any better remains to be seen. (185)

But van der Tuuk also defended his fellow critic. "Multatuli seems to be deaf and dumb. Is he still holding forth? Because you dislike him you can't see his virtues. I'll say again that his piece about Father Jansen is masterful, but I'll also grant you that he can sometimes be as tedious as an old bag" (193). After he had heard of Multatuli's death he asked "are they going to publish the complete works of Multatuli? I mean a cheap edition. But there is a lot in him that is unpalatable and was only written to fill both a page and his pocket. He sometimes bullshits a lot" (207). And it is also not surprising that the linguist in van der Tuuk had a good laugh at the expense of Multatuli's dubious explanations and derivations of Javanese and Malay words. He called them "capricious." "They tickle the funny bone with the result that what's good goes down the drain as well" (212).

Finally, a passage from a letter to D'Ablaing, Multatuli's publisher and a militant freethinker.[45] The text illustrates once more van der Tuuk's dis-

like of Holland, Christianity, and Calvinism, as well as his typically aggressive style and character.

If *Dawn* wants some excerpts from missionary reports I'll be glad to supply a
selection that will make your hair stand on end. That you are busy I can well
understand but that you cannot read my letters I refuse to accept. I suspect that
you received my letter when you were in a bad mood because I remember dis-
tinctly that I took special care to write out very clearly the titles of the books I
wanted.[46] Multatuli could produce more if he weren't so conceited. *Asmodee*[47]
said: if M. has money he doesn't want to work, and if he doesn't have any he can't
work. When he sold his countenance[48] and displayed it (in your shop) I thought
that he'd gone crazy, or rather, that he didn't understand the Dutch. His idolaters
couldn't bear the thought of paying 10 guilders for a portrait when, as they said,
2.50 was a good enough price for it. No matter how much he hates mankind M. is,
generally speaking, too much of a simpleton when it comes to knowing his countrymen. He should have been born in France—or, in any case, not in Holland—
which is also true for Roorda van Eysinga.[49] I am often surprised that people like
you who still have French blood in their veins are so respectable and solemn. Calvinism seems to have left an ineradicable impression. It is true, I must say, that it is
no small matter to have been a Calvinist without having suffered from it. Calvinism has the same effect as opium: even when you have licked it you're still
stuck with being skinny and having blue lips. One could say that Calvinism has
the same effect on someone's brains as being hit by a windmill has on someone's
skull. You never recover. The dent is there once and for all. I am not coming back
to Holland, although I have enough money to resign and cut coupons. If I go back
I'm going to live in Naples. That won't be entirely pleasant, since I'll be shut off
from any news from Holland or the Indies but, on the other hand, I won't be
bothered by calvinistic claptrap covered with a sauce of Dutch slobber. What a
place, that Holland! I remember a windy and rainy day when I went to *De Pool*[50]
on the Rokin to grease my mortal bones. When I felt the necessity to rid myself of
what I had consumed, I found that two hands weren't enough: to hold on to your
hat (stovepipe), cigar, umbrella, and your tool, resembled a circus act.

While reading some Buddhist texts I noticed that "the religion of Love" is the
illegitimate child of Daddy Jehovah and Mommy Buddha. Even Dante's hell was
stolen. That holy mothball Xavier[51] wrote to Portugal that when he attended a
church service in India for the first time he felt that the Devil had fooled him by
giving a performance of his one and only blessed religion. Christ as an incarnation
of God (*awatara*) is a lousy replica of Vishnu who keeps on returning to earth to
rid the world of monsters (*raksasas*, and other evil creatures, which represent so
many manifestations of the Devil). The Jews gave the religion from India a Jewish
color, and it is now palmed off as christianity. When it's christmas, catholic coun-

tries display the birth of Christ and rock a cradle. The same thing happens in India with *Kresna* as child. The host of little shepherdesses who attend Kresna have been transformed into one fallen woman (Mary Magdalen). And the many monsters Vishnu did battle with have been turned into a single Devil. What was a plurality in the religion from India has been reduced to a single item in christianity. The Jews were under the heel of one despot and the people from India under many. Vale! (182–84)

DESPITE his belligerent assertions, van der Tuuk never moved to Naples to cut coupons, although he left a sizable estate. He died in August 1894 in Java, in a military hospital in Surabaya, a victim of dysentery (which had plagued him throughout his life in the tropics) and the indifferent medical care on Bali. He remined true to himself till the very end. When the doctor who treated him during his final illness wanted to clean a glass to give him a drink, van der Tuuk snarled: "Stop that. That glass has never been washed before" (222). On his last walk to the boat he was dressed in a frock coat and held a cigar box filled with silver money under his arm.

He left a sum of nearly 135,000 guilders, a fortune in those days. His work, which was of more lasting value, was found scattered "throughout the house and the back porch." The movable goods were estimated at "883 guilders; including provisions and drink worth 660 guilders; two donkeys, worth 50 guilders; and three geese worth 3 guilders. The bamboo house covered with *atap* (dried palm leaves) is estimated to be worth 10 guilders" (225). This only indicates that van der Tuuk, consistent to the end, lived in accordance with his own sense of priority.

His life's work is represented by the Herculean labor of his Kawi-Balinese dictionary which, in effect, he never finished. Like Murray, the first editor of the *Oxford English Dictionary*, van der Tuuk was "caught in a web of words." He found himself confronted by insurmountable problems of verification. Variants multiplied endlessly and like the tasks of the sorcerer's apprentice, van der Tuuk's lexicographical labor got out of control and overwhelmed him. Only death was able to put an arbitrary stop to it.

Van der Tuuk will be remembered as one of the pioneers of the study of Indonesian languages and comparative philology. He was something of a legend in his own time. People came to visit him on Bali to satisfy their curiosity about his eccentricity and traveled from Europe to pay homage to his scholarly reputation. Yet he found greater satisfaction in being honored by the native population as one of their own. It has been reported that, after his death, van der Tuuk's *njai* lived for years in the same little house and welcomed visitors with: "Ini Gusti Dertik punya rumah, masuk sadya tuan" ("This is the house of Sir van der Tuuk, please enter, mister").

NOTES

1   Van der Tuuk's major publications are all linguistic works. They are a grammar of the Batak language, *Tobasche Spraakkunst*, 2 vols. (Amsterdam, 1864 and 1867); a Batak dictionary, *Bataksch-Nederduitsch Woordenboek* (Amsterdam, 1861); a reader of the Batak language: *Bataksch Leesboek, bevattende stukken in het Tobasch, Mandailingsch en Dairisch*, 4 vols. (Amsterdam, 1860–62); and a dictionary of Old Javanese and Balinese, *Kawi-Balineesch-Nederlandsch Woordenboek* (Batavia, 1897–1912). He also published countless technical articles. But it is his correspondence that is most important in presenting a full portrait of the man and his mind. It is distributed among four institutions: the Bijbelgenootschap in Friesland, the University Library in Leyden, the Royal Institute of Linguistics and Anthropology in Leyden, and the files of the Multatuli Society in Amsterdam. A selection of his letters was collected and transcribed by R. Nieuwenhuys: Herman Neubronner van der Tuuk, *De Pen in gal gedoopt. Brieven en Documenten*, ed. R. Nieuwenhuys (Amsterdam: Van Oorschot, 1962). A second, revised edition of this volume was published more recently: Herman Neubronner van der Tuuk, *De pen in gal gedoopt. Een keuze uit brieven en documenten*, ed. Rob Nieuwenhuys (Amsterdam: Em. Querido, 1982). Parenthetical citations in text will be to this second edition. I have kept van der Tuuk's idiosyncratic capitalization.

2   *Malacca* refers to both the town and the territory on the west coast of peninsular Malaya. The Portuguese conquered Malacca in 1511 and it remained a Portuguese possession for over a century. It was from Malacca that Albuquerque organized the voyages to the Moluccas or Spice Islands, and it was there that St. Francis Xavier established the first Christian mission in Malaysia. The Dutch held Malacca from 1641 to 1795, when England took it over. It was returned to the Dutch in 1818, but in 1824 it became a permanent British colony in exchange for Bengkulen and other possessions on Sumatra.

3   *Affonso d'Albuquerque* (1453–1515) was a Portuguese explorer known as "the Portuguese Mars." He was responsible for early Portuguese settlements in India, especially Goa, for the first European exploration of the Red Sea, and for the capture of the island of Ormuz in the Persian Gulf. In the present context his significance is restricted to his subjugation of Malacca in 1511, which established a strong Portuguese influence in the East Indies for a long period.

4   J. J. A. Muller, "Junghuhn als topograaf der Bataklanden," in *Gedenkboek Franz Junghuhn 1809–1909* (The Hague: Martinus Nijhoff, 1910), 85–86.

5   *Bakkara* was the name of both the valley and the capital of that portion of the Toba region, situated on the southwestern shore of the lake. Van der Tuuk went there specifically because Bakkara was the seat of the "priest-king" of the Bataks, called Si Singa Mangaradja.

6   *Si Singa Mangaradja* was both a temporal and a spiritual ruler of the Toba-Bataks. The name, which means "the great king who resembles a lion," seems to have been a title that was inherited by individuals of aristocratic rank. The power associated with the title seems to have been more spiritual than political, for the ruler's influence seldom extended beyond his own district. The tenth and last one died in 1907 fighting the Dutch. The legendary descent from the gods and the strange life of the first Singa Mangaradja can be read in the translation of a Batak text that was among van der Tuuk's papers: "Singa Mangaradja, de heilige koning der Bataks," ed. and trans. C. M. Pleyte, *Bijdragen tot de Taal-, Land- en Volkenkunde van Nederlandsch Indië*, 7 (1903): 1–48.

7   Van der Tuuk's notes from his journey to Toba Lake, which are translated after this letter, suggest that the term *Si Pokki* was a Batak variant for the *padris*. Perhaps some essential facts concerning the *padris* will make this byzantine intrigue somewhat more comprehensible. Atjeh and the Batak lands were mentioned in the text as two major ethnic realms. One should add to them the realm of Minangkabau on Sumatra's west coast, below the Tapanuli residence. The Minangkabau were a remarkable people who claimed descent from Alexander the Great (*Iskander Dzu'l Karnain*). The proud, freedom-loving Minangkabau were known for their elaborate houses with saddle-shaped roofs reminiscent of Chinese architecture and for their matrilineal society. Their religion was a form of animism and they were not hospitable to Islam.

In the early nineteenth century some Islamic zealots from the Padang region returned from Mecca and formed an orthodox Muslim party. Its members were mostly *tuankus*, or Muslim preachers, better known today as *mullahs*. Their fanatical orthodoxy was particularly opposed to the matrilineal society of the Minangkabau, as well as to other traditional customs and rituals. Their demand for stricter adherence to Islamic law and the Koran was met by opposition, which the *tuankus* countered with extravagant punishment, violence, summary justice, and, finally, open warfare. A recent analogy can be found in Iran where the ayatollahs and mullahs have instituted a similar system of orthodox theocracy.

The word *padri* was not derived from either Dutch or Malay, but most likely came from "padre," and was used in that sense by Raffles to refer to the padris. See G. W. J. Drewes, "De etymologie van *padri*," in *Bijdragen tot de Taal-, Land- en Volkenkunde* 138 (1982): 346–50.

For a short time the padris restricted their efforts to the general region of Minangkabau. They demanded the abolition of opium use, drinking, and *sirih* chewing. Cockfights and dice games were forbidden and women were forced to wear the *chador*. The men were expected to wear only white to distinguish them from the "enemy." These laws were enforced with Draconian measures. It is said that one padri killed his aunt when he caught her chewing *sirih*.

The padri movement gained influence and adherents and soon embarked on a campaign of conquest under the banner of holy war or *prang sabil*, in Arabic *jihād*. The fearsome effects of piety soon forced local supporters of *adat*—or traditional law and customs—to seek European protection. The padris considered such people (including the Bataks) infidels and either executed them or sold them as slaves. Chiefs from the Minangkabau region first asked protection from Raffles's interim British government, but nothing was really done until the Dutch colonial government, reinstated after the Napoleonic wars, engaged the padris militarily. This was necessary because the padris' ruthless conquest had been successful and they had subjugated a large area. The padri wars lasted from 1821 to 1838. The Islamic zealots fought the Europeans ferociously, convinced they were engaged in a full-fledged prang sabil against Islam's traditional infidels, yet the Dutch military campaigns finally succeeded in defeating the padris and in restoring order and normalcy. One of the ironies, however, is that the Minangkabau had negotiated their independence away in return for military aid, and after the completion of the pacification ceased to function as a sovereign state.

Although most historians restrict their accounts of the padri wars to the Padang, Minangkabu, and Rau regions, it is known that the padris also ventured to the north. Van der Tuuk's descriptions make it clear that the movement managed to penetrate even to the shores of Toba Lake but, though besieged by the Islamic Achinese in the north and the padris from the south, the Bataks had little inclination to welcome Muhammadanism.

Documents pertaining to the padri wars can be studied in E. B. Kielstra, "Sumatras Westkust van 1819 tot 1825," *Bijdragen tot de Taal-, Land- en Volkenkunde van Nederlandsch Indië*, 5 (1887): 7–163; "Sumatras Westkust van 1826 to 1832," idem, 5 (1888): 216–380; and "Sumatras Westkust van 1833 tot 1835," idem, 5 (1889): 161–249, 313–79, 467–514.

8   The *Rau region* was situated above Padang in central Sumatra, in a low valley of the Bukit Barisan which is part of the mountain range that extends the length of the island. Its lower elevation causes the region to have many swamps (*rau=rawa*=swamp). A high incidence of malaria, many tigers, and difficult access made the region, though fertile, an inhospitable backwater. The same features, however, provided the padris with natural protection against the Dutch military campaigns. Nevertheless, in order to eradicate them, the Dutch were forced to engage the padris in the Rau region, where they finally succumbed. Hence it was in a sense true when the Bataks told van der Tuuk that "Si Pokki" (i.e., the padris) had been "killed" in the Rau region.

9   Van der Tuuk's incredulity that the Bataks could not see that he was a European is amusing. His appearance was more Asiatic than Western. Photographs show a face that is almost Chinese, and Rob Nieuwenhuys told me that he has it on authority of one of van der Tuuk's relatives that his coloring was quite dark. Hence it is not surprising that the local people in Sumatra as well as in Bali thought he looked much closer to them than to the European *orang blanda* or "white man."

10   The *fortresses* referred to should not be envisioned as large citadels with battlements and bulwarks. The Bataks lived in permanently settled villages, or *huta* as they called them, which they surrounded with earthen walls. What made these walls sturdier than one might think was a hedge of impenetrable bamboo which was planted on top of the walls, constituting a formidable hindrance.

11   *Toba na sae* is Batak for "the treeless Toba region." This is but one example of how the Bataks designated areas of their region by simply adding specific features to the name of their lake. This region borders the lake itself, has indeed few trees, and may be described as a vast plateau of arid soil, resembling a steppe.

12   When the Bataks told van der Tuuk that he was on the "southeastern shore of the lake" they made a mistake. He was on the south*western* shore, and the lake stretches in effect from south to north. If one adjusts for this error, everyting else he described is verifiable.

13   *Samosir* is a large island in Toba Lake of nearly 500 square miles. Like the Toba na sae region it is treeless and the rain runs off it, almost immediately into the lake. Despite this unfavorable condition it was probably the most populated region in the Indies. The Bataks on Samosir were isolated from Dutch colonial influence for a long time and were not susceptible to Islamic proselytizing. They made a living from piracy and raising livestock. Samosir was particularly praised for its horses. The population once had the reputation of widespread opium addiction, slavery (not abolished until 1914 under Dutch rule), and an unshakable devotion to the "priest-king" Si Singa Mangaradja.

14   *Dolok Sanggul* was a town southwest from the lake. *Dolok* means *mountain* in Batak.

15   Although one can understand van der Tuuk's accusation of greed, it is perhaps more understandable why the robbers would try to take the "Chinese box" away from him when one knows that the Bataks kept jewelry in similar boxes, and that they, like the Navajo, measured wealth by the amount of jewelry one possessed or could display.

16   A *pustaha* was a book made from long strips of tree bark softened in rice water. After such a strip had been written on, it was folded and secured between two small planks serving as covers, in accordion fashion. These books were found mostly among the Toba-Batak and contained texts on divination, astrology, magic, and soothsaying. Much less frequently did they contain stories or historical accounts. They somewhat remind one of the books of the Maya, such as the *Popol Vuh* or the *Prophecies of Chilam Balam*. The pustahas were in

possession of either the aristocracy or the sacerdotal caste called *datu* by the Toba-Bataks. These texts were difficult to decipher even for the datu, because they contained a fairly large number of Sanskrit words and expressions.

17 *Nai Pospos* was a region with forbidding mountains, in the southeastern portion of the Batak highlands.

18 The *Silidung region* was a large and populous subdivision of the Tapanuli residence, south of Toba Lake. It was considered the most important region of the Toba-Bataks, rich in agricultural crops such as rice. Its residents steadfastly adhered to its traditional religion.

19 *Burton* was a British missionary who traveled in Sumatra in the 1820s.

20 *Sopo* was a Batak word to indicate either a small structure to store rice or, more often, a particular building in a Batak town. It served as a storage place, a covered forum or law court, or as a dormitory for celibate males. The sopo also used to be a respository for trophies, pustahas, and magic batons. Because it was used as temporary quarters for travelers as well, it was the logical place for van der Tuuk to do his research. In former times the trophies in a sopo included skulls of wild boars and humans and the smoked and dried hands of enemies defeated in battle.

21 *Zahn's Bible stories* refers to the *Biblische Historien* (Biblical stories) that F. L. Zahn (who died in 1890) published in 1832, and that were translated into many languages. Zahn was a German Evangelical pedagogue.

22 Generally speaking, a *radja-muda* was the person who ruled in the name of a *radja*. One should not, however, ascribe to the position the aura of splendor the title evokes in popular imagination because of the legendary rulers of India. *Radja* derives from the Sanskrit word *radjan*, meaning *monarch*. In the Indies, however, the title was also given to village chiefs and, in Sumatra, even to harbormasters. Only the title of *maharadja*—which means *king of kings*—could also in the Dutch East Indies be associated with power and grandeur. The king of Minangkabau used to be addressed as such, though the title was subsequently usually reserved to indicate the king of the Netherlands.

23 *Sjarif* is the old Malay spelling of the Arabic word *sharif* (*noble*), a title granted only to descendants of Muhammad. In the Muslim world they were also known as *sayyids* or *lords*. The sharifs or sayyids represent a special class of Muslims, distinguished by their right to wear green turbans. They were held in reverence and had a great influence. The government or *sharifate* of Mecca was always held by one of these descendants of the prophet.

24 *Sombaon* were revered spirits who were thought to live in tall trees and dark and somber places. They were held in great esteem because they were thought to police mankind's behavior. They normally revealed themselves to people in the shape of snakes.

25 *Sirih* is the general Malay word for either the leaves or the fruit of the pepper plant of the genus *Piper betle*, family of the *Piperaceae*. The Batak name is *napuran*. It forms the main ingredient of sirih chewing, a common habit not only in the Malay archipelago, but throughout most oriental nations where it is known by its English name as "betel chewing."

26 *Arbaan, Parbotihan*, and *Aèk Godang* were small towns at some distance southwest in the mountains below Toba Lake. These names have changed or are spelled differently, but I am assuming that Aèk Godang is the same town the *Atlas van Tropisch Nederland* (1938) calls "Aeknagodang."

27 *Tanku Rao* was one of the *padri* leaders mentioned before (n. 7). *Tuanku* was a title accorded a teacher of Islam, while *rao*, I would think, stands for *rau*, the region where the *padris* fought their final battle, under the leadership of the "Tuanku Imam" (whose real name was Malim Basa) in 1837.

28 The stone coffin van der Tuuk examined gives an indication of how serious a role the dead played among the Bataks. They worshipped the *bégu* or *shade* (soul) of the corpse. To

158 Herman Neubronner van der Tuuk

ensure that the *bégus* would not interfere with the living there were elaborate ways to make them lose track of where their relatives were living. The sarcophagus van der Tuuk described refers to a more ancient way of entombment, clearly one that was reserved for notables. More normal was burial in the ground, though some Batak peoples cremated their dead or let them decompose on open platforms in the fields. There are several photographs of such a sarcophagus in F. M. Schnitger, *Forgotten Kingdoms in Sumatra* (Leiden: E. J. Brill, 1964).

29   The *Royal Institute* referred to is the "Royal Institute of Linguistics and Anthropology" (*Koninklijk Instituut voor Taal-, Land-, en Volkenkunde*) now housed in Leyden, but founded originally in The Hague in 1853.

30   Van der Tuuk's sensible remarks about cannibalism are given later in the text. From whatever is known about it, the Bataks' cannibalism seems to have derived from their peculiar sense of justice. It does not appear to have been a form of ritual eating but rather a form of punishment reserved for recidivous criminals, adulterers, mortally wounded prisoners of war, and traitors. The latter category included spies, as van der Tuuk found out to his dismay. Eating a victim seems to have represented a form of insult and when, after his flesh was consumed, his bones were pulverized and strewn among the dogs and pigs, it was felt that he had died twice and was irrevocably cast into nothingness.

31   Anglo-Dutch rivalry in the Indies dates from the seventeenth century and is the result of two maritime nations vying for control of the seas and for a monopoly of trade routes to the Far East. The British tried as early as 1624 to establish a rival or "anti-Batavia" in the Malay archipelago, but did not succeed until the early nineteenth century. British influence and political intrigue were mostly confined to Sumatra, Borneo, and the Malay peninsula. However, from 1795 to 1815 Holland was under the aegis of France, and Britain, committed to an anti-French policy, saw its chance to unseat Holland as a rival colonial power with a semblance of legitimacy.

Holland's experiment as a revolutionary republic (1795–1806), inspired by the American War of Independence and the French Revolution, turned out to be disastrous and left the nation with greatly diminished resources and political clout. Under Napoleon's reign French dominance increased until Holland was annexed and governed by Napoleon's brother, Louis, from 1806 to 1810. By the time the French emperor abdicated for good (1815), the Dutch nation was in a sorry state; it was described in 1808 as a "hollowed-out willow, only living on its bark." The exiled Dutch government had asked England to administer its colonies during the interim, and this political opportunity coupled with the stricken state of the nation provided England with the impetus to bring to a profitable conclusion the endless rounds of negotiations the two nations had been conducting concerning territorial, maritime, and commercial supremacy. The British extended their control in Sumatra, and in 1811 invaded and conquered Java where Thomas Stamford Raffles (1781–1826) ruled as lieutenant governor from 1811 to 1816. Napoleon's demise forced a return to former boundaries. British presence in Sumatra, however, did not wane and Raffles, who nurtured an intense dislike of the Dutch, sought to increase its sway when he governed British territories in Sumatra from 1818 to 1823. During that time he finally realized his dream of establishing an "anti-Batavia" by obtaining the island of Singapura in 1819. It was a political stroke of genius because the harbor of Singapore soon controlled a major trade route to the Far East and it soon rivaled Batavia as a trade center.

Dutch resistance to the British presence was relatively slight and ineffectual during the time the nation was rebuilding from the Napoleonic disaster. Therefore, it was not surprising that van der Tuuk encountered a fairly strong sentiment favoring the British, because they had made their presence known in Sumatra for a long time. During the previous century, England had constantly solicited the favors of the lords of Atjeh, and by the second decade of the nineteenth century they had gained a hold not only on Atjeh, but also on Sumatra's west coast, the Benculen region, and the cities of Palembang and Padang. The latter city, criticized by van der Tuuk, was under British control from 1795 to 1819.

The endless diplomatic campaigns between the Dutch and the British can be studied in Nicolas Tarling, *Anglo-Dutch Rivalry in the Malay World 1780–1824* (Sydney: Cambridge University Press/University of Queensland Press, 1962), while there is a recent study of revolutionary Holland: Simon Schama, *Patriots and Liberators: Revolution in the Netherlands 1780–1813* (New York: Knopf, 1977).

32 *Benzoin* refers to an aromatic resin derived from the *Styrax benzoin* tree. An old, but incorrect, English name for it is "gum Benjamin." It has a very pleasant scent, reminiscent of vanilla, and is used primarily for perfumes. The Malay term for benzoin is *menjan*, whereas its Arabic name (from which the present word is derived) clearly indicates its prominence as a lucrative product of the Dutch East Indies: *ban jawi* or "frankincense of Java."

33 *Statute labor*, or in Dutch *heerendiensten*, was a system of forced labor based on, and perpetuating, native aristocratic rights. The subjects of an overlord were compelled to provide a work force for his private requirements as well as for the construction of public works such as roads and waterways. When the Dutch came to the Indies they did not attempt to eradicate this feudal system, but added to it. The results were almost inhuman demands made on the native individual. An exorbitant amount of time was required to satisfy the demands of the native lord and those of the Dutch authorities, which left very little time or energy for the labor required to sustain life. From 1854, the Dutch government began to ease this burden, but progress was slow and statute labor was never entirely revoked. Raffles's interim government abolished statute labor in 1813, but the proclamation was never put into practice.

34 Van der Tuuk is referring to *T. W. J. Juynboll* (1802–61), a theologian and Semitist, whose specialty was the literature and history of the Samaritans.

35 Van der Tuuk gives a different meaning for this word while making the interesting observation that the Malay spoken in Batavia contained a great deal of Balinese.

> As you know, the original population of Batavia consisted largely of Balinese who were employed by the VOC as either slaves or soldiers. Even the housekeepers of those pious gentlemen of the Company were Balinese slaves. That is the reason why to this very day the native housekeeper of a European is still called *"njai."* This word is in Bali the normal term for addressing a young woman from the lowest class in a friendly manner; it means "younger sister." (154–55)

36 P. Voorhoeve, *Critical Survey of Studies on the Languages of Sumatra.* "Bibliographical Series 1 of the Koninklijk Instituut voor Taal-, Land- en Volkenkunde" ('s-Gravenhage: Martinus Nijhoff, 1955), 9–14.

37 One example of van der Tuuk's extraordinary erudition is that, in the midst of a polemic with the prestigious professor Taco Roorda, he formulated almost casually two new phonetic laws for Indonesian languages. These later were accepted as the foundation for more advanced research.

38 The Lampong district covers the southernmost region of Sumatra. During the scant year he traveled in this district, van der Tuuk learned enough of the language to lay the foundation for its future study. He published a number of Lampong manuscripts and wrote several articles about its linguistic aspects. Van der Tuuk considered the language important because he believed that it represented a transitional stage between the languages of Sumatra and Java, and felt that its study would increase knowledge of Old Javanese or Kawi.

39 Nias is a fairly large island off the western coast of Sumatra.

40 The *culture system* was introduced in 1830 to invigorate Holland's economy which was

in dire straits after the revolutionary experiment and Napoleonic dictatorship. In principle it meant that the native farmer was required to cultivate one-fifth of his acreage with crops designated by the colonial government. In practice it meant that only those crops that were profitable on European markets were grown, such as sugar, coffee, and indigo, and that a much larger portion of the land was used than was originally planned. The reason for this was the government's insistence that the Indies *had* to show a profit no matter what, and the result was that there was not enough land left to plant rice, and not enough of a labor force even if sufficient land were still available. The system was only beneficial for a colonial gov-ernment that was intent on having an annual credit balance (*batig saldo* in Dutch), but it was disastrous for the native population of Java. Whole regions were starving when a great deal of arable land became useless for rice because other crops such as indigo and sugar cane had exhausted the soil. After two decades of this blatant exploitation, the culture sys-tem was gradually abolished during the 1860s.

41   *W. H. Engelmann* (1836–68), was a fellow linguist who almost rivaled van der Tuuk's endowments. At first a theology student, his interest in languages displaced an interest in dogma and Engelmann went to Leyden to study Semitic languages. In 1858 he received a doctoral degree on the basis of his scholarly edition of an Arabic poet (Al Hadirah) with translations and notes in Latin. He also did comparative work on the relationship between Arabic and Spanish. To earn a living he became, first, a tutor to the children of a rich family, and was then hired to represent the Bible Society in the Sunda district on Java. Engelmann must have met van der Tuuk in Amsterdam, probably in 1863. In the fall of 1864 he arrived in Java and settled in Bandung, but he was to be in the Indies for less than four years. The sentiments van der Tuuk expresses in this letter were shared by most people who had met Engelmann.

42   The *Seputik* is a river in the Lampong district. Its name means *white river*. The other place names in this paragraph refer to various towns in that residency. *Telokbetong* was the main harbor on the most southern coast or Lampong Bay.

43   This anecdote was also used by E. du Perron, who described van der Tuuk in his novel, *Country of Origin*, without mentioning his name. See *Country of Origin* (Amherst: Univer-sity of Massachusetts Press, 1984), 261–62.

44   *Multatuli* was the pseudonym of Eduard Douwes Dekker (1820–87), Holland's most famous critic of the colonial system and its most important writer of the nineteenth century. His masterpiece is *Max Havelaar* (1860); it was published in this series. The *Ideën* van der Tuuk refers to are seven volumes of prose, ranging from pithy epigrams to installments of a never-finished novel. They were published between 1862 and 1877.

45   Rudolf Charles *D'Ablaing* van Giessenburg (1826–1904) was Multatuli's publisher from 1862 to 1866. The name of his firm was R. C. Meijer. He was a well-known free-thinker and president of the freethinker organization *De Dageraad* (or Dawn), from 1856 to 1865. This organization had been founded by Junghuhn and D'Ablaing in 1856. Its jour-nal of the same name printed Multatuli's first publication: "Geloofsbelijdenis" (Credo) in 1859, now to be found in the first volume of his collected works: *Volledige Werken*, 7 vols. (Amsterdam: Van Oorschot, 1973).

46   It is amusing to find van der Tuuk refusing to admit that his handwriting was nearly illegible. Anyone who has taken the trouble to read it will vouch for the heroism of his long suffering correspondents who had to decipher his impossible squiggles.

47   *Asmodee* was a journal published in The Hague and, later, in Amsterdam from 1845 to 1900.

48   It is true that Multatuli tried to "sell his countenance." Though a lionized author since the publication of *Max Havelaar* in 1860, Multatuli made little money. In 1864 he con-

ceived the bizarre scheme of selling his portrait to admirers. A photographer in Brussels took his picture and from this likeness a lithograph was made. The photograph sold for fifty guilders and the lithograph for ten. Multatuli was living at the time in some rooms that members of the *Dageraad* organization had fixed up for him in the attic of his publisher's house in Amsterdam. When the portraits were finished (the photographer was never paid) a cubicle was hammered together in the bookshop of his publisher, D'Ablaing van Giessenburg. Multatuli sat in this cubicle waiting to write quotes from his own work on each signed copy of his portrait. The business turned out to be a flop because the prices were too high. See W. F. Hermans, *De raadselachtige Multatuli* (Amsterdam: Boelen, 1976), 113–15.

49 *Roorda van Eysinga* (1825–87), a reformer and relentless critic of colonial practices, had a life of almost tragic futility. Born in Batavia, he was the son of a minister and was educated in Holland. He returned to the tropics and stayed for nineteen years. During those years he was an officer in the colonial army, ran a tobacco plantation, was an editor of a newspaper in Batavia, a surveyor in government service, and an engineer for the project to establish the first railway system in Java. Although he was competent in all of these occupations, he usually managed to incur the displeasure of his superiors. Described by someone as "his own worst enemy" Roorda van Eysinga lacked a sense of compromise and pragmatic realism and, like some chivalric knight, consistently involved himself in controversy regardless of the consequences. He has the rare distinction of having been banished from the colonial Indies. The immediate cause was because he printed accusations that a prominent Dutch banker in Semarang was guilty of graft. The man had highly placed friends and persuaded the governor-general to punish Eysinga. The accusation itself would not have been sufficient justification for the extreme measure that was taken, but Eysinga also had a friend who, as the political rival of the governor-general, was railroaded out of his position. Embroiled in a political assassination campaign not of his own making, Eysinga already had a reputation as a vociferous critic of colonial policies, and he fell victim to the purge.

Back in Holland he barely managed to support himself with free-lance journalism, translations, and the writing and printing of brochures intended to justify his own case or to criticize the government. He married late in life and moved to Switzerland both for economic reasons and to deprive Holland of his presence. His political opinions became increasingly more radical until he finally embraced anarchism. It is possible he knew Kropotkin, and it was inevitable that he came to know Multatuli. He did not have Multatuli's genius as a writer, nor did he receive the public notoriety and acclaim Multatuli enjoyed. Yet his labors in defense of the Javanese were essentially in the same spirit as Multatuli's. Roorda van Eysinga was simply at the wrong time in the wrong place, and he lacked superior talents to compete with his celebrated compatriot. Multatuli's writings also diminished Eysinga's own literary efforts. He thought that he would be immortalized by the rhymed philippic "Last Day of the Dutch on Java" (written in 1860) and by his scurrilous pamphlet attacking King Willem III, entitled "Concerning the Life of King Gorilla" (first published in brochure form in 1887). But his dubious immortality is restricted to Multatuli's praise in one of the footnotes—the fifth one—he added to later editions of *Max Havelaar*.

Roorda van Eysinga wrote his own melancholy epitaph when, in a letter to Multatuli, he described himself as "a failed soldier, failed engineer, failed man of letters, and, if I hadn't married, a failed human being." The most recent biography is Hans Vervoort, *Sicco Roorda van Eysinga: zijn eigen vijand* (Amsterdam: De Engelbewaarder, 1979), which includes a bibliography.

50 *De Pool* was another name for Cafe Polen in Amsterdam, which was frequented especially by brokers from the stock exchange.

51 The *holy mothball* van der Tuuk refers to was probably the greatest Catholic mission-

ary ever to work in the East Indies. Franciscus Xaverius (St. Francis Xavier) was born in Basque country in 1506. A brilliant student, Xavier was already a professor and reputable philosopher when Ignatius Loyola persuaded him to join the newly created Society of Jesus, better known as the Jesuits. Under Portuguese auspices he sailed for India in 1541 and reached Goa in 1542. Xavier never stayed anywhere for very long, content with pioneering the spread of Christianity and then leaving it to other missionaries to firmly establish the work he had started. After nearly three years in India he traveled to Malacca and, in 1546, to the Moluccas or Spice Islands. There he preached on Ambon, Ternate, Banda, Tidore, and other smaller islands. In 1547 he was back in Malacca and returned to Goa in 1548. In 1549 he traveled to Japan and established the first outpost of Christian mission work in that country. In 1552 Xavier intended to spread the gospel in China, but he died on an island off its coast. His historical importance derives from having single-handedly pioneered missionary work in all Southeast Asia. What van der Tuuk refers to is the astonishment of St. Xavier when he witnessed a Hindu religious ceremony. The various elements of this religion showed some (uncomfortably) close resemblances to the Christian pantheon.

Bas Veth

Bas Veth (1860–1922) wrote only one book—*Het Leven in Nederlandsch Indië* (Life in the Dutch East Indies), published in Amsterdam in 1900—but on the strength of that single publication he has the rare distinction of living on as a feminine noun. His lexical canonization is as the substantive *basvetterij,* which is glossed as a colonial synonym for *gekanker.* The latter is a participial noun from the verb *kankeren;* it acquired the specific meaning of complaining during the nineteenth century, and is said to be a usage peculiar to colonial society in the Indies. *Kankeren* is an intransitive verb meaning "to find fault," "to grump or gripe," but there is really no satisfactory translation because the verb includes the entire emotional range from grumbling to what in the American vernacular is called "grouching."[1]

This sense of unmitigated dislike, as in Veth's work, was particularly associated with colonial society in the Indies, but was also, and still is, the preferred state of mind of Dutch intellectuals and writers. To this very day, polemics is a literary activity much favored in Holland. There are instances of people who write under several pseudonyms simply to be able to expand their verbal shot to include more targets. Du Perron, a major colonial writer, considered literature "sublimated polemics," a dictum with which many contemporary Dutch authors would wholeheartedly agree.[2]

Kankeren was once considered a particular colonial vice. The greatest representative of Dutch colonial literature was Multatuli, a writer who energized his entire literary career from a choleric contempt of the colonies, if not of Dutch society as a whole. Other examples are the bitter criticism of Beb Vuyk, the disparaging fiction of P. A. Daum, and the chivalric police actions that E. du Perron conducted against the colonial tastemakers of the twenties and thirties (all three are represented in this series). In the present volume one will find the peevish eloquence of H. N. van der Tuuk and Alexander Cohen, the brilliant pessimism of Willem Walraven's lifelong quarrel with the Indies, and François Valentijn's self-serving attacks on his detractors. It almost seems as if the finest colonial writing depended on a kind of intellectual prickly heat, even though the literary eruptions it caused would no more cure one of the disease than would scratching the inflammation that was caused by what was once called "tropical lichen."

One of the most accomplished of colonial *kankeraars*—the latter being the noun indicating a person who by his utterances conjugates the verb— was Walraven (see below). Forty years after Veth's controversial book, this brilliant but bitter journalist became Veth's most fervent defender. As can be surmised from the section devoted to Walraven, the later author agreed with almost everything Veth had to say, though for far more complicated reasons. "I can't find anything in [Veth's book] that I haven't seen myself in the Indies either today or in the past." Walraven considered veracity the hallmark of literary *kankeraars*. Only "Philistines" thought of them as crabs because they were basically utter realists: "The *kankeraar* tells me the truth about life and the world, and it is the truth I'm looking for." Walraven considered Sinclair Lewis a prime example, a *kankeraar* who felt stifled among the "American Philistines" "even though he won a Nobel Prize." And the Philistines will always hate a man like Lewis or Veth because they are allergic to the truth. "Let us, therefore, *kankeren* for the love of truth, if possible in a literary fashion, perhaps even with a bit of genius. The greatest [*kankeraars*] have never done anything else and were therefore maligned by the plebs. All of them were *kankeraars* and that is why we still know them and why we will never forget them."[3]

A similar basis of reality is claimed by satire, a literary genre easier to detect than define. A full attempt at definition is not within the scope of this section, but it is possible to circumscribe Veth's work in terms of some characteristic elements of satire. *Het Leven in Nederlandsch Indië* is an angry indictment, written from a standpoint that is essential to what Northrop Frye assumes to be satire's "militant attitude to experience."[4] Veth never hides his feelings. He opens his attack with a straightforward confession.

The Dutch East Indies is the incarnation of misery for me. The twelve years I spent in those regions of exile are like twelve horrible dreams. I found nothing uplifting there; there I found everything that depresses. Good people became bad; never the bad ones good. Everything fresh that arrives there fades, what blooms pales, what flowers withers, what shines dulls, what glows is extinguished: ideas, feelings, thoughts, illusions, the body and soul of the Europeans who have to live there, in short, everything that comes from the far west called Europe, and alights in the far east called the Dutch East Indies. Begin in Atjeh, follow the string of volcanos across Sumatra, Java, the Moluccas, Celebes, and end at the northernmost tip of the Sangir Islands, and you will find the same thing everywhere: degeneration, the decomposition of the pure European temperament.[5]

Nothing changed his opinion by the time he finally managed to escape: "I kicked the dock for the last time and I probably swore when I did it" (171). The book ends with a stichomythia of indignation, similar to the end of Multatuli's *Max Havelaar*.

> I planned revenge all the time.
> I wanted to settle accounts, completely.
> I wanted to square accounts, once and for all.
> I wanted to settle with that life in the Dutch East Indies, completely, so I
>   would never have to return.
> I wrote this book.
>
> (171–72)

Veth's blistering contempt has a bitterness that classes his effort with Juvenal's misanthropic satire and not with the more tolerant subtlety of Horace. There is, for instance, no irony in Veth's assault. Because he felt that he had been infected by the colonial "pest microbes" (22), Veth used invective as a prophylactic with the hope that potential victims who were still safe and healthy in Holland would take heed of his warnings to avoid future contamination. There is, therefore, and this is often true of satire, no ambivalence in Veth's work. He does not want to amend vice, as Dryden claimed to have done, but prefers rather to lance moral cancers, particularly those diagnosed as cupidity and hypocrisy. Yet he can also become more mundane and denounce the colonial cuisine or sanitary habits.

The method of Veth's satire is akin to that genre's fundamental practice of reducing the complexity of life to simple terms. Satire is tyrannical and has no use for democracy; fairness and relativism would only dissipate the energy needed to better the enemy. Satire aims to draw blood and scorns negotiation, hoping to be, in Puttenham's phrase, "like the Porcupine that shoots sharpe quils out in each angry line." Satire's denunciation is exclusive, and though this is by design and necessity, it is often the cause for branding the satirist a snob and his preferred society as conservative. Selective overstating, a device much favored by politicians as well, is a proper tool for "sham-smashing," as H. L. Mencken called the objective of his American brand of literary bloodletting. The satirist feels no compunction in pronouncing his opponent guilty on the basis of circumstantial evidence. Veth, for instance, condemns the Dutch colonial on the basis of what he eats and drinks, the hotels he frequents, and the physical condition of his dogs and horses. There is no doubt that the satirist is biased but he cannot be otherwise because the desperate diseases of folly and vice require desperate measures. But there must be skill in his cauterization. The patient should not succumb, but should survive to live on as a warning.

Satire has no fixed style. Juvenal called its mode of expression a *farrago* or *hodge-podge* (*nostri farrago libelli*), and any stylistic weapon is allowed. Though Veth is not as great a writer as some of those mentioned before, he did have considerable talent and an impressive stylistic arsenal. Besides straightforward execration, he made use of distortion (usually hyperbole), anecdotes, satirical lists (a device perfected by Rabelais), reductio ad absurdum, repetition, parody, neologisms, Billingsgate rhetoric, and the mixing of colloquial with literary Dutch. It is a deliberate style that is well aware of what it wants to do and how to do it. But it seems doubtful that Veth drew sustenance from the classic ages of satire such as Greek and Roman antiquity, the Middle Ages (when Dutch literature contributed such masterpieces as *Reynard the Fox, Till Eulenspiegel,* and Erasmus's *Moriae Encomium*) or the entire seventeenth and first quarter of the eighteenth centuries which produced some of the greatest satirists both on the Continent and in England. His master, it seems to me, was Multatuli and, in general, the Romantic movement; the latter provided him with the supreme examples of Byron and Heine—Veth quotes both—as well as Crabbe in England and Jean Paul in Germany.[6] Crabbe's satiric method, for instance, was based on realism and the firm belief that life was "a progressive disillusionment"; Veth's perception of life in the Indies was the same, and he too considered his method a realistic one, necessary to counsel prudence to young Europeans contemplating a career in the tropics.

Although Veth is prejudicial in his selectivity, hence untrue to actual experience, which is, of course, a falsehood all art is guilty of, there is a compositional and symbolic order to his anatomy. His account is framed by the arrival of the innocent newcomer, his progressive disillusionment, and his repatriation which, rather than a joyous homecoming, has all the signs of a desperate flight. Besides this obvious design, copied from actual experience, there is an oblique substratum indicative of Veth's negative attitude. It is manifested by associating static imagery with the Indies and kinetic imagery with Holland. This becomes especially clear in Veth's experience of nature.

Tropical nature is alien and oppressive. In what to many people[7] would be a perverse inversion, tropical nature's fecundity and overpowering energy are reduced by Veth to a sepulchral immobility; it is "heavy, broad, still, always tranquil [and] close . . . the landscape of the Indies does not provide joy" (35). The emblem of this inert torpor is the *waringin* tree which, described by Veth's neologism, is always "dead-dumb" (*stil-stom*). In contrast, European nature is a vivacious joy of exuberant good spirits, a Heraclitean *panta rhei*. The waringin tree in question was in the middle of the native market (*pasar*) in the town of "Payacombo" (in Dutch more commonly spelled Pajo Koemboeh) in western Sumatra.[8]

A waringin tree is an incredibly large tree, very venerable, the patriarch of tree people. Strings of aerial roots are suspended from its branches, its leaves are tiny, but it has millions of them. At first I felt nothing but admiration and I kept on contemplating those waringin trees. The first time I saw them they stood there dead-dumb, dead-dumb in the pasar. Not a leaf stirred and the aerial roots hung down limply and languidly, immobile. And I left Payacombo full of respect for those magnificent waringin trees. They seemed to me to be symbols of the tropics' luxuriant nature. Such power! Such an abundance of creative potential. In Europe a waringin tree would shade a city square. I experienced a feeling of holiness and I began to understand why a childlike people considers the waringins sacred.

And again I partook of the banality of mercantile life. A year later I was in Payacombo for a second time and I was stretched out in a long chair on the hotel's front veranda. The waringin trees stood dead-dumb in the pasar. Not one of the millions of tiny leaves stirred and the aerial roots hung down limply and languidly, immobile. I was in Payacombo in 1887, 1888, 1889, 1890, 1891, and for the last time in 1897. The waringin trees stood there always and always dead-dumb in the pasar and not one of the millions of tiny leaves stirred and the aerial roots hung down limply and languidly, immobile. I have seen it rain in Payacombo, have seen it thunder, and seen lightning, there was even a breath of wind now and then. But those waringin trees stood there always, always dead-dumb in the pasar. Not even the wind seemed able to move them and there never issued a mysterious whispering from that army of leaves, no matter how hard it blew. And one afternoon, while I was dreaming in my long chair with those dead-dumb waringins in front of me, I fell asleep and I suddenly saw a row of poplars moving deliciously back and forth, nodding their heads in a stately fashion, I heard the language of rustling leaves in a wood of beech trees, there was a stirring in a forest of oaks and acorns fell, bouncing so marvelously on the dry fallen leaves, a bird sang and white clouds floated in a blue sky. There was a murmuring wind and fresh air.

And I lamented: take me away from here and put me under a willow tree near a ditch in Holland, but let me not waste away under these dead-dumb waringins. . . . Do you understand now why I think that European nature is more beautiful than the one in the Indies? The rice fields and other crops do indeed bring life and variation, but without them, and without the monkeys in the jungles, there's wellnigh the silence and peace and loneliness of the grave, even if everything is green and a formidable hot sun is burning. (38–39)

It doesn't take long for Veth's dislike to become all inclusive.

And it is always hot, hot, hot, and again hot, always. Nature and climate ruin the European. That eternal green and boring blue do not inspire him but numb. The vernal smile is not known in the Indies, but they are well acquainted with the dazed, apathetic tropical grin. I am not a great admirer of Indies's nature. She is almost always boring, she does not comfort, she does not inspire, because she does not speak to us. To be sure, she is magnificent now and then, but it is a dead magnificence. Nothing sways there, nothing rustles, there is no stiff breeze, there are no skies, no beautiful drifting clouds, no mingling of shades. (20)

As with Kay in Andersen's tale "The Snow Queen," a piece of the demon's mirror seems to have lodged itself in Veth's soul. Even a splinter of it could turn a person's heart into a lump of ice, make the most beautiful landscape look like "boiled spinach," and distort "everything they looked at, or made them see everything that was amiss." For Veth even manages to turn the tropics into a kind of winter. He asserts that for the returning European, the mere promise of Holland is enough "to thaw the glaciation of the Indies" (107). The snow and ice of the long northern winter were like an elixir to Veth, an opinion not shared by everyone. I. P. C. Graafland (1851–1918), who wrote under the pseudonym Creusesol, expressed the opposite point of view in a book published in the same year as Veth's.

You over there in Java, you who rightfully maintains that it is warm there, can you, after you've been there for several years, can you still recall for even a moment how it looks here in Holland during the last days of December, the shortest days of the entire year? I think that, without harming either one of us, we can simply envy one another. Over there you enjoy a day of twelve hours, with a profusion of clear sunlight in a blue sky . . . which I so much want to see again. Here we have a maximum of night time and during the day it seems that the sun is too lazy to shine and that the sky in its anger about that stretches a gray tent, not a blue one, over the chilly earth. And on top of that it snows! The gray sky is littered with hundreds of thousands of those white little flakes that only lend a poetic mist to the landscape or city if we can enjoy it at home with a glass pane of several centimeters thick between our face and the air outside, while we're looking at the wondrous whirling that the *udjan kapok* ["rain of kapok"] presents to our eyes that stare in wonderment because they are no longer used to such a display.

And contrary to Veth's opinion, it is winter's oppression that gives Creusesol the feeling of "wanting to rebel, to strike out, to make everything bigger, roomier, more alive. No more of that silent room that seems twice as silent because it is dark, no more of that downpour of the white stuff, that 'udjan kapok,' that shredding of the gray sky which looks exactly like a bell jar and that is as gray as the dust that the maid forgot to clean because it is Christmas." [9]

Since it is the natural heir to the stultifying environment, the native population can do no more than show the same torpid invariability. As far as Veth is concerned, the natives all "loaf," are indolent, indifferent, and undignified. But Veth is not really interested in them. The only Asians that rouse his ire are the Chinese, a prejudice shared by many colonials in both the Indies and British India. They are corrupt money grubbers, "low life" (99), "well fed and fat from stolen cash" (47). Their main aim in life is finagling money and business privileges from dishonest Dutch officials. But except for his discussion of the Chinese, Veth's entire focus is on the way the European lives in the Indies. This one-sidedness was the main reason why Du Perron rejected Veth's account; he felt that Veth argued exclusively from the nominally "superior" European point of view. For Du Perron, Veth was "a cheap *kankeraar* about the Indies," and he dismissed Veth's "warning" as nothing more than a "desperate attempt of a European who tries to wash himself clean" after assuming that the Indies had "soiled" him. [10]

Consistent with the general reductive pattern of Veth's satire, one will find that the lifelessness of tropical nature is duplicated by the physical deterioration of the Europeans, particularly the women. They strike Veth, "almost without exception," as suffering from "severe anemia" that is evident in "their dull, hollow eyes, in the limp, colorless ears [and] in their vacant expression" (45). Their life in the Indies is a living death. "European women who go to the Indies in good health impress those who see them upon their return after several years' residence 'as if they have died already.' They died while they lived in the Indies. They return like ghosts" (109). The same thing happened to the British woman in India. She too was not considered a true "memsahib" until "she has lost her pretty color—that always goes first, and has gained a shadowy ring under each eye—that always comes afterwards." [11]

In Veth's Stygian Indies, domestic animals fare no better than women. The carriage horses would make Rosinante look like a robust steed. They are poor excuses for a horse, "those small, spindle-shanked, unkempt, down-in-the-mouth creatures, hitched to mylords and dos-à-dos.[12] Neglected and utterly miserable these equine ghosts stand there dazed, wretchedly waiting for their burden of kicks, whiplashes and, believe me, even having stones thrown at them, whereafter they attempt either to schlepp along or get up to a desperate gallop and bungle their way to where they are tortured to go" (50).

The native dog or *gladakker* was worse. Like the pariah or pi-dog of British India, the gladakker was a canine outcast that belonged to no one. The peculiar word is a Dutch bastardization of *geladak* in the phrase "djaran geladak," *djaran* being the Javanese word for *horse* (normally *kuda*) and *gladag* for someone who carries something.

Gladakkers aren't normal dogs, they are Indies dogs, hence degenerate degeneration. The ugliest and hungriest cur in the filthiest neighborhood of a European city is, even at the worst stage of neglect, a beauty compared to a gladakker. And such a European cur has at least decent dog manners. He can bark, raise his head when you call him, wag his tail, and run away at a nice trot. He has decent eyes and ears. But gladakkers are the most repulsive, abject creatures in existence. They are sneaky and incredibly treacherous filthbeasts that can only howl, that have the sunken, dirty-yellow eyes of assassins and ears like dishrags and that, at the sight of a stick or whip, creep away with their limp, watered-down rope of a tail down between their legs, only to commence an excruciating howling behind a hedge or fence. Gladakkers arouse a profound disgust. The lowest point the canine race has fallen to was when it lent the gladakker a countenance. A gladdaker is impossible in Europe, he can only thrive in the Indies. Decent dogs soon die in the Indies, which is a good thing because the company of gladakkers would only turn them into scum. (49)

But the center piece of Veth's description is the "Indies man" and everything pertaining to him. Veth is not referring to a person of mixed blood, as was the more normal meaning of that term at the time, but to a full-blood European, or *totok*. There is the same confusion here as with the term *Anglo-Indian* in colonial India. It originally referred exclusively to British people living in that colony, but by the end of the nineteenth century it meant specifically a person of mixed blood, later known as *Eurasian*. Using one of satire's favorite techniques, Veth reduces the "Indies man" to a robot in the service of Mammon.

The real reason the Dutch are in the Dutch East Indies is business, business in the larger sense of trade, agriculture, industry, and mining. If the Indies no longer produced coffee, sugar, tobacco and other products, and if the millions of Natives [*sic*] preferred to walk around naked or in clothes they manufactured themselves, and there was no more gold, petroleum, or tin, then all the Europeans would pack their bags and leave the place, never to return. The bureaucrats, the officers, and the merchants would simply be gone. We're in the East in order to buy products and to sell articles made by European industry. The hordes of bureaucrats and officers are only in the Indies because there is coffee, sugar, tobacco and manufactured goods to deal in. Every European in the Indies wears a trademark. Every European only goes there to earn money, hopefully a lot of money. The traditions of the old East India Company, when every bureaucrat was also a merchant, those traditions are still very much part of the bureaucratic scene, particularly that of the top bureaucrats. Because what all of them really want to do is play at being a merchant in some way or another. It sometimes spreads to their wives as well, and they will sell sarongs, or loan out money at exorbitant interest rates to poor shopkeepers. You will find this business mentality in even the lowliest of clerks. In the Indies you have to do business. If you understand that, no matter how, you probably can stand being there. . . .

He who earns a salary or makes money in the Indies looks upon the Indies as a cow who gives milk, indeed a lot of milk for him who has enough nerve to push the others away from her teats. And so, get going, push and shove for the gold-milk from she who provides. (153−54)

Still using satire's technique of freezing the enemy into a uniform type, Veth expands his portrait of the "Indies man" by fitting him into a larger classification. Its members were best observed in hotels. There "everybody is treated equally, everybody pays five or six guilders a day, and the gin that's on the front veranda is offered free to moderate drinkers as well as alcoholics, to the high and mighty as well as to the little man. There is one class, one gin for *all* the guests in the Indies hotel. Such democracy!" (129).

The Indies man's favorite stomping ground (besides the club) was an abomination for Veth. "Oh, that hotel life in the Indies! It's simply awful, only pigs and insensitive Indies people can feel comfortable there" (131). The bill of fare only made it worse. "What an unsavory pool stinks in an Indies hotel! And the food! The rijsttafel in a hotel . . . is simply awful; the steak and potatoes that follow later taste of rancid coconut oil. You get up even hungrier than when you sat down. And some of the guests have such weird mugs! We apparently become strange and peculiar creatures after we've been in the Indies for several years" (131).

Like Valentijn before him, and like Walraven several decades later, Veth found Indies food some kind of swill. Anyone who has ever had a decent rijsttafel will find his fury incomprehensible, if not pathetic. But to disenchanted Europeans, food seems to have been a form of compensatory infantilism. Although native food was plentiful and delicious, there were enough colonial households where European food was preferred. Because it had to come from Europe in tin cans there was, besides the expense and inevitable tastelessness, the very real threat of botulism. Yet Dutch foodstuffs were transported to the Indies as early as the seventeenth century and for many years to come dinner could consist of a peculiar combination of Dutch and Indonesian dishes.

Veth found hotel accommodations as objectionable as their menu. It should be mentioned that the following targets were to be found in every house in the Indies. A *mandi* room, for instance, was the room where one bathed. It was separate from the toilet. It contained a large square cistern that was kept full of water by means of a conduit—often a hollow bamboo—that led to the source outside. One stripped, poured water over one's body with a small bucket, soaped, and then rinsed (*siram*). The bucket, called a *gajung*, had a wooden grip fastened below the rim, and resembled the New England bucket used for collecting the sap from maple trees. One *never* took a bath by getting *in* the water. "Mandi rooms! The floor and the plank in front of the cistern are muddy and sticky. The smell of the toilets next door vie with the smell of urine inside. The predecessors of the man who wants to take a bath seem to have used the room as a urinal. Good god!" (131).

The condition of the toilets was even worse. Veth has been called an "aesthete," but he relinquished that rarified domain when he chose to become a satirist. As is so often the case with satire, Swift's, for instance, scatology is a favorite topic because it is reductive, degrading, and very effective in deflating posturing. But the power of its effect is relative, of course, and depends on time and place. Writing at the turn of the century, Veth knew perfectly well that bodily functions were taboo. Hence the most brutal reduction in his book was downgrading colonial existence to the level of a toilet. His description is essentially correct, even if sanitation was not much better in, say, Paris. The means of cleaning oneself was using water from a bottle, a procedure called *tjebok*.

Imagine that there's a tropical rainstorm. With a native pajong [parasol] over your head, and wading through puddles, you arrive all muddy at a row of small buildings, meant for a certain purpose, all miserable shacks, filthsties. The door hangs from one hinge, and there's a wooden latch to close that door very unsatisfactorily. It's leaking inside and you're sorry that you've left the pajong outside. I shouldn't hold back now and must tell everything.

The seat of the water closet—one understands that the term "emperor" is just as far removed from "ragpicker" as the word "closet" is from an Indies "convenience"—the seat of the water closet is an ordinary plank with a round hole in it. It seems to be inevitable that the seat is wet—from using the bottles filled with water or from something else. The unlucky hotel guest won't *sit* on the seat but stands on top of it, whereafter he squats down over the opening. Having to use an Indies "closet" in this manner has become such a habit that in a hotel in one of the major cities, where they happened to have a real john, I saw a sign that said: "please do *not* stand on the seat"!

There's also another reason to use an Indies comfort station in such an uncomfortable fashion. If you were to sit down on the seat, as you are used to doing in Europe, it wouldn't take long before you felt the antennae of several cockroaches against those parts that are bared on such an occasion. (129–30)

Sexuality was another taboo that Veth used only in order to illustrate in yet one more way how the European male could fall prey to the Indies. He is not concerned with the fate of the native woman, and seems to regard her association with a white male as a form of iniquitous vengeance. Clearly, succumbing to a native woman is tantamount to surrendering to a dangerous lure.[13]

Let Native men live with Native women according to their customs—which can be sweet at times, naive, even pure. There's much that's holy in their rites and in the simplicity of their lives, as long as they've not been tainted by European contact, and hence instructive to us westerners. But I'd rather see a European keep a marvelous dog or a fine horse than a Native woman. Where it concerns a man and a woman living together I pay no attention to class, nor do I really care about racial differences. I will acknowledge all relationships, but I will never approve of a European associating with a Native woman. It is a relationship that dishonors both. Whatever beauty a European lodges in his soul cannot be expressed when he lives with a Native woman. Whatever beauty lodges in her soul cannot be expressed when she lives with a European. The two are worse than strangers. They are spiritual enemies. The majority of young European men have a need, an urge to be with a "woman," and when there simply isn't one available they search restlessly for something that, in their erotic imagination, resembles a woman, at least physically. The fateful aspect of the sex drive is here clearly in evidence. Because there's nothing one can do about the fact that young Europeans—and unfortunately a large number of older ones as well—are driven by that urge and won't have anything stop them. It's just as impossible to hold back the sea. And so they "go" to a Native woman because, given the circumstances, they can't find a European one. But *all* such relationships are miserable. And perhaps the most horrifying is that, as far as the European is concerned, he only wants to satisfy the most disillusioning lewdness in the most vulgar fashion. He goes to an Indies female the way he'd go to. . . . you know where, reader. (112–13)

Veth's reduction of the "white barbarians" (82) to a mechanism is not restricted to greed or sex. Colonial society also strikes him as being a collection of puppets manufactured to demonstrate an absurd form of etiquette. They will "introduce themselves to the most impossible people at the most impossible time and place" (116). "In the Indies you only become a person after you have introduced yourself" (122). Veth provides a grotesque list of instances when this ceremony will take place, illustrated by a number of anecdotes. One of them—and Veth, as any satirist would, swears it is the truth—took place in the Moluccas. Some naval officers were introduced to a "clump" of ladies during an official reception. One of the officers found himself next to a woman who had joined the reception *after* he and his fellow officers had been introduced. He was not aware of that, yet he was cold shouldered. When she turned her back on him he asked what he had done wrong, and "there issued a snarl from the mouth of the beauty: 'You are not permitted to speak to me, you have not been introduced. I don't know you'" (122).

This mania was part of the larger curse of protocol and hierarchy, what Veth calls the "pretensions of rank." This was by no means restricted to the upper echelons of the colonial administration, but was practiced with a vengeance by the "little bureaucratic gods" (68) as well.

The wife of a head master has to greet the wife of an assistant resident first; it has been calculated that an assistant resident holds a higher rank than a head master, so, ladies, don't you forget it. Now it once happened in an outlying district that the wife of the head master—a much older lady—did not greet the spouse of the assistant resident first and, therefore, was not greeted herself by the peacock wife of the assistant resident. The next day the assistant resident saw the poor head master and addressed him: "If your wife cannot show my wife the proper consideration then *I* will no longer greet *you*." (71)

Though this is bad enough, adherence to a hierarchical order was far worse in the British colonies, particularly India. British colonials studied *The Warrant of Precedence* (or *Civil List*) up to the Second World War, and probably thereafter. This was a document listing social status according to rank in both the civil and the military service, further divided into a nomenclature of classes and subclasses quite as rigorous as Linnaeus's index of the natural world. Such a rigid system, in both Java and India, bred arrogance, and whereas the Indian Civil Service officials were denounced as "the pedestal mob" and "tin gods on wheels," the same could apply also to the Dutch governor-general's "court" at his official residence in Buitenzorg.[14]

Such affectations are nothing but vulgarities to Veth. He is, if anything, consistent in his denunciation. The only time an Indies man mentions God is when he swears (62); his only social criteria are money and social position (60); he is an inveterate booze hound; he has no class, no style, no culture; he loves dirty jokes and his notions about women are on a level with a "quadruped" (77).

Veth's interpretation of life in the Indies was grossly distorted of course. There is no need to catalog the good aspects of that colonial existence such as the hard work, the generosity, and the hospitality of Indies society, or the morality that was far more relaxed and lenient than it ever could have been in Holland. Veth, however, can only approve of two things. Like Valentijn, he admits that musical performances were surprisingly good (146), though what he is referring to, of course, is European music and not to Javanese music, which had its own rich heritage. The only other aspect of colonial life to elicit Veth's approbation was the club, or *soos* as it was called by the Dutch. It was the one institution that he considered to have status and the only place where he felt "European" (138). But otherwise, Veth would have subscribed to Mencken's vitriolic dismissal of the South (in the essay entitled "The Sahara of the Bozart," published in 1917) as being equally valid for the colonial Indies. Mencken asserted that the South "for all its size and all its wealth and all the 'progress' it babbles of, is almost as sterile artistically, intellectually, and culturally as the Sahara Desert. There are single acres of Europe that house more first-rate men than all the states south of the Potomac. . . ."[15]

How true was Veth's anatomy? As is the case with the best satire, there was an incontrovertible basis of veracity. A good gauge of this is the victim's reaction, and Veth was denounced with outraged vehemence. His book—it had four printings, which made it something of a best-seller in those days—"unleashed a stream of letters to the editor, articles, brochures, and pamphlets" that continued for years.[16] The fury of his detractors proves the point made by one of his defenders, Otto Knaap (1866–1917), who felt that Veth "had hit the nail on the head."[17] And even a cursory glance at Dutch colonial literature, particularly P. A. Daum's fiction, which is roughly contemporary with Veth's, would vindicate Veth's malediction. But the real cause for his vitriolic portrait is not known. Veth was a businessman who dealt in *ongeregelde goederen*, which I take to mean that he bought and sold liquidation stock from businesses that were bankrupt. If so, he could not have been very popular, and the desperate owner would have looked on him as something of a mercantile scavenger. Veth did business in the tropics for twelve years and returned to Holland when he was forty. Not much else is known about him, yet one is left with the feeling that he had suffered a personal insult that asked for retribution, and he certainly didn't suppress his need for vengeance.

BAS VETH'S glacial anatomy of tropical life in the colonial Indies is a book of death. Sin, sorrow, decay, and death are the loathsome consequences if a man leaves the Eden of Holland for the benighted wilderness of the Indies where his pursuit of money is nothing but an excremental vice. Life in the Indies is an inhumation. Most appropriately, Veth ends his Stygian account with the real blackness of death. It fits the symbolic pattern of his book by turning the natural, moral, and societal quarantine of the colonial island realm into a real, but infernal archipelago. To be sure, he allows himself to escape, but for most inmates the captivity became permanent and ended in physical death. This ineluctable reality returns us to the realism of satire when, as Swift did so masterfully, the mocking mask is removed to display the mirthless face of fact. And sudden, swift death from tropical disease was a cold certainty for the European usurpers. As a repatriated Englishman wrote in a melancholy poem about India: "death and sickness" is "the tribute that we pay . . . as the price of Oriental sway." [18]

The four vignettes of colonial life given below, which Veth used to round off his deliberate composition, are four snapshots of death and disease. They illustrate the power of "blackness" and, in terms of style, represent Veth's best writing. That this is a deliberate device is clear: Veth's first view of the Indies was the harbor of Padang in western Sumatra. [19] Veth experienced little enthusiasm, perhaps due to his melancholy realization that his sentence of exile seemed without parole. The last vignette of life in the Indies takes place in Padang as well, and it also describes the arrival of a ship, but this time it is a hospital ship. Its passengers are beriberi sufferers. [20] This is the final leveling down to a democracy of death. The patients are Europeans as well as "Native soldiers," not to mention convicted criminals. For all of them it is the end of the line; the grimace has turned grim and *kankeren* discloses itself as a real and lethal disease. It is the bleak fulfillment of the book's motto, taken from the inscription above the entrance to Dante's Inferno: "Abandon all hope you who enter here." In a larger sense it also prophesied the ultimate demise of European colonialism.

VIGNETTES OF THE INDIES
Blackness

I

It was dusk. A procession hurried along Nipah Avenue—the avenue of swamp palms.[21] In front walks a Native mandur[22] from the chain-gang barracks with a badientje[23] in his hand, a small stylish walking stick, and with a white band around his arm.

Then, as if floating in the air, a somber object: a wooden, triangular roof, painted black, two meters long, bouncing on top of several bamboos that rest on the shoulders of black, human shapes—chain-gang convicts who are acting as pallbearers. Underneath that black roof lies the corpse, the corpse of one of their comrades who has just succumbed to cholera:[24] he is the tenth casualty today in the chain-gang barracks.

The corpse was quickly wrapped in a piece of Madapollam,[25] soaked with carbolic acid, laid on a tikar (mat) and put under the black roof. And one, two, three, the roof floats in the air already, bouncing on the bamboos that creak and squeak under the weight. And now at a trot to the graveyard, to the graveyard for convicts. Behind the bouncing roof follow two laconic grave diggers, also chain-gang convicts, who very cleverly carry their spades on their shoulders as if they're playing soldier. Every so often the procession goes faster and the bamboos squeak louder and the roof heaves up and down as if at sea and the grave diggers shuffle along with the spades on their shoulders.

From the Nipah Avenue, along the Muara,[26] to the beach, that's where the convicts' graveyard is. Dusk has almost turned into night. The sea is black and the black waves beat against the beach. The hurried procession has arrived. Quickly the grave diggers take the spades from their shoulders and dig a grave right next to the waves. The black object has been put on the ground; it is lifted off the bamboos and the corpse is shoved into the hole next to the waves. The hole is quickly kicked full with sea sand, some stamping down with the feet and a couple of blows with the flat of the spades.

Finished.

They all march back to the barracks where the cholera is raging. Tomorrow the mandur and the laconic grave diggers will take the same route—but they might be under the black roof themselves, and be buried on the beach, where the black waves splash.

II

The cholera raged in epidemic proportions. In the kampongs the Natives died like rats and mice. In the Chinese quarter things weren't quite right either—every day there were five, six, ten cases. But the cholera had still spared the European population of the place.

At night the conversations were all about this macabre subject; and around the gossip table it was said that as many as a hundred Natives were dying each day, dying from cholera. They had seen them drop, saw them die in convulsions before their very eyes. A lot of cognac is consumed.

Suddenly: a shock, a shudder went through the European community. Did you know: Mr. A. has cholera. The first European to be attacked by the hideous disease. And that afternoon Mr. A. is dead, dead from cholera. It's as if everyone is overcome by terror. They are oh so afraid.

Even the undertakers shrink back from their task. The corpse of the cholera patient is not removed and the families who live next door to the deceased complain to the assistant resident of police, whining from cholera fear, claiming that the corpse is stinking already and that the stench is driving them from their homes. And a note is written to the warden of the jail: "Provide a couple of convicts to bury Mr. A's corpse around eight."

At eight, Native prisoners carry a rough black box into the room where the corpse of the cholera patient is lying. With great indolence—fatalism, the chains and their somber lives lead to indolence—with great indolence the unfortunate chain-gang convicts put the corpse in the box.

And now to the European graveyard. Quick.

Neither kith nor kin, neither friend nor foe, follows the somber procession, wait, yes, there's one, one lone friend. A grave has been hastily dug in the European cemetery. Around nine o'clock, in the dark of night, the procession of blue-clad convincts approaches the cemetery with the cholera corpse.

A lantern in front, a lantern in the rear, two crocks of carbolic acid. The graveyard supervisor and the warden are standing by the hole, waiting for the procession.

Javanese oh-sounds from the mouths of the convicts, the pounding of footsteps approaching, approaching the grave.

Dull lanternlight. The black box. Lower it into the hole as quickly as possible; the crocks of carbolic acid cluck while they're emptied over it. Everything taken care of. Burial of a cholera victim; the first case among the Europeans of the place.

No friends, no flowers, no minister. Sinister removal to the graveyard, then hiding it beneath the earth.

III

I had taken my bath at six in the morning and was drinking my cup of coffee and reading the paper in my long chair.

"Tuwan." I look up. A Native boy with a piece of paper. "Mr. W. died last night. The funeral will be at five this afternoon." And a name under it. Must be a friend. Mr. W. Yes, I knew his liver had been bothering him for some time. He complained a lot when I saw him recently. Oh, there's B., a good friend of W., riding into my yard; he's got to know more about this affair. "Good morning; you've heard already, right? W. is dead. Happened sooner than people thought. Had to have an operation because of a liver abscess. The operation yesterday went very well, but W. died last night from some complication that the doctors hadn't counted on. Well, he's dead."

"You're also going to the cemetery this afternoon?"

"Yes."

Had to go out burying this afternoon. Came home from work at four, an unusual hour. Black pants and jacket, black gloves, white tie, top hat. It's still very hot. Sweating in the black suit, drove to the house of the deceased in a dos-à-dos. The box was just being carried outside.

Funeral procession.

Walk through the cemetery to the grave.

Box carried by undertakers.

The friends behind it, also the minister.

Everyone has been called away from work or has just gotten up from his siesta.

In full daylight, at five in the afternoon, the faces look remarkably disheveled, so yellow, so tired, so funereal. The cohort itself looks like a succession of corpses behind a corpse. And the costumes that are supposed to be black! Many suits are green-gray, brownish instead of black. A display of old clothes. Hardly anyone fits in his black jacket and the trousers are too short. And in those green, gray, brown-yellow, old-fashioned mourning clothes the ashen friends follow the box, some of them wear round hats that are brown or gray.

The minister speaks by the grave.

That's the way it's supposed to be, they say.

The friends and acquaintances around it.

The hole is half filled with water; it rained during the night and in the morning. The box is lowered into the hole, plop, disappears about halfway into the filthy liquid.

Some flowers are tossed in; a few spadefuls of earth on the already wet lid of the box.

The corpse of the man who we were yesterday congratulating around five on his successful operation plops today at five into a grave half full with water.

IV

They signal the boat from Atjeh[27] from the tall signal post on the other side of the Padang River.

The people who rent out carriages saw the signal and hurried to get the my-lords, victorias, and calèches out of the sheds that are supposed to be coach-houses—old, rickety, dilapidated, faded vehicles and coachmen hasten to harness the miserable nags, those equine ghosts of Rosinante.

And then the ferocious rush to the landing by the Muara, over the roads of Padang, and if it hasn't rained for a long time the clouds of dust whirled behind the vehicles, dust that penetrated everywhere, into all the houses along the road. The cracking of whips and the shouts of the drivers. A wild chase. And soon after the signal, rings were hoisted on the signpost, black rings. One, two, three, four, five.

From the hospital they were keeping an eye on the number of rings that were raised. And they hurried to collect tandus—litters—and chain-gang convicts to carry them. Every black ring on the signpost meant that there was a need for ten or twelve tandus, and they kept on adding new black rings—six—seven. They stop hoisting them: seventy tandus. That is to say: seventy sick or severely wounded men were on board the boat from Atjeh, and they were so ill or infirm that they could only be transported by litter from the wharf to the hospital.

And those carriages—the worst of Padang's carriage trade—serve to transport the sick who can still walk a little, just enough to go down the wharf to the Muara.

And little by little everything is collected near the Muara. And now it's nothing but wait, wait by the moorings. The big steam launch that was sent to the Atjeh boat, now anchored in the roads of Pulu-Pisang, still hasn't come back. Finally, finally the steam whistle is heard behind Monkey Mountain and the launch comes around the Whale—the large, smooth rock at the foot of the mountain—to go up river, and docks. Then the sick and wounded are carted off.

Many hang down limply, they can't move anymore. Most are beriberi suf-ferers—European and Native soldiers, and convicts as well. Those who can still walk a little are put in the carriages. The seriously ill, those who are near dying, and those who have died already, are carried in the tandus.

The drivers are back on their seats.

Cracking of whips. And they proceed along the Muara. The beriberi patients who are riding are driven at a gallop to the hospital. They're followed by the pro-cession of tandus. It goes calmly, very calmly. One after the other, the tandus pass by very slowly. And in each tandu is a seriously ill patient or a dying one, or a dying beriberi patient.

There are countless tandus. Another one, another, and yet another. And yes, finally the last one, the last one that disappears through the gate of the hospital.

The beriberi procession is over.

NOTES

1 The etymological discussion is based on: *Van Dale Groot Woordenboek der Nederlandse Taal* (1961); *Franck's Etymologisch Woordenboek der Nederlandsche Taal* (1949); Jan de Vries, *Nederlands Etymologisch Woordenboek* (1971).

2 E. du Perron, *Verzameld Werk*, 7 vols. (Amsterdam: Van Oorschot, 1955–59), 2:746.

3 W. Walraven, *Eendagsvliegen, Journalistieke getuigenissen uit kranten en tijdschriften* (Amsterdam: Van Oorschot, 1971), 315–20.

4 Northrop Frye, *Anatomy of Criticism* (1957; reprint, New York: Atheneum, 1968), 224.

5 The text used is a new edition. Bas Veth, *Het Leven in Nederlandsch Indië*, ed. Rob Nieuwenhuys ('s-Gravenhage: Thomas and Eras, 1977), 17. It is a shortened version of the original text published in 1900. Hereafter page numbers will be given in the text. I have attempted to preserve Veth's idiosyncratic style with its numerous inversions, neologisms, implied but not stated verbs, and peculiar syntax. He often leaves out clear references to antecedents, and I have maintained this style. I have kept his haphazard italicizing and explanation of Malay words.

6 I consider Multatuli a Romantic; see my afterword to Multatuli, *Max Havelaar Or the Coffee Auctions of the Dutch Trading Company*, trans. Roy Edwards (Amherst: University of Massachusetts Press, 1982), 338–78.

7 Aldous Huxley, for example, in what seems to me a correct view of tropical nature vis-á-vis the European or British one. See his essay "Wordsworth in the Tropics" in *Collected Essays* (New York: Harper and Row, 1958), 1–10.

8 *Pajo Koemboeh* was the name for both the town and a district in western Sumatra, above the median of that large island, in the mountains of what used to be called the Padang Highlands. This area was much favored because of its mild climate, which was due to its elevation of some sixteen hundred feet above sea level. Abundant rain made it ideal for growing such lucrative crops as coconuts, tobacco, and cacao. After several good roads had been built and a railroad connection had been established, the town of Pajo Koemboeh became an important marketplace, where thousands of people from the Minangkabau region came to buy and sell on Sundays. The huge waringins in the *pasar* or central market were famous. The name derives from *pajo,* "a swamp," and *koemboeh* (*kumbuh*), a kind of reed-like grass. Veth's peculiar spelling, "Payacombo," looks British to me. I have the notion that Veth was an Anglophile. This peculiar spelling is one indication, another is his occasional use of English words such as *plenty* (134) or his assertion that the curry from British India was more *savory* (134) than the Indonesian variety. He also quotes British authors, such as Byron and Shakespeare, in the original. Although this is difficult to prove conclusively, Veth's attitude to the colonial tropics strikes me as similar to the British one, particularly in India. If my notion is correct, it would be somewhat ironic, because the British were far more rigid than the Dutch.

9 The Creusesol passage is from a selection printed in an anthology by Rob Nieuwenhuys:

In de schommelstoel, Nederlandse letterkunde over Indonesië van 1870 tot 1935, ed. Rob Nieuwenhuys (Amsterdam: Querido, 1975) 83–84.

10   Du Perron, *Verzameld Werk,* 2:634; 7:40; 2:634.

11   Michael Edwards, *Bound to Exile. The Victorians in India* (1969; reprint, New York: Praeger, 1970), 161.

12   *Mylords* and *dos-à-dos* were carriages. A mylord was a four-wheeled vehicle, somewhat like a victoria in that it had room for two passengers, a convertible top, and a perch for the driver. A dos-à-dos, French for "back to back," was a two-wheeled vehicle with a canopy over the space where the passengers sat. It was more commonly called *sado.*

13   See my introduction to one of the novels in this series: Louis Couperus, *The Hidden Force* (Amherst: University of Massachusetts Press, 1985).

14   Edwards, *Bound to Exile,* 97–98.

15   For a comparison between the Dutch colonial Indies and the American South, see my introduction to Daum's novel, *Ups and Downs of Life in the Indies* (Amherst: University of Massachusetts Press, 1987).

16   Nieuwenhuys in his anthology, *In de schommelstoel,* 62.

17   Quoted by Nieuwenhuys in ibid., 76.

18   Quoted in Edwards, *Bound to Exile,* 220.

19   *Padang* was the capital of a district by the same name on the west coast of Sumatra. In Veth's time it had about forty thousand inhabitants. Padang became a fairly prosperous trade center toward the end of the nineteenth century, because railroad service was extended between the city and the surrounding country, and because of the construction, between 1887 and 1892, of the Emma Harbor in Queen's Bay. The latter was necessary because it was impossible for ships to dock directly in Padang. They came to anchor in the roads behind a small island called "Banana Island" or Pulau Pisang, where they were safe from storms coming from a westerly direction. The island was to the southwest of the mouth (*muara*) of the Padang River, also known as the Arau or Harau River. On board ship one could see neither the city nor the river. People and goods were transported on a launch and only when the passengers rounded the cliff called "The Whale" could they see the shore. From the shore it took forty minutes by carriage or twenty by train to reach Padang. The city was hidden from view by the tall Apenberg or Monkey Mountain, part of the Padang mountains. It got its name from its large population of long-tailed monkeys (*kera* in Malay) that had become quite tame because numerous hikers fed the animals bread and bananas. On top of Monkey Mountain was a sign board to indicate the arrival and departure of ships.

20   *Beriberi,* once a dread disease in the Indies, was particularly virulent among military personnel and prisoners. This was because the rice they ate was "polished rice," i.e., rice that had been buffed to make it shinier. In the process the outer fleece was removed, and with it some important vitamins, particularly vitamin B_1. The subsequent deficiency affected the peripheral nerves. Symptoms were paralysis of the limbs, insensitivity to pain, and severe weight loss. Death was sudden. Young males were particularly susceptible to the disease, especially young native men. It could be cured very simply by feeding the victims unpolished rice, fresh meat, vegetables, and fruit. It is remarkable that the seventeenth-century naturalist Rumphius (see the volume entitled *The Poison Tree* in this series) mentioned *katjang idju* (or *idjo*) as a remedy. It is a bean (*Phaseolus radiatus*) that was often eaten like our peas. It was discovered in this century that *katjang idju* is rich in vitamins, but in Veth's time this was not common knowledge. Ironically, Europeans could be stricken too if they ate much European food from tin cans because the contents had lost all nutritional value and were well-nigh devoid of vitamins.

21   Nipa(h) palms are the *Nipa fruiticans* palms that have short trunks and grow mainly in

swampy areas in brackish water. Their leaves were used as *atap,* the most common of roof-ing materials.

22   *Mandur,* from the Portuguese *mandador,* was the title of a native overseer or foreman.

23   *Badientje* is the Dutch spelling of the French *badine.* It refers to a small stick or riding crop, usually made of rattan. It was flexible and light.

24   *Cholera* was particularly lethal to the European population. Caused by the cholera bacillus, it was a very contagious disease that most often resulted from drinking contami-nated water and unhygienic contacts with cholera patients. Symptoms were severe diarrhea, vomiting, cramps, dehydration. Cholera was, in Veth's time, usually fatal.

25   *Madapollam cloth* was a stiff, heavy, calico cotton cloth originally woven near the town of Madapollam in the Madras residency in India.

26   Although Veth capitalizes it, *muara* is not a proper name but was the general term in Sumatra for the mouth of a river.

27   *Atjeh* is the name of a region and sultanate in the northern section of Sumatra. The people of Atjeh were devout Muhammadans and fiercely anti-Dutch. Atjeh was the last re-gion in the Indies to be "pacified," yet it was involved in almost continuous warfare from 1873 to the beginning of the Second World War.

Alexander Cohen

$\mathbf{A}$LEXANDER COHEN(1864–1963) is primarily important to this anthology because he spent four years as an ordinary soldier in the Dutch colonial army during the penultimate decade of the nineteenth century. He also epitomizes those who were the best, and perhaps the most interesting, among colonials: those outsiders who made a home of exile, the combative mavericks who refused to yield, and the passionate nonconformists who made dissenting a way of life. Cohen consistently went against the grain as if he had been born to the task. He was the son of an orthodox Jew from Leeuwarden, the capital of Friesland, Holland's northernmost province. Though this birthplace seems a most unlikely cradle for a son of Zion, Cohen shared the Frisians' proverbial stubbornness and intractability, and he seems to have committed himself to an unconventional life at an early age.[1]

Cohen, the second son of Aron Heiman Cohen Jzoon, was born 27 September 1864; his elder half-brother was from his father's first marriage. Alexander's mother, Aron's second wife, gave birth to two other sons as well as three daughters. In 1873, when Alexander was nine, she died from tuberculosis. Cohen lovingly remembered her as a "beautiful, quiet, soft, [and] friendly woman" who was unable to guide his upbringing because she was "worn out" from relentless childbearing (9). To my knowledge the only other time Cohen wrote about someone with similar tenderness was after the death of his wife in 1959.[2] I would assume that he considered the two women to be kindred spirits, and he was well aware of their selfless devotion to men who were often hard to live with.

Cohen's father married for the third time in September 1875. His stepmother treated Alexander well and often tried to intervene on his behalf during the relentless war of attrition between father and son. To no avail.

The father was a hard taskmaster who firmly believed in corporal punishment, withholding food, and verbal abuse. Playing was not allowed,
toys were taboo, and pocket money out of the question. Fighting was permitted, providing clothes were not damaged, but all in all little love was
given. When young Cohen fell through the ice one winter, a poor fish
hawker hauled him out and brought him home. "My father gave the man
a quarter, which was quite amazing. 'But—' says he to my noble res-
cuer—'if you leave him there the next time, I'll give you a dollar'" (26).

No matter how "senseless" the father's "authoritarianism" (23), the
son did not knuckle under. He stole money to buy toys, lied to cover his
truancy, and was expelled from three schools for bad behavior. He dis-
avowed the authority of his orthodox religion and declared that his favorite biblical personages were the dispossessed—Cain for instance. Cohen
wondered why God "liked roasted lamb chops better than radishes" (14).
Esau was preferred because he had been "neglected and deceived and had
a pretty bad home life too." And Moses appealed to him because he had
been "had" by God when he was allowed to look at but not enter the
Promised Land, even after wandering for forty years with those "rowdy
and unmanageable children Israels" (15). Cohen finally renounced his religion entirely, although he was baffled when one of his more tractable
brothers did likewise, only to become a Lutheran instead. "What kind of
attraction, for Heaven's sake, can there be in protestantism, a religion
that purged itself of all poetry—be it primitive, refined, or barbarian—
very rigorously, as if it were delousing itself" (19). Even Catholicism was
preferable because it had not entirely forbidden ardor and emotion. Cohen opted for what the Mexican poet and essayist Octavio Paz has called
a "warm civilization."[3] Hence his abiding love of France. "When I move
among the people in the Bois de Boulogne I am struck once again, but
now even more strongly, with what I had already noticed in Ghent: how
much the unconstrained, loose, airy, pleasant, and also Catholic, peoples
who live farther south, distinguish themselves from my penned-in, stiff,
heavy-handed, joyless compatriots." This difference is even apparent
within the military. Whereas Dutch soldiers are "clumsy and stiff as a
poker," the French ones are "lively, lithe and quick"—an impression
aided by the latter's colorful uniform of "red trousers, dark blue tunic,
white puttees, and their shako with a colorful pompon" (145). Cohen felt
a similar liberation when he was in the Indies for, even though there was
nothing to recommend the colonial army, he had no quarrel with the
tropics.

While still at school, his favorite subjects were history, geography, and
languages. He was, however, an utter failure in everything else. His flair

for languages served him well; after he moved to Paris, he wrote in Dutch for Dutch newspapers, in French for Parisian gazettes, translated the Dutch colonial writer Multatuli into French, rendered one of Zola's novels into Dutch, produced French versions of Nietzsche and Gerhart Hauptmann's play *Einsame Menschen* (*Lonely People*), and his Malay remained good enough to converse with Javanese dancers at the 1889 World's Fair in Paris. Many years later he could still recite entire poems in Frisian as well, for Cohen seems to have been blessed with a phenomenal memory. But his scholarly career was short; when he was around fourteen, he was permanently barred from any further formal education because of his recalcitrant behavior.

His subsequent days as a good-for-nothing turned the parental home into an armed camp. The son's only "asylum" was the attic where he had found a bookcase filled with books. Because his hideout was difficult to get to and because Cohen was extremely cautious, his father never discovered him there. Among the forgotten books in this remarkably well-stocked case, he read, besides nineteenth-century Dutch literature, Shakespeare, Scott, Heine, Thiers, Alexander Dumas, and the novels of Victor Hugo. Though these works became definitely more enticing because they had to be read in secret, they were not unusual fare for a rebellious youth like Cohen. Yet in Cohen's case they also seem most appropriate, for he remained in many ways a combative romantic rebel all his life, one who practically made a profession out of contrariety, whose political hero was Napoleon, and whose literary master was Multatuli, Dutch literature's most brilliant malcontent.

The relative leisure he experienced during this time was short-lived for this precocious nihilist. After several failed attempts to find his son some sort of employment in Holland, Cohen's father decided in 1880 to apprentice him to a German tanner. The experiment was an utter failure, but the brief encounter with Germany (no longer than three months) left a lasting impression. Cohen's employer lived in Sonsbeck, a small town in the Rhine province, to the west of Wesel, between the Dutch border of the province of Limburg and the west bank of the Rhine. With his customary wit, Cohen later wrote that he never could stand people with "pointy elbows and hook noses" (51), but the main reasons for the debacle were that his employer was as authoritarian as his father, that he hit his apprentice (and Cohen promptly responded in kind), and that he did not like the aspersions the Dutch boy cast at a German nation that was still basking in the success of the Franco-Prussian War. For the rest of his life, and he lived to be nearly a hundred, Cohen never lost his intense dislike of Germans. When he once met a sympathetic one, Cohen commented that this had to be "one of the six or seven exceptional Germans, put into circulation by the good Lord once every thirty-three years, for the duration of one generation, in order to prove that there were also 'good ones' among them" (51). During the First World War, disgusted with pacifism and enraged at Germany, Cohen wrote a scathing article about "bochophile pacifisme." He included Mata Hari in his criticism. This Dutch "choreographic artist," as the French press gallantly called her, had also been born in Leeuwarden (as Margaretha Geertruida Zelle) in 1876. She escaped from the same stultifying environment as Cohen's in 1897 by marrying a much older captain in the colonial army and, like Cohen, she preferred living in Paris to wasting away in Holland. But spying for Germany—"that dishonorable trade *for money* [sic] without the excuse of patriotic passion"—justified, according to him, her death by firing squad on 15 October 1917. Furthermore, Cohen felt that her "exotic dancing" was vulgar and a travesty of the refined and chaste beauty of Javanese dancing. He concluded his article: "In truth I can tell you that *art* lost nothing when she was executed yesterday. There's merely one less German spy in the world."[4] Neither his pugnacity nor his prejudice ever softened.

Declared undesirable by the tanning industry—Cohen insisted that he always "preferred cathedrals to factories" (52)—and the German nation, Cohen was sent back to Holland and a furious father. It was quickly decided to make him a sailor next. Cohen's father felt that a steamer would not do because "they returned so quickly" (53) so he looked for a sailing ship in Rotterdam harbor and found one bound for Nova Scotia. Alexander deserted before the ship set sail. Back in Leeuwarden, the generational armed camp deteriorated into open warfare. The son ran away to Belgium, was arrested, imprisoned, and returned to the Netherlands. Everything else having failed, going to the Indies was mentioned as a last resort. The Colonial Ministry had just created the new position of military clerk, and Cohen's father consented to his son's request because of this more "respectable" job. At the time his permission was required by law because a child had to be eighteen in order to join the colonial army (one was not considered adult until twenty-three years of age). Cohen was accepted, signed up for the mandatory six years, and left Holland three weeks before his eighteenth birthday in September 1882.

Cohen lived as a soldier in the Indies from October 1882 to January 1887 when, almost two years before the contractual termination of his enlistment, he was dishonorably discharged. Of those four years he spent more than three—from June 1884 to Christmas Day 1887—in a military prison on Java. When he exchanged the parental prerogatives for the even more inflexible imperiousness of the military, he made a serious, though understandable, miscalculation. At the time the service was a way out for him; it gave purpose and shape to what looked like a chaotic future and it still had an aura of bravado and audacity. Cohen courted adventure all his life—adventure in the romantic sense of trying one's luck, seeking out risks in a novel and exciting fashion, or committing oneself to an impetuous action that flouts prudence. Cohen was to find out several years later that adventure can also be intellectual, but either physically or mentally, an adventurer goes against the grain and is the exception to the norm; adventure is mutability. During these early years Cohen pursued adventure as a form of mobility, but he later came to understand it as a mental limberness as well. In both cases Cohen's adventuring took the form of originality and spirited individualism. Societal rule cannot allow such imtemperate high spirits as his, and for good reason: one cannot command a disarray of mavericks to be a herd. Alexander Cohen was never corralled. He characterized his life as "an exploration of Adventure" (6) and praised Napoleon because he was "an immense adventurer, a semi-divine adventurer, but an adventurer nevertheless, and one who remained separate from the French people, for whom this same people had been first and foremost the tool of his glory, Napoleon who, in his innermost self, had never identified with this people" (143). This lack of identity was true of this most unlikely Dutchman who was a hotspur as well, albeit without the hyperboles, and who lived the greater part of his life as a stranger among the French. But during the youthful years of the 1880s Cohen found himself pitted against military rule. His description of that contest is included below. Suffice it to say at this point that the colonial army fared no better than his father.

In February 1887 he was living once again in Leeuwarden, but at the end of that summer, when he finally came of age, Cohen left his father's house for the last time. In the fall of the same year he found work with a socialist paper, *Recht voor allen* (Justice for everybody), in The Hague. For the next forty years he worked as a free lance for a variety of publications in both Holland and France. His debut as a journalist was in June 1887; most appropriately he published a series of articles in a radical paper in Groningen that was a polemic against a recruitment pamphlet that the Colonial Ministry was distributing to attract volunteers for the military. He remained a polemist all his life, never giving quarter or asking any.

Cohen is part of the Dutch tradition of *kankeraars* that Bas Veth belonged to, a tradition that seems to have thrived so well in the colonial Indies. But, as in any field, not everyone can obtain excellence. Menno ter Braak, a Dutch critic from the thirties, pointed out: "In order to 'swear'

well, one needs talent; in order to insult one's opponents one needs to
know human nature so well that one is really capable of hitting the offend-
ing target; in other words, one has to be a personality who can vouch for
his own standards (even if they are 'merely' the standards of a knight errant), and one can only discover the personality of a polemist in his style.
Such a polemic personality who wrote an excellent polemic style is Alexander Cohen." Cohen's style is nimble and surprisingly colloquial, even
after he had lived more than a half century in France. It is informal, lively,
limber, and very much his own. Especially in his autobiographical work,
Cohen displays a fine sense of humor and, like Valentijn, he had a love for
the droll and anecdotal. It is remarkable that his descriptions of even the
most distasteful experiences manage to retain a cheerfulness, a sense of
indomitable good spirits. As Ter Braak put it so well: Cohen "had too
great a sense of humor to be a prophet of rancor." [5] Except for his dislike
of Germany, there was no malice in Cohen the man or the writer. One
may even detect a kind of naiveté in him, as Ter Braak did, but that is
probably due to his sincerity and his refusal fo succumb to bitterness—a
surrender that would have only diminished him and shown the enemy
that his methods had been successful. Resilience in the face of bitterness
indicates a core of integrity and self-confidence that is most disheartening
to the opposition; there is nothing more unnerving than a cheerful rebel,
as Cohen appears to have realized.

It seems to me that, despite his misfortunes in the colonial army, Cohen
did not entirely dislike the military. Some of the best times of his youth
were in the company of soldiers. When he was nearly fifty he joined the
French army during World War I with a certain excitement. That readi-
ness to do battle is also evident in his writing; Cohen was what the French
so expressively call *un écrivain de combat*, a phrase that retains some of
the flavor of danger and excitement usually associated with military life.
Cohen saw his combat duty as opposing anything that smacked of conformity, authority, the status quo, or, perhaps better said, anything that
was counteractive. One can imagine that such a stance did not earn him
much favor, particularly with ideologues whose posturing did not sit well
with Cohen's amazing appetite and stamina for dissent. The titles of four
of his major works speak for themselves: *Uitingen van een reactionnair*
(Expressions of a reactionary), 1929; *In opstand* (Resistance), 1931; *Van
anarchist tot monarchist* (From anarchist to monarchist), 1936); and the
anthology of his articles and essays entitled *Een andersdenkende* (Dissenter), 1959.

Cohen had enlisted in the battle with society at an early age. The only
difference was that after 1887 he put his dissenting opinion into words as

well as action. He joined the Dutch socialists at that time only because they were a rebellious opposition force (126). On 6 September 1887, he shouted at the passing King William III in the Hague: "Down with the gorilla, long live socialism." The simian epithet he derived from a lampoon about the Dutch king written by Sicco Roorda van Eysinga (1825–1887), a friend of Multatuli and an officer in the colonial Corps of Engineers, who was banished from the Indies and was living in voluntary exile in Switzerland.[6] Cohen was arrested and tried. He was his own defense counsel and his sarcastic plea was printed in a number of radical publications. He was sentenced to six months in jail for lese majesty and, unenthusiastic about enduring incarceration again, he fled to Belgium in March 1888. The Belgian authorities did not respond to Dutch demands to extradite him and, at his own request, Cohen was allowed to take the train to Paris. He arrived in the French capital on 12 May 1888 and never left France again except under duress or for professional reasons. The beginning of his long career as a journalist for both Parisian and Dutch papers and journals dates from that year.

French authorities also declined to extradite Cohen though he was kept under surveillance. He made a meager living from his job as a paid correspondent for *Recht voor allen* (Justice for everybody), signing his articles with the pseudonym "Souvarine," the name of the nihilist in Zola's novel *Germinal*. Desperate to make more money, he translated pamphlets by the Dutch socialist leader Domela Nieuwenhuis into French and translated Zola's novel *Au bonheur de dames* into Dutch for the Flemish newspaper *Vooruit* (Forward). In the meantime he felt more and more sympathy for the anarchist movement which, in the final decade of the nineteenth century, was a force to be reckoned with. Again a reflection of his uncompromising nonconformism and individualism, Cohen had come to dislike the socialists because of "their lust for power, their corporalism,[7] their sectarianism, their denial of all individuality, their conception of man as a herd animal that stuffs itself at the communal trough, their coarse materialism, and their imperviousness to all abstract beauty and all aestheticism" (159). Anarchism which, after all, was against everything, was more akin to his own volatile personality. Although he never joined the anarchists officially (just as he had never joined the socialists and was never to be an official member of anything), his articles for various French anarchist publications made him guilty by association in the authorities' eyes. He was arrested in December 1893 after Vaillant's bombing of the Chamber of Deputies in the Bourbon Palace. Despite efforts by the writer Octave Mirbeau, by the actor and director Lugné-Poe, and by Zola, Cohen was expelled and forced to go to England.[8]

During the same eventful year Cohen met Elisa Germaine (Kaya) Batut

(1871–1959). Cohen shared his life with this seamstress from August 1893 until her death more than sixty years later. They were not legally married until 1918, twenty-five years after they met. Together they lived in poverty in London where Cohen could only get sporadic journalistic work, including a few articles for *The Torch of Anarchy*. But his desire to get back to Paris was powerful, and in August 1895 he was able to slip back into France illegally. He managed to be acquitted of the criminal charges lodged against him, and the sentence of twenty years at hard labor was dismissed as well. He still could not stay in France, however, and he was once again forced to leave. Out of sheer desperation he went with Kaya to Holland. In the fall of 1896 he was arrested by the Dutch authorities and was forced to serve his previous six-months' sentence for lese majesty. While in prison he translated Multatuli into French. In the summer of 1899 he was back in Paris and during the first decade of the new century he finally succeeded in becoming a naturalized French citizen.

Cohen continued to work as a free-lance journalist. In France he contributed regularly to such publications as the *Mercure de France* and *Figaro*, and in Holland to the large daily paper *De Telegraaf* (The telegraph). During their final years he and Kaya lived near Toulon. Cohen died there in 1963, less than four years after Kaya's death, at the age of ninety-nine.[9]

Menno ter Braak noted that "it is just as possible to be an adventurer in journalism as it is to be an adventurer in the jungle."[10] Cohen's intellectual venture never ceased. He repudiated anarchism when it became oppressive and opted during the latter part of his life for monarchism—French of course—a most unpopular choice to be sure. But he knew that revolutionary movements always become ossified, that the original promise of individual liberty is soon trammeled by the heavy exoskeleton of doctrine. Like the hermit crab, Cohen wanted to remain free to choose new domiciles when he had outlived the one he presently inhabited. And what, paradoxically, was so true of the best of the colonial spirit, was true of Cohen: he registered his independence time after time to make sure that both he and the world (even if it did not care) knew that he was not institutionalized yet.

In the end he called himself a "reactionary," not in the simplistic pejorative sense, but in the original sense of one who "reacts"—one who causes and experiences a stimulus. He made his position clear when he distinguished between "revolution" and "resistance."[11]

Revolution, a turning over, takes place within the limited borders of time and space, and its action expires and is smothered like spent, exhausted waves on a soggy beach. Resistance is eternal and infinite. Revolution brings to power other, sometimes new, and usually more ruthless, because not yet satiated, masters. Resistance neither fosters nor accepts a lord. Revolution is made to order. Resistance is an elemental force. Revolution is collective and, because its ultimate goal is to rule and oppress, of low quality. Resistance is individual, disinterested and superior. (161–62)

Alexander Cohen lived according to his nature and would not be defrauded. His exhilirating individualism that saw a constant need for disobedience bears some resemblance to Thoreau's. He did not possess the latter's unstinting love of nature, but they did share a sense of humor, practical humanism, and the need for a vigilant nonconformity. Cohen was an enthusiastic dissenter without theory or dogma. Abstraction was anathema to his reflections that were sturdily footed in reality. He always gave his political disquisitions a human face and found giving offense a refreshing tonic. Cohen leveled with the world and with himself; honesty was a habit he wore well. There was something of a knight errant about him; his lance was not for hire and he took pleasure in lopping off cant wherever he encountered it. That he finally sided with dead French kings is yet another quixotic gesture of a man who would rather pursue the impossible than conform to the presumption of likelihood. Camelot is a better place to linger than a consortium.

THE colonial army Cohen joined in 1882 was more nearly a foreign legion than a national fighting force.[12] This had been the case from the very beginning of Holland's colonial empire in Indonesia. For the almost two centuries that the VOC, or United East India Company, ruled the Indies it had relied on what amounted to a private army. This perpetually inadequate force was made up of crews from the Company's fleet, a number of recruits from Europe, slaves or other impressed natives, and auxiliary forces supplied by Indonesian sovereigns allied with the Dutch. Because of a policy of parsimony—which remained in force for the nearly three and a half centuries of Dutch colonial rule, and was matched only by that of the British government[13]—and the appalling casualty rate, it was always difficult to maintain an adequate combat force. In 1637 Governor-General Van Diemen appealed to the Company's headquarters in Amsterdam to send him more men because he was unable to maintain a force of more than 3,000 to 4,000 men.[14] As a result, Dutch recruiting officers signed up just about anybody, a method that forced another governor-general in 1819 to lament that he had to rely on troops that were "the scum of foreign armies."[15]

The need for such "scum" increased after 1813. In 1798 the commercial enterprise of the Company became a colonial empire and the government decided to extend its authority in the Indies. Napoleon intervened, however, and Holland lost its colonies to England. Restored in 1813, Holland resumed its policy of extending its direct control in the Indies, an effort that required more troops. Because it was not deemed advisable to have an entirely native army—although the colonial army always consisted of almost two-thirds native troops—the necessary percentage of European men had to be found somewhere. It was difficult to find enough volunteers among the Dutch population. The Dutch have always been averse to soldiering as a profession, and their dislike of regimentation makes them very poor candidates for the military. Hence the colonial ranks had to be filled from elsewhere.

The first source was Holland's own national army—not until 1830 was there a complete disassociation between the armed forces of Holland and the Indies—especially its most disreputable element. In 1814 a standing order was issued to retrain convicted military criminals for service in the tropics, a plan that was soon extended to include hard-core criminals from civilian prisons. This dangerous practice was nominally abolished in 1841, but between 1846 and 1847 convicted criminals still represented seven percent of colonial replacement troops.[16] When this source did not suffice, recruiters turned to others. After the Napoleonic wars, a sizable number of unemployed veterans were available in Europe, and they were eagerly sought by the Dutch. One must remember that fighting forces were made up of volunteers only; conscription was not introduced in Holland until 1918, and in England only two years earlier. During the first half of the nineteenth century, a large number of French-speaking soldiers joined the Dutch colonial army: Frenchmen, Belgians, and Swiss. Official military language had a disproportionate number of French words, and they were still in evidence during Cohen's time. French-speaking soldiers were so numerous that they were known by special names. A Frenchman was a *didong* from the phrase "dites donc" ("look here") and a Belgian was a *stengan didong* or "half didong," *stengan* being Malay for "half."

After 1877 large numbers of Germans joined up, as Cohen found out to his dismay. He notes that during his tour of duty in the 1880s, a substantial percentage of the cadre was German. Between 1855 and 1894, 73,000 troops left for the Indies; 45,000 were Dutch and the other 28,000 were men from every European country except Ireland, Iceland, and Turkey.[17] Although Ireland had a very poor population—and poverty was a better recruiter than patriotism—there were no Irishmen in the Indies because they constituted the bulk of the British rank and file.[18] The most unusual colonial troops were Africans. In 1837 the government sent a major to the Gold Coast in west Africa to buy the freedom of black slaves and bring them to Java for military service. By 1841 there were 1,500 Negro soldiers, divided in several all-black companies. After they revolted in Sumatra, the *blanda itam*, as the Indonesian soldiers called them (meaning "black Europeans"—*belanda* was the general term for a Dutchman and, by extension, any European, and *hitam* meant "black"), were dispersed throughout the army. Black troops were noted for their cleanliness, height, and bravery. Over the years their numbers dwindled, even though an effort was made during the 1860s to recruit freedmen. Only thirty were left in 1899, and by 1915 not a single one remained on active duty. Most had stayed in Java; for a long time there was a black district in the Javanese city of Semarang.[19]

The major reasons for joining the Dutch colonial army were economic or to escape criminal charges. Defoe put it succinctly: "The poor starve, thieve, or turn soldier."[20] There was also an element of adventure and romanticism that decided some in favor of a tour of duty in the tropics. As was the case with the French Foreign Legion, the Dutch colonial army could boast of a small number of foreign aristocrats who had to leave their native country and foreign officers who had been dismissed from their own armies for a variety of reasons. They were the equivalent of the British army's "gentlemen rankers"—of whom perhaps the most famous was T. E. Lawrence—who, in Kipling's words, were "the legion of the lost ones [and] the cohort of the damned." A recruit quickly felt he was a member of that legion as soon as he reached the main depot in Harderwijk, a harbor town in northern Holland.

Harderwijk was popularly known as "the sewer of Europe." It did not take long for a recruit to realize that he was now part of a confraternity of outcasts. The young women in Harderwijk deliberately held handkerchiefs to their noses when they passed a soldier, who was invariably dressed in his "iron suit" or "jailbird suit," as he called his gray uniform.[21] It is obvious that these nineteenth-century recruits were not of the best quality. Enlistment standards were steadily lowered because men were so difficult to come by. Their physical condition could be poor, they did not have to be more than five feet tall, and they could join until they were forty-four. For the first few weeks they could still believe they had done the right thing after they received the *handgeld* or "bounty," which had been the recruiter's greatest lure. In 1848 the amount was twenty-four guilders for a Dutchman and nine for a foreigner. But because of increased military activity in the colonies, this amount kept increasing until a bounty was worth 300 guilders in the 1870s for an enlistment of six years.[22] Cohen states that he received 350 guilders, which was a large sum at a time when 5 guilders a week was considered a decent wage. There was, however, a catch that most recruits did not know about: having accepted the bounty, a soldier was henceforth barred from becoming an officer.

Reality soon dispelled whatever romantic notions a recruit might have harbored. The humiliating attitude of Harderwijk's civilian population contributed to this sobering effect, but even more authoritative was the information provided by returning veterans who had reenlisted. Their presence was considered a serious demoralizing influence. In 1857 an attempt was made to keep such "old sweats," as Kipling called them, from going to Harderwijk because "their appearance is usually so dismal and miserable that they inspire fear and regret in those men who have signed up for the Indies, and who see the others return in such a pitiable condition from the very country that is their own destination. This repatriated personnel give the men in the barracks a very bleak picture of the East Indies."[23] Desertion suddenly became a very attractive alternative, as the military authorities were well aware. The new troops were marched to the transport ships under armed guard, usually by marines with fixed bayonets. No one was allowed to leave the ship after embarkation, including noncommissioned officers. (Due to a similar fear of desertion in the British army, only officers were allowed to disembark in Cape Town when ships stopped there on their way to India.)[24] Needless to say, it was considered better to try to desert before leaving the continent than to wait until one had arrived in the strange and alien tropics. Favorite places for escape were the Channel and, after the Canal had been opened, in Suez. Mutiny also was not uncommon on board troop ships, though it rarely succeeded and was always brutally suppressed.

The voyage to the colonial capital of Batavia in Java took three months; after the Suez Canal opened in November 1869, this was reduced to five or six weeks. When the recruits arrived in Java, they were brought to the depot in Meester Cornelis, a suburb south of Batavia, now known as Jatinegara. Here the craftsmen were separated from the general mass and assigned to special detachments; the rest were trained to become foot soldiers.

The ordinary soldier called himself "Jan," "Fusilier" (more often combined as "Jan Fusilier") or "Jantje Kaas" ("John Cheese"), the equivalent of the British army's "Tommy" or "Thomas Atkins." The native soldier called the European trooper *oom* ("uncle"). Another common name was *koloniaal* ("colonial"), and the entire army was referred to as "Jantje Kaas" (this came to include the entire colonial government as well) or "Jan Compagnie" ("John Company," leftover from the days of the voc).

The pay of "Jan Fusilier" was scandalous. Cohen mentions that he received the equivalent of a quarter a day when he arrived in Java, but that he was quite happy with it. By 1909, more than thirty years later, it had been increased to seventy-five cents. In 1909, a European sergeant who was married and had three children was paid 1.25 guilders a day, with twenty-five cents "indemnity."[25] On the positive side, there was the promise of a pension, a rarity in the nineteenth century. This one item indicates that there is some truth to the saying that the army was the state's "only welfare system,"[26] even if it was totally inadequate by modern standards. After twelve years of continuing service, a pension in Cohen's time amounted to 200 guilders a year.[27] In 1909, for a corporal who had thirty years' service, the amount was 330 guilders, and for a soldier, 275.[28] Such a sum was not enough to live on in Holland and a considerable number of retired personnel chose to stay in the Indies, where their pensions had more buying power. No matter how little this may seem to us, the Dutch veteran was better off than his British counterpart. In England, "in the early nineteenth century, the old soldier turned beggar was a common sight, dressed in shoddy old clothes with medals pinned on the left breast, their ribbons frayed and faded. Mendicancy was regarded as the normal, almost the only trade of the old soldier."[29]

Pay for native troops was lower than for their European counterparts. In the 1870s, a native fusilier was paid 6.30 guilders a month as compared with the 9.90 a European received. By the beginning of this century a married native soldier earned a quarter a day (paid every five days) plus foodstuffs.[30] Except for Ambonese and Menadonese troops, native infantry were not issued footwear until 1908.[31] Despite a ratio of three natives to one European soldier, there were practically no native officers.

The common dogface soon found out that, in the Indies too, the "other ranks," as the British officers condescendingly referred to the grunts and cadre, were even less welcome in civilian society than they had been in Holland. Even during the First World War, hotels and restaurants in Java refused admission to all military men except officers. It was not until 1934 that public notices were removed that stated that "military personnel below the rank of noncommissioned officer are not permitted in [this] establishment." The same held true in Victorian Britain, and any American who has been an enlisted man on active duty has encountered similar hostile disdain from civilians. In colonial society, the soldier was very much a pariah. Officers were tolerated, but not Jan Fusilier. It has been said that he preferred combat with the enemy to the animosity of the European population.[32] The soldier's sobriquets for civilian colonials indicate the social scale as perceived by the underdog who, as a popular British rhyme noted, is "adored when [the nation] is at the brink of ruin [but when] the danger is over, God is forgiven, and the soldier is slighted."[33] The colonial soldier called a civilian *buikje*, or "pot," because of his prosperous girth, and "politician," and one can be sure that the twain rarely met. And as if the civilians' distaste was not enough, the government also went out of its way to treat the recruits like animals. After 1830, the colonial military were no longer part of the Dutch national army but fell under the jurisdiction of the Colonial Ministry which was not known for its liberal disbursement of funds to the colonies. As ever cost-conscious, it, like the British government, preferred to replace efficiency with economy. The result was an undermanned, poorly equipped, disgruntled fighting force. Many military expeditions failed because of insufficient manpower and lack of equipment. At one time, authorities went as far as declaring underwear a luxury. Not until 1849 were undershorts replaced as regular issue.[34] In such a vast archipelago as Indonesia, troops had to be transported by ship as a matter of routine. They were always consigned to be deck passengers, and if cattle were taken on board, the soldiers had to share the deck with the animals.

The odds for survival in colonial military service were very poor, but disease, not combat, was the main killer. In one of the most ferocious and certainly longest military campaigns—the war with Atjeh (a realm in northern Sumatra), which lasted from 1873 to 1913—only 2,000 soldiers were killed, but more than 10,000 died from epidemical diseases, especially cholera and beriberi. Bas Veth's description of the arrival of a hospital ship from Atjeh depicts what was, unfortunately, a regular event. In 1876 it took 17,000 men to maintain a fighting force of 8,000.[35] These numbers were true for all Western armies. A report about the mortality rate of Dutch colonial troops from 1814 disclosed that out of a hundred men no more than seven were still alive after thirteen years, and, after twenty years, not a single one. In 1826 the mortality rate was twenty-one percent, in 1827 it was twenty-six, and in 1828 nearly thirteen percent.[36] If neither the enemy nor tropical disease killed a man, the medical corps would. An official report from 1881 admitted that the majority of medical officers in the colonial armed services were foreign rejects who spoke little or no Dutch. For over half a century there were never more than two hundred physicians on active duty in the entire archipelago,[37] and most were criminally incompetent.

One physician, while drunk, removed the uterus of a woman thinking it was a polyp, and the patient died. After his trial, the government recruited him for service in the Indies at a substantial salary. In his new function, he applied pure carbolic acid to a burn and administered twenty grains of "tart. emetic" to a native soldier who was suffering from asthma. One doctor died from delirium tremens and another from addiction to chloral hydrate. Two doctors committed suicide, several were dismissed for alcoholism, one for certified insanity, and seven had to be given medical furlough because they were unfit to serve after a very short time in the field. Cohen does not seem to have known that medical officers were seldom seen in uniform. They made their rounds in tails, white vests and pants, and hats.[38] In Nieuwenhuys's [E. Breton de Nijs] *Tempo Doeloe* one will find a curious photograph of a surgeon ready to operate on a patient *outside* a building, dressed in the way just mentioned, with a gardener looking on.[39] Lower hospital personnel were made up of recruits judged unfit for active duty. It is not surprising that the troops were more scared of being sent to hospitals than of facing the enemy.

And their foe was formidable. For over a century, say from 1816 to 1926, there was constant fighting in the colonial East Indies. Most of that fighting was guerrilla warfare. Driven by a fanatic courage and what in some cases amounted to a disdain for death, the Indonesian nations fought with a ferocity that did not allow for the sentiment of mercy. The most bitter fighting was in Atjeh and against the Balinese. Several cases have been recorded when Balinese aristocracy, both male and female, put on their best clothes and ornaments and attacked their colonial enemy en masse until the Balinese had all been killed.[40] The colonial army fought just as ferociously, for they knew that no quarter was given. To sustain this type of relentless combat for such a long period of time, a great number of native troops had to be recruited. They came from all over the archipelago, though the largest contingents were Javanese, Menadonese (from northern Celebes), and Ambonese. The latter two groups were considered outstanding fighting men and held a position of respect comparable to the Gurkha battalions in British India.

Besides the fact that they did a great deal of the fighting, native personnel was also invaluable for advising the European upper echelon. Even if not immediately implemented, their advice was generally heeded. In this respect the Dutch were far more progressive than the British high command.

In the bitter and brutal Atjeh War, any real success for the colonial army came only after they had adopted native tactics for counterinsurgency purposes. Outside Java, patrols came to be of a standard strength (called a "brigade") of eighteen men and a sergeant. Cumbersome and useless bayonets were abolished and the indigenous troops were armed with carbines and *klewangs*, a kind of saber that was also used by the Atjeh warriors. (European soldiers were never relieved of their ineffective bayonets.) Because most of the fighting was hand-to-hand combat, patrols thus armed became very effective, and there is no doubt that the Dutch finally gained the upperhand because their "small units, numerically weaker than the enemy," had become adept at using their opponents' weapons and fought on equal footing with courage and willpower.[41] The *benteng* was another device copied from native strategy. In practical terms, a *benteng* consisted of some sheds built in native fashion, surrounded by a bamboo palisade. Such outposts were not difficult to construct, and, if they were taken, they were not indispensable. In this manner the Dutch military presence could be prominently established outside large population centers.

The nature of this tropical warfare required a durable psychological cohesion among military personnel, a bond that had to be strong if it were to survive. Such a bond was only reinforced by the disapproval of the European civilian population who, as is attested to over and over again, regarded the "other ranks" as something akin to lepers. By force of necessity, the colonial army became a separate (but never equal) social structure. Its motto could well have been similar to that of the French Foreign Legion: *legio patria nostra* or "the Legion is our fatherland." As Alfred de Vigny (1797–1863), the French poet who spent thirteen stultifying years as an officer in the French army, knew: "The army is a nation within the Nation." Cut off from normal European social intercourse and at an enormous distance from their homeland, the European rank and file had to rely on each other for the companionship and human interaction that even soldiers need. The society of the native troops was closer and more solid than that of their European colleagues. The ethnic differences produced some curious reverse prejudices. Although all troops ate the same polished rice, native soldiers were proportionately less likely to contract beriberi because they were allowed to eat their rice with the customary *sambalan*, a native condiment made from hot peppers that have a high vitamin content. Although Europeans were flogged or caned even in the late nineteenth century, I have not run across any mention of the same punishment being meted out to native troops. It is likely that it was not used because public corporal punishment was such a disgrace to the native soldier that a man so disciplined became totally unreliable and would have to be discharged. Finally, the black African troops always marched at the rear of a formation—not because they were considered inferior but because their superior height would otherwise obstruct the vision of the smaller native and European soldiers coming behind them.

The colonial military "nation" was a world all of its own, with its own code of behavior, its own taboos, its own particular (and marvelously inventive) slang, and its own vices. The vices, were like those of any other armed service, be it American, British, or French. It is a triad familiar to anyone who has ever served: alcohol, women, and gambling. Of the three, drinking was by far the easiest escape from the harsh reality of military life. Drinking was officially sanctioned by the Dutch military authorities, as it was also by the British, although the Dutch were far more generous in their allotments. Recruits received a ration of "jenever," or Dutch gin, as soon as they had been quartered in the Harderwijk depot. When, in 1850, these same newcomers disembarked in Batavia, they were welcomed with a glass of arak and a dry bun.[42] Arak is a distillate of either molasses, rice, or the sap of the areca palm.

Liquor was also made available while the troops were at sea. An order issued in 1864 stipulated that on board chartered ships, gin was to be distributed as follows: "for European, African, and Ambonese noncommissioned officers and troops, and for European women: in the morning 0.075 Dutch 'kan' of jenever; in the afternoon 0.075 'kan' jenever; in the evening 0.075 'kan' jenever." A "kan" was about a liter, hence this was equivalent to a ration of a quarter cup three times daily. In Atjeh, during the 1880s, a sergeant or another NCO walked along the lines of men standing at formation and poured a glass of gin from a square, green bottle. The soldier that the glass was handed to had to down it with one gulp and pass it on to the next man. The gin rations were reduced over the years; by 1899 it was a deciliter per day, or about half a cup. One reason that alcohol rations remained in vogue is that gin was considered an effective medicine. A medical directive from 1863 strongly supported it because "recent experience has taught us that the administration of a certain amount of strong spirits retards the passage of food through the intestines, with the result that a man remains sated for a longer period of time. This is important for long marches when a man might be without food for a long time."[43]

There were, understandably, a considerable variety of colorful expressions for a drink of jenever. Perhaps the oldest was *soopje* or *sopie*, a term for a shot of gin already current in 1737. Another old expression, which became part of standard Dutch vocabulary, was *oorlam*, from the Malay phrase "orang lama datang," or "a person who arrived a long time ago," an "old hand." Most of the terms are untranslatable, but a few can be mentioned. Among the twenty-five I counted that were associated with jenever, I found "parrot soup" (*papegaaiensoep*), a "fat head" (*dikkop*), "hopping water" (*huppelwater*), "seawater" (*zeewater*), "straight up and down" (*recht op en neer*), and, because it warmed the stomach, a "bite of peasoup" (*hap snert*). The first drink was "incoming" (*inkommertje*) and the last one "outgoing" (*uitsmijtertje*, with a pun on the Dutch word for a bouncer, *uitsmijter*). Having a drink before going to bed was called either a "mosquito net" (*muskietennetje*) or "to put on a mosquito vest" (*een muskietenvest aantrekken*) because one presumably did not feel the mosquitoes after the drink. "Silverneck" (*zilvernekkie*) was a term for a good brand of beer, and "to conquer a captain" (*een kapitein veroveren*) referred to polishing off a bottle of Chabanneau cognac, a brand that had three stars on its label in the same configuration as the three stars on the collar of an infantry captain. A crate of jenever, manufactured by the A. van Hoboken & Sons Company, was simply called "a crate of A.V.H." (*een kist A.V.H.*) and such an empty crate came to be known as "an empty organ with 15 pipes" (*leeg orgel met 15 pijpen*). But the most curious expression was "to suck on the monkey" (*de aap zuigen*), a term originally invented by the navy. It referred to young coconuts whose milk had been removed through a small hole, which were then refilled with a wine called *saguer*. On the outside, the coconut looked intact and could be easily smuggled on board a troopship. Once at sea, the alcoholic content was sucked out with a straw.

The official ration was seldom enough. Because a trooper could not buy much gin, even if it was cheap, on thirty-five cents a day, he turned to native brews such as the aforementioned arak, tuwak, and saguer, which the British spelled "sagwire," a king of strong wine made from the sap of the arenga palm, a drink similar to what the British knew as "toddy." A European male who did not drink—and Cohen did not—was a rare phenomenon.[44] To the Indonesian population, drunkenness (*mabok*) became synonymous with being a Dutchman. A native woman considered herself lucky if she found a European man who was not *mabok* all the time when off duty, and who did not love the "square lout" (*vierkante lummel*, or jenever bottle) above anything else.

Relationships between Europeans and native women were both common and officially sanctioned. One reason for what has been called "concubinage," was the abysmal pay scale, which made it absolutely impossible for "other ranks" to support a family. Officers also fared no better during the nineteenth century. A royal proclamation from 1824 stated that officers, from captain down, would not get permission to marry unless they could prove "that one of the future marital partners, or both together, possessed the unencumbered property of a first mortgage valued at 10,000 guilders in silver, on a real estate property in the Dutch East Indies that has also been assessed for a ground tax of at least 20,000 guilders."[45] This was, to say the least, an absurd restriction. Even when the amount was lowered to 7,000 guilders in 1869, it remained an insurmountable obstacle. If a man had that kind of money he would be a man of substance and most likely would either not be in military service or be still living in Holland. The situation gradually got a little better for officers but it remained hopeless for the other ranks. Besides the bad pay, a married soldier lived in the barracks (commonly known as *tangsi*) in a small space separated from other inhabitants by only a sailcloth. Kitchen, toilet, and bathing facilities were shared communally with all the other married couples. Despite the high mortality rate, there were no insurance provisions for next of kin. Not until 1908 was a modest pension enacted for the widows and orphans of the other ranks. Because any such "improvement" was considered too costly, one will find that as late as 1900 only three married men of the other ranks were allowed per battalion. The colonial soldier had no alternative but frequenting brothels or, if he could afford it, keeping a native woman as a mistress.

In his memoirs, Cohen mentions how easy it was to obtain such a woman. In his case it would have taken a gift of a few clothes, some kitchen utensils, and a little money, amounting together to no more than one hundred guilders. Although the usual colonial term for such a mistress was *njai*—a Balinese word that originally meant "housekeeper"— among the military, especially in Java, the common expression was *muntji*, the Javanese word that also meant "housekeeper." Cohen remarks in a newspaper article that soldiers slept with their *muntjis* in the barracks in bunks that were no more than an arm's length away from the next man's, and without any separation to give even the illusion of privacy.[46]

With a hyprocrisy that was typical of relations between the military and civilian societies, such practices were decried in Holland as offensive, and the colonial army was considered "a training school for immorality." From what has already been noted about a soldier's life in the colonies, it is understandable that a single Dutch woman would never consider going to Java in order to marry a common infantry man. This could have been simply remedied by more money, but the Dutch government was far too niggardly to allocate funds for raising military salaries. In 1913 the colonial minister stated that his department "would put an end to the licensed barracks-concubinage among European and Christian native soldiers in the future, albeit very gradually"![47]

What was worse, the military command felt that European women would be a far greater liability in the barracks than native ones. "The presence of a large number of full-blooded European women would make it very difficult to maintain peace and order in the camps. Whatever the acknowledged failings of Indo-European and native women, they nonetheless possess, without exception, the quality of being able to preserve an outward appearance of modesty. . . . This modesty is generally foreign to full-blooded European women from the milieu from which most of the lower ranks come. For this reason, any significant importation of such women would inevitably give rise to situations which, far from promoting good morals, would seriously undermine them and, consequently, would undermine the discipline of the men as well." [48] Even if this Dutch general's opinion was wrong, the common foot soldier would not have found many matrimonial prospects. In most European nations, families were horrified if a daughter contemplated marriage with a military man, particularly if he was a member of the other ranks, and it seems there was not much enthusiasm for such a notion among the Indonesian population either. This certainly is the major reason why soldiers preferred to choose their partners from socially less accepted circles.

No matter how one looks at it, it remains a fact that "sex and liquor were the two primary concerns of the enlisted man." [49] In the Dutch colonial army, this fact was openly acknowledged and acted on accordingly; however, the fate of the native woman and her Eurasian offspring was lamentable. Her man could leave her for any reason, and if he returned to Europe after his tour of duty was up, he very rarely took his *muntji* and her *liplap* children along; they would only be an embarrassment in the morally "superior" society of nineteenth-century Holland. Such illegitimate children were known in the Indies by the delicate phrase *kepaten obor*, or "extinguished torch," since they "fell outside the circle of light that was provided by the burning torch of the legal and paternal acknowledgment of the father." [50] These children were often abandoned by *both* parents and faced a very bleak future, but in the last decade of the nineteenth century a Dutchman from Haarlem came to the Indies hoping to alleviate their misery. In 1893 Johannes van der Steur (1865–1945) opened a home for such children in Magelang, a garrison town and military depot in central Java. The Dutch government assisted his admirable work with sporadic, meager subsidies, yet the "Oranje-Nassau Institute" was still in existence after the Second World War. Another philanthropic attempt— though perhaps more self-serving—was a rather unique military academy, established by Lieutenant-Colonel Von Lutzow in 1847 near Purworedjo in central Java (it was later moved to Gombong). It became known as the "School for Wards" ("Pupillenschool") and was in operation until 1912. It took in abandoned boys and educated them in a military fashion. Most of the boys joined the same army their unknown fathers had served in, and a large number of them became noncommissioned officers.

The life of a native woman whose husband was a native soldier was not necessarily any better, as can be surmised from *Anak Kompenie*, the sober, knowledgeable account of life in the colonial barracks by Lin Scholte. The majority of native troops were married, and they made up two-thirds of the professional fighting forces. Since the life of a married native trooper had much in common with that of his (much rarer) European counterpart, it may be useful to mention a few particulars. All unmarried soldiers, the *budjangs*, and all married native troops below the rank of noncommissioned officer lived in large camps called *tangsis*. Married native NCOs lived in small houses outside the *tangsi*, and the "heavenly bodies," that is anyone who wore stars, i.e., officers, lived even further away. In the barracks, called *chambrees* by the Dutch, separate living quarters were indicated by sailcloths that were strung on wires like curtains. In the present century the chambrees were separated by a low wall, with their openings onto the common area covered by an olive-green curtain, nicknamed the "morality curtain." The main piece of furniture was the bunk bed, known in the nineteenth century as a *slaaptafel* or "sleeping table." It had a metal frame that held two plank beds with *tikars*, or mats, on them, which was the case in normal village life. A family had often more than one child, and the children slept on *tikars* on the floor and under the bunk bed. That space under the bed was known as *kolong*, hence the common name for *tangsi* children was *anak kolong*, the colonial version of our "army brat." This specialized language was part of what constituted a self-contained and singular world that perpetuated itself. Daughters married soldiers, and sons became soldiers in their own right. *Tangsi* life was regulated by military rules and regulations. During the morning the women did all their cooking and washing in a separate building popularly known as the "women shed." At noon the families were reunited in the chambrees to eat and have the requisite tropical siesta. At three in the afternoon, women and children had to leave again while the men performed their duties. After 5 P.M. the families were once again together in the chambrees until next morning's reveille at six.

The Dutch colonial army was not alone in having to face the constant problem of desertion. Both native and European soldiers went over the hill. The Dutch fusilier was particularly likely to buck the system and frustrate discipline. Cohen was not remarkable in this respect, except for his obdurate persistence, wherein he resembles Prewitt in James Jones's *From Here to Eternity*.

Military law at the company level was rather arbitrary. Every territorial commander was ordered to announce a perimeter around the camp outside of which a soldier was not to go. If caught outside this radius he could be punished with disciplinary action at the pleasure of his commanding officer. More often than not the culprit was busted, forfeited his pay, and was caned with a rattan, not to exceed fifty strokes. A soldier could appeal such a sentence, but Cohen's experience shows how little that mattered. As if to remind him of what was in store for him a soldier saw every day the physical affidavits of the penal code. They came in the shape of "bears," convicted native hard-core criminals who acquired that name because they wore shackles and reminded people of chained bears at country fairs. Their reddish-brown uniforms probably contributed to this impression as well (the same uniforms were the reason that they were also known collectively as "the red battalion"). "Bears" were to be found throughout the archipelago performing most of the nasty or dangerous chores. Their major task was to act as bearers for military patrols. They also made roads, carried the litters (*tandus*) made of a piece of sailcloth that was slung between two bamboo poles and used to transport cholera and beriberi patients, as Bas Veth described, or buried the dead, particularly those who had died from contagious diseases. If they performed particularly dangerous chores they were rewarded with a reduction of their sentences. One example of such a chore was associated with the "walking ambush" in Atjeh. This referred to armored freight cars with vents in the sides for the twenty soldiers inside to fire through. Such a car was propelled by four "bears" whose upper bodies were chained inside the car while their legs stuck out below and whose job it was to push the contraption down a narrow-gauge railroad track.[51] There were also more congenial chores: "lampbears" took care of the lamps when a unit was on bivouac, "teabears" made tea for the lieutenant, and the "kitchenbear" had perpetual KP duty.

A native criminal was not the only one who found himself in chains. As late as the last decade of the nineteenth century, the colonial army could still sentence *any* man to "ball and chain," a punishment one would have thought to have vanished with the Middle Ages. In Cohen's account of the Pontjol military prison in Java, one will find a description of that punishment, as well as the chilling fact that a prison commandant could order it at will and for as long as he felt necessary. The list of punishments a soldier could incur was quite long, and it appears that Cohen experienced almost all of them.

Keeping all the aforementioned evils in mind, not to mention the horrendous mortality rate, it is no surprise that many troopers loved to get a "red passport," a document that indicated they had been dishonorably discharged. Cohen got one of these. Men would go to great lengths to escape *de laatste vernieuwing* ("the last renewal," i.e., a coffin) that would bring them to the military graveyard, known in the last century by the expressive phrase *kampong dièm*, Malay words that mean "the quiet vil-lage." One ploy in Atjeh was to acquire the swollen legs so typical of beri-beri patients. If one managed to fake them long enough, a man became a medical reject, though a sign was tatooed on one of his buttocks to make sure he would not reenlist.[52] Another, tougher, way out was to deliberately provoke disciplinary action that resulted in incarceration in the stockade at Ngawi in Java. After a man had been there 365 days, he was discharged from the service.[53]

And yet, despite all the particular afflictions here mentioned, the life of a soldier was not any better in other armed forces. Every army had its own version of the disciplinary hell. The British army in the Victorian era was loath to abolish flogging; it was still on the books in 1914.[54] Another punishment, the whirligig, was a wooden revolving cage that was whirled around with great velocity. The person inside it always became violently ill. Along with flogging and being put in stocks, the whirligig was also a punishment for women.[55] Corporal punishment in the French Foreign Le-gion was infamous. The following passage from William Jay Smith's mem-oir, *Army Brat*, summarizes the life of the American soldier at about the same time as Cohen's experience, and recapitulates everything we have noted about the Dutch colonial soldier.

At the turn of the century the Army enlisted man in the United States was treated as an outcast, a worthless individual. Soldiers were not allowed to enter respect-able places of entertainment, and respectable young women would never be seen with them in public. The number of desertions during the fiscal year ending June 1889 had increased at such an alarming rate that something clearly had to be done. To investigate the situation Frank L. Woodward of the St. Louis *Post-Dispatch* en-listed at Jefferson Barracks, and in a series of articles, collected in *The Dogs of War* (1890), he made some sensational charges. The officers of the post, he said, were unnecessarily cruel and overbearing; the food was unfit to eat; vermin in-fested the quarters; and men were placed under arrest on the most trivial charges and confined to the guardhouse, which was indescribably filthy.[56]

In light of all these circumstances it is surprising but nonetheless true that some remarkable men volunteered for the colonial army. It should be mentioned again that they were not drafted and that there was no con-scription. The most famous volunteer was not Dutch. Arthur Rimbaud (1854–91) signed up in 1876 as a fusilier at the age of twenty-one. He left Harderwijk in June and arrived in Java in July. He was assigned to the First Infantry Battalion stationed near Salatiga. He deserted in August of the same year, having been a colonial fusilier for less than three months.

The two greatest naturalists of the colonial era were the Germans Rumphius (1628?–1702; see the volume in this series entitled *The Poison Tree*) and Junghuhn (1809–64; included in this anthology). Both volunteered for service in the colonial army. Rumphius was an "ensign" in what was still the private army of the VOC and Junghuhn went as a health officer and was in the service from 1835 to 1845. An iconoclast somewhat in the spirit of Cohen, Sicco Roorda van Eysinga (1825–77) served as an officer in the Colonial Corps of Engineers from 1844 to 1855. He was praised by Multatuli for his vociferous criticism of colonial policy and was the author of the political lampoon about King William III that indirectly caused Cohen to be tried and sentenced for lese majesty. Another man who, like Van Eysinga and Cohen, became a journalist after his military service was Willem Walraven (1887–1943) who is also represented in this anthology. Two other remarkable figures associated with the colonial army were Pieter Bleeker (1819–78) who became a famous ichthyologist and published a standard work on Indonesian fish, and Eugène Dubois (1858–1940) who, like Bleeker, was a doctor in the army, and who between 1891 and 1892 discovered the famous Java Man, the fossil remains of *Pithecanthropus erectus,* once considered the missing link in the evolutionary development of mankind.[57]

Finally, there was C. Eijkman (1858–1930) who served briefly as a medical officer in Java but returned home because of ill health. He went back to the Indies as part of a team charged by the government to find the cause of beriberi. While his colleagues pursued the wrong clues, Eijkman discovered that there had to be a substance in the fleece of unpolished white rice that prevented people from contracting the disease. He published his researches in 1896, and his theory, which had been based on work with chickens, was applied to humans in various prisons in Java and Madura and proved to be correct. Yet Eijkman encountered a great deal of resistance from his colleagues and he returned permanently to Holland in 1896. His work gradually found more and more acceptance, particularly in the United States. Eijkman received the Nobel Prize in 1929 for his work on what in 1911 had been called "vitamins."

One must admit, however, that when all is said and done, remarkably little has been written about the daily life of the colonial soldier not engaged in combat. One will find some officers in a number of novels, particularly in Daum's fiction, but they are no more than dapper extras in the theatrical parties of the colonial upper class. An exception is Du Perron's portrait of Arthur Hille, in chapter twenty-five of *Country of Origin* (1935; published in this series), a tough but admirable officer who served in Atjeh. There are a few war novels, such as Székely-Lulofs's *De hongertocht* (Journey of Famine, 1936) but those are not what I have in mind. *Halfbloed* (Halfcaste, 1946) by J. Fabricius was one attempt to describe the life of the ordinary infantryman when not on campaign, but it is an indifferent novel. The only firsthand account of *tangsi* life is Lin Scholte's *Anak kompenie* (1965); it is well written (though not very accessible to foreign readers because of the large number of Malay expressions) sober, and successful in its attempt to be objective. That it is written from the viewpoint of a *muntji* makes it all the more interesting.

M. T. H. Perelaer (1831–1901) wrote a long autobiographical novel about his life as a career officer. Primarily dealing with his many years of service in Borneo, the tetralogy was published between 1884 and 1885 as *Een kwart eeuw tussen de keerkringen* (A quarter of a century between the two tropics). In 1881 Perelaer published a curious novel entitled *Borneo van Zuid naar Noord* (Borneo from south to north). It purportedly tells the adventures of four deserters of the colonial army—two Swiss, a Belgian, and a native trooper—during their harrowing trek through the jungles of Borneo. The novel contains a great deal of information on the Dayaks, culled from Perelaer's scientific study *Ethnographische beschrijving der Dajaks* (Ethnographical description of the Dayaks), published in 1870. Perelaer's novel was published in a translation by Maurice Blok in this country under the silly title *Ran Away from the Dutch or Borneo from South To North* (New York, Dodd, Mead and Co., 1887). Another officer who used his experiences for literary purposes was W. A. van Rees (1820–98). Considering that he began writing after he retired he wrote a great deal, but from a literary point of view his work is not distinguished. As a source of information about the colonial army it still has some value, especially *Herinneringen uit de loopbaan van een Indisch officier* (Reminiscences of a career colonial officer, 1862).

Dutch colonial literature does not have a writer like Kipling who was able to present the British colonial Tommy with sympathy and affection in the collection of stories *Soldiers Three* (1895) and the narrative verse of the *Barrack Room Ballads* (1892). If one excludes novels about soldiers in war, American literature does not have that many examinations of G.I. Joe's life either. Two outstanding exceptions are James Jones's *From Here to Eternity* (1951)—the title was taken from Kipling's poem "The Gentleman-Rankers"—and Smith's *Army Brat* (1980). Such paucity of chronicles about barracks' life makes Cohen's account all the more valuable, particularly because descriptions of military hoosegows are even rarer. That, besides Cohen's lively style, is the reason for its present inclusion.

THE soldier has always been an outcast, an expatriate in his own country as well as in any other nation he has been ordered to invade. He is, as Alfred de Vigny noted, both "victim and executioner, the scapegoat who's daily sacrificed to his people and for his people." [58] An invisible man, he does not find approval or honor in society at large and is forced to make do with his own kind. His is a hard life that requires bitter talents. Napoleon was well aware of that. His prescription (in *Maxims of War*) for a successful military man would hardly be touted on a recruiting poster: "The primary necessity of the soldier is the steadfastness with which he can bear fatigue and privations; bravery is only secondary. Poverty, privations, and misery are the tuition of a good soldier."

Ironically, there is a certain resemblance between the soldier and the European colonial. From the point of view of Europe the colonial was considered an inferior alien. His labor made governments wealthy, yet when the chips were down he found out that he was quite expendable. He too was asked to obey and serve and never question his mission. Alfred de Vigny made an observation about military life that applies to both soldier and colonial: "We must deplore the servitude, but we should admire the slaves."

✦❦✦

The steamer *Patuah* brings me to Palembang; the couple of days at sea were wonderful despite the fact that I was a deck passenger, and they were followed by a couple of hours going up the river Musi.[59] Cholera was raging in Palembang at the time—against a wall behind the hospital a stack of coffins was ready for use—and I don't see more of it than the *benteng* where I spend a week waiting for further travel orders. The city, the *kota*, is off limits.

I seem to remember the journey from Palembang up the Musi River to Rantau-Bajur. From there, together with some other personnel, I make the trip up the Lematang River to Muara-Enim on board a small paddle steamer that, because of the many curves in the two rivers, steams very slowly and carefully. To pass the time, the captain shoots every so often at crocodiles that lie with their dirty yellow snouts gaping wide on the mud near the banks. Whether it's hit or not, the beast shoots rapidly into the water while lashing it with its tail. At night we ride at anchor in midstream and hear the hoarse roar of tigers.[60]

I disembark in Muara-Enim because the boat doesn't go any farther, sleep one night in a "passanggrahan," [61] and leave the following morning, before daybreak, for Lahat in a "kahar sapi," a small cart pulled by a cow. The path leads for the most part through virgin forest where the thick foliage filters the sunlight to a semi-darkness. Large, dark monkeys (*lutungs*)[62] vault through the trees high above my head, and their shrill cries echo in the immense silence.[63] I am drunk on Robinsonism and, while still in this mood, I reach my destination after two days.

Lahat is situated on a plateau near the swift and, at this point, not navigable Lematang River. On the other side stretches a lowland—the Passumah lands I think—that was considered "unsafe" at the time. Wilderness and jungle surround the little town in three out of four directions. In the distance, halfway between. Lahat and the southern coast, the enormous, blunt cone of the Dempo looms. This is exactly the landscape I wished for in my dreams.

The garrison—two companies, the second and third, of Sumatra's Eastcoast garrison battalion, plus the crews of four muzzle-loading cannons and a couple of mortars, commonly known as "cat heads," say six men and a gunnery sergeant— is billeted in bamboo barracks that are inside the earthen ramparts that surround the *benteng*. Also inside the *benteng* is a small hospital built of wood, while outside it are the three offices of the major, who is the garrison commander, the lieutenant-adjutant, and that of the lieutenant-quartermaster. The latter office is where I work, along with a civilian clerk, the Ambonese Noja.

My superior is Lieutenant Kempers, a young man of around thirty. He is quiet, shy, and melancholy. I never saw him laugh. He treats me kindly and sometimes asks me one thing or another, thereby indicating that he has some interest in me: where I come from, what I know, where I got the notion to come to the Indies when I am still so young, and so forth. Once in a while I go by his house to get some papers signed. He's married and his wife who, like him, has no pretensions, lets me play with their child sometimes. Lieutenant Kempers lends me a magazine or a book from the reading box[64] occasionally. All in all, I couldn't be better off.

I do the same thing as in Meester Cornelis and Weltevreden: writing out vouchers for suppliers . . . so many times so many grams, that is so many kilos meat, rice, bread, coffee, or salt. For the rest I make up reports: weekly reports, monthly reports, and trimester reports. Monotonous? To be sure. But I've got a lot of time off. I go for walks in the woods, and spy on birds, monkeys, snakes—there are emerald, purplish-red, and vermilion ones, also some that are leaf-green with a red tail, and some with black and white squares—bronze grass lizards, flying lizards, and stick insects.

I also learn Malay because I want to know it better than what is normal among European soldiers. [. . .] While in camp I prefer to be with the native soldiers who interest me far more than my own kind because, generally speaking, the latter's limited conversation has little to recommend itself. But outside I am every day overwhelmed by my never diminishing fascination for the glorious mother-of-pearl dawn, when the sun rises over the thin, pink mist at daybreak and is greeted by the languid cooing of the *perkututs*;[65] or the melancholy dusk that descends very rapidly and melts all the colors and hues into a somber velvet, and the imposing silence of the night that is made more profound and solemn by the rustling hum of a myriad insects, and the bronze resonance of the giant toads. I muse, I dream, I'm happy. I succumb to a pantheistic piety.

And so several months go by, months without incident, months of passive bliss. Except for the lieutenant-quartermaster, I've little to do with anybody else. Except for my administrative chores, I have no fatigue duty. There is, of course, reveille at five in the morning, lights out at nine P.M., lining up for chow, and the monthly inspections. But those regulations don't bother me, nor do they even displease me. After all, the rest of the time I'm a free man!

But then occurs that little business that brings an end to all those delightful things, while its consequences gradually drag me down into a whirling maelstrom of unpleasant tribulations. I am not complaining about what happened, never did, nor do I have any regrets. Because, before anything else, you've got to pay the price in this world. And what is too high for the rare jewels that are known as self-respect and independence? Perhaps I could have done it at less cost. But I was proud and sensitive, in the double meaning of "sensible" and "susceptible." [. . .] It all came about because of Dr. Prochnicz, the medical officer, and my de jure justified but de facto impractical inflexibility.[66]

The doctor, a Pole, is always in civilian clothes when he makes the rounds of the hospital or when he's off duty. I don't blame him for that. But I can't stand that he never returns my salute. My point is that, if I salute him it is pure politeness on my part, because I don't have to salute an officer in mufti. The first time I thought it likely that the doctor hadn't seen me, or perhaps he was absentminded, which can happen to the best of us. But some days later he didn't return my salute again. I'm becoming irritated, but decide to try it once more. A couple of weeks or a month later I meet him again. I salute him as correctly as possible—"the open right hand against the garrison cap while looking at him, my superior in rank, with pride and respect"—but with the same negative result: he does not return my salute. That's it, he can go to hell as far as I'm concerned. And I can go to hell myself if I ever salute him again, unless he's in uniform.

Some time later I meet the doctor again, at night, on the main road. He is, as always, "in mufti." We pass each other no more than three feet apart. I look him straight in the eye—not for anything in the world would I have pretended that I had *not* seen him, or pretend that my thoughts had been elsewhere—and I don't salute him. He looks at me with surprise, the way a man does when he can't believe his eyes, but doesn't say anything, at first. But I'm not more than a few steps past him when he calls after me: "Fusilier! . . . fusilier!" I don't look back and keep on walking. I am *not* a fusilier. I am a company clerk! Not that I would take advantage of that. Good Lord, no. If he had tried to flatter me and had called: "General!, general!" I still would have kept on going. He yells another couple of times: "Fusilier! . . . fusilier!" then turns around, overtakes me, stands in front of me and says:

"Didn't you hear me call you?"

"No!"

"You want to tell me you didn't hear me?"

"No, not that! I *did* hear you. . . . "

"Then why did you keep on going?"

"You called 'fusilier,' and I'm not a fusilier."

"You're not a fusilier? What are you then?"

"I'm a company clerk."

"I see. That's why you kept on walking?"

"Yes!"

"Fine! . . . Tell me mister clerk, don't you know who I am?"

"Yes, I know."

"And who am I?"

"The doctor."

"So you *do* know. Why didn't you salute me?"

"Because I don't have to."

"You don't have to?"

"No! I don't have to salute you when you're in civilian clothes."

"I see, that's what you think?"

"No, I don't think so, I know so!"

"I'll teach you otherwise."

"No, you won't. I don't have to salute an officer in civilian clothes. . . . As far as you're concerned, I've saluted you over and over again, but you've never saluted back. You never did. That offends me. . . . "

"So, mister clerk is offended. That's too bad."

"Yes, it is. That's how you offended mister company clerk. I was polite to you when I didn't have to be, and you don't respond to my politeness. I won't salute you anyore."

"You'll be hearing from me."

"Fine."

The next morning the sergeant in charge of quarters tells me that I've got to report to the commanding officer. That is done at nine, so I go as usual to my office where I have to be at seven. My superior, the lieutenant in the quartermaster corps, who comes in an hour later, has already heard about it, and while shaking his head, tells me I've done something crazy and that there's no doubt I'll get punished for it.

On the stroke of nine I report to the office of the major. He appears after a moment, settles a couple of things, and then asks curtly:

"Why don't you salute your superiors?"

"But I *do*, sir."

"No, you don't. You didn't salute the doctor last night and you also had a big mouth about it. . . . What dya got to say for yourself?"

"The doctor was in civilian clothes, Major, and he never returns a salute. . . . "

"That's none of your damn business. You salute your superiors even if they're walking around in pajamas. Understand?"

"Yes sir, but . . . "

"Shut up. . . . Eight days guardhouse[67] for not saluting a superior. You can go."

I do my office work as usual but when I'm through in the evening I'm locked up in a cell in the guardhouse, a dank hole where I also have to stay for two entire Sundays.

When my eight days are up, I ask permission to see the commander. I "raise objections"—that is the official phrase—to the punishment I received and want to appeal to the immediate superior of the person who imposed the penalty, in this case the commander of the garrison battalion at Palembang. The major gives me a nasty look:

"Ah, so now we're an appellant too. . . . Do you really think you'll accomplish anything with that?"

"Well, at least I'd like to try, sir. I was unjustly punished. . . . "

"Shut your trap. I'll submit your appeal. Dismissed!"

A week or so later I have to report to him again and Major Van den Broek tells me triumphantly that my appeal was considered unfounded by the battalion commander who, due to the "unfounded appeal," sentences me to fourteen days in the guardhouse.

"I'm sure you've had enough now," the major presumes sarcastically.

"I'm not sure yet, sir. I'll think about it."

When my fourteen days are up I ask again permission to see the major.

"Now what you want?" snarls he.

I answer that, because I feel aggrieved by the fourteen days detention, I want to appeal to the Court of Military Review.[68]

"You want to bring this to the Court? Have you thought about this?"

"For fourteen days."

"Do you know that this means restriction to quarters until there's a decision from the Court?"

"Yes, I know. But it's worth it."

"You insist on appealing to the Court of Military Review?"

"Yes."

"Fine. Then you're restricted to quarters from this moment on. Dismissed."

Again a couple of months pass. During that time I can't put a foot outside the *benteng* except to go to and return from the office of the lieutenant-quartermaster. Because ten or twenty times a day between five A.M. and nine P.M., between reveille and tattoo, they sound the bugle for muster for those men who're confined to barracks.[69] It is the signal that invites me to report without delay to the sergeant in charge of quarters—the NCOs have been ordered to keep a sharp eye out for me—who inspects me every time very carefully. And if, as once happened, I arrive for muster with one of my uniform buttons only half or even a third through a buttonhole I get the sarcastic and hyperbolic advice that it would be better if I "appeared bare-assed" and am put on report and punished for appearing "in undress" at muster.

It rains punishments: detention in the guardhouse, stockade, solitary.[70] They're out to "get" me, as they say, and nothing is easier than catching me.

Major Van den Broek's face shines, and his usually creaky, wooden voice is ecstatic when he reads me one morning the decision of the Court of Military Review:

"The Court convened etc.; considering, etc.; declares that the appeal of clerk Cohen, serial number 15527, concerning the penalty imposed by the Commander of the garrison battalion Sumatra East Coast, is without grounds, and imposes twenty-one days of detention."

The major asks me if I got what I wanted and expresses once more his assumption that I must have had enough of appealing.

"No," I tell him. "I'm just getting to like it. The rest you'll know after I'm through with my twenty-one days."

He bursts out laughing, but it seems rather forced to me.

"So, you're just beginning to like it? Me too. We'll cut you down to size yet. You can go."

No! I'll be damned if I will. I'm not going to let it pass. I was unjustly punished from the very beginning. I didn't have to salute the doctor, and I want to see if there's any justice to be gotten, even if every stone has to be turned.

The major narrows his cold, gray eyes down to slits when, after my time is up, I ask to see the major again, of course, and inform him that, since I'm not satisfied with the decision of the Court of Military Review, I want to appeal to the Court of Military Appeals in Batavia.[71]

[That court decides in Cohen's favor, but he is still locked up.]

At the time of the Court of Military Appeals' decision I am in preventive detention for an upcoming court martial due to repeated insubordination. The reason is that I've gone crazy during the long months prior to the judgment, crazy from all the pestering, and I've now become completely wild. My emotional state is similar to that of a man who's run amok. The more they punish me, and the worse it gets each time—stockade, and then solitary, that is to say, locked up every day on water and rice, or locked-up-every-other-day-on-water-and-rice, with my right hand shackled by means of a short chain to my left foot, or my right foot to my left hand—the more indifferent I become to *all* punishment. I couldn't care less about being restricted to quarters, and leave the *benteng* to go into the forest whenever I feel like it. And though I do not drink—not because I'm virtuous but because I don't like the taste of jenever—I'm put on report by I don't know which one of the subaltern[72] sycophants for "being intoxicated" and am punished for it despite my protest against the false accusation. When my four days stockade are up I walk, although I am restricted to quarters, to the canteen outside the *benteng*, and gulp down, despite gagging, two "thick heads," which is to say two times ten centiliter [i.e., about a cup] of jenever and a moment later I bump on purpose into the lieutenant-adjutant: "Okay, lieutenant, now can you punish me for being drunk. Now I'm *really* drunk."

If, at a given moment, I've got to do, say, thirty-six days stockade and solitary at a stretch, and during that time have to "stand bediri"[73] again for something or another, I tell the major while he's giving me an additional eight days: "If I were you I'd make it an even fourteen."

I keep on smashing everything in the guardhouse to smithereens: the trestles of my bunk, the bunk itself, the lock of my chains, along with the chains. I demolish the barred wooden door. When I leave for Palembang in May or June of 1884 in order to appear before the Court of Military Review, I've run up a debt "to the nation" of over sixty guilders, and a record so bad that there couldn't be many like it in the East-Indian army. I've paid a heavy price for my triumph, but they couldn't break me.

I don't want to give the impression that I encountered in Lahat only injustice, harshness, and viciousness. There were a couple of good men among the officers. There was first of all my immediate superior, the lieutenant-quartermaster who, without saying one word of course, or without making any gesture that I could have interpreted as agreement with my resistance, did whatever he could to moderate my bitterness. For instance, in order to give me a chance to break the monotony of my endless restriction to quarters, he came up with the following: he sometimes ordered me to deliver personally the vouchers I had written to the various suppliers rather than have the civilian clerk, the Ambonese Noja, do it. The trips back and forth between the camp and the *kampong* where the bread Chinese, the rice Chinese, the meat Chinese, etc., lived were "duty," because of the lieutenant's order, and therefore not punishable. But the success of Lieutenant Kempers's friendly trick was unfortunately of short duration. After it had been reported a couple of times that I had "been seen outside the *benteng*" and been "absent at the detainees's muster" and, in order to clear things up, had argued that I had been out on official business, Major Van de Broek, the commanding officer, put an end to this partly illegal hooky playing after a ferocious dressing down of my poor, timid boss.

Another officer who was sympathetic to me was the commander of the third company, Captain Stevels. He was a big fellow who loved a "pop"[74] and was idolized by his men, both European and native. When he was the duty officer of the week and had to come to ask the prisoners every day if "they had any complaints," he had the opportunity to ask me the same standard, but in practical terms, useless question. He always did so by addressing me in a soldierly but well-meant fashion:

"Goddammit kid, you're in the clink again? What a mess. I wish I could keep you outa here. I'm sure that if you'd been in my company, it never would have gone this far. I would've talked with the doctor. But I can't do anything about it now."

And Captain Stevels, who sported an enormous ash-blond handlebar mustache, would throw up his hands in despair and walk away. [. . .] But I should not forget fusilier Heinzl, my bunk mate, i.e., my neighbor in the barracks during the rare times I slept there and not in the hole.

Heinzl, who comes from Luxembourg where he had been a miner, is my only friend. He's almost twice as big as I am, and twice as old. He has a short red beard, luxuriant flaming-blond hair that stands straight up, and enormous hands. Heinzl doesn't say much, and if we go for a walk on Sundays we sometimes walk beside each other for half an hour or more without ever saying a word. I love Heinzl and look up to him because he's such a good man. He can tell me anything he wants and I will never take offense. He's constantly scolding me. As far as the business with the doctor is concerned he thinks that I was completely wrong. If I didn't want to salute him, I should have looked the other way and pretended that I hadn't seen him. And as far as my appeals are concerned—to the battalion commander, the Review Court, the Appeals Court—I should never have started with it. Heinzl does not condone my conduct. But when I'm in the clink and he's the one to bring the chow—and he sometimes swaps duty with somebody else in order to get that job—he gives me all kinds of food, though he's in danger of getting caught and liable to severe punishment. He does it like this: the provost sergeant unlocks the various, dimly lit cells in succession and, without saying a word, Heinzl gives the temporary inhabitants their chow. When he comes to my cell he quickly steps inside, loudly slams the mess kit[75] on the bunk I'm lying on, snatches at the same time the garrison cap off his head and puts it back on almost immediately, and a small package of sambal, a couple of fried bananas, a fillet of fried fish, or a meatball falls next to or on top of me. Heinzl is out of my cell at once and the sergeant, who stayed outside and hasn't noticed a thing, locks the door again.

Good, noble Luxembourger Heinzl! Together with the German Oskar Raffauf and the Frenchman Bastier—the last two were fellow inmates at *Fort Prince of Orange*, popularly known as Pontjol near Semarang—these men constitute the international trio who helped make life over there, that hard and bitter but also proud existence, bearable to me.

There was one thing that might have kept me from taking that dangerous route that started with my intentional refusal to salute the doctor. [. . .] And that would have been taking a "housekeeper." "Housekeeper" was the virtuous official definition for a native girlfriend. The soldiers talked less euphemistically of a "broad."

I had seen in the *kampong* a beautiful child who, though she was still at home, I would have gladly elevated to the rank of my "njai." Officially there was nothing against such a thing. But I lacked the capital, the measly sum I needed for Djuwita's modest trousseau: a couple of colorful *badjus*,[76] one or two sarongs, a mattress filled with kapok instead of straw, and the indispensable kitchen utensils. I wrote my father for one hundred guilders, but I did not mention that I needed the sum for setting up a household. I think I hinted at wanting to buy some Malay grammars, some civil service regulations, and such other passionate literature. At my request, Lieutenant Kempers was kind enough to add a few words to my letter. He certified that I "had ambition and wanted to get ahead," which was all true. I had an enormous ambition to get to Djuwita.

Three months later I received a registered letter . . . with twenty-five guilders. Farewell matrimonial notions. Farewell my graceful Djuwita. I had sworn from the bottom of my heart, I don't know how many times, that her divine body was as slim as the *pinang* palm, her voice as melodious as bamboo leaves rustling in the evening breeze, her eyes as soft and deep as the eyes of the *kidang*, her teeth as white as the fruit flesh of the *mangistan*, that her down skin had the golden luster of a ripe *langsep*, and that her blue-black hair shone like the plumage of the *mentjo* bird, also known as *beo*.[77] . . . During our second or third meeting I had given her a European *slendang*, . . . the talleth that I had seldom used and is, therefore, in almost pristine condition. My pious stepmother had put it in my leather trunk on the last day of my home leave, along with a complete set of prayer books and my tefillin, because she was convinced that they would come in handy one day. Well, I got a lot of fun out of my "talleth." So did Djuwita. Every time she went to the market she draped the "slendang blanda" around her body and used the four white satin "tsitsis" bags at the corners to keep the cents, half nickels, dimes, and quarters separate.[78]

The passionate company clerk poses, but the Good Lord disposes. If my father had sent me the hundred guilders instead of twenty-five, my idyl with Djuwita would probably have never ended and I, weakened by the pleasures of Venus— love, *durengs*, and *gamelan* music[79]—would have put up with all sorts of things. Who knows, I might have saluted the boorish, nongreeting doctor till my dying day, and would have humiliated myself forever. But the way things went, with me incapable of setting up housekeeping in any solid, material sense, I was forced to take back my word . . . Selamat tinggal, Djuwita. Selamat tinggal, hati ienten.[80]

[Cohen was sentenced to two and a half years of imprisonment for repeated insubordination and was sent to the military prison called *Fort Prince of Orange* in Java, where he arrived at the end of June 1884.]

I can't say that my first look of my new residence—with its tarred black walls and the deep, dry moat around it—put me in a good mood when, between two fusiliers with rifles and fixed bayonets and with a sergeant at my heels, I walked over the bridge and entered below the arch of the gate. But inside it wasn't as bad as I had imagined while in custody in Palembang or in the awful House of Detention in Batavia.

Covered with tar down to three feet off the floor, with the rest painted white, the vaulted barracks in the square fort were all connected without doors or bars, and received light and air their entire width from an opening, like a half circle, in the wall that looked out on a spacious courtyard with four trees in it. The iron berths with their bedding, consisting of a straw mattress, a pillow, and a spread, were the same as in ordinary barracks. The internees, who wore their own uniforms, still had their regulation leather trunk and, if they wanted to, could have a wooden chest as well to hold their personal belongings.

If you didn't know you were in a prison you would not have been able to guess differently from the look of the barracks. Nor would you have known it from the chow, which was like that in regular camps and, generally speaking, no worse. If a man had money, i.e., if he was paid for his work, he could between 5 P.M. and 5 A.M. buy additional food from the "housekeepers" who were allowed to go into the fort: fruits, *sajorans,*[81] *sambalans,* eggs, fried fish, and so forth. Smoking was permitted in one's free time and all of Sunday, but not in the barracks.

In order to be finished with the subject of "treatment," let me mention that for the tractable ones, life in Pontjol was quite bearable. A man who does his work—making clothes or shoes, or whatever fatigue duties he might have—and who keeps his mouth shut when a superior rants and raves, who does not protest, who is completely devoid of anything that even remotely resembles imagination, and especially a man who arrives at *Fort Prince of Orange* without a record like mine, such a man can easily get along. Duty, to give a name to the forced labor, is not excessively hard. For men sentenced to a maximum of six months, it usually consists of such ambulatory chores as cutting grass for Piet, the bowlegged horse of the quartermaster, sweeping up leaves, weeding the inner courtyard, sawing and chopping wood for the kitchen, filling up the stone purifiers with water,[82] and the like. If he's got six months to two years, a man is usually assigned to the tailor shop where, after a short apprenticeship, he is set to making blue cotton tunics and pants, serge coats, and garrison caps for the army. Shoes are made by internees and the "chastised" ones who've got to do more than three years.

The so-called chastised—a picturesque term—are delinquents sentenced to a minimum of five years with loss of rank, due to theft or some other common law offense, or because of military delicts such as deserting to the enemy, or actual insubordination.[83] They're dressed in uniforms that have every kind of military insignia removed from them. Their barracks are no different from those of the military internees, and there is no partition of any kind to prevent or hinder an exchange between the two categories of inmates, although neither is allowed in the other's quarters. It is an injunction few obey and which, for that matter, makes little sense because in the workshop, or while doing any kind of work, both categories are always in contact with each other.

The workshop is about 150 feet from the fort. It is a huge shed, with an *atap* roof, and is surrounded by an iron fence. Men work there every day, except Sundays and holidays, under the professional supervision of a sergeant and a corporal tailor, a sergeant and a corporal shoemaker, while discipline is maintained by several "overseers,"[84] two sergeants and several corporals. There is a deafening noise of about a hundred sharply clicking sewing machines, the rumbling and banging of the press—for the shoeleather—and the tapping of tens of shoemakers' hammers.

Around the inner courtyard, below the living quarters, are the various magazines, as well as the laundry room, the dank *mandi* room, the latrines, and the holding cells which I quickly become acquainted with and where I will spend many a day. And if the reader also knows that *Fort Prince of Orange* was surrounded by a *rawah*, or swamp, and that when there was a flood, this courtyard was sometimes inundated—when I was in Pontjol a giant turtle once swam inside, was captured and killed in a gruesome fashion, and became part of the chow—then he might have some idea of the place that for two and a half years was my compulsory domicile.[85]

My first meeting with Captain Hamel, the commanding officer, was anything but affable. We made a most unpleasant impression on one another: I because of my horrendous personnel file—they had not removed the unlawful sentences but rather, with perfect malice, had underlined them with red ink—and he because of his repulsive appearance and unnecessarily hostile tone of voice.

Captain Hamel was over sixty, a broad-shouldered, big fellow with green-gray eyes that stared at you as coldly as those of a fish, with shaved jowls, a mustache of rusty wire, and on his pimply temples spitcurls he had greased and flattened with brilliantine. He had the soul and intelligence of an adjutant, a "chien du quartier" or "barracks dog" as such creatures are called in the French army, and I think that he had only been kicked upstairs from adjutant to captain in order to lend some prestige to his function as a prison warden.

When I was presented to him at muster the day after my arrival, he immediately began to lash out at me. He banged furiously with the back of his right hand on my file that he was holding in his trembling left hand and which he had apparently just read that morning. He assured me that, no matter what, they'd know how to cut me down to size, and that he'd keep a sharp eye on me and that nothing—"You understand soldier?"—nothing whatever would be overlooked. He finally recommended me to the special care of the subalterns: "Adjutant, you

don't let that man out of your sight. He's to report to me for the least little thing."
He spat at me like a cat a little longer—"You've been warned"—and decreed that
I would be trained to become a tailor, the one job I had never felt any inclina-
tion for.

Fifteen minutes later I was brought to the tailor shop by the corporal tailor, a
fat slob of a tallow German who was called Fatzke or Pratzke or something like
that, and who was constantly tripping over his saber. I was instantly put to the
task of ripping apart outmoded garrison caps that were to be restyled. He told me
that I'd better be careful not to cut either the cloth or the piping with the sharp
shoemaker's knife that I'd been entrusted with, or he'd put me "auf rapport."
That would also happen if I failed to take apart less than the minimum number of
topis[86]—ten or fifteen a day, I think.

Corporal tailor Fatzke, or Pratzke, who indeed put me "auf rapport" several
times for professional mistakes or oversights, is not Pontjol's only NCO representative of the Teutonic fatherland. The cadre is almost all Germans! A German, a
Saxon, sergeant Lange, a pockmarked, sneaky *sbir*[87] with an ash-blond beard
who speaks a pidgin Dutch. He has the physiognomy of a rain-drenched bat who,
in order not to be heard when he's snooping around for trespasses or when he
tries to listen to our conversations, takes off his shoes and puts on felt slippers so
he can slide noiselessly through the barracks. Other Germans are the corporal
"overseers" Ahrens, Frasch, Clemens, and Pauli; the last two, one a Rhinelander,
the other from Hanover, are decent fellows who do not take advantage of their
position and try very hard not to report people.

The cadre has only three Dutchmen. One of them is Adjutant Engers, from
Groningen, and is another one you can have. Captain Hamel's order to keep an
eye out for me he has taken to heart with a warmth that deserves a better cause.
Then there's Sergeant Berton, or Berdon, from Limburg, who's usually drunk but
leaves us alone, and the sergeant tailor, a hairy, bowlegged dwarf, in love with his
gold stripes. When he emerged from his magazine one morning and walked into
the yard, he was hit on the head with a pole[88] by Bout, a "chastised" one, who he
kept putting on report for all kinds of nonsense, and was knocked out cold. Bout,
who already had to serve ten years, got another five, but he said that he couldn't
care less. As far as the sergeant tailor was concerned, he became not only *post
hoc*, but as *propter hoc* as possible, perhaps not a better, but certainly a wiser
man, who didn't pester anybody anymore and seldom put a man on report.[89]

[As was to be expected, it rains punishments on R. 5215, as Cohen is
known in Pontjol. One of them is rather surprising.]

The "ball and chain" punishment meant that the penitent for whatever number of
days, or a month, or two months, or for "an indefinite period of time," was forci-

bly loaned an iron ball of about sixteen pounds with the requisite chain about five foot long, with the understanding that the chain was to be fastened to the left or right ankle, according to what the party in question preferred, by means of a three-inch wide iron cuff with a heavy lock.

To tell the truth, I found this trinket, which you had to wear at night as well, a little bit of a problem at first. But you get used to anything, even to what is most unpleasant, as long as you've made up your mind not to give in. I had already noted with understandable interest what other prisoners did to make the punishment more bearable. They would wrap a piece of seam material around the cuff in order to prevent the leg from being chafed raw, or fasten the heavy lock to their calf by means of an ingenious device of shoemaker's thread and a little strap, or keep the chain at hip level, again with a piece of seam material, and the ball had become, quite literally, bearable. I won't go so far as to say that this punishment was fun, and that I didn't feel much lighter during the twenty minutes, out of every twenty-four hours, I was rid of the iron ball, chain, cuff, and lock, so I could take a bath, that is to say, pour lots of cold water over myself in the *mandi* room, otherwise known as a bathing facility. But I've always been quick to adapt and with one, two, or three and a half months of constant practice in how to handle the ball, it became a habit, as if second nature. My virtuosity in juggling my sixteen pounder was soon without equal. While you were working, the thing was on the ground of course. But while marching, or when coming to and going from the workshop, or at chow call, etc., one normally carried the ball on one's shoulder. And it wasn't long before I didn't even have to hang on to the ball when I balanced it on my left shoulder while I walked. It was a triumph of the spirit—the spirit of resistance—over brute force when I became the only one who after work was over in the evening and while defying punishments and penalties, climbed with my stumbling block the small stone steps that came out onto the safe roof of the fort. Once up there, I made the rounds several times with my hands in my pocket and the ball on my shoulder. From the roof I could see the sea, the sea wherein, according to Baudelaire, the free man sees the reflection of his emotion.

I am treated, of course, to the entire gamut of punishments that Captain Hamel has at his discretion. There is no restriction to quarters in Pontjol, nor being put in the guardhouse. The lightest sentence is the hole or solitary, usually with only water-and-rice. The hole is a narrow cell, about seven feet long and just over three feet wide. It contains a narrow plank bed, a chamber pot, and a water jug. [. . .] But let me recall some of my comrades.

There was Hubscher, from the Hague—quiet, silent, kind Hubscher. I would never have understood how he got five years if he hadn't told me that, when he was drunk, he had done bodily harm to a sergeant. He was my bunkmate in the barracks, just like Heinzl, who resembled him temperamentally. And just like Heinzl but with equal lack of success, he berated me for my rebelliousness. "What good does it do, man? They'll simply destroy you." And he counseled me to be resigned and to have patience. But his friendship was not restricted to words. When I was shackled with the ball and chain and therefore somewhat hampered in my movements, he'd do my laundry for me: "Come on, gimme your dirty stuff. I've got to do a laundry anyway, so it makes no difference." For that matter, I seldom had the necessary couple of cents to buy a bar of soap because for most of the time my weekly wages amounted altogether to nine cents. And they regularly subtracted half from that pittance, say four cents, to pay back the debt of some sixty guilders I owed the government.

Payday, when we received our "pocket money" and our wages—five, ten, or fifteen cents per workday, according to the capacity and industry of the prisoners—payday was on Sunday morning, near the Gate. The first time when I, burdened with my ball and chain and therefore "devoid" of wages, was to receive the princely sum of five cents I caused the lieutenant who was present—because there was also a lieutenant who, I think, was called Verbeek, an insignificant fellow who gave me eight days in the hole once for "looking disrespectfully" at him—I caused him fits of indignation that time when I, with a grand gesture, deposited the five cents I had just received in the collection box for the band that was hanging on the wall behind his chair. Because Pontjol boasted of a military band made up of half a dozen internees who several times a year, especially on the King's Birthday and on Christmas, obliged us with performances that were both deafening and heartbreaking, though full of good intentions.

Just as quiet as Hubscher and, like him, sentenced to five years detention for insubordination, is the Frenchman Bastier. He is a pleasant fellow, uneducated but civilized by nature as so many Frenchmen are, and who can't tell me enough about France, the country I have yearned for ever since childhood. Because of him I can perfect my French, and he learns some Dutch from me, a language that had enough interest for him to ask me, after my sentence expired, if I would send him a French-Dutch and a Dutch-French dictionary. I kept my promise in Leeuwarden and added a pipe—one I paid for with honest money—to the two dictionaries.

Besides Bastier, there are two other Frenchmen in Pontjol: the two "chastised" ones by the names of Durand and Mauléon. Durand is a tall, skeletal man from Paris with frizzy hair and a face that's almost black from working in the sun. After serving seven years in Algeria, he wound up in Harderwijk and signed up for the "East." When he had served four of his six years he got an inheritance of 20,000 francs. He bought a substitute[90] for the two years he still had to serve, caught the boat to Marseilles, from there a train to Paris, and spent all his money in a couple of months, except for the sixty francs he needed for a train ticket to Harderwijk. Ten months later he was in Pontjol, sentenced to five years and reduction in rank. He always called me "Moïse" [Moses], and it was by this name that he called out to me some years later on the boulevard des Batignolles where, covered with two sandwichboards, he was eating a piece of bread on a bench. I took him home with me and we had lunch together and talked about Pontjol. What else would we talk about? I never saw Durand again.

Mauléon—"le petit père" or "daddy Mauléon" as he was called by us and by his own people—Mauléon is a very short, luxuriously overgrown little man, with graying hair and beard, and a crooked nose that makes him look very distinguished. He maintained that he'd been a captain in the merchant marine, in command of his own ship. But he'd had some "bad business" that brought him, by land, to Harderwijk where he signed up as a colonial soldier. Once he arrived in the Indies he thought he had gotten himself into some more "bad business." In order to get out of it he'd stolen something—some shoes from the garrison's clothing depot I think—and sold it, which got him five years and the desired discharge from military service, after serving his sentence, of course. He found life in Pontjol, where they'd put him to making shoes and where he spent his free time solving problems in algebra and geometry, far more congenial than when he was still with his company and had to drill, go on patrol, stand guard, have barracks inspections, have to shine his buttons, maintain his rifle, and all that sort of stuff. And when I bumped into him now and then and inquired how he was—"bonjour capitaine, comment allez-vous"—he almost invariably answered: "comme un rat dans un fromage, mon ami!" which for him represented a social position—that of "being a rat in a cheese"—that was the most enviable.

Again I have been sidetracked. I was talking about the various punishments I received in Pontjol.

The reader is now acquainted with the ball and chain, and solitary is less of a mystery to him than it was for Sergeant Laheur and his cronies. But the reader has not been introduced yet to caning, a corporal punishment reserved for extremely serious offenses. Such an extremely serious offense usually referred to the fact that you had been "cocky," that is, you didn't keep your mouth shut when you're being abused by some sergeant or corporal or other, or by the adjutant, or by the "old man" himself, Captain Hamel. And thus it happened that I, too, came "to lie on the bench" three times because I never could keep my mouth shut when something was bothering me. Once I got ten lashes, and twice I received twenty. The first time I resisted forcefully, but I was grabbed by four "chastised" ones who had been commandeered for this, was overpowered, and tied to the bench. The next two times I thought it better, because more dignified, to take it stoically and laid down on the bench after giving the adjutant, who was acting as sheriff, and the two "overseer" corporals, Ahrens and Frasch, an unmistakable look of contempt and defiance. They got back at me for that. The adjutant did by counting as slowly as possible . . . one! . . . two! . . . three! . . . ," thereby prolonging the punishment as much as possible. His two helpers got back at me by wielding their finger-thick rattans, which they had put in water the day before to make them supple, as hard as they could, raising them as high as possible before coming down on my behind that was only covered with a thin cotton pair of pants. This was child's play for Ahrens, a brute six foot tall, who enjoyed his work immensely. But Frasch, who had a case of hydrocephalus not from water but from gin, had boiled-fish eyes and an enormous red mustache, Frasch is rather small and in order to get better leverage he has to jump several inches off the floor every time. This lends it a comic air, although the punishment is otherwise hardly that and extremely painful. After it's over, the patient is locked in the hole for twenty-four hours so he can think it over and repent. He's given some grub and a bucket of water to cool off his behind that is black and bruised from the lashing.

I get more and more used to the ball and chain, it hardly bothers me anymore. And if Captain Hamel expects—which he does—that, after an indeterminate amount of time (say a week or so) and while promising to behave better, I will request to be "dismissed" from the thing, then he's dealing with the wrong person, i.e., my stubbornness. Ask for mercy? Never! It makes the "old man" sad, while it is also, to a certain extent, damaging to his reputation. My obstinacy, that is no secret to anybody, gives a bad example and breaks all the time-honored rules of the place that say that an "indefinite one"[91] keeps walking around with his sixteen pounder until, after six or eight weeks, he has finally succumbed and with his tail between his legs comes to ask for *ampon*. But to ask for *ampon* or "mercy" never occurs to me and I'm becoming something of a problem. Because they can't keep me shackled to a ball and chain until the end of my sentence—I mean detention—simply because I refuse to humiliate myself.

One morning when I'm busy sweeping up leaves, the adjutant addresses me:

"Hey Cohen, how long you've got that ball and chain now?"

"I'm not keeping tabs, but I bet it's something like three weeks."

"You're nuts, man? It's at least over two months!"

"If you know it so well, why'd you ask me for?"

"Oh, well, no reason. . . . If I were you I'd ask to go see the C.O. and request to be dismissed from the ball and chain. Perhaps the captain will grant it."

"No, I won't. If the captain thinks that's been long enough then he can remove the thing himself. But I will never ask him."

"Whatever you say, I couldn't care less. It don't bother me."

And in order to show that it doesn't bother me either I grab the sixteen pounder which, while we'd been talking has been lying on the ground, and swing it by its chain onto my left shoulder with the grace that comes with long practice, and walk away. Between parentheses I should mention that my shoulder had a cushion of calluses many years after I had been "dismissed" from the ball and chain, from Pontjol, and from the colonial army.

My work at that time was making buttonholes, and I earned ten cents a day, which meant that on Sundays I received sixty-nine minus thirty-four, or thirty-five cents pay. But I much preferred the other kind of work: sweeping up leaves, cutting grass, sawing or splitting wood for the kitchen, etc., that only brings in five cents a day. Every so often I was perfectly willing to incur eight days solitary or fourteen days of the ball and chain, in order to be busted from tailor back down to an ambulatory forced laborer at half pay.

Captain Hamel had another "bête noire" besides me; the "chastised" Vetter who, like me, was considered a fantast. Once I was on muster with him when the captain—after he had ascertained that the regulation shoes Vetter had made weren't sufficiently elegant—wanted to know what my neighbor had been in civilian life. That was his stereotypical question of anyone who had to report to him because of negligence or indifference in the workshop. And depending on the answer—bricklayer, exotic dancer, grinder, fisherman, eelsmoker, house painter, or pianist—the sentence was: so many days solitary or so many days ball and chain. The sentence would either be light or severe depending on whether Captain Hamel—who divided mankind in two categories: that of shoemakers and tailors—felt that the man who was standing in front of him had had in "civilian life" more to do with making shoes or making clothes.

"What did you do in civilian life, soldier?"

"Sword swallower, captain," answered the "chastised" Vetter calmly and with the straightest face in the world.

Captain Hamel was speechless for a moment. Sword swallower! That man in front of him had been a professional sword swallower. It never occurred to him that Vetter was pulling his leg. He was dumbfounded because he couldn't see a connection, right there and then, between sword swallowing and shoemaking, yet it had to exist as a "given" for him in order to be able to appreciate the man's transgression and figure out the commensurate punishment.

After half a minute of silent reflection, he brought his hand to his spitcurl. He had seen the light! A sword equals a shoemaker's knife. If a man could handle a sword, and in such an unusual way as that, requiring the utmost caution, then that man would also be able to wield a shoemaker's knife. And if he didn't do it properly then it was obviously unwillingness on his part.

"Fourteen days ball and chain! And don't let me see you again soldier!"

But he did see Vetter again some time later when he sentenced him to eight days in the hole because he had been "in improper uniform at evening muster." The "improper uniform" had consisted of a bunch of cock feathers in Vetter's ass, who had otherwise been stark naked and covered with shoe polish from top to toe and polished to a high gloss by one of his buddies. He had acted the wild man before a large and enthusiastic crowd and bitten off the head of a live rat as part of his act. Enthralled by the performance, not a single man had remembered muster until we suddenly saw Sergeant Laheur and Corporal Frasch in our midst. Vetter jumped headlong from the wooden crate he was parading on and came to attention in all his glory. It was so funny that even Laheur couldn't suppress a smile, an exceptional manifestation of rapture on his part, though it didn't prevent him from reporting the rat swallower, along with ten other military internees he'd caught in the barracks that had been off limits to them.

I mentioned in passing the "housekeepers" who, between sundown and sunrise, were allowed to enter Pontjol and could sell all kinds of food they'd brought with them from the outside. Only prisoners with the most irreproachable conduct, of course, were allowed to have a housekeeper and of that select group, only four or five were honored with the semi-official title of "whoremaster." A whoremaster was very popular with the men. It was a matter of course that he got a corner spot in the barracks and he was the only one who, with tacit agreement of the cadre, was allowed to enclose his extramarital couch with a mosquito net, read: a bedspread hung from a piece of rope. He loaned out his girl to the men for cash only, at an approved rate—one guilder for an hour, three for the night—and would graciously make his corner bunk available to his clientele. But only the bunk, not the mosquito net. Because it was live and let live, and the latter was the Walloon Lardennois's business. He functioned as the "tukan klambu" or "mosquito-net man" who, for the modest sum of a dime, ensured that the couple was shielded from the indiscreet glances of coming and going personnel by means of three bamboo slats attached to three of the bed's four legs, a couple of ropes, and two bedspreads. I should mention for the sake of truth, that, to my knowledge, neither a corporal nor a sergeant (including Laheur) ever disturbed anyone's amorous sport when he was making his nightly rounds. For this discretion they will be forgiven a great deal in the Hereafter.

We have a whoremaster in my barracks as well. His name is de Hondt, an enormous, blond Belgian who, when he left Pontjol several years after me, must have left with quite a nestegg. Because his girl was the youngest and nicest of the four or five housekeepers (hence had the most clients) who, as delegates of the fair sex in *Fort Prince of Orange*, brought a little poetry into our prosaic existence. De Hondt is a scrupulous man and an inexorable opponent of any kind of favoritism. First come, first serve, if I may put it like that. He keeps strict records of the requests he receives, and serves everybody in chronological order. The only one for whom he breaks the rules now and then is me, due to my particular situation as an outlaw who's never sure about tomorrow night and who, in all likelihood, might wind up in the hole or be hobbled by the ball and chain. It's true that the latter does not entirely prevent me from having a delectable tête-à-tête, but it isn't very cosy either. That's why that good soul de Hondt, who's always susceptible to reason, allows mercy to replace justice when I've sold my bread for a period of ten days or a month and as a result am in possession of one or of three guilders and come to ask him if Innôh is free that evening and if she might be inclined to "go out" with me, so to speak. He begins immediately to object, has to consult his agenda first. [. . .] But when, as a matter of principle, he has upheld the motto "everyone's got to wait his turn" for a while, he succumbs in the end to my argument [. . .] and changes the order of the sequence after he has very diplomatically consulted with the other men who also crave a "night of love."

About ten months before my time was up, and being sick and tired of getting the ball and chain and solitary for all kinds of nonsense, yet still as indomitable as ever, I had the original notion of putting my objections to Captain Hamel's conduct in writing and sending them to him. Because whenever I reported to him I never succeeded in getting anything through his thick skull, and all my attempts richocheted off the fellow: "Shut your trap man!" and usually resulted in more punishment. I felt that there was nothing left but to put it black on white.

I took a big chance doing so, and there probably was no precedent for this in the annals of Pontjol. In the letter I accused Captain Hamel of making it impossible for me to stay out of harm's way because he kept recommending me to the cadre's disfavor, and insisted on punishing me with heavy sentences for what were often piddling offenses and breaches of discipline, most of which I had never committed. I further told him that I was only in *Fort Prince of Orange* in order to serve the two and a half years of military detention I had been sentenced to, but not to be punished ad infinitum for my behavior in Lahat, behavior that had nothing to do with him and which, for that matter, had been the result of a series of unwarranted disciplinary punishments that had been interpreted as such by the Court of Military Appeals, something that he must have seen in my personnel file. I assured him, in case it still escaped him, that the punishments he gave me wouldn't reform me or make me repent, and I announced that as soon as I was free again I would make public, by means of newspapers (the journalist had already reared his head), how he had mistreated me.

I read my letter over again several times, changed a few things here and there, and thought that it was good. But being infinitely more pretentious than the Creator of heaven and earth who otherwise had also been much pleased by his Handiwork (see Genesis 1:4, 10, 12, 18, 21, 25), I was not satisfied with this conceited epistle and, in order to make a greater impression on Captain Hamel, I added without blushing that I "had talent, even an infernal talent" (I still recall those exact words) and was sure, therefore, to find a hearing for my future disclosures.

And that is that. My letter is finished. What will be will be. After all, things couldn't get any worse. He would punish me, of course—I counted on getting twenty strokes with the rattan—for this unheard-of display of lack of discipline. But I am sure, intuitively sure, that I will be left alone after that, or, at least, they wouldn't be "after" me anymore. And so . . . come what may.

But there still remained the problem of how I would get the letter into Captain

Hamel's hands. He would never accept it at muster. That was unthinkable. Nor was it possible to entrust my epistle to the sergeant in charge of quarters, as we had to do with our normal correspondence (unsealed of course). The man would have refused to accept it because there simply couldn't be any kind of correspondence between an internee and the remote commandant of *Fort Prince of Orange*. Besides . . . not for anything in the world did I want the cadre to know of my daring attempt to intimidate their boss, the captain of the "overseers." [. . .] The opportunity for sending my letter presented itself fairly soon. I entrusted it to a comrade whose time was up and who promised me that he'd mail it that same day in Semarang. And so, with understandable anxiety, I waited to see how things would work out.

[Cohen's scheme worked. He was allowed to work in the prison library and was left alone for the remainder of his sentence.]

My time was up on Christmas Day 1886, and I left *Fort Prince of Orange* early in the morning, after I'd heard the good news the day before from Captain Hamel. At his request, I was to be discharged from the army as "completely unmanageable" with a passport Letter B.[92] Good old Captain Hamel!

I stayed eight days in Semarang, but on the second of January 1887 I boarded the *Gelderland* and arrived in Rotterdam on the nineteenth of February. Along with around twenty other repatriated soldiers, I left the same day for Harderwijk in order to be mustered out at the Colonial Recruiting Depot.

I would much rather have stayed in the Indies and look for a job there. I loved the Indies, while there wasn't much that attracted me in Holland. But, unfortunately, I didn't have enough money to stick it out, no matter for how short a time, until I'd find employment. Hence I was forced to return to Holland. But I wept when I saw Java's coast recede in the distance.

NOTES

1   Biographical material is based on the first volume of Cohen's autobiography: Alexander Cohen, *In opstand* (Amsterdam: Van Oorschot, 1976). Subsequent page references to this work are given in the text. Further material is taken from *Alexander Cohen. Uiterst links. Journalistiek werk 1887–1896*, ed. Ronald Spoor (Amsterdam: de Engelbewaarder, 1980), hereafter abbreviated as *Uiterst links*; and from *Alexander Cohen. Uiterst rechts. Journalistiek werk 1906–1920*, ed. Max Nord (Amsterdam: de Engelbewaarder, 1981), hereafter abbreviated as *Uiterst rechts*.
2   *Uiterst rechts*, 14–16.
3   Octavio Paz, *Conjunctions and Disjunctions*, trans. Helen R. Lane (New York: Seaver Books, 1982), 37.

4 *Uiterst rechts,* 8, 193–95. It is a nice irony that in Atjeh, *mata-mata* referred to people who spied for the Dutch colonial government; see the Van Dam article listed in note 12 below.

5 Menno ter Braak, *Verzameld Werk,* 7 vols. (Amsterdam: Van Oorschot, 1950–51), 6:360.

6 For Van Eysinga, see *Sicco Roorda Van Eysinga. Zijn eigen vijand,* ed. Hans Vervoort (Amsterdam: De Engelbewaarder, 1979), and my note 49 to the chapter on Van der Tuuk, above.

7 I am not sure what Cohen meant by this term, in the original *korporalisme.* Perhaps it refers to an excessive interest in the material, i.e., corporal, aspects of life?

8 *Octave Mirbeau* (1850–1917) was a novelist, playwright, and polemist. He was a fierce controversialist who loved to cause scandal. His political trajectory was the obverse of Cohen's: he started out on the right and ended up on the extreme left. He was an anarchist, an antimilitarist, and against organized religion. A. M. *Lugné-Poe* (1869–1940) was an influential director, actor, and author who brought controversial contemporary works to the French stage, often at great risk because of censorship.

9 For Cohen's love of France and his last years near Toulon, see: Max Nord, "L'amour d'Alexander Cohen pour la France," *Revue de culture néerlandaise* 10:2 (September 1981): 32–37.

10 Ter Braak, *Verzameld Werk,* 6:363.

11 In the original, "resistance" is *opstand.* This may be translated as "revolution" but that clearly was not Cohen's interpretation of the word because he used it as the opposite of "revolution."

12 This section is based on information from the following sources. The article "Leger" in *Encyclopaedie van Nederlandsch-Indië* (ed. D. G. Stibbe, 2d. ed. in 4 vols. and 3 supplements [The Hague: Nijhoff, 1917–32], 2:545–62) is primarily useful for listing the endless but ineffective reforms during the span of more than a century; abbreviated as *Encyclopaedie.* This work is supplemented by H. L. Zwitzer and C. A. Heshusius, *Het Koninklijk Nederlandsch-Indisch Leger 1830–1950* (The Hague: Staatsuitgeverij, 1977), abbreviated as *KNIL.* One of the most useful sources for the history and language of the colonial soldier in the nineteenth century is J. J. M. Van Dam, "Jantje Kaas en zijn jongens. Bijdrage tot de kennis van den Ned.-Indische soldatentaal in de 19e eeuw," *Tijdschrift voor Indische Taal-, Land- en Volkenkunde* 82, no. 1 (1942): 62–209. Van Dam is the source for all the military terms I have used, except where noted.

13 Byron Farwell, *Mr. Kipling's Army* (New York: W. W. Norton, 1981), 20.

14 *Encyclopaedie,* 2:546.

15 Van Dam, "Jantje Kaas," 68.

16 Ibid.

17 *KNIL,* 12–13.

18 Farwell, *Kipling's Army,* 80.

19 H. J. de Graaf, *Wonderlijke verhalen uit de Indische historie* (The Hague: Moesson, 1981), 123–26.

20 Quoted in Farwell, *Kipling's Army,* 85.

21 Van Dam, "Jantje Kaas," 69, 92, 142.

22 *Encyclopaedie,* 2:559. See also the article by Fred Lanzing, "Gedane veldtochten, bekomen wonden, uitstekende daden, bijzondere verrichtingen en ontvangen belooningen," *Maatstaf,* no. 5 (1982): 1–7. It is an account of the author's grandfather who enlisted at the age of fifteen! The article has some inaccuracies.

23   Van Dam, "Jantje Kaas," 88.

24   Farwell, *Kipling's Army,* 242.

25   Data from Van Dam, "Jantje Kaas," 85, 89.

26   Farwell, *Kipling's Army,* 85.

27   Paul van't Veer, *De Atjeh-oorlog* (Amsterdam: De Arbeiderspers, 1969), 160.

28   Van Dam, "Jantje Kaas," 85.

29   Farwell, *Kipling's Army,* 190.

30   Lin Scholte, *Anak kompenie* (The Hague: Moesson, 1965), 5.

31   *KNIL,* 10.

32   Van Dam, "Jantje Kaas," 74, 90.

33   Quoted in Farwell, *Kipling's Army,* 93.

34   Van Dam, "Jantje Kaas," 78.

35   Van't Veer, *De Atjeh-oorlog,* 118.

36   Van Dam, "Jantje Kaas," 79.

37   *KNIL,* 136.

38   Van Dam, "Jantje Kaas," 80–81, 137.

39   R. Nieuwenhuys [E. Breton de Nijs], *Tempo Doeloe. Fotografische documenten uit het oude Indië* (Amsterdam: Querido, 1973), 82.

40   Mochtar Lubis, *Het land onder de regenboog. De geschiedenis van Indonesië* (Alphen aan den Rijn: A. W. Sijthoff, 1979), 129.

41   Van Dam, "Jantje Kaas," 98; *KNIL,* 49, 99.

42   Van Dam, "Jantje Kaas," 71.

43   Van Dam, "Jantje Kaas," 83.

44   This was (is) no different in the American army. As William Jay Smith observed in his fine memoir of American army life in the 1920s and 1930s: "Over the years drinking became a matter of pride and a badge of merit" (*Army Brat: A Memoir* [New York: Persea Books, 1980], p. 42).

45   Van Dam, "Jantje Kaas," 85.

46   Cohen, *Uiterst links,* 61.

47   Van Dam, "Jantje Kaas," 86, 87.

48   Hanneke Ming, "Barracks-Concubinage in the Indies, 1887–1920," *Indonesia,* no. 35 (April 1983): 84–85.

49   Smith, *Army Brat,* 153.

50   Scholte, *Anak kompenie,* 47.

51   Van Dam, "Jantje Kaas," 149–50.

52   Van't Veer, *De Atjeh-oorlog,* 162.

53   Van Dam, "Jantje Kaas," 148.

54   Farwell, *Kipling's Army,* 99.

55   *The Rambling Soldier: Life in the Lower Ranks, 1750–1900, through Soldiers' Songs and Writings* (Harmondworth: Penguin Books, 1977), 65–66.

56   Smith, *Army Brat,* 66.

57   For a survey of anthropological research in the Indies prior to the Second World War, see Robert von Heine-Geldern, "Prehistoric Research in the Netherlands Indies," in *Science and Scientists in the Netherlands Indies,* ed. Pieter Honig and Frans Verdoorn (New York: Board for the Netherlands Indies, Surinam and Curaçao, 1945), 129–67. See also Gert-Jan Bartstra, "Some Remarks Upon: Fossil Man from Java, his Age, and his Tools," *Bijdragen tot de Taal-, Land- en Volkenkunde* 139, no. 4 (1983): 421–34.

58   The quotes by Alfred de Vigny are from his memoir about French army life, *Servitude et Grandeur Militaires* (1835), published in various editions. All translations are mine.

59   The present text is an edited translation of chapters seven, eight, and nine, from Co-hen's book of memoirs *In opstand*. The switching back and forth between the present and the perfect tenses is peculiar to Cohen's style, at least in this book. In translating the termi-nology for military life in the colonial army during the nineteenth century, I have tried to furnish American equivalents, but they cannot always be exactly the same. When there is a problem, I have indicated it in the notes. In order to distinguish Cohen's ellipsis from my own, which I use to indicate a passage left out, I have put the editorial ellipsis between brackets.

60   Cohen's trip to Lahat begins in Palembang, which was the largest city and trading cen-ter in Sumatra. Lahat was built on a number of islands formed by various smaller streams which branched off from the large Musi River. The city was situated inland, at a distance from the lower eastern coast of Sumatra, across from the island Banka. The native popula-tion descended largely from Javanese who invaded this region of Sumatra in the fifteenth century. Palembang became a prominent harbor because two rivers—the Musi and the Lematang—joined at a confluence west of the city. Both rivers were navigable (which is not always the case in Sumatra) and allowed a great deal of river traffic inland. The Lematang and Enim rivers met at Muara-Enim (*muara* is the term for a river's mouth), the most im-portant trade center at the time in the Palembang Highlands. In Cohen's day Muara-Enim was as far as one could go by major transportation; a railroad was not built until the present century. From Muara-Enim travel became very difficult. Lahat, Cohen's ultimate destination, was, despite being the district capital of the Palembang Highlands, a very small town with no more than several hundred inhabitants. About 360 feet above sea level it was situated on the left bank of the Lematang River and controlled a crossroads. The first military post in the interior region of the Palembang district was established in Lahat in 1831. The garrison was billeted in a square earthen redoubt within Lahat, and in a cantonment outside it. The military post was abolished in 1912. Lahat can be said to be in the foothills of the Bukit Barisan mountain range that stretches the length of the island, parallel to the western coast. This range has many high mountains and volcanoes. One of the latter is the Dempo, a vol-cano still active in Cohen's time. One of its peaks, Gunung Merapi, is over a thousand feet above sea level and is the second highest mountain peak in Sumatra. The Bajau River origi-nates on the northwestern slope and is part of the Musi River basin. The local population believed that Dempo's pinnacle was the abode of their dead and the residence of their pro-tective spirit called Pojang. The volcano was first climbed by Europeans in 1780.

61   A *pasanggrahan* was a temporary dwelling for people traveling on official business. It was maintained by the regional administration. Private citizens were also permitted to use it.

62   *Lutung*, also spelled *lotong*, is the black, long-tailed monkey *Semnopithecus maurus*. When full grown it has long black fur, a slender body, a very long tail, a large face, and hind legs that are considerably longer than the front paws. The *lutung* lived primarily in Java and southern Sumatra, from the coastal plains up to high in the mountains.

63   In the original, Cohen used the French verb *voltiger* for "vault," which is just one ex-ample of his liberal use of French phrases and expressions.

64   "Reading box" for *leestrommel*, a metal box that circulated among the European population and contained popular magazines and novels.

65   The *perkutut* is a member of the large family of turtledoves that can be found all over the archipelago, but are particularly associated with Java and Sumatra. Turtledoves are highly prized by the local populations. They are kept in bamboo or wooden cages that have no door, though four of the wooden bars can be moved up or down to give access to the cage. At one time it was believed that the dove's droppings would turn into gold and people used to put a piece of cotton under the cage to collect them. It was also believed that if a bird

became one hundred years old it would lay a golden egg every day. The dove Cohen is referring to is the barred ground-dove *Goepelia striata*, also known as *ketiran, katiran,* or *katitiran*. It prefers to live on the ground and feeds primarily on seeds. About the size of a blackbird, it has gray feathers in various shades, its belly is white, and it has a number of thin, black rings around its neck. These tame, sweet doves have a small head and an elegant body and are still prized for their lovely call, reminiscent of our mourning doves.

66   *De jure* is a legal phrase meaning "by law," "by right," as opposed to *de facto* which means "in fact," "in reality."

67   *Guardhouse* for *politiekamer*. Meaning literally "police room," it was a detention cell in the barracks (*kazerne* in Dutch) where a soldier was locked up for a short period of time.

68   *Court of Military Review* for *krijgsraad*. This was a court convened to try cases of individuals who fell under military jurisdiction. In Holland it was the court of first resort, made up of military officers and presided over by a civilian judge.

69   *Muster of men confined to barracks* for *het geconsigneerdenappel*. Use of the French verb *consigner* is typical of the large number of French terms used in the colonial army. In Dutch usage, *consigner* indicated that a soldier was forbidden to leave the barracks.

70   The first punishment I already noted, but the last two are troublesome terms. I translated *provoost* as *stockade* because it once stood for a "soldier's prison" although it also could refer to a military punishment. *Cachot*, yet another French word, is harder to pin down. I opted for *solitary* (or "the hole") because it was a term for a cell as well as a prison, and because of Cohen's subsequent description of one.

71   *Court of Military Appeals* for *Hoog Militair Gerechtshof*, which was the highest and final court of appeals in the military. The Court of Military Appeals has that same function in the U.S. army.

72   *Subaltern* was the same in the Dutch and British army: a commissioned officer below the rank of captain.

73   "To stand bediri" for *bediri staan*. The first word is Malay in the phrase *berdiri tegak*, or "to stand upright," i.e., "to stand at attention." In the original text, Cohen deliberately refuses to use the customary second-person formal form of address "U" and addresses the major only with the informal "jij."

74   *Pop*, our slang term for a drink. In the original *spatje*.

75   *Chow* for *potje*, i.e., *potje met eten*; mess kit for *etensblik*.

76   *Badju* was a jacket or bodice worn by women with a sarong.

77   Cohen is imitating Malay love poems or *pantuns* which were very popular. *Pantuns* were rhymed quatrains. The first couplet usually presents a statement of fact, while the last conveys the author's real meaning. Many *pantun* images became clichés, including the ones Cohen used for his seduction. Comparing the loved one to a *perkutut*, for instance, was one of them. The *pinang* refers to the areca palm, a very graceful tree. Its fruit, *pinang*, is a mild stimulant chewed with betel leaves (*sirih*). The *kidang* is the barking deer (*Cervulus muntjac*). It is small, with small horns; the male has strongly developed canines that show outside the upper lip. Also known by the Malay word *kijang* (*kidang* is Javanese) or the Sundanese *mentjek*, this little deer stands no taller than three feet. Its back is a dark chestnut color. *Kidangs* normally live in couples on open terrain. The *mangistan*, known in English as "mangosteen," is the *Garcinia mangostana*, a favorite fruit that has white lobes embedded in the thick, dark rind. *Langsep* or *langsat* is the fruit of a large tree (*Lansium domesticum*), and it was much prized. The peel is a pale yellow, and inspired the popular simile *kulit langsep*, or to have "a skin like the pale yellow one of the langsep." Such a complexion was much admired and was preferred to darker skin color. *Mentjo* or *beo* (*Gracula javanensis*) is the

mynah bird. It was admired for its blue-black or green-black shiny plumage, and its ability to mimic human speech.

78   *Slendang (selendang)* is a kind of stole worn over one shoulder. When Djuwita refers to a *slendang blanda* she means a "European slendang."

Talleth (Hebrew spelling), *tsitsis* (Yiddish), and *tefillin* are three accessories for prayer in the Jewish religion. The talleth is a prayer shawl, tsitsis a ritual garment with fringes at the four corners, and tefillin are leather phylacteries. I do not know what Cohen means by "four satin tsitsis bags," because the tsitsis has fringes at the four corners but nothing, to my knowledge, that can contain anything.

79   I am supposing that *dureng* is a misprint for *durian*, also known in Sumatra and Borneo as *duren*. This is a celebrated fruit (*Durio zibethinus*), that smells horrendously but has a delicious pulp. The native population considered the durian an aphrodisiac. See *The Poison Tree*, 93–111, in this series.

Gamelan refers to the music produced by a Javanese orchestra for wajang performances and court dances. The orchestra usually included a *rebab*, a kind of violin with two strings, a *suling* or bamboo flute, and gongs and drums. The most extensive study in English is J. Kunst, *Music in Java: Its History, Its Theory, and Its Technique*, ed. E. L. Heins, 3d enl. ed., 2 vols. (The Hague: Martinus Nijhoff, 1973).

80   The Malay sentence means "Goodbye Djuwita. Goodbye, sweetheart."

81   *Sajoran* is the Indonesian word for "vegetables."

82   *Stone purifiers* for *lekstenen waterfilters*. A *leksteen* was a stone that allowed water to drain through, and was synonymous with "filterstone."

83   *Chastised ones* is a troublesome, though colorful, term in the original. The Dutch word, *afgetuigden* has various connotations. *Aftuigen* was originally a verb meaning to "unharness" or "take down" something, such as the rigging of a ship. In a figurative sense it can mean "to get undressed," but its most common modern meaning is to beat up somebody, to berate somebody either physically or verbally, to denigrate a person. Because of the latter, I chose "chastised" because that connotes at least the last two meanings of both physical and mental abuse.

84   *Atap* was a common roofing material made from the leaves of the nipah palm, or other palm trees.

Overseer is a compromise for the untranslatable word *stokkenknecht*, which Cohen says was an official designation. Literally it means "stickman," the second syllable in the sense of a "subordinate." It probably derived from *stokbewaarder* which was an old term for a prison guard or overseer.

85   *Compulsory domicile* was in Latin in the original text: *domicilio coatto*. I take it that the last term is a misprint for *coacto*.

86   *Topi* was the Malay word for "hat," i.e., a tailored hat as opposed to a cloth wrapped around the head.

87   *Sbir,* commonly spelled *sbire*, is French slang for a police officer.

88   *Pole* for *pikol*. Normally spelled *pikul*, it can refer to a specific weight of 137 pounds, the verb "to carry" (*mempikul*), or to a carrying pole that was balanced on a man's shoulder and had a basket hanging from each end, attached to the pole with strips of rattan.

89   *Post hoc (ergo) propter hoc*, a Latin phrase meaning "after this, therefore that," to indicate the false assumption that something has caused an event simply because it preceded the event.

90   *Substitute* for *remplaçant* in the original. It was common practice in nineteenth-century France to pay somebody to take a recruit's place in the service. There was even a

"Bureau de remplacement" that a person could turn to. The practice was abolished in 1872.

91 *Indefinite one* for *onbepaalde* which, I assume, refers to a person who is being punished in some way or another for an indeterminate amount of time.

92 *Passport Letter B* was the same as a "red passport," i.e., a document indicating a dishonorable discharge from the service.

Kartini

KARTINI (1879–1904) was the daughter of a Javanese aristocrat who was the regent of Djapara.[1] The Djapara district, one of four that together formed the Semarang residency (in 1901), was situated on the northern coast of central Java. The island narrows into a "waist" between the harbor cities of Cheribon and Semarang. East of Semarang the land widens again and juts out into the Java Sea. The Djapara regency was the northwestern section of that bulge. The region was no longer prosperous during Kartini's life but in the sixteenth century its main city, also known as Djapara, had been an important Javanese trade center that connected the trade routes between Malacca and the Moluccas. Djapara fought with other Javanese regions against European influence, particularly that of Portugal, primarily in western Indonesia. Toward the end of the sixteenth century, Djapara was absorbed by the expansionist realm of Mataram and became the center of subsequent negotiations between the Dutch VOC and Mataram. During the seventeenth century Djapara was a haven for Dutch ships which found abundant and cheap provisions there—although, as Kartini mentions, the district was constantly threatened by food shortages toward the end of the nineteenth century.[2] The Dutch established a trading station in 1615 when Mataram aligned itself with the VOC.

Djapara was a favorite anchorage because, situated on the western coast of that protrusive section of Java and shielded by mountains from eastern winds, it provided a fine natural harbor for ships (which at that time were always hugging the coast), before they tackled the dangerous waters around the northernmost headland of the district. Two small islands, Pulau Pandjang and Pulau Kelor, protected Djapara's bay from western and northwestern winds as well. Political and economic relations between the Dutch and Mataram blew hot and cold during the seventeenth century and Djapara began to decline when the Dutch moved their main office from Djapara to Semarang in 1708. Gradually the bay silted up until Kelor Island became part of the mainland, and even small vessels could no longer anchor near Pulau Pandjang. In Kartini's day the old town was no more than an hour's distance from the coast.

No longer a harbor or trade center, Djapara became a sleepy town in a district that was not easily accessible by train, that suffered from severe flooding in the west monsoon and from scorching heat the rest of the year, and that had a rather unhealthy climate. These aspects of life in Djapara are reflected in Kartini's letters where she shows a real compassion for the plight of the ordinary people (*wong tjilik* in Javanese). The main livelihoods in Djapara were fishing and the industry connected with coconut plantations. The district was also known for its fine wood carving and furniture making, two crafts that Kartini hoped to revive and make known to the world at large (180–83).

Radèn Adjeng Kartini, or simply Kartini as she preferred to be known, was the second daughter of the regent of Djapara, Radèn Mas Adipati Ario Sosroningrat. Titulary was a social reflection of what in Kartini's time was a rigidly controlled world of hereditary customs and laws known as *adat. Radèn* was a title applied to Javanese aristocrats who were not necessarily descendants of royalty. It could, in fact, be conferred by the colonial authorities on a native regent. The word *mas* in *radèn mas* indicates a male aristocrat and is an abbreviation of *kamas* or "older brother." *Adipati (hadipati)*, from the Sanskrit word indicating a "paramount administrator," referred to a Javanese ruler or administrator (regent) of the highest class of nobility. The honorific *Adjeng* that preceded Kartini's name indicated that she was an unmarried female aristocrat; after a woman married she was known as *Radèn Aju.* Her name indicates that Kartini was a noblewoman but not a princess. The English title of her correspondence (*Letters of a Javanese Princess*) is both misleading and inaccurate.[3]

Kartini's father had two wives. Although polygamy was sanctioned by Islam, it had been "customary among Javanese nobility for centuries before Islam came to Indonesia," and was therefore both legal and common.[4] Because the world of Javanese aristocracy, known as *prijaji,* was very sensitive to social discrimination, a distinction was made between a wife who came from the same social level as her husband (she was known as the *patmi*) and those (known as *selir*) who did not. The *patmi* did not need to be the first woman her husband married, and the *selir* were *not* concubines. Kartini's mother was her father's first wife. Her name was Ngasirah, and her father was a copra merchant who had been to Mecca, and who hence had the right to be called a *hadji*. Kartini's father and this *selir* wife had eight children including his five sons. After his two oldest children, both sons, had been born, the regent married a woman of requisite aristocratic standing; she became the *patmi* and was known as the radèn aju.

The radèn aju had three daughters. As prescribed by *adat*, each legal wife had her own role and function in the household in accordance with her social rank, but no distinction was made among the children.[5] This is clear from Kartini's description of the way children had to obey specific rules of behavior.

One of my younger brothers or sisters may not pass me by unless he or she does so by creeping along the floor. If a younger sister is sitting on a chair and I pass by her, she must instantly slide down to the floor and remain sitting there with her head down, until I am well out of sight. My younger brothers and sisters are not allowed to use *jij* and *je* [informal second-person singular] when addressing me and can only use High Javanese [i.e., formal or Krama Javanese],[6] and after each sentence has passed their lips they have to "sembah" to me, that is bring both hands together and raise them to just below the nose. If my little brothers and sisters speak about me to other people, they have to use High Javanese when they refer to anything that belongs to me, for instance my clothes, the place where I sit, my hands, my feet, my eyes, and everything that pertains to me. They are strictly forbidden to touch my honorable head, and can only do so after I've given my exalted permission and they have "sembah'd" several times. If there are some dainties on the table, the little ones are not allowed to touch them before it has pleased me to partake of them. (12)

The injunctions here have to do with age, not geniture. The deference due to an older person, particularly in terms of different generations, was rigidly enforced and caused Kartini a great deal of suffering because she was torn between her duty to her father whom she loved and admired (see 70–71, 84–88, 133–34, 149–50), and her intense desire for individual liberty. The lack of distinction between the children of the *patmi* and those of the *selir* is demonstrated in the closeness of Kartini, her half-sister Rukmini, and her full sister Kardinah; Kartini very often used the first-person plural in her letters and referred to this sisterly triad as the "three-leaf clover" who collectively wrote sketches for a Dutch magazine under the name "Tiga saudara" or "the three sisters."

Life in the *kabupaten,* the family compound and official residence, was circumscribed by *adat,* but for a *young* female child, it was a happy and carefree existence surrounded by servants and with few restrictions. Although it was far from common, a little girl might even attend a Dutch primary school. Kartini went to such an ELS school where she learned to read and write Dutch and was exposed to Western ideas. This liberal existence ceased around the age of twelve. Having arrived at the nubile age, the female *prijaji* was barred from liberty of movement and thought and was incarcerated in the gilded cage of the *kabupaten* (18, 57). From then until she was expected to get married, at around fifteen or sixteen, a girl's existence was entirely monitored by *adat,* by what was *pantes,* i.e., proper and fitting. "A real jewel of a Javanese girl is silent and immovable like a wooden doll; she speaks only when it is absolutely necessary and does so in a whisper of a voice that is inaudible even to ants; she walks step by step, like a snail; she laughs soundlessly without moving her lips, because it's so unseemly when the teeth can be seen, that's when you look like a 'luwah' or fox" (57; also 13). A girl learned to efface herself almost literally, to subborn herself to the will of her father, her older brothers, and her future husband. The father arranged a marriage and a daughter had absolutely no voice in choosing the man she was to share her life with; she was supposed "to follow meekly, be it to heaven or to hell" (in Javanese: "sargo nunut, meraka katut").[7] The reason for child marriages was utterly pragmatic: the younger the bride the less she was liable to insist on a choice based on her feelings and affections. This notion was succinctly expressed in the Javanese saying that "when the heart has ripened, it no longer allows itself to be molded."[8]

The young Kartini rebelled vehemently.

I was always in trouble with my older brothers and sister because I chose not to obey what they deemed right unless I thought it was fair. And so I, a child of barely twelve years old, stood there all alone facing a hostile force. But even then God did not desert me. He helped me get through that very difficult time. Bitter, very bitter tears were shed by us children. . . . My eldest sister married, my eldest brother left, and from that moment on we started a new existence. The motto was: "freedom, equality and *sisterhood!*" We want to be loved and *not feared.* (264)

The fact that she did not get married until she was twenty-four says a great deal. She must have had a strong character and an indomitable will, for what she engaged in amounted to a war of attrition within the impregnable walls of the *kabupaten.* Kartini's oldest brother and sister were her worst enemies. For an entire year not a single word was exchanged between Kartini and one of her brothers (431). Kartini's mother, the *selir*, Ngasirah, also failed to see the justice of her daughter's objections (59). It has been suggested that, ironically, the radèn aju, the *patmi* wife who had experienced the life of a *prijaji* girl, was more likely to comprehend Kartini's suffering than her own *selir* mother who had grown up outside this restrictive society.[9] It must have been a difficult situation for everyone concerned. Every so often Kartini's letters hint at the disapproval of the *prijaji* world around her. Her parents and older siblings were criticized and derided for harboring such an improper rebel as Kartini.

This is said more often: "We want to marry a Dutchman!" One time that statement was made during a dinner at some family of ours—made by a European. Everybody amused themselves at our expense and one said: "They want to have it easy." They were good enough to let Mother know all about it, and she was very upset. And there was a so-called *friend* of ours at that dinner, one who has stated time and again to love us so much, and our friend calmly allowed them to throw mud at us. So we've already had quite a few experiences that can be useful to us. Even worse things have been said to me personally, but we think they're so low that we don't even take the trouble to defend ourselves. And they get even angrier because we remain so calm. (430; see also 241)

Kartini would not surrender to the pressure. Her third brother was sympathetic and after the oldest sister had married and left, Kartini was bolstered by the ardent support of two "accomplices," her sisters Rukmini and Kardinah. From about 1895 on, these three were as inseparable as the three musketeers in their battle for emancipation and personal liberty. Kartini also received some qualified support from her father, a loving but besieged ally. One must remember that only "a tiny proportion of the indigenous elite" received any kind of Western education. "Many natives were just not interested in such education; they regarded it as unnecessary and probably dangerous, bringing with it the risks of cultural alienation and possible conversion to Christianity."[10] But some *prijaji* families did believe in European training, and the most famous one was the Tjondronegoro clan, Kartini's father's family. His father, Pangeran Ario Tjondronegoro, had been the regent of Demak (a neighboring regency to the south of Djapara) and had hired a Dutch tutor to educate his four sons. They all reached the rank of *Bupati,* or regent. One of Kartini's uncles wrote articles and books in Javanese; another studied railroad engineering in Holland. Her own father was known as "an advocate of better education and conditions for government *prijaji* . . . and he and his brothers became the classic examples of the enlightened *prijaji* by the end of the nineteenth century."[11] Despite persistent opposition by his peers, Kartini's father followed family tradition and allowed all his children, particularly his sons, to receive a "modern" or "progressive" education. He could not deny his Javanese heritage entirely, however, and made some concessions to tradition, particularly where it concerned his daughters. Nevertheless, he supplied Kartini and her sisters with Dutch books and magazines, allowed his favorite daughter to correspond with various Europeans, both male and female, and, after the sisters were approximately sixteen, gave his permission for occasional excursions into the world outside the *kabupaten*.

Most important was that the regent permitted his daughters to enjoy social intercourse with Europeans on a personal level. Kartini maintained these relationships for the rest of her life because she was permitted to correspond with her friends in Dutch. She wrote to ten Dutch people over a period of five years, from 1899 to 1904. Except in one case, she had become personally acquainted with all her correspondents in Djapara. The exception was a young woman about her own age, Stella Zeehandelaar, with whom she came in contact after Kartini placed a notice in a Dutch feminist magazine asking for a pen pal. This was, of course, against the grain of traditional Javanese society wherein a *prijaji* woman eschewed public exposure and notoriety. Most of her correspondents were in the vanguard of social change, even in Holland. From about 1894 to 1899, Kartini frequently met with Mrs. Ovink-Soer, a dedicated socialist and feminist who was the wife of the assistant resident in Djapara. Her "pen pal" Stella was another ardent feminist. Mr. and Mrs. van Kol were similarly inclined; Van Kol was one of the founders of the Dutch Socialist party and a member of Parliament. But Kartini's friendship with Mr. and Mrs. Abendanon was perhaps the most decisive. J. H. Abendanon was the director of the Colonial Department of Education, an influential liberal who fought for a more "ethical" direction of Dutch colonial policy. He and his wife were ardent believers in women's education and women's rights, and he helped Kartini with her dream of opening a school for *prijaji* daughters. Unfortunately, after Abendanon had sought out support in government circles, the plan for such a school had to be abandoned because of strong opposition from other Javanese regents (106, 111). As a meager substitute, Kartini and her two sisters ran a small school for village children in her father's *kabupaten,* until Kardinah's sudden marriage, in January 1902, undermined that modest venture as well.

In 1902 Kartini managed to persuade her parents to allow her and Rukmini to study in Holland. She submitted an official request for support to the Dutch authorities, and for a while things looked quite promising. But in January 1903 Abendanon visited her in Djapara and convinced her to abandon her plans because her father was old and sick, because she would find it difficult to live in an alien environment such as Holland, and because she might become too Dutch and find that *prijaji* parents would not send their daughters to such a person for schooling.[12] This represents a curious turnabout for Abendanon and it must have been very difficult for Kartini to give in to his arguments. She opted for study in Batavia, a decision that her parents must have seen as the lesser of two evils. She was granted a government subsidy for this purpose, but she turned that down as well because of her impending marriage.

During the summer of 1903 Kartini had agreed to marry the regent of Rembang who had written to her father asking for his consent. One can imagine how agonizing this must have been for a woman who had been so vociferously opposed to the *prijaji* conception of marriage. Although the regent of Rembang was a progressive man who had studied in Holland, he had not renounced polygamy.[13] Her parents argued that it was providential that a man in his position wanted to marry such a notorious trouble-maker as Kartini, a woman who was already twenty-four years old. He could also be invaluable to her plans because, as his radèn aju, she could enlist his influence and support. Kartini gave in on the condition that this matrimonial prospect would not stand in the way of her further education or prevent her from realizing her desire to educate the daughters of native chiefs. Radèn Adipati Djojoadiningrat acceded to her demands and Kartini married him on 8 November 1903. There is little doubt that the main reason for Kartini's surprising surrender was the precarious health of her beloved father.[14]

Her brief marriage to this man whom she had never seen before her wedding turned out to be better than expected (368). In March 1904 she discovered she was pregnant. The child, a boy, was born on 13 September 1904, but Kartini died four days later.

On 3 August 1964, Sukarno, the president of the Republic of Indonesia, declared Kartini a "Heroine of National Freedom." Her holiday, *Hari Kartini*, is on 21 April. She is remembered in Indonesia as one of the first champions of women's rights. In Indonesia the emancipation of women is closely allied to the emancipation of the entire population, and Ibu Kartini ("Mother Kartini") has been canonized not only as a defender of her "sisters" but also as a patron saint for all modern Indonesians.[15] In what follows, I have attempted an interpretation of the symbolic reasons why the struggle for women's rights can easily expand to include the amelioration of an entire civilization.

In terms of the male world, woman represents "the Other," an embodiment of dissimilarity that is not praised but deemed inferior and unequal. European usurpers often represented a colony as a woman; Las Casas, the champion of the Indian population, referred to Mexico as a female who should be saved from "unnatural fathers" (i.e., the conquistadors) "and given to a husband who will treat her with the reasonableness she deserves." [16] Submission and colonization were reciprocal terms. Reaction to colonization often took the form of proclaiming an individual liberty that delighted in its otherness, an inequality that was creative and progressive because it was motivated by change. Such a transitive view of existence can only be a threat to a society that has institutionalized conformity by means of a ritual order that is satisfied with being unalterable and intransitive. The latter can often be associated with a male, the former with a female modality. In Kartini's case, the first impulse for dissension had nothing to do with colonialism but was a personal struggle for recognition as a woman and an individual.

The *prijaji* world she was born into was a society dominated by men and by past traditions and ritual known collectively as *adat*. Woman, individuality, and change were of necessity excluded. The *prijaji's* fear of alterity is indicated by Kartini in terms that connote stasis, artificiality, and an injunction against spontaneity and naturalness. As soon as she became nubile, i.e., became a woman, Kartini was incarcerated: "My prison was a large house with an extensive yard around it, but the latter was surrounded by a high wall, and it was the wall that held me prisoner. No matter how spacious our house and yard, if you *always* have to stay there, it can only become stifling" (18). In another letter the "closed square space" of the *kabupaten* is identified with a "cage," a gilded cage to be sure, but a "bird cage" nevertheless (57). At the age of twelve the natural freedom that we consider the mandate of childhood is stifled; jumping, climbing trees, bouncing up and down rather than walking, even laughter is prohibited and replaced by unnatural control. She is told to become a "wooden puppet" who is voiceless and without emotion (57). Along with her individuality, any resemblance to life has been removed, and she is now a thing that men can manipulate according to an authority invested in them by the past.

To realize such a disjunction from nature and humanity requires degradation. A puppet is not a person, hence inequality is not an issue. Its relevance is only expressed in terms of its usefulness for him who controls it. Kartini is told that "women are nothing," that they have "been created for the pleasure of men" who can do with them "what they will" (62). "We Javanese women have to be compliant and submissive first and foremost; we should be like clay that can be given any form one likes" (70). Again and again Kartini testifies bitterly to woman's inferior position in Javanese society (11, 61, 69, 70, 106, 127, 166, 168). She is not allowed to be a woman and she is also not allowed to be an individual; in fact she is not even thought of as human. In the Indies, woman "has for centuries been considered and treated as a creature of a lower order, indeed, and why shouldn't I say it, as an object without a soul," something that has no "right to an independent conscience or to the freedom of thought, feeling, and action" (111). When context is everything and content irrelevant, such exponents of individuality as emotions and passions cannot be allowed expression. Affection has to be inferred (60) but cannot be demonstrated; there is no intimacy between parents and children (63); Kartini's deep and abiding love for her father must remain mute because "strict Javanese etiquette stands coldly and coolly between the two of them" (63).

It is not surprising that Kartini regarded "indifference" as the worst state a human being can be reduced to (68), and indifference was precisely what a Javanese woman had to cultivate when she entered a polygamous society as a matrimonial prospect. Indifference became an external reflection of what was, after all, an enforced process of dehumanization. Kartini's most impassioned indignation was roused by the "hideous injustice" (52) of polygamy. Marriage, which should be "a calling," is in reality nothing more than "an occupation" (127). Kartini summarized the desperate plight of the married Javanese woman in a story about Fatima, the prophet Muhammad's daughter.

Fatima's husband took yet another wife and she was asked by the Prophet how she felt about it. "Nothing, Father, nothing," she professed. While she said this she leaned against a banana tree and its leaves, which had once been fresh and bright, wilted, and the trunk which supported her body turned to charcoal. Once again the Father asked how she felt, and once again she professed: "Nothing Father, nothing!" The Father gave her a raw egg and asked her to press it to her heart. When he asked it to be returned he broke it open: the egg was cooked! The heart of the Oriental woman has not changed since then. This little story teaches us the opinion of many women about this cruel right that men have. (128)

Kartini's rebellion against the condition of the Javanese woman took the form of resistance to the demand that a woman must, almost literally, forget her self. She had to deny her emotions and her humanity, and acquiesce to being an inferior and alien creature, an embodiment of Otherness that had been domesticated. It is reasonable to assume that Kartini was not the only Javanese woman who felt that way. What sets her apart, however, is that she voiced her opposition and proposed a solution.

An equally important factor is that in her case we find a different perspective of colonialism. Whereas she encountered intransigence at home she discovered tolerance in the West. In his study of the symbolic implication of the Spanish conquest of Mesoamerica, Tzvetan Todorov makes it clear why this is not surprising. The paradox of Europe's success in colonizing was based on two things that are wellnigh mandatory for a successful development but are also elements that a ritualized, tradition-bound society cannot allow. One is "the Europeans' capacity to understand the Other," and the second is that Europeans also "exhibited remarkable qualities of flexibility and improvisation." Todorov considers improvisation a hallmark of European civilization, but it is a quality also associated with woman. "The cultural model in effect since the Renaissance, even if borne and assumed by men, glorifies what we might call the feminine side of culture: improvisation rather than ritual, words rather than weapons. Not just any words, it is true: neither those that designate the world nor those that transmit the traditions, but those whose raison d'être is action upon others." Todorov's exemplary figure who embodied these traits during the Spanish conquest of Mexico is the much maligned Malinche. Quite rightly it seems to me, Cortès's female interpreter represents for Todorov "the first example, and thereby the symbol, of the cross-breeding of cultures; she thereby heralds the modern state of Mexico and beyond that, the present state of us all, since we are not invariably bi-lingual, we are inevitably bi- or tri-cultural." [17] Although this statement needs to be modified, it should be already clear that Kartini's example offers some important collaboration.

Without language, Kartini's guerrilla warfare with Javanese *adat* would have remained a courageous but mute event that would not have reached beyond the walls of the Sosroningrat *kabupaten*. If, as has been asserted, language is the "companion of empire," [18] it was in Kartini's case also the companion of freedom. The verbalization of her thoughts was the result of a cross-cultural collaboration. Kartini wrote in Dutch, a language she had learned as a small girl in a Dutch school. She perfected her knowledge by reading Dutch books and magazines and by sporadic conversations with Dutch people. She poured out her heart and examined her convictions in the language of the colonizer, addressing her epistolary improvisations to European women with whom she could identify not because of national or political imperatives but because of the kinship of gender. Letters are improvised communication with the Other, and Kartini used them as weapons in her struggle for individual liberty.

Letters play a large role in our lives, we have to thank them for almost everything; without our correspondence we would never have gotten as far as daring to break with ancient traditions and customs. You don't know, or perhaps you do, what the letters of our friends, superior in spirit and soul, have meant to us. They effect a purifying and exalted influence; they develop our spirit and emotions. So much beauty, loveliness and preciousness has reached us by mail, pearls, precious stones, of both heart and head. Oral conversations can be etched in our soul, but you must admit that time pales many a word even though the syntax remains un-altered; but letters faithfully repeat every word for all time, and as often as you want. (249; see also 285)

Kartini's Dutch was not impeccable, but she knew her adopted lan-guage remarkably well. Her style was influenced by a form of writing that today is considered sentimental and effusive. She used a great deal of ex-clamations and italicized emphasis (which I have retained) as well as a romantic rhetoric, but in this her style was not much different from the average literary production of her time. She admired Henri Borel and Au-gusta de Wit (220) both of whom wrote a cloying prose, but she was also well acquainted with Multatuli's work (21, 30, 42, 44, 159; his novel *Max Havelaar* was published in this series) and with that of Holland's other great novelist of her day, Louis Couperus (44, 292; his novel *The Hidden Force* also appeared in this series). She also mentioned that she had read Bas Veth (220) and Frederik van Eeden (221). It should also be mentioned that the occasional clumsiness, abrupt shifts in subject, and unnecessary repetitions are partly because these were private letters, often written on the spur of the moment, and never polished with an eye to future publication.

Kartini's "gems," so precious to her own development, would have re-mained intrapersonal instruments of no use to the community if they had not been made public, that is, printed as a book. A book is a subversive paradox. On the one hand, mass duplication can make a text communal property, but a book is also an individual act of cognition outside the im-perative of a group. A book is both transitive and intransitive. In Kartini's case this crucial transformation from the personal to the collective was brought about by a Dutchman in Holland. After he retired from his offi-cial function as director of the Colonial Department of Education, J. H. Abendanon (1852–1925) collected the letters Kartini had written to various individuals and published them in 1911 under the title *Door duisternis tot licht* (Out of darkness into the light). The book was a suc-cess (a fifth edition was published in 1976). It was translated into Malay and published in Java in 1922 and again, in a different translation, in

1938 (the sixth printing was in 1968). A Javanese translation appeared in 1938, an English one in 1921 (with a second edition in 1964), and a French one in 1960. The verbal improvisations became an international means of communication.

Emancipation requires communication and knowledge. In Kartini's case both were supplied by European civilization. It is understandable that the Dutch language, Holland, and, by extension, European civilization, represented liberation for Kartini. "Knowledge of the Dutch language disclosed for us an inexhaustible source of pleasure; it disclosed for us so much beauty that we had no idea existed" (208). Dutch is to be "the salvation" (83) of the Javanese population (see also 8, 13, 47, 59, 66, 83, 135, 183, 222, 397). Language is so important because it equals communication, and communication means knowledge. "Knowledge of Dutch is *the* key that unlocks the treasuries of Western civilization" (397; see also 27, 46, 47, 76, 83, 299, 396). Knowledge is power, and language is woman's weapon which, in the long run, can be more effective than man's use of force. The *prijaji* world appears to have intuited that language is dangerous. "I don't know any modern languages, alas!—*adat* does not tolerate that we girls learn more languages—it is already bad enough that we know Dutch" (8). Because Malay was the lingua franca of the archipelago it would make sense to translate important texts into that language, but, writes Kartini: "It would be useless because there are few Javanese women who can read Malay. Only men do" (19). There was a tacit acknowledgment by the egocentric male world that language is feminine and powerful and capable of becoming "allocentric" (from the Greek "allo" which means "other").[19] If that were allowed, woman would cease to be the ceremonial puppet that centuries of ritualized pressure had forced her to become and she would reassert her individuality, that is to say her difference, which could only be interpreted as a threat. "And to have a language in my power would not be of much use to me now, because I am *not allowed to think aloud*" (136). Such resistance only indicates the efficacy of what is forbidden, and Kartini was well aware that language was her strongest weapon. "Oh, how I ardently, ardently, wish to have the power of one language, be it my own or Dutch, in order to state clearly what I think and feel about so much that invokes my admiration, or that fills me with indignation, such as that misery that my own people honor and support, the men from egotism and the women from powerlessness, and that has sprouted from ignorance. I have in mind something biting and sharp about 'Ideals.' And there are times when I'm itching not to write these thoughts down only for myself or for my confidants, but want to fling them into the faces of the other ones" (135).

There is also delight in Kartini's love for languages, though to a static authority delight can be subversive as well. A ceremonial society employs language as a device of concealment and restraint, ultimately turning language into silence. But the passionate embrace of language by an individual such as Kartini is joyful and spontaneous, is generative. Kartini had an appetite for languages and was a linguist quite as remarkable as Malinche. She was fluent in Javanese, Malay, and Dutch (21), and as we have seen, she bemoaned the fact that she did not know any other languages (245). Her linguistic sensitivity is expressed in the following remark about the attempt she and her sisters made to learn French. It is also a nice example of how cultural cross-pollination can stimulate the imagination with a fresh insight. "Rukmini once claimed that she dreamt in French; she was with Chateaubriand in Louisiana, that wondrously beautiful country that he described. The French language has much in common with ours [i.e., Javanese] as far as syntax is concerned, and their 'h' is the same as ours" (83).

If we concede that language is feminine, we will find all the more validity in the notion that woman is the transmitter of culture and civilization. This was definitely true with Kartini, but because in her particular case language and civilization were to a large extent European impulses, we have the curious inversion whereby the colonizer has lost his customary association with male conquest and becomes a disburser of alternative affections, has in fact become "feminized." But other needs of life which we usually identify as "feminine" could also only be satisfied by Europeans. Kissing, or any other display of emotion, is alien to Javanese society and identified solely with Europeans (22). Love and justice have to be learned from them as well (45), including the crucial need to base marriage on mutual respect and affection between husband and wife. Hence Kartini's affective needs were to be satisfied by the West, though it is customary to assign such gratification to the East.

There is no gainsaying that Western culture provided Kartini with certain emotional and intellectual values that she yearned for. This does not mean, however, that she disparaged her own culture to the point of identification with its alternative. Nor did she succumb to the lure of equality because to have done so would deny difference and alterity, two cultural mandates that, as we saw, are particularly associated with woman and that are decisive for the vitality of a civilization. Due to her superior intellect and feeling, Kartini never lost sight of the unique character of either Javanese or Dutch society, and she was able to do this because she remained cognizant of her "otherness" as a woman, as a Javanese vis-à-vis the Dutch, and as a promulgator of European civilization in the conservative world of the Javanese *prijaji*. Such insight can only enrich because, as Todorov points out, "self-knowledge develops through knowledge of the Other."[20]

In 1902, Kartini wrote derisively to her Dutch pen pal that the praise she had been accorded from certain Dutch quarters was only due to the fact that they "find a Javanese woman who writes in Dutch *interesting*" (186). She was well aware that the reason was the attraction of the Other.

The professor thought us to be partial savages and discovered ordinary people; what was strange was only skin color, clothing, and environment, and these conferred a peculiar cachet on the ordinary. Don't we feel pleasantly moved when we discover our own thoughts in another person? And if the other is a stranger, someone of a different race, from a different continent, different blood, color, mores and customs, then this can only enhance the attraction of spiritual congeniality. I am convinced that people wouldn't take as much notice of us if instead of a sarong and kabaja we wore dresses, had Dutch instead of Javanese names, and if European instead of Javanese blood flowed through our veins. (96–97)

Kartini was also mindful of the danger of becoming Europeanized (114), and rejected this possibility for herself.

People often maintain that, at heart, we are more European than Javanese. A melancholy thought! We might be imbued with European thoughts and feelings—but that blood, that Javanese blood, that lives and warmly flows through our veins cannot be silenced. We feel it when there's incense and the scent of flowers, when the gamelan sounds, when the wind murmurs through the coconut palms, when the perkututs coo, when people blow on rice stalks as if playing a flute and when you hear the pounding on the wooden rice blocks. (116)

Nevertheless, in order to escape the confinement of Javanese society "we have to go to an entirely different environment, in a different country, with entirely different mores, customs, habits, and conditions. We expect from Europe that it will prepare us better, equip us better for the work we have to do; that it will steel us, armor us against the many poisoned arrows which many of my people will surely shoot at us because we dare to be different from them" (225). But for Kartini the search for knowledge was always an emotional and intellectual trajectory that was circular not linear, a retrograde action that *had* to return to her Javanese heritage in order to be of any use.

Really, we expect nothing, nothing from Europe that is in anyway similar to what European girls dream of: "happiness"; nor to find much friendship and sympathy there; nor to feel *happier* in a *European* environment. We only hope to find this one thing that we *need* for our *goal: knowledge* and *education*. That is the *only* thing we think of. What does it matter if we don't like it in Europe, or if we will never feel comfortable in Dutch surroundings, if only we get what we are *looking* for and *need* for our *goal?* That's why we come, not to enjoy ourselves. (299; see also 300–305, 313)

Experiencing the Other, therefore, is a process of edification of both her own self and of the communal self of her nation. "It may sound strange, but it is a fact nevertheless; you Europeans have taught me to love my own country and people. Instead of alienating us from our own nation, European education has brought us closer to it; it has opened our eyes and heart to the beauties of our people and country, and also . . . for their needs . . . their wounds. We love our country and people so very much!" (202). And a month later, in a letter from April 1902: "And we so much want to give that beauty of other peoples to our own people, not in order to drive out its own beauty and replace it with an alien one, but in order to ennoble it!" (208; see also 219, 223–24, 299).

What Kartini wanted to do for Java is, according to Todorov, what Malinche did for Mexico. "La Malinche glorifies mixture to the detriment of purity . . . she does not simply submit to the Other . . . [but] she adopts the Other's ideology and serves it in order to understand her own culture better, as is evidenced by the effectiveness of her conduct." Like Malinche, Kartini hoped to perform "a sort of cultural conversion." [21] "By crossing different plants and animals one acquires ennobled types of plants and animals. Wouldn't it be the same for the mores of different peoples? When the good of one is mixed with the good of the other, wouldn't this engender nobler mores?" (224).

Kartini wanted to be a mediator between the European and Javanese cultures, hoping to dispel their ignorance of each other. "How can they [the Dutch] judge us [the Javanese], judge our ways? Do they know us? No, nor do we know them!" (36). But such ignorance can be eradicated by communication, by language.

A European, no matter how long he has lived in Java, and being ignorant of Native circumstances, can't be conversant with everything in our Native world the way the Native is. Much of what is still obscure and a riddle for Euopeans I could solve with a few words, and where a European is not permitted to go, the Native is welcome. All the subtleties of the Native world which are unknown to even the greatest European scholar can be brought to light by the Native. (17)

Knowledge of the Other engenders knowledge of one's self, communication is the imperative for understanding, and language is its vehicle. After having mastered the Dutch language and having acquired salient aspects of European culture, Kartini returns to her own with greater understanding and appreciation. Trying to convey her love for Java to the young Dutch woman who was her confidant, Kartini now hopes for a linguistic reciprocity. "Oh Stella, we heard such a treasure-trove of beauty from the mouth of the people; wisdom, truths, so clear, in such simple but oh so melodious words! To really command your language and then make that beautiful and sacred music comprehensible to you! . . . If I could only teach you my language so you would be able to enjoy our beauty in its original state" (251–52). "How would you feel about learning the Javanese language? It is difficult to be sure, but she is so beautiful! It is the language of feelings and is full of poetry and . . . wit" (258; see also 251–55, 271).

Kartini embodied in both word and deed her country's need for transformation. "Oh how marvelous it is that we live precisely in this age!, which is the transition from the old to the new!" (43). A time of transition demands adaptation and improvisation, demands communication. But a collective recalcitrance that does not allow the individual, the Other, to exist cannot communicate. It can do little more than repeat injunctions. Kartini began by defying that norm only to find that interpersonal communication was impossible. To satisfy that craving she went to school with Europeans who, as Todorov pointed out, were masters of that kind of exchange. And in the process of coming to know herself as a viable individual, as a woman, she also came to master that other kind of communication as well: "The interaction that occurs between the person and the religious universe."[22] Kartini returned to the core of her being, an essence that she had been forbidden to know.

Woman is the transmitter of culture because she represents change, that is to say, growth. Woman literally embodies the Other, yet this intimacy does not confine but rather expands into a consanguinity with the world. The fundamental consequences of life are borne by women, not men, and are the foundation of civilizations. This might well be because woman represents the paradox of continuity and change, permanence and alterity. Where men may fashion a context, women engender content: nutrition is more important than a napkin. We will find that Kartini had little trouble expanding her individual plight into the larger need of her nation. She could do so because she came to understand that woman is not capable of indifference, that there is a community of interest more profound than *adat*. She described this simple realization in the form of a story about herself and her sisters which she included in a long letter to Mrs. Abendanon:

Little brother made her open the gates of her heart to Mother again. Little brother taught her: what a *mother* is, and what a child owes her. Mother had dark rings under her eyes, looked weak and worn, and little brother did that, little brother, who never left her in peace and who woke her up at night over and over again. And yet, no matter how difficult little brother was, she never saw a trace of resentment on Mother's face; when little brother made a hue and cry for her, she was with him in a minute and she'd pick him up tenderly and would not put him back until he was once again peacefully asleep. And hadn't she once been as helpless and small as little brother? And had her mother not slaved for her as well? (64)

This little scene, narrated as if it happened to someone else, seems to me to be the epiphany for Kartini's larger faith. Two years later she argued for a more comprehensive interpretation of maternity: nurturance of the spirit as well as the body.[23]

How conceited of us to play "mother" often with "children" who are older than we are. But what does age matter? Every person needs love, the graybeard as well as the child. Does a woman really come into her own only and exclusively through marriage, come to the complete development of her emotions because motherhood is a woman's greatest glory and fulfillment? But is it absolutely necessary for a woman to have her *own child* in order to a be a "mother" in the sense that that word ought to mean: a creature that is all love and devotion? If that is true, how pathetic is the attitude of the world that says that one can *only love a piece of oneself* with the complete surrender of one's ego! For aren't there many mothers who are only called "mother" because they've brought children into the world but who otherwise are not worthy of that name? A woman who gives herself to others with *all* the love she has in her heart, with all the devotion she's capable of, such a woman is in a spiritual sense a "mother." We place the spiritual mother higher than the physical one. (274)

Though she suffered a great deal because of men and their *adat*, Kartini was able to include them as well (47, 289), though she remained firmly convinced that "Woman is the bearer of Civilization" (100). The provenance of this largesse we have already surmised: women are better prepared to transmit culture because "mother Nature herself has put it into their hands: *mother*—the first *nurturer* of human kind" (289). She uses *nurture* here in the old double meaning of "nourishment" as well as "education." "The human being received from woman its very first nurture— in her lap the child learns to feel, think, and speak; and I realize more and more that this earliest of educations is *not without meaning* for one's entire life" (100; see also 45, 127, 325). Clearly, woman is the matrix of sensibility and mentality (it was once known as "mother wit"), because she is the first one who imparts them. Hence it is not surprising that Kartini strongly felt that education should not be restricted to the accumulation of facts. Her opinion is yet another instance of the demand for content over context. "Besides the head, the heart should be guided as well, otherwise civilization remains superficial" (135; see also 99, 172).

In a few short years Kartini progressed from the need for interpersonal communication to seeing the need for what Todorov considered the communication between the individual and the world. Nature once again became solace and sustenance: "Mother Nature has never failed to comfort us when we came to her to have our spirits raised" (99; see also 110–13, 118). Gardens raise her spirits as well (75–76) and she caught herself wishing that she could be removed from society in order to be alone in and with nature (132). And, as a child from coastal Djapara, Kartini always felt regenerated by the sea (176) who was her "greatest friend" (with a feminine ending in the original; 363).

Kartini felt at first that religion was a curse rather than a blessing for mankind (21). After all, religion (Islam) sanctified *adat*. But she gradually came to learn that "it is *not religion* that is loveless but that it is people who turn the original divine beauty into ugliness. And we think that the highest and most beautiful religion is *Love*. And is it really absolutely necessary to be a Christian to live according to this divine command? For the Buddhist, the Brahman, the Jew, and the Muhammadan, even the heathen, can also lead a pure life of love" (311). In the same way that she cut through the pretense of *adat* by saying to her correspondent "just call me Kartini" (9), she also stripped religion of its guile by reducing it to a fundamental truth: "I call sin all those deeds that make a fellow human being suffer" (16).

KARTINI became a Javanese ideal as well as a symbol for modern Indonesia. Her example befits modern Javanese society, a society that has recently been praised by a scholar as possessing "an ability to accommodate to and tolerate conflicting norms and ideas, the capacity to entertain in coexistence ideas and values that would seem incompatible in many Western settings, an unusual capacity for sympathetic toleration in social behavior."[24] Kartini should be seen as a symbol of a larger truth, one that indicates that an amalgamation of diverse cultures can soften cultural rigidity and even lead to a rediscovery of what may be the best in the respective civilizations. Todorov posed a similar situation when discussing Spanish colonialism: "Is any influence, by the very fact of its externality, detrimental? . . . Can the history of any country be other than the sum of the successive influences it has undergone? If there really existed a people who rejected all change, would such a will illustrate anything but an impulse of hypertrophied death instinct?"[25]

As Kartini's example so clearly illustrates, a foreign influence need not be declared a priori harmful. Nor does accommodating it have to mean betraying one's origins. There should be a more rewarding glory than chauvinism. Our present idea, as Todorov understands it, is that "we want equality without it compelling us to accept identity; but also difference without it degenerating into superiority/inferiority . . . we aspire to rediscover the meaning of the social without losing the quality of the individual."[26] At the threshold of this century, Kartini showed that this greater good, if not comprehensible by reason, is apprehensible by sense.

To Stella Zeehandelaar   May 25, 1899

I have longed to make the acquaintance of a "modern girl," that proud, independent girl who has all my sympathy, and who, happily and cheerfully, makes her way through life, quickly and firmly, full of enthusiasm and good spirits; working not only for her own well-being and happiness, but also for the greater good of mankind.

I am full of enthusiasm for the new era, and I can truly say that, as far as my thoughts and feelings are concerned, I do not partake of this time in the Indies, but am completely involved with my progressive white sisters in the distant West.

If the laws of my land permitted it, I would like nothing better than to give myself completely to the work and struggle of the new woman in Europe. But ancient traditions that cannot be broken just like that, keep us imprisoned in their strong arms. One day those arms will release us, but that time is still far away, infinitely far. It *will come,* that I know, but not until three, four generations have passed. Oh, you do not know what it is to love this young, this new age with heart and soul, and still be bound hand and foot, chained to all the laws, customs, and conventions of your country which you can *not* escape. All our customs and conventions are directly opposed to the progress that I want so much to see introduced in our society. Day and night I think about the means that would allow me to escape my country's rigid mores after all . . . but, even though the old Eastern traditions are staunch and strong, I'd be able to shake them off and break them were it not that another bond, stronger than any ancient tradition could ever be, ties me to my world: that is the love I bear for those who have given me life, and whom I have to thank for everything. Do I have the right to break the hearts of those who have given me nothing but love and kindness all of my life, and who surround me with the tenderest care? I would break their hearts if I gave in to my desire and did what my entire being yearns for with every breath and every heart beat.

But it was not the voices alone which reached me from that distant, that civilized, that reborn Europe, which made me long for a change in existing conditions. Even in my childhood, when the word "emancipation" had no sound or meaning yet, and writings and books that dealt with this were far beyond my reach, even then there awakened in me a longing that kept on growing: a longing for freedom and independence. Conditions in my direct and indirect environment broke my heart, and made me cry with a nameless sorrow for the awakening of my country.

And the voices which kept on coming to me from the outside ever louder and louder made the seed which my profound sympathy for the suffering of those I love had planted in my soul, made that seed sprout, take root, and made it grow strong and vigorous.

But that's enough for now—some other time more. Now I must tell you something about myself so that you can make my acquaintance.

I am the eldest, or really the second, daughter of the regent of Djapara, and have five brothers and five sisters—what a profusion, right? My grandfather, Pangeran Ario Tjondronegoro of Demak, was a great leader in the progressive movement of his day, and the first regent of central Java to unlock his door to that guest from far across the sea: Western civilization. All his children who had a European education, have, or had (many of them are no longer with us) inherited a love of progress from their father; and they gave their children the same upbringing which they themselves received. Many of my cousins and all my older brothers have gone through the H.B.S.—the highest institution of learning that we have here in the Indies; and the youngest of my three older brothers has been studying for three years in the Netherlands, and two others are in the service of the government. We girls, as far as education goes, are still fettered by our ancient traditions and conventions, and have profited but little from these advantages, as far as education is concerned. It was already a great crime against the customs of our land that we should be taught at all, and because of that have to leave the house every day to go to school. Because the *adat* of our country strictly forbids girls to go outside their houses. We couldn't go anywhere else, and the only educational institution our little town can boast of is an ordinary grammar school for Europeans.

When I reached the age of twelve, I was kept at home—I had to go into the "box." I was locked up at home, and cut off from all communication with the outside world, whereto I would never be allowed to return except at the side of a husband, a stranger, chosen for us by our parents, and to whom we are married without really knowing about it. European friends—this I heard much later—had tried in every possible way to change my parents' mind about this cruel decision about a young and spirited child like me, but they were unable to do anything. My parents were inexorable: I went to my prison. I spent four long years between four thick walls, without once seeing the outside world.

How I got through that time, I have no idea—all I know is that it was terrible. But I was left one source of happiness: reading Dutch books and corresponding with Dutch friends were not forbidden. Those were the only bright spots in that awful somber time. Those two things meant everything to me, and without them I might have perished, or what is worse: my spirit, my soul, would have died. But then came my friend and deliverer, the spirit of the age, and his footsteps echoed everywhere. Proud, solid, ancient structures shook on their foundations at his approach. Strongly barricaded doors sprang open, some as if by themselves, others with great difficulty, but nevertheless they opened, and let in the unwelcome guest. And wherever he went, he left his traces.

At last, in my sixteenth year, I saw the outside world again. Thank God! Thank God! I could leave my prison as a free person and not chained to a husband who had been forced on me. Then several events followed that returned to us girls more and more of our lost freedom; and last year, at the time of the investiture of our young queen [Queen Wilhelmina], our parents gave us "officially" our freedom back. For the first time in our lives we were allowed to leave our native town and go to the capital where the festivities were held in honor of the queen. What a great and priceless victory that was! That young girls of our position should show themselves in public was something unheard of here, and the "world" was amazed. Tongues began wagging about this unprecedented event, our European friends rejoiced, and we, we were as rich as no queen could ever be.

But I am far from satisfied. I want to go further, still further. I've never desired to run after parties and other frivolous amusements. That has never been the reason for my longing for freedom. I wanted to be free, to be allowed or to be able to make myself independent, not to be beholden to any one, and, above all, never to be obligated to marry.

But we must marry, *must, must*. Not to marry is the greatest sin a Muhammadan woman can commit; it is the greatest disgrace for a native girl and for her family.

And marriage here, oh, miserable is too feeble an expression for it. How can it be otherwise, when the laws are entirely for the man and never for the woman? When both law and convention are entirely for the man, when he is allowed to do *anything, anything* at all?

Love, what do we know about love here? How can we love a man or he love us when we don't know each other, are not even allowed to see each other? Young girls and men are kept strictly separated.

Yes, I would love to know all about your occupation, it seems very interesting to me. And would you also tell me about your preparatory studies before you got your job? I would also love very much to know more about your Toynbee evenings[27] and also about your teetotal organization that you support so ardently. We don't have things like that in the Indies, but I'm very interested in them. Could you sometime describe a Toynbee evening for me? I really do wish to know more about this work for our fellowmen than the little that magazines and newspapers tell me about it.

Thank God that we don't have to fight the drink demon in our Native society—but I fear, I fear that once—forgive me—your Western civilization has gained a foothold here, we will have to contend with that evil too. Civilization is a blessing, but it has its dark side as well. The tendency to imitate is inborn, I believe. The masses imitate the upper classes, who in turn imitate those of higher rank, and these again follow the best ones—the Europeans.

There is no successful feast unless there's drinking. These days, when the Natives are celebrating—unless they are very religious (and usually they are Muhammadans only because their fathers, grandfathers, and remote ancestors were Muhammadans—in reality, they are little better than heathens), one will see one or more square bottles, and they are not sparing in the use of these.

But there's an evil here greater than alcohol, and that is opium. Oh! The misery that that horrible stuff has brought to my country! Opium is the *plague* of Java. Yes, opium is far worse than the plague. The plague does not remain forever, sooner or later it goes away, but the evil of opium, once established, grows. It spreads more and more, and will *never* disappear, never, simply because it is protected by the Government! The more general the use of opium in Java, the fuller the treasury. The opium tax is one of the richest sources of income for the Colonial Government. What does it matter if it is good or bad for the people?—the Government prospers. This curse of the people fills the coffers of the Dutch East-Indies Government with hundreds of thousands, with millions in gold. Many say that the use of opium is not evil, but those who say that have never seen the Indies, or else they are blind.[28]

What else are our many murders, incendiary fires, and robberies, but the direct result of the use of opium? True, smoking opium is not an evil as long as one can get it, when you have money to buy the poison; but when you can't, when you don't have the money to buy it, and you're addicted, then you become dangerous, then you're lost. Hunger will make a man a thief, but the hunger for opium will make him a murderer. There is a saying here—"At first you enjoy opium, but in the end it will devour you." And this is so very, very true. It is terrible to see so much evil around you and be powerless to fight against it.

I loved all of that marvelous book by Mrs. Goekoop, and must have read it three times. I can never grow tired of it, in fact I love it more every time I reread it. What would I not give to be able to live in Hilda's environment. Oh, if we were only as far in the Indies, that a book could cause such violent controversy, as "Hilda van Suylenburg" did (and still does) in your country.[29] I would not rest till

H. S. appeared in my own language to do good, harm if necessary, in our Native world. It is a matter of indifference whether it be good or bad, as long as it made an impression, for that shows that one is no longer sleeping. Java is still in deep slumber. And how can we ever be awakened when those who should serve as examples still love sleep so much.

It is a fact that the majority of European women (and I'm not speaking of the *Dutch women* who live here) living in the Indies care very little, or not at all, for the work and the cause of their white sisters in the Fatherland. And the most recent event in the world of Dutch women has proven it. Didn't the ladies from the Dutch East Indies participate diligently in the National Exhibition of Women's Labor in the Netherlands? We also received an invitation to participate, and we accepted very gladly. The grand work that women are doing has all my sympathy, we are burning for the good of the cause, for the noble endeavor of the courageous women in your country, and we were so happy to be able to contribute just a little seed to the construction of that gigantic mountain which shall and *must* be a blessing to all women, white and brown.

We also received *prikkaarten*.[30] It was impossible to get even one contribution from my own people. No matter how much we explained the cause, they would not, nor did they want to, understand us. Out of desperation we simply went for help to the Europeans. We sent cards and wrote letters asking for support from well-known and not so well-known ladies.

I must admit it was quite daring on our part—we Javanese going to Europeans to speak for a European cause, such pretensions!—people could really have resented this, but we didn't think about that at all. We had only one thought, one goal, to serve the cause with heart and soul. And—we were helped a great deal! It seemed they thought it was cute that we, little Javanese women, asked for their help and perhaps . . . But enough, they donated a lot, even those women who had sworn not to do anything for the exhibition were persuaded to open their purses a little wider.

Only one lady took exception to our behavior—but we didn't let that bother us. And though later on our participation in the exhibition didn't end quite as well for us, we were never sorry for even one minute that we had been part of that Labor.

Please tell me everything, everything about the work and the struggle, the thinking and the sentiments of today's woman in the Netherlands. We are extremely interested in *everything* that concerns the Woman's Movement!

I don't know any modern language, alas!—*adat* does not tolerate that we girls learn more languages—it is already bad enough that we know Dutch. I long with heart and soul to know languages, not so much to be able to speak them, but rather to be able to enjoy the many beautiful works by foreign authors in the original. Isn't it true that no matter how fine a translation is, it can never be as good as the original? That is always better, more beautiful. We love so much to read, to read beautiful works is our greatest pleasure. We, that is, the younger sisters and I. The three of us have grown up together, and we are always with one another. There's only one year difference in our ages. There's really no discord among the three of us. Of course, we have little differences of opinion now and then, but that does not weaken the bond between the three of us. Our little quarrels are wonderful, I think—I mean the reconciliations that follow. It is the greatest lie—don't you think so too?—when people maintain that two human beings should have the same opinion about *everything*. That can't be, people who say that must be hypocrites.

I have not yet told you how old I am. I was just twenty last month. Strange, that when I was sixteen I felt so frightfully old, and felt depressed so often. Now that I have two decades behind me, I feel young and full of life, and pugnacious, too.

Just call me Kartini; that is my name. We Javanese have no family names. Kartini is my given name and my family name, both at the same time. As far as "Raden Adjeng" is concerned, those two words are the title. When I gave my address to Mrs. Van Wermeskerken, I could hardly give only Kartini. People would find that strange in Holland, and to put 'Miss' or something like that before it, well, I have no right—I'm only a Javanese.

Well, for the moment you know enough about me, right? Next time I'll tell you about our life in the Indies. If you want to be informed about any aspect of our life in the Indies, just let me know. I am more than happy to give you whatever information you want about my country and my people. [. . .]

To Stella Zeehandelaar   August 18, 1899

Thank you, thank you so much for your deliciously long letter, for your cordial words that warmed my heart. Shall I not disappoint you when you get to know me better? I have already told you that I am very ignorant, that I know nothing, nothing! Compared to you I feel like a complete zero. But you are well informed about Javanese titles.

Before you mentioned it, I had never given much thought to the fact that I am, as you say, "highly born." Am I a princess? No more than you. The last prince of our line, from whom we directly descend in the male line, was, I believe, twenty-five generations back. But Mama is still closely related to the royal house of Madura. Her great-grandfather was a reigning monarch, and her grandmother was a hereditary queen. But we don't care at all about that. To my mind there are only two kinds of aristocracy, the aristocracy of the mind, and the aristocracy of the soul. I think there is nothing sillier than people who pride themselves on their so-called "high birth." What virtue is there in being a count or a baron? My poor little brain can't comprehend it.

Nobility and noblesse, twin words with almost the same sound and with entirely the same meaning. Poor twins! How cruel life is to you, because it almost always keeps you ruthlessly apart. If nobility were ever to be what it means, yes, then I would be honored to be "highly born." But now?

I remember how mad we were last year, when, in the Hague, the ladies at the Exposition of Woman's Labor called us the "Princesses of Djapara."

In Holland they seem to think that everyone who comes from the Indies who is not a "babu" or a "spada"[31] must be a prince or a princess. Here in the Indies, Europeans seldom call us "Radèn Adjeng," but usually address us as "Milady." It could drive me to despair. I don't know how many times I've said that we were not "miladies" and still less princesses, but they simply don't listen to me and obstinately keep on calling us "Milady."

Not long ago a European, who seemed to have heard about us, came here and asked our parents if he could be introduced to the "princesses." This was allowed, and oh the fun we had.

"Regent," he softly said to our father, though we could hear him clearly—there was much disappointment in his voice—"princesses, I thought of glittering garments, fantastic Oriental splendor, but your daughters look so simple." We could hardly suppress a smile when we heard this. Good Heavens! In his innocence he had paid us the greatest possible compliment by thinking that our clothes were simple, because so often we're afraid that we are prudes and vain.

Dear Stella, I am so glad that you consider me like one of your Dutch friends and that you treat me like one, and that you find me a kindred spirit. [. . .]

I have always been an enemy of formality. I am glad that for once I can throw off the burden of Javanese etiquette, now that I have a little chat with you on paper. The formulas, the little rules, that have been instituted by people are an abomination to me. You can hardly imagine how heavy a burden mother etiquette is to the Javanese aristocratic world. You can't move a muscle or that nasty lady will stare grimly at you. But in our household, we don't take all those formalities so seriously. We honor the golden saying: "Freedom is happiness."

Among ourselves, beginning with me, we'll dispense with all formalities, and we'll just have to listen to our own feelings to see how far we can go with our liberal tendencies.

Formalities are simply awful with us Javanese. Europeans who have lived for years in the Indies, and who have come in close contact with our native dignitaries, cannot understand Javanese etiquette at all unless they have made a special study of it. I've often explained all of this to my friends, but after I've talked myself hoarse for a couple of hours they still know just as much about our formalities as does a newborn babe.

In order to give you some idea of how oppressive our etiquette is, I'll give you a few examples. One of my younger brothers or sisters may not pass me by unless crouching down and creeping along the floor. If a younger sister is sitting on a chair and I pass by her, she must instantly slide down to the floor and remain sitting there with her head down until I am well out of sight. My younger brothers and sisters are not allowed to use *jij* and *je* when addressing me and can only use High Javanese, and after each sentence has passed their lips they have to "sembah" to me, that is bring both hands together and raise them to just below the nose.

If my little brothers and sisters speak to other people about me, they have to use High Javanese when they refer to anything that belongs to me, for instance my clothes, the place where I sit, my hands, my feet, my eyes, and everything that pertains to me. They are strictly forbidden to touch my honorable head, and can only do so after I've given my exalted permission and they have "sembah'd" several times.

If there are some dainties on the table, the little ones are not allowed to touch them until it has pleased me to partake of them.

Oh, you'll shudder if you happen to come into such a distinguished Native household. You speak to your superiors so softly that only those standing next to you can hear it. When a young lady laughs, she must not open her mouth. (For Heaven's sake, I hear you exclaim.) Yes, Stella, you'll hear more strange things if you want to know everything about us Javanese.

If a girl walks, she must do it decorously, with little neat steps and oh so slowly, like a snail. If you walk a little fast, they'll call you a galloping horse.

Toward my older brothers and sisters I observe all forms scrupulously because I don't want to deny the good right of any one, but beginning with me, we are doing away with all formality. Freedom, equality, and fraternity! My little brothers and sisters behave toward me, and toward each other, like free and equal comrades. There is no stiffness between us,—only friendship and affection. The little sisters use the informal mode of address to me, and we speak the same language. At first people disapproved strongly of the free, untrammeled relationship between us brothers and sisters. We were called "uneducated children," and I was a "kuda koree," a wild horse, because I seldom walked but was always jumping or skipping along. And they called me names because I often laughed aloud and showed an unseemly number of teeth! But now that they see how close and affectionate the relationship is between us, and mother etiquette has taken flight before our freedom, they're jealous of our harmonious union that binds the three of us so closely together.

Oh Stella, you should see how, in other *kabupatens,* brothers and sisters live past each other! They are brothers and sisters only because they are children of the same parents; no other bond unites them except the relation by blood. You see sisters live past each other who, except for a family resemblance in their faces, you would be unable to tell that they meant anything to one another.

Thanks, dear Stella, for your nice compliment that pleased me as if I were a child. I love your language so very much and as far back as my schooldays it has always been my most fervent wish to know it well, know it really well. I'm still so far away from fulfilling that wish . . . but that I've come one step closer is clear from your flattering compliment. Besides, I can't be spoiled anymore. I have been horribly spoiled both at home and by my friends and acquaintances.

Oh Stella, I thank you so much for the friendly thoughts you have for us Javanese. From you I did not expect anything else, but that for you all people, white or brown, are equal. From those who are truly civilized and educated we have never experienced anything but kindness. If a Javanese is ever so stupid, unlettered, uncivilized, the kind of people you belong to will always see in him a fellowman, whom God has created too; one who has a heart in his body, and a soul full of sensitive feeling although his countenance may remain immovable, and not a glance betray his inward emotion.

Whereas your synopsis of "Hilda van Suylenburg" made you very sympathetic to me, and your first letter increased the good feelings I have for you, your last piece of writing gained you a fixed and permanent place in my heart.

At home we speak Javanese with each other; Dutch only with Dutch people. Now and then we may use some Dutch with each other, for example when there's a pleasantry that cannot be translated without losing most of the humor.

To Stella Zeehandelaar   November 6, 1899

Certainly, Stella, I cannot thank my parents enough for the liberal way they raised me. I'd rather have my whole life nothing but strife and sorrow than be without the knowledge which I owe to my European education. I know that many, many struggles await me, but I am not afraid of the future. I can't go back to the old ways but neither can I go any further with the new, thousands of ties still bind me to my old world. What will happen? All my European friends ask themselves this question. If I only knew myself, dear people, I would gladly tell you. They all know and understand how precarious our situation is, and yet they say that my father was wrong to give me the education I had. No!, no! don't blame my dearest father. No, and again no! Father could neither help nor foresee that the same upbringing he gave to all of his children would have had such strong effect on one of them. Many other regents gave their children the same education we had, and it never resulted in anything more than native young ladies with European manners, who speak Dutch. Nor did civilization go any further with many an educated European woman. "What is going to happen?" everybody who met us asked Mrs. Ovink-Soer. All of them know that, sooner or later, we have to return to the society wherein we no longer can be happy.

There's nothing we can do about it; one day it will happen, it *has* to happen that I will have to follow an unknown husband. Love is nothing but a fairy tale in our Javanese world. How can a man and a woman love one another when they see each other for the first time in their lives when they're already tied to each other by marriage?

I shall *never, never* fall in love. To love, there must first be respect, in my opinion, and I can't have any respect for the Javanese young men. How can I respect somebody who is *married* and a *father,* and who, when he has had enough of the mother of his children, brings another woman home, and is, according to the Muhammadan law, *legally* married to her? And why shouldn't they? It is no sin, and still less a scandal. The Muhammadan law allows a man to have four wives at the same time. And though it may be a thousand times not a sin according to the Muhammadan law and doctrine, I shall forever call it a sin. I call a sin all those deeds that make a fellow human being suffer. Sin is to cause pain to another, whether man or beast. And can you imagine how a woman must endure the tortures of hell when her husband comes home with another whom she must recognize as his legal wife and her rival? He can torture her to death, mistreat her as he will; if he does not choose to give her back her freedom, she can go whistle for her rights. Everything for the man, and *nothing* for the woman, that is our law and custom.

"Noblesse oblige," you said in your last letter. What a fool I was to think that spiritual nobility goes hand in hand with nobility of character!—that to be spiritually superior is the same as moral superiority! How bitterly disappointed I've been about that.

Do you understand now the deep aversion I have for marriage? I would do the humblest work thankfully and joyfully, as long as it prevented me from that and made me independent. But I can do nothing, nothing, on account of Father's social position.

If I choose to work, it would have to be something that suits me! But work we would like and that wouldn't be a disgrace to my high and noble family (a series of regents from Java's east coast to central Java) is so terribly far beyond our reach. It would demand a long stay in the West and we can't afford that. We have aimed too high and now we have to take the consequences. Why did God give us the talents, if we lack all the means to develop them? My two sisters, without any guidance, have done very well with drawing and painting, according to those in the know. They would love so much to go on with their studies. But there is no opportunity here in Java, and we *cannot* go to Europe. To do so we need the consent of his Excellency, the Minister of Finance, and we don't have it. We'll have to rely on ourselves, I guess, if we want to get ahead.

Oh Stella, do you know what it is to long for something so much and yet to feel powerless to obtain it? Could Father have done so, I have no doubt that he would not have hesitated to send us to your cold and distant land. I draw and paint too, but I'm far more attracted to the pen than to the brush. Do you understand now why I'm so anxious to master your beautiful language? No, don't try to fool me. I know my limitations all too well. If I could master the Dutch language, my future would be assured. A great number of opportunities would open up for me, and I would be a true child of humanity. Because, you see, I, as a born Javanese, know *everything* about the Indies world. A European, no matter how long he has lived in Java, and being ignorant of Native circumstances, can't be conversant with everything in our Native world the way the Native is. Much of what is still obscure and a riddle for Europeans I could solve with a few words, and where a European is not permitted to go, the Native is welcome. All the subtleties of the Native world which are unknown to even the greatest European scholar can be brought to light by the Native.

I feel my powerlessness all too well, Stella. Everybody would burst out laughing if they could look over my shoulder and read this little sheet of paper. What a crazy idea of mine, right?, I who do not know anything, has learned nothing, and yet would venture on a literary career? Still, even if you also laughed at me, and I know you don't, I will *never* give up the idea. It is indeed a desperate undertaking, but "nothing ventured, nothing gained" is my motto! Forward! Let's dare to do and try! Three-fourths of the world belongs to the bold ones.

I sent you my little article in the *Contributions of the Royal Institute of Linguistics and Anthropology*. I wrote it some four years ago and never looked at it again, until, a little while ago I saw it again when I was sorting some old papers. Just at that time Father received an invitation for a contribution from the staff of that Institute. Father sent them the little article and after some time I received a bunch of offprints. I thought it might interest you, so I sent you one.

Another little piece about batik, which I wrote last year for the Women's Labor Exposition and had never heard from again, has been included in a standard work on batik that will soon be published. It was nice when I unexpectedly heard about it. I had already forgotten about the whole business.

You ask me how I came to be put between four thick walls. You probably thought of a cell or something like that. No, Stella, my prison was a large house, with an extensive yard around it, but the latter was surrounded by a high wall, and it was the wall that held me prisoner. No matter how spacious our house and yard, if you *always* have to stay there, it can only become stifling. I remember how I often, from mute despair, would throw my body against the permanently closed doors and the cold stone wall. No matter what direction I took, at the end of every walk was always a stone wall or a locked door.

When our young queen was crowned, the doors of our dungeon were permanently thrown open, but the event had been prepared for a long time already. For years, European friends had been banging and hammering on those sturdy walls that locked us in. At first they resisted forcefully, but a steady drip will hollow out a stone. And bit by bit the walls began to crumble until, with the Coronation festivities, our Parents pulled us out of the rubble and brought us out into God's wide, free spaces!

Lately Mrs. Ovink often says to me: "Child, did we do the right thing when we got you out from behind those high walls of the kabupaten? Perhaps it would have been better if you had remained in the kabupaten. Because, what's going to happen, what's in store for you?"

And when she saw us drawing and painting she cried out full of distress: "Children, children, is there nothing else for you but this?"

No, the best solution would be if the three of us were blown up, and Father and Mother would forget that they ever had us. Luckily, I am optimistic by nature, and don't hang my head very easily. If I cannot become what I so much desire to be, I'll become a kitchen-maid. You should know that I am a "brilliant" cook. My family and friends don't have to worry about my future, don't you think? A good kitchen-maid is always in demand, and can always get along.

The salaries in Holland seem so small compared with those in the Indies. Yet they're always complaining here about the low pay. Here a person is entitled to a pension after only twenty years of service, and clergy after only ten years. Don't you think that the Indies is an El Dorado for officials? And yet, many Dutchmen vilify it as a "horrible monkey land." I become furious when I hear them talk about the "horrible Indies." They forget all too often that this "horrible monkey land" fills many empty pockets with gold. [. . .]

It would be useless to translate "Hilda van Suylenburg" into Malay. Who can read that language, besides men? There are so few Javanese women who can read Malay. And before the book can do any good for them, they will first have to be prepared for it. They would only think that it was nice story and nothing more.

There *will* come a change throughout our native world; the turning point is foreordained; but when will it be? That is the big question. We cannot hasten the hour of revolution. And to think that it is us who have such rebellious thoughts in this wilderness, so far away in the interior with no land beyond it. My friends here say that we'd be smart if we slept for a hundred years or so, and when we woke up, the time would be just right for us . . . and Java would have become what we want it to be.

"Work among the People of The Indies" I have. Mevrouw Zuylen-Tromp sent Father the book as a present, and he gave it to me. That lady sent it to Father with a request to comment on it and to ask if we wanted to contribute anything. She wanted to publish a book on Javanese women. But I declined. I have much to say about Javanese women, but I am still too young, and have had so little, pitifully little, experience of life. The subject I was supposed to address is far too serious and sacred to me to be taken lightly. I could write what they wanted now, but I know that I'd regret it if I did. Why? Because after four years I'll have a better and clearer idea about various things, and I would have a better grasp of the host of ideas that flit through my mind.

I cannot tell you anything about the Muhammadan law, Stella. Its followers are forbidden to speak about it with those of another faith. And, to be honest, I am a Muhammadan only because my ancestors were. How can I love a religion that I do not know, and am not allowed to know? The Koran is too holy to be translated no matter what the language is. Here no one knows Arabic. You're taught to read from the Koran, but what is read no one understands. I think it's crazy to teach someone to read without teaching the meaning of what is read. It is as if you were to teach me to read an English book, one that I would have to know by heart, the whole thing, without your telling me the meaning of a single word. If I want to know and understand my religion, I would have to go to Arabia in order to learn the language. Nevertheless, one can be a good person without being pious, isn't that so, Stella?

Religion was intended as a blessing to mankind—to create a bond between all the creatures of God. We are all brothers and sisters, not because we have the same human parents, but because we are all children of one Father, of Him who is enthroned in the heavens above. Oh God! I sometimes wish that there had never been a religion. Because this one, the one that was supposed to unite mankind, has through all the ages been a cause of strife, discord, and the most horrible bloodshed. Members of the same family threaten each other because of the different manner in which they worshipped the very same God. People whose hearts are united by the tenderest love have turned with hatred from one another. Different churches, though they call upon the same God, have built a wall between two throbbing hearts. I often ask myself uneasily: is religion indeed a blessing to mankind? Religion, which is meant to save us from sins, how many sins are committed in thy name?

I own "Max Havelaar," though I do not know "Show me the place where I have sown." I shall ask about it, because I love Multatuli very, very much.

I'll tell you another time about the relationship between the people and the ruling classes. I have written too much already, and that is a subject that cannot be dealt with so quickly.

What do we speak at home? What a question, Stella, dear. Naturally, our language is Javanese. We speak Malay with foreign orientals, either Malays, Moors, Arabs, or Chinese, and Dutch only with Europeans.

Oh Stella, how I laughed when I read your question: "Would your parents disapprove if you should embrace them warmly without their permission?" Why, I have yet to give my parents, or my brothers and sisters, their first kiss! Kissing is not customary among the Javanese. Only children from one to three, four, five, or six years of age are kissed. We never kiss one another. You are astonished at that! But it's true. Only our Dutch girlfriends kiss us, and we kiss them back. And even that is only recently. At first we let ourselves be kissed, but we never kissed in return. We have only learned to kiss since we became such good friends with Mrs. Ovink-Soer. When she kissed us, she would ask for a kiss in return. At first we thought it was strange and did so very awkwardly. But you learn that pretty quick, don't you? No matter how much I should love somebody (always a Dutch woman, we Javanese never kiss), it would never occur to me to kiss her without being asked. Because, you see, I don't know if she would like it. It is pleasant for us to touch a soft white cheek with our lips, but if the possessor of that pretty cheek would also find it pleasant to feel a dark face against hers is another question. People can think us heartless, but we would never embrace anyone of our own accord.

If, as you say, I can hold my own with many Dutch girls, it is principally the work of Mrs. Ovink, who used to talk to us as though we were her own sisters. Associating with such a cultured and well-bred Dutch lady had a beneficial influence upon the little brown girls. And now "Moesje" knows very well that, though time and distance may separate us, the hearts of her daughters will always belong to her. Father had promised us—or rather, Mrs. Ovink made him give his word of honor—to let us go to Djombang. Mr. Ovink wanted to take us then and there. We love them so much, so much, almost as much as our Father and Mother. We miss them terribly. Even now I can't quite realize that they are actually gone. We experienced so many things together. We shared our family existences so warmly and for so long.

To Mrs. Ovink-Soer   *Beginning of 1900*

You know how much we have always longed for Europe. We were content to study here, because Europe was beyond our reach. Last year we would have been awfully happy if it had only been Batavia, although even then our thoughts were always directed to Europe. We want to ask the Government here to send us to Europe at government expense. Rukmini would study art in order to devote herself later on to the revival of Indies art, which is one of the ways to promote the welfare of the people. Little One [i.e., Kardinah] would go to an institute for Home Economics in order to teach future mothers and housewives the value of money and thrift, a virtue that the careless, vain, and pomp-and-circumstance loving Javanese so badly need to learn. And I to study education, in order to teach the future mothers, besides science, the notions of *love* and *justice,* the way we learned them from the Europeans.

The Government wants to bring prosperity to Java, teach the people frugality, and wants to begin with its officials. But what good will it do if the men are compelled to put some money aside, when the women, who are responsible for the household, don't understand the value of money? The Government wants to educate and civilize the Javanese people and, for a start, forces the upper class, which is the aristocracy, to learn the Dutch language. But is an intellectual education everything? To be truly civilized, intellectual and moral education must go hand in hand.

And who can do the most for the latter, contribute the most to raising the moral standard of mankind: the woman, the mother, because in her lap a human being receives its first nourishment. There the child learns first to feel, to think, and to speak. And that earliest education cannot be without significance for one's entire life that's yet to come.

The most serious fault of our people is *idleness*. It is a great drawback to the prosperity of Java, and we can only alleviate it with *moral education*.

So *many forces* that could be of use and a benefit to the country and the people remain unused because their possessors chose not to use them because of indolence. An aristocrat would rather suffer abject poverty and misery than be well off because he had to work without the golden pajong to protect his exalted head. The aristocracy despises anything that isn't covered by that coveted item: golden parasols![32]

Our people are not very amenable to ideals; we have to astonish them with an example that *speaks* to them and that would *force* them to follow it, if we want to achieve our goal of progress and enlightenment. For that reason we want more than anything else to go to Holland to study. Little Mother, help us!

When we have finished and have returned to Java, we shall open a school for the daughters of the nobility; if we cannot get the means from the Government, then we will work for it privately in some other way, start a lottery or something. The means will be found when we are ready to do the work—but for the moment our hardest struggle is here at home. If we could get Father's consent we would be richer than a king. Oh if only we could get that!

Oh, it hurts so much, so much. It is awful to be a Javanese girl who is sensitive. Poor, poor parents, what fate caused you to have such daughters! We hope and pray fervently that they may be blessed with a long life, and that later on they will be proud of us even if we do not walk around under glittering golden parasols.

Help us friends to get away from here so we can work at realizing our ideals. Because there would finally be a beginning to end that great injustice that has caused the hearts of women and children to bleed.

I will work hard at learning the Dutch language so I have complete control of it and can do with it what I want—and then I shall try, by means of my pen, to arouse the interest of those who are able to help us improve the lot of Javanese women.

"Poor fools," I hear you say, "just the three of you want to shake that gigantic structure and tear it down?"

We will shake it, little Mother, with all our strength, and even if only one stone falls down, we shall not have worked in vain. But first we are going to try to find the cooperation of the best and most enlightened men in Java, even if there's only one. We want to get in contact with our enlightened and progressive men, try to gain their friendship, and after that their cooperation. We are not fighting the men, but those old traditional conventions, *adat,* that are not worthy of the Javanese of the future, that future of which we (and a few others) are the forerunners. Throughout history, the pioneers of no matter what course have always suffered a lot, *we know that.* It is marvelous to have an ideal, a calling. Call us mad, foolish, what you will, we cannot help it, it is in our blood.

Grandfather was a pioneer when, half a century ago, he gave his sons and daughters a European education. We have no right to be *stupid,* to be *nothing.* "Noblesse oblige." Excelsior! We cannot make common cause with the men of the younger generation yet. If we did, we would be distrusted at once. Friendship between unmarried women and men, who are either married or not, is considered impossible. Later, when we have gained our independence, it will be different. My brother knows them all, either personally or through correspondence. We know that there are men who appreciate civilized, thinking women. I heard a man say once (he was a highly placed native official) that it is such a great help and support to a man if a woman is civilized and educated.

To Stella Zeehandelaar   August 23, 1900

Believe me Stella, if I, if we, ever make it in the sense that you and I mean by "making it," then it will be on your conscience. I'm not just writing this, I mean this with all my heart. You have taught me a great deal and your encouragement has been a sweet support, a force. I shall, I will fight for my freedom. I will, Stella, I will, do you hear me? But how shall I be able to win it, if I don't fight? How shall I be able to find it, if I do not seek? Without struggle there can be no victory. I shall fight, and I shall win my freedom. I am not afraid of the burdens and difficulties, I feel strong enough to overcome them, but there is one thing I am afraid to face squarely. Stella, I have often told you that I love Father so very, very much. I don't know whether I will have the courage to persist if it will break his heart that is so full of love for us. I love him incredibly much, my old gray Father, old and gray because of worrying about us, about me. And if one of us should be condemned to unhappiness, let it be me. Here too lurks egoism, for I could never be happy, even if I were free, even if I gained my independence, if by attaining that, I had made Father miserable.

But, you ask, aren't you a bit too gloomy about the future? Oh, if that were true! I was already optimistic when I hinted at a possible solution! Shall I tell you something? For Javanese girls, the road through life is shaped and formed according to one and the same plan. We are not allowed to have *any* ideals; the only dream we are allowed to dream is: to become today or tomorrow the umpteenth wife of some man or other. I defy anyone to disprove what I've said.

Thinking about Javanese and European conditions and comparing one with the other, you'll have to admit that it is hardly any better there than here insofar as the morality of the men is concerned. Women are just as unfortunate there as over here, with this difference however, that over there the great majority of women follow the man into marriage of their own free will, while here the women have no say at all in the matter, but are simply married according to the will of their parents or guardians, with whomever those in power deem to be right.

In the Muhammadan world the approval, indeed, even the presence, of the woman is not necessary at a wedding. Father can come home any day, for example, and say to me, "You are married to so and so." And I will have to follow my husband. True, I can refuse, but that gives the man the right to chain me to him for the rest of my life, without his ever having to concern himself about me. I am his wife, even if I don't follow him, and if he doesn't want to divorce me, I am tied to him for the rest of my life, while he is free to do as he pleases, marry as many women as he wants, without having to concern himself about me at all. If Father should marry me off in that manner, I would simply kill myself. But Father will never do that.

God has created woman as the companion of man and the calling of woman is marriage. Fine, this can't be denied, and I gladly acknowledge that the greatest happiness for a woman, even for centuries after us, is a harmonious cohabitation with the man of her choice.

But how can one speak of a harmonious cohabitation if our marriage laws are the way they are? I will give you an example. Shouldn't I automatically hate marriage, despise it, because it wrongs a woman terribly? No, fortunately not every Muhammadan has four wives, but in our world every married woman knows that she is not the only one, and that the man can bring home a companion any day, who has just as much right to him as she does. According to Muhammadan law she is also his *legal* wife. In the directly ruled territories the women don't have as hard a time as their sisters in the principalities of Surakarta and Djokjakarta.[33] Where we are, women are already miserable with only one, two, three or four other wives. There, in the Principalities, the women call that child's play. Over there one will hardly find one man with only one wife. Among the nobility, especially at the court of the emperor, men have as many as twenty-six wives, if not more.

Should these conditions continue, Stella?

Our people have grown so accustomed to them that it doesn't bother them anymore, but that does not alter the fact that those women suffer terribly. Almost every woman I know curses this right of the men. But curses never help; we have to act.

Come, women and girls, rise up, let us extend our hands to one another, and let us work together to change this unbearable situation.

Yes, Stella, I know that in Europe too, the morality of men is awful. I agree with you, let us honor the young men who turn their backs on temptation and inveterate habits, and let us feel disgraced by the modern girls who knowingly follow men whose lives are sullied. The young mothers could do the most about this, as I have said so many times already to my sisters.

I would like to have children, boys and girls, in order to bring them up and turn them into people after my own heart. First of all, I would get rid of that miserable habit of favoring boys over girls. We should not be surprised at a man's egoism when we consider that as a child he was already favored over a girl, his sister. As a child already, a man is taught to despise girls. Many times I heard mothers say to their boys when they fell and cried: "A boy who cries is just like a girl!"

I would teach my children, both boys and girls, to regard one another as equals and always give them the same education, depending, of course, on their ability.

For instance, I would *not* allow a daughter of mine to study if she has neither aptitude nor desire for it, simply because I want her to be a new woman. But neither would I cut her short in order to give priority to her brother, *never!*

And I would also remove the barriers which so foolishly have been maintained between the two sexes. I am convinced that if they were removed, it would be especially beneficial to men. I cannot and will not believe that educated and civilized men purposely avoid the company of women who are their equals in culture and education, so they can throw themselves into the arms of disreputable women. What keeps many men from the company of civilized women is that a gentleman can hardly ever be nice to a girl or she will immediately think of marriage. All of this will disappear when a man and a woman can freely mingle from childhood on.

You say, "We girls can do a great deal about steering young men in the right direction, but we are allowed to know so little about their lives." All that will change in time, but we have to work hard, very hard, otherwise that time won't come. Here in Java we are only at the brink of the new age. But do we have to go through all the different phases you over there have already gone through, in order to arrive at the stage you're already living at in Europe? [. . .]

To Mrs. Abendanon

Blood is thicker than water. I set great value and importance on the origin of whatever surrounds me. I have the notion that I will be blessed by objects that belong to people who I revere, love, and respect.[34] I am sure that I will learn far more easily and diligently from the books you sent me. Don't you think I'm foolish? I'm only a big child who wants to love so much, who wants to *know* so much in order to *understand. That's* what we want!

To understand is a very difficult art, isn't that so dearest? It is a very difficult thing to learn for a person who was not born with it as a gift.

Understanding makes you judge more mercifully, makes you forgive, and makes you *good.* My deepest gratitude, dearest, that both of you want to teach us to learn how to understand!

It's Friday evening, the gamelan evening, they're playing our favorite pieces. The crust of ice around our hearts has melted, the sun has kissed our cold hearts to be warm again! Now they are once again susceptible to emotion. The sweet, serene tones which are brought to us by the soft evening breeze from the *pendopo* cause our souls to soar up high to the blue skies of our imagination![35]

Dream on, dream on, dream for as long as you have dreams! If there were no dreams anymore, what would life be, reality is hard enough most of the time.

Perhaps people are right when they say that we really should be living alone on an uninhabited island.

But that would be pure egoism, right? We have to, I believe, live *with* and *for* people. *That* is the aim of life—to make Life beautiful.

Suffering purifies, that is, if the person is of good caliber, because in the opposite case this would not be true. We too have changed—in what way, the future shall know. We only know that we're no longer those carefree children anymore.

We've given away all the little knickknacks from our room, and made the children happy with them. The room of the happy girls is no longer, that place where so many dreams were dreamt, where we mooned so much, and thought, felt, and were jubilant, where we struggled and suffered. Only our bookcase is the same, and our old friends still smile at us in their friendly, familiar, and encouraging way! One of those is our best friend, an oldie that not many people pay any attention to anymore because it is so old-fashioned. Yet it shows itself immediately when its domicile is opened. Our sweet, faithful oldie. Many people would sneer at it, but we love him, our old friend, who has never deserted us, who rejoiced with us during the happy days and who comforted us and lifted us up when there was sorrow and the days were somber. It is . . . de Genestet.[36] He has comforted us so much lately!

To Mrs. Abendanon   March 5, 1902

Do you know who draws those wajang figures for us all the time?[37] You'll never guess. One of our gamelan players! It's amazing how the man can do it, and so neat too. But it seems that the art of drawing is native to Djapara; little *katjungs,* the little boys who tend the buffaloes, draw neat wajang figures in the sand, on the wall, on bridges, and on bridge railings.

The wall behind our house is always covered with wajang figures. If they'd paint the bridge railings white today, they'd be covered with wajang figures tomorrow, drawn by muddy, naked little monkeys either with charcoal or with a piece of red brick.

It's very convenient for us to have a draughtsman around; if we want something or another, we only have to tell him and explain it to him.

At present the woodcarver is making something very beautiful: a bookcase out of djati wood with edges made from sono wood.[38] The door, made of one single pane of glass, is going to be set in a double frame: two narrow carved strips of sono wood joined at intervals by wajang figures and djati wood. At the bottom the two frames are joined by means of snakes that are rushing at each other. The top is going to be carved with wajang figures, and it will also have scroll work. The top part of it rests on two small jambs near the door, which have been carved and fitted with inlaid carvings of sono wood. We saw something like it in Mantingan, the Tomb of the Sultan of Mantingan (it's about half an hour away from here). It didn't have any wood carving, instead it was stucco that had been set into the walls. There were antiquities from China, where the Sultan had been. There's quite a story connected with it.

It is a sacred tomb, and we've gone there several times. A Chinese man had followed the Sultan back home. He also lies buried there. Next to his grave is a *patjè* tree.[39] Miraculous powers are ascribed to that tree. Women who are childless and who long to have a child visit the tomb and bring flowers and incense for the Sultan. If a *patjè* fruit falls on the grave of the Chinese, a woman has to pick it up, make a *rudjah* with it, eat it, and her wish will be fulfilled.[40] They've told us the names of people who profited from it.

Edie is right, the Javanese people are fond of myths and fairy tales.

They say that the children the Sultan of Manbingan blesses the childless couples with are all girls! Poor childless people! We'll have to look for a sacred tomb that will bless the world with boys; there are already too many women in the world!

Good heavens, did I ever wander. I was writing about that bookcase and completely forgot about it. That beautiful piece of furniture is for our sister Kardinah, a present from the Ovink family. Sis was really lucky!

Last month they finished two fire screens. They were for a controleur who's going back to Holland.[41] They're beautiful things, also with wajang figures. The one consists of three leaves entirely made of djati wood, and the other is made from one piece of djati wood framed with dark sono wood. It's simply beautiful.

How marvelous that there's such a demand for our Djapara wood carving. Try to imagine what happened here. Djapara's wood-carving industry has been spoiled because the daughters of a prominent Native official keep on telling the carvers to work after European models and motifs. It was in one of the papers. We were dumbfounded when we heard it, because we had always thought that the wajang figures were specifically Indies. But now it appears that we were wrong, that it's something European, because the models and motifs came from the kabupaten. But to err is human, right, and we're only human, and only Javanese at that. It took quite some doing to get our artists to carve wajang figures. They were scared to death that the wajang spirits would be angry with them. They would only do it after Father assured them that he would take full responsibility, and that the wrath and revenge of the spirits would only come down on him, because he was the man who had ordered them, and not on them, who were only carrying out his will. It was amusing, but that's the way it is with many things.

It was also very difficult to take photographs in the villages. Superstition says that one's life is shortened if one has one's portrait taken, and a photographer is a great sinner. All the portraits he has taken will ask him for their lives in the hereafter. When we came with a photographer into a village, several women began to cry. But when, finally, there was one courageous one who *dared* do it, they dried their tears and when we came back at another time, they offered to have their pictures taken. That's the way it is with everything, isn't it, somebody has to *dare*, make an example!

Sis Rukmini is busy making a portrait of sis Kardinah as a bride. She's drawing from memory. The upper lip and the nose aren't going too well, but the rest can pass. She was particularly good at the bridal ornaments. She's going to try if she can duplicate it in clay, the way you told us. She has a nice little portrait of Kardinah in her sketchbook. It's so nice that she can do all these things, though she has never been taught. But she is, of course, a child of Djapara where even the little shepherd boys know how to draw. Djapara is really privileged. You can't imagine how proud we are of our dear home. Yet there are many who, because they *have* to be here, curse their fate that brought them to this impossible place. Question of taste!

Now a few words about the "vanity problem." Recently I asked a Dutch writer for her opinion about . . . my Dutch. Last week I received a letter from her that included one from another Dutch lady who had just been giving her opinion about my Dutch when she received my letter. That was purely by accident, yet, how nice! I was glad, of course! A week earlier I had an offer from another Dutch lady, via a friend of mine, to become a contributor to a progressive woman's journal that she was running. Write a letter for it every two weeks. My friend had spoken about us to that lady, and she felt sympathetic to our cause, and would gladly do something for the Javanese women with her magazine. She too was of the opinion that a child of the Javanese people should make her own voice heard in order to make the Dutch have a better understanding of the Javanese, and elicit their sympathy for that people. I really want to, of course, but I first have to ask Father's permission, and I'm pretty sure I'll get it.

To Stella Zeehandelaar   August 15, 1902

[. . .] We are busy collecting Javanese fairy tales for Nellie [Mrs. Van Kol], and Rukmini is busy making illustrations for them.

O Stella, we've heard such a treasure-trove of beauty from the mouth of the people: wisdom, truths, so clear, in such simple but oh so melodious words! To really command your language and then make that beautiful and sacred music comprehensible to you! If only you knew the soul of my people, you would be so much drawn to us. We are so close to nature, to the source; our wisdom does not require that you rack your brain in order to understand it. In simple words, but oh, how beautiful of sound and rhythm.

If I could only teach you my language so you would be able to enjoy our beauty in its original state. The deeper I penetrate to the very soul of our people, the more superior I think it to be. Among you, wise men and poets usually come from certain classes, and culture is only found among certain classes. But the great majority, that is to say the common people, are—may I say it?—crude. There are some superior spirits among the lower classes, but the bulk of them Stella? You know them better than I.

But come along with me and let's wander through kampongs and dessas: enter the meager huts of the poor, listen to them speak, hear their thoughts.[42] They're all unschooled people, but what wordmusic murmurs from their lips, what a beautiful soul is expressed in it. Tender, discreet by nature, simple and modest! If I am ever with you I will tell you so much about our gentle people, about the way they think and the way they see things. You have to know and love them as we do. There are so many poets and artists among them, and when a people has a feeling for poetry, the most beautiful thing in life, it can *not* lack an inner civilization.

Everything that is exalted and beautiful in life is *poetry*. Love, devotion, truth, faith, art, *everything* that *elevates* and *ennobles* is *poetry*. And poetry and the Javanese people are inextricably united. The least, the very humblest of Javanese, is a poet. What do you think of the profound respect that children have for their parents, or the touching piety of the living toward the dead? At every joyful occasion the dead are remembered, and their blessing and the blessing of heaven is invoked. We always commemorate our dead, be it with joy or sorrow.[43]

And the name of mother—how holy that is! In the hours of pain and doubt, the pale lips always murmur that name. It is Mother, and again Mother, who we call upon if we need help or support. We venerate motherhood when we call upon her in desperate moments of grief. Why do we not call upon our father, why just our mother? Because from the beginning of childhood, we instinctively feel that mother represents a world of love and devotion.

Mother hood

Each object that falls from our hands is picked up while saying: "Oh, Allah, my child." Do I have to explain to you what that means or implies?

Stella, I shall work very seriously at your language, that I may master it some day, and be able to make you understand all that is beautiful in our people. I am also seriously studying my own language, because I want to teach our people about the white race, as I know it in its finer and nobler aspects. They must learn of your great and noble people, honor and love them. They must. I want to do so much that sometimes I wish I had another pair of hands. The will is great, but the strength is little. I can't risk my health, that would be a stupid thing to do. And yet I am often stupid, I often work late at night, and that is not good for me. I may defeat my own purpose; I want to do a great deal of work, but the end of the story could be that I can't do any work at all because I'm physically too weak. That would be terrible. That's why I am trying very hard to be more moderate and live more sensibly.

To Mrs. Abendanon   October 27, 1902

Oh, if we could only tell you the tenderness we feel every time we receive another proof of your love for us. Despite all our misery we consider ourselves *privileged* creatures. There are oh so many poor souls who are in far worse circumstances than we are, who have to struggle through life *alone,* without a friend, who never hear a friendly word, never see a sympathetic glance, never receive a warm hand-shake. We feel ourselves *richly blessed* because we have a friendship and love such as yours.

Keep on loving and trusting us little Mother, that's what makes us happy. We thank you deeply, deeply for your love and sympathy.

You can see that we've recovered somewhat. We waited for this before we answered your last letter, one which we have absorbed and will keep as a relic.

Oh please, we beg you and pray that you won't think so much about our happiness. We've told you so often, we *don't* seek *our* happiness, but that of *others*.

Believe us, we don't expect, either from *Europe* or from our *own future,* to gather roses for ourselves. We have only one dream, one illusion of Europe: that it will equip us well for the fight that we are engaged in for the salvation of our people, our sisters.

Really, we expect nothing, nothing from Europe that is in any way similar to what European girls dream of: "happiness"; nor to find much friendship and sympathy there; nor to feel *happier* in a *European* environment. We only hope to find that one thing that we *need* for our *goal: knowledge* and *education*. That is the *only* thing we think of. What does it matter if we don't like it in Europe, or if we will never feel comfortable in Dutch surroundings, as long as we get what we are *looking for* and *need* for our *goal?* That's why we come, not to enjoy ourselves.

The highpoint of our stay will be to be together again with our dearest brother, to whom we are attached not because of blood ties but also from an affinity of spirit and soul!

We really do not expect the European world to make us *happier*. The time has long gone when we seriously believed that "the European is the only true civilization, supreme and unsurpassed."

Forgive us, if we say this. But do you yourself think that the civilization of Europe is perfect? We should be the last not to be grateful and appreciative of the great good that is part of your world. But will you deny that over against all that is beautiful and exalted in your society there is much that ridicules the very name of civilization?

We complain about pettiness and narrow-mindedness in our own environment, but don't think that we don't expect to find such *pettiness* as well in that world we hope to go to so we can achieve our goal. [. . .]

You know better than we that, among the *thousands* who are called "civilized" by the world, there are only very *few* like that in *reality;* that not every European is broad-minded, although one can and does expect it from him; and that even in the most elegant, exclusive, and brilliant salons *prejudice* and *narrow-mindedness* are by no means a rarity.

We do not think of Holland as an ideal country. On the contrary. Judging from what we have seen of the Dutch over here, we can certainly be assured that we will see and experience *much* in their small, cold country that will *wound* our sensibilities and *bitterly grieve* us. We Javanese are blamed for being born liars, for being untrustworthy, and ingratitude personified. We have not only read this, but we have heard it said many times, and that is a good test of the person's degree of sensitivity.

We only smile when we read or hear such pleasantries. To ourselves we think of European social life that so often gives brilliant proof of the truth and sincerity of those many Europeans who look down with scorn upon the lying and unreliable Javanese.

We hardly came in contact with Europeans until a very few years ago. The first time we found ourselves in a European crowd was at the time of the coronation of Her Majesty. Oh, how can we describe how moved we were when we realized for the first time how admirably they play comedy in the European world, and not on stage either!

It was during that feast that my reverence for Europeans received its death blow. We saw two ladies in animated conversation holding each other by the arm, their heads confidentially close, and heard affectionate words going back and forth. Good friends, we thought. A gentleman came and broke up the tête-à-tête. As he walked away with one of the ladies, we heard her say to him: "What a harridan!" while the other one said to a woman next to her: "That silly creature, she's decked out like an idiot!" A minute earlier she declared that the "dear one" was so charmingly dressed.

We received blow after blow that evening, from this and other "uplifting" little scenes. We saw red-faced men—"gentlemen"—who exuded the horrible stench of alcohol when they spoke. And, oh, the noise and racket everywhere! Our hearts grew *cold,* and we were dying to get away from that "civilized" environment. If we had been mean and had told what these *friends* said of one another, a civil war would have broken out!

Just a little while ago a girl wrote us about a visit which she had made to a mutual friend. She had been so charmingly and so cordially received. A little later we met this friend and we thanked her for her kind reception of our little friend. And what did she say? "I think she's an *awful* girl. She's such a sour puss. She's never friendly or sweet, but she always *snaps* at you."

Innumerable times we witnessed disgusting kissing displays between persons whom we knew *hated* each other. And it was not the despised "nonas" who did this, but white people of unmixed blood, educated, and well brought up.[44] We also saw how innocent, simple "nonas" were made a fool of by clever, civilized Dutchmen.

The Javanese is a *born liar,* and is *completely unreliable.* We leave it at that. We only ask that when a *child* sins through *ignorance,* and an adult thinking person commits the same sin *deliberately,* which of the two is the most guilty? We sometimes do ask ourselves, what is *civilization?* . . . Is it . . . mastering . . . hypocrisy?

Oh, what have we done, what have we said? Forgive us little Mother. You know that it is not our intention to hurt you or insult you, we only want to be *honest.* Is it not true that honesty is the basis of our friendship, of our love? It is often not polite to be honest. We do not enjoy being impolite, unless we *have* to. We are Javanese, for whom "courtesy" is a particular trait.

It is *your* light that has made us see and ask: "What is form without content?" We think that you ought to know our opinion about some things in your society, because you seem to think that we look upon the European world as our ideal. What we consider *true civilization* you already know: and we know that you think the same: *true civilization* is by no means the property of all the countries of the civilized world. The *truth* can also be found among the peoples that the bulk of the white race, convinced as it is of its own superiority, looks down on with *contempt.*

Our people have faults, certainly, but they also have virtues which could very well serve as examples to the "civilized nations." We already have degenerated, as you can see, otherwise we would never have said this, which does not give a good impression of what always has been considered one of the particular qualities of the Javanese people: "modesty."

Father said to me once, "Ni, don't think that there are many Europeans who *really* love you. There are very few of them." Father did not have to tell us that, we already knew that *very well*. We could count on our fingers, and we don't have to use two hands either, those who really are our *true* friends. Most of them *pretend* sympathy for effect, or they are counting on something. It's ridiculous! The best thing to do is to look at the humorous side of things, then they won't bother you as much. People often do such foolish things. Don't you think that many of those who now talk about Native art, only do it to be part of something, and not because they have any real appreciation for it. A few *important people* are interested and soon *everyone* is mad about it. Is it from conviction? But that doesn't matter, if the *goal* of the real friends of Java and Javanese art can be reached.

Do you think that no matter how *innocent* we might be, we don't know why the *Echo* is so eager to publish our articles? It makes for good *advertisement* for that paper. The *Dutch Lelie* placed its columns at my disposal, and time and again the editor asked for letters from me.[45] Why? For publicity. Letters from a true daughter of the Orient, from a "real Javanese girl," thoughts from such a half-wild creature, and written by herself in a European language, how terribly *interesting!* If we, out of despair, cry out loud about our miseries in the Dutch language, then we are so very "interesting again." And if, God forbid, some day we should die of our broken hearts, because of our murdered ideal, then that too will be so terribly "interesting." Oh, there are people who think that only being interesting is desirable. [. . .]

There is much that is beautiful in Javanese ethics. It is only a pity that not everybody *understands symbolism.*

People take the things that the wise men preach, *literally.* For instance, they abstain from food and sleep; as now interpreted it means, that one must *fast* and sleep as little as possible and all will be well in this life and in the hereafter. The real idea escapes them. "*Not* eating and sleeping are the *goals* of our *life.*"

I am a child of Buddha, and that alone is reason enough not to eat animals. As a child I was very ill. The doctors couldn't help me, they were desperate. A Chinese convict, who had been friendly with us children, offered to help me. My parents consented, and I was *healed.* What the medicines of learned men could not accomplish was done by "quackery." He healed me simply by making me drink the ashes of the burnt offerings dedicated to a Chinese idol. By drinking that potion, I became the child of that Chinese divinity, Santik-Kong of Welahan. A year or so ago we made a visit to the holy one. It is a small golden statue that has incense burning in front of it day and night. In times of epidemic it is carried around in state to exorcise the evil spirits. The birthday of the holy one is cele-brated with great pomp and Chinese come from far and near. Old Chinese resi-dents have told us the legend of the golden statue, which for them really lives.

Our land is full of mysticism, myths, fairy tales, and legends. You must have heard many times about the enviable calmness with which the Javanese meets the most frightful blows of destiny. "It is tekdir" (fate), they say, and this gives them peace and resignation. The fate of every man is determined, even before he sees the light of day. Good fortune and bad fortune are meted out to him before his birth. No man may turn away from what God has decreed. But it is a duty to try everything to prevent it *before* misfortune happens, and when it happens anyway, despite their efforts, it is "tekdir." And against "tekdir" *nothing* in the world can prevail.

Do you know what this tells us? We have to be *steadfast, keep going,* and let happen what will happen, and they will submit calmly to the inevitable, and say it is "tekdir." That is why our people will be against us, *before* it has actually hap-pened. Brought face to face with the fact, they are confronted by "tekdir" and will *resign* themselves. God give us *strength.*

It is *very sad;* we are preparing to estrange ourselves from our loved ones, to break the bonds which up till now have been our greatest happiness. But better a *sound* little hut than a castle in ruins, better a perfectly sound little skiff than to drift on the wreckage of a magnificent steamship.

For a long time now I have had to go to bed without Father's special goodnight for me. Until a few months ago, Father never went to bed without stopping first outside our room, poking his head around the door so he could see his little daughter once again, and calling her name before he went to bed. If my door was locked, he would knock softly; his little daughter had to hear that her dearest one had not forgotten her.

Gone now is that dear, dear time. I have had *much* love, perhaps *too much.* And when one person has *too much,* someone else must have *too little.* Now it is my turn to do without; for too long I've had abundance.

It is *hard* for me, but I *hope* and *pray fervently* that he, *my Father,* my *dear one,* will *be able* to banish me from his heart. My poor, dear sweet one will be spared much misery that way. I shall always love him dearly. In spite of everything he has remained as dear to me as before, it's only that . . . I have to get used to loving without the luster of the ideal. It was so beautiful, so very beautiful. I have to thank that ideal love for some very wonderful, really happy years! But for my poor Father, it would be better had I never become a child of Buddha, he would then possess me *entirely,* if only in memory.

What Nellie said is true: "Life brings more cruel partings than death. Those whom death takes away from us in the bloom of love and friendship remain more surely ours in spirit than those whom life leaves to us."

My poor, dear Father, that he should find this out in his old age and from his favorite child!

It is terribly hard for him, may God forgive me. But he is not the only one who has suffered and who will suffer; we too have striven and suffered. We pray God fervently that he won't suffer too much because of us and that in the course of time he will have good reason to be proud of his little daughters. That will reconcile him to the great disappointment we are causing him now.

NOTES

1   Biographical information is from J. H. Abendanon's article "Kartini" in *Encyclopaedie van Nederlandsche-Indië*, ed. D. G. Stibbe, 2d. ed. in 4 vols. and 3 supplements (The Hague: Nijhoff, 1917–32), 2: 279. (This unsigned article can be attributed to Abendanon on the basis of the article on Abendanon [6: 2–3], which was written by his son.) The most accurate and up-to-date information can be found in four texts written by Cora Vreede-De Stuers: *L'Émancipation de la femme Indonésienne* (Paris: Mouton & Co., 1959); "Kartini: feiten en ficties," in *Bijdragen tot de Taal-, Land- en Volkenkunde* 121 (1965): 233–44; "Een nationale heldin: R. A. Kartini," *Bijdragen tot de Taal-, Land- en Volkenkunde* 124 (1968): 386–93; and "Boekbespreking," *Bijdragen tot de Taal- Land- en Volkenkunde* 136 (1980), 390–95.

2   Because there is no reliable uniform edition of Kartini's letters in English, the page references in the text refer to the most recent Dutch edition: Radèn Adjeng Kartini, *Door Duisternis tot Licht. Gedachten over en voor het Javaanse volk*, ed. Elisabeth Allard, 5th ed. (Amsterdam: Gé Nabrink & Zn., 1976), 30.

3   Radèn Adjeng Kartini, *Letters of a Javanese Princess,* trans. Agnes Louise Symmers (New York: Alfred Knopf, 1920); this first edition had a foreword by the Dutch novelist Louis Couperus. The same translation was reprinted in 1964 with a brief preface by Eleanor Roosevelt; it was edited and had an introduction by Hildred Geertz: Radèn Adjeng Kartini, *Letters of a Javanese Princess* (New York: W. W. Norton, 1964). Though I have referred to this translation occasionally, one should be warned that Symmers's text is less than satisfactory. For one thing, she leaves out sentences, paragraphs, even entire pages of the original, for what seem to be purely arbitrary reasons. She also adds her own emphasis where there is none in the original and often leaves out Kartini's peculiar usage. Furthermore, I would guess that Symmers's knowledge of Dutch was far from thorough. One example of innumerable ones is her translation of *van kant maken*. It means "to commit suicide," but Symmers translates it as "I should find a way out at the beginning, one way or another." Her faulty knowledge of Dutch is probably why she apparently failed to notice Kartini's irony and it may also have contributed to her inclination to make Kartini sound far more sentimental and "sweet" than she actually was. Kartini's tough-mindedness and resiliency is not easily discerned in Symmers's translation. I would also submit that Symmers's use of English is far from ideal, or even idiomatic. This poses an additional problem because Kartini, not being a native speaker, shows some lapses in her style, particularly syntactical ones. We have, in Symmers's edition, a case of the blind leading the blind. In my translation below I have preserved Kartini's awkward phrasing in those instances when there was no reasonable alternative, short of rewriting her text; when I could surmise what was meant, even if it was not completely clear, I have translated accordingly. In sum, Symmers's translation should never be relied upon, and the introductions to both English editions contain some biographical errors.

4 The information comes form a study by the Javanese cultural anthropologist Koentjaraningrat; quoted by Vreede-De Stuers "Kartini," 234.

5 Ibid., 242.

6 "High Javanese" and "low Javanese" require an explanation too complicated for full discussion here. Suffice it to say that there exist different kinds of speech and style based on social relationships. Basic Javanese ("low"), with the largest number of words, is Ngoko; formal ("high") Javanese speech is called Krama. Falling between the two is a usage called Madya. Each level has refinements. Ngoko has four variations, Madya and Krama each have three degrees of formality. As Clifford Geertz put it: "In Javanese it is nearly impossible to say anything without indicating the social relationship between the speaker and the listener in terms of status and familiarity." A number of words have, besides their denotative meaning, a "status meaning." Even the manner of speech changes according to the level used: "The higher the level one is using, the more slowly and softly one speaks and the more evenly. The high language levels, when spoken correctly, have a kind of stately pomp which can make the simplest conversation seem like a great ceremony." See his excellent explanation of what he called "linguistic etiquette": Clifford Geertz, *The Religion of Java* (1960; reprint Chicago: University of Chicago Press, 1976),248–60. See also Elinor Clark Horne, *Javanese-English Dictionary* (New Haven: Yale University Press, 1974), xxxi–xxxiii.

An interesting interpretation of the use of Ngoko and Krama in dealing with matters surrounding death is provided by James T. Siegel in his article mentioned in note 43. Death is said to be the most perfect achievement of social decorum because the immobility of the corpse no longer allows any "mistakes."

7 Vreede-De Stuers, "Een nationale heldin," 392.

8 Vreede-De Stuers, *L'Émancipation,* 30.

9 Vreede-De Stuers, "Kartini," 239.

10 Heather Sutherland, *The Making of a Bureaucratic Elite: The Colonial Transformation of the Javanese Priyayi* (Singapore: Heinemann, 1979), 46.

11 Ibid., 47–48.

12 Vreede-De Stuers, "Boekbespreking," 393–94.

13 Ibid., 391. This is important information because it was assumed for many years that the regent of Rembang was a widower with no other wives.

14 Vreede-De Stuers, "Een nationale heldin," 391.

15 Ibid., 387, and "Boekbespreking," 391–92. The notion that the emancipation of women has a direct impact on the emancipation of the nation is taken quite seriously by modern Indonesia. President Sukarno published a book on the important role of women in the fortunes of the republic: *Sarinah, Panitya penerbit Buku-buku karangan presiden Sukarno* (Jakarta, 1963). It was translated into Dutch: *De taak van de vrouw in de strijd van de Republiek Indonesia* (Amsterdam: Van Ditmar, 1966). Cora Vreede-De Stuers argues for the same affinity in her study of the emancipation of the Indonesian woman; see *L'Émancipation,* xiii. A novel that portrays the problems of a modern educated woman during the last years of Dutch colonial rule is Soewarsih Djojopoespito, *Buiten het Gareel* (Utrecht: W. De Haan, N.V., 1940). The title may be translated as "beyond constraint." Javanese women are in the vanguard again today. In an island that has 88 million inhabitants, birth control is desperately needed, and to get any results, the government found it essential to enlist the aid of Javanese women at the local village level; see Richard Critchfield, "Discovering Indonesia's Women," *Asia* 2, No. 4 (November/December 1979): 8–17.

16 Tzvetan Todorov, *The Conquest of America: The Question of the Other* (New York: Harper and Row, 1984), 171. This study was first published in Paris in 1982 as *La Conquête de l'Amérique*.

17. Ibid., 248, 92, 101.

18 This statement by the fifteenth-century Spanish grammarian Antonio de Nebrija is quoted in ibid., 123.

19 Todorov's term, ibid., 109.

20 Ibid., 254.

21 Ibid., 101, 100.

22 Ibid., 69.

23 Such an interpretation of maternity might also be due to the experience of having several "mothers" in a *prijaji* family (165). In her argument that a woman need not be a biological mother in order to be maternal, Kartini was taking issue with the importance the Javanese attached to bearing offspring. Even when a *prijaji* woman was married, she remained known as a *nganten* (abbreviation of *pengantèn*, or a "bride") until she had given birth to a child. She could be called a "bride" all of her life if she never produced offspring (201).

24 Quoted from the introduction by George McT. Kahin to Benedict R. O'G. Anderson, *Mythology and the Tolerance of the Javanese*, Monograph Series of the Modern Indonesia Project: Department of Asian Studies at Cornell University (Ithaca, 1965), iii.

25 Todorov, *Conquest of America*, 177.

26 Ibid., 249.

27 *Toynbee evenings* refers to meetings of people who subscribed to social ideas promulgated by the British historian Arnold Toynbee. The primary goal of the meetings was to educate the working classes and they often took the form of what we would call "adult education" classes.

28 Opium was particularly used by the Chinese in the Indies, but its use spread to the general population. The Dutch colonial government realized as early as the beginning of the seventeenth century that there was money to be made from controlling the opium traffic. In 1893 it decided to control the entire process of buying, shipping, preparing, and selling opium for a profit. By 1904 this policy was extended to the entire archipelago.

29 *Hilda van Suylenburg*, published in 1898, was a novel about the emancipation of women, by Mrs. Goekoop-de Jong van Beek en Donk. Of little literary value, it had some social significance at the time.

30 A *prikkaart* was a way to collect money for charitable causes. It involved a card (*kaart*) with a number of squares printed on it. After someone made a financial contribution, the volunteer would make a hole (the Dutch verb: *prikken*) in a square to indicate that money had been given.

31 *Babu* was the general word for a female servant.

32 *Golden parasols* were the *pajongs* that were carried by a servant behind the nobleman or a high official. The pajong was used less for shade than to indicate rank, and its use was restricted to the highest rank of Javanese nobility. The Dutch colonial officials imitated the custom until it was abolished in 1904.

33 *Directly ruled territories* and *Principalities* are translations for the Dutch phrases *Gouvernements landen* and *Vorstenlanden*. The first, representing the greater part of Java, were ruled directly by the colonial government in Batavia; the latter were ruled nominally by Javanese royalty, though in reality they were indirectly controlled by the Dutch government.

34 What Kartini is referring to here is the notion of *pusaka,* which was very much part of the Indonesian world. Although often translated as "heirloom," a *pusaka* is, probably, more correctly translated as a sacred relic. Many regions in Indonesia used to have regal ornaments that were revered as holy objects by the population. In reality a *pusaka* can be any kind of object that has special, spiritual, or magic significance to an individual, family, ruling dynasty, or an entire region.

35 A *pendopo* was a kind of pavilion in front of the regent's house. It had no walls and consisted basically of a large floor covered by a roof supported by pillars. The *pendopo* was used for ceremonial events or for any other occasion that required a large amount of space.

36 *De Génestet* refers to the nineteenth-century Dutch poet Petrus Augustus de Génestet (1829–61). He was a very popular poet of religious verse, narrative verse, and verse that described the ordinary life of the bourgeois. Both his wife and child died of tuberculosis, and he died of the disease two years later.

37 *Wajang* (or wayang) *figures* refers to the flat puppets made of leather that are used in the performance of shadow plays. Based primarily, though very loosely, on the Mahabharata epic, the wajang plays present traditional material and a great deal of improvisation. It is popular among both the common people and the *prijaji*. The latter discern a philosophical or psychological symbolism in wajang, while the former enjoy it as a form of entertainment and as a religious representation. Wajang is generally considered quintessential Javanese. Some good studies in English are Anderson, *Mythology and the Tolerance of the Javanese;* Geertz, *Religion of Java,* esp. pp. 262–78. A good explanation and an English translation of three plays can be found in James R. Brandon, ed., *On Thrones of Gold: Three Javanese Shadow Plays* (Cambridge: Harvard University Press, 1970).

38 *Djati* wood was also known as "Java teak," a dark wood used particularly for making furniture and building ships. *Sono* wood comes from the *Sono keling* tree (*Dalbergia latifolia*), also known as "sun wood" or "rose wood." It is a tall wide tree, originally from India, that grows primarily in central and eastern Java. Its wood is highly prized for making furniture.

39 The *patjè* tree, also known as *mengkudu,* is a low tree (*Morinda citrifolia*) that was cultivated for the peel of its roots which was used as a dye in the batik industry. Young tender leaves and the juice from the fruits were used as a medicine. When the fruits were partially ripe they were used to make a *rudjah*.

48 *Rudjah* (*rudjak*) is a kind of fruit salad made from a large variety of fruits, peppers, spices, and sugar. It may be served at *selematans,* a ritual religious feast that often includes a communal dinner.

41 *Controleur* was the third highest rank of colonial regional government, below resident and assistant resident. Originally the controleur's main task was overseeing agricultural activities but his responsibility expanded during the nineteenth century until he became the main adviser on native life and conditions for his immediate superiors.

42 *Kampong* and *desa* both mean "village." The first word is Malay; the second, Javanese.

43 For a contemporary discussion of the Javanese attitude to death, see James T. Siegel, "Images and Odors in Javanese Practices Surrounding Death," *Indonesia,* no. 36 (October 1983): 1–14. Given the present context, it is interesting to note that the proper attitude to death is to be *iklas* or detached, and that a corpse is considered the ideal expression of social decorum because it cannot show any outward signs of emotion.

44 *Nonas* refers to women of mixed Asian and European blood.

45 The *Echo* and the *Lelie* (Lily) were women's magazines.

Willem Walraven

WHETHER at home or abroad, Willem Walraven (1887–1943) was an outsider. Like some of the best minds of the Indies, he was caught in an intellectual and spiritual nomansland. The despair one finds in his letters and in his work is not so much the product of either the Indies or Holland, but is rather a reflection of what was essentially his own personality. Nevertheless, Walraven's example illustrates salient aspects of colonialism.

Walraven was born and raised in Dirksland, on the island Goeree-Overflakkee, in the province of Zeeland. His father began as a humble peddler and worked his way up to a respectable merchant. Perhaps due to his father's material success, Walraven came to see his parent as a symbol of the status quo whose life represented a defense of a stable society where anything not the norm was unwelcome and dangerous. In the days of Walraven's youth, Zeeland was a cultural and geographical backwater. The combative provincialism, which defended its isolation as a virtue, became anathema to this recalcitrant boy and Walraven fled to the more invigorating cosmopolitanism of Rotterdam. Little is known about his youth, but the few facts that can be gleaned from his later correspondence make it clear that certain fundamental traits of his character were formed in those early years and did not significantly change during the rest of his life.

He aligned himself ethically and politically with the still-heady revolution of socialism and Marxism. Revolutionary socialism, with its stated desire of improving the lot of the masses, was, psychologically speaking, against the parental norm, was of necessity against imperialism, applauded "modern" developments, and detested the straitjacket of religion. True to the revolutionary form, Walraven was critical of the colonial

system, against Calvinism, and a champion of ideas that pitted a new ethics of a younger generation against what was inevitably seen as petrified
conservatism of the parental enemy. But there were some anomalies in the
stance Walraven took. Though certainly more "progressive" than his native community, he objected to such untraditional innovations as films
and jazz, and the nostalgic sketch of his years in Rotterdam betrays a
yearning for an era irrevocably gone rather than praise for the new era of
progress. This apparent contradiction anticipates his later fascination
with the decay of colonial society with its attendant romanticism of failure and wasted dreams. This man nevertheless committed the revolutionary act—at least at that time—of marrying a native woman, acknowledg-
ing in public that he cherished her as much as any European wife, even
admitting that in some ways she was his superior. In later years, however,
Holland became for Walraven a promised land (he was never to see it
again), and the Indies came to typify the status quo and a stubborn
conventionality.[1]

No longer able to stomach either Zeeland or his staunchly bourgeois
parents, Walraven immigrated to the North American continent in 1909,
staying for five years in both Canada and the United States. As was true
for many immigrants, Walraven worked in a variety of menial positions,
such as dishwasher, ranch hand, and factory worker. It seems he also
bummed around. Although little is known of these crucial years, we can
infer that Walraven experienced the loneliness that most newcomers to
this continent have had to endure. Of Canada he particularly remembered the "monotony of pines and snow; a country filled with Christmas
trees but without the gay decorations. I remember those sad and monotonous mountains especially at sunset, sad because of their desolation and
monotonous because of the sparse vegetation. Pine trees and more pine
trees, endlessly" (E 92–93). At a later date he added that these were
"landscapes that made you either cry or commit suicide" (B 393).

Of the United States, too, he could praise only the physical beauty of
the land; he found the American people as bad as his colonial enemies.
"Only nature is beautiful, though monotonous. But I have no idea what
someone from Europe could admire in its cities or its people, unless it is
some sort of curiosity for the ridiculous. That's only for stupid people
who don't know anything about anything, who have not developed intellectually, who have no need for culture. America and the Indies (and
especially America) are countries where you'll starve intellectually" (B
293–94). His American experience betrays some revealing ironies. Because of the libraries that Andrew Carnegie, that paradigmatic capitalist,
built all over the country, he was able to do a great deal of reading. He

read Heine there, for instance, and preserved a lifelong admiration for the poet. And though America was the epitome of modernism to the younger European generation of the first two decades of this century, Walraven despised it as a cultural wasteland, typified by its movies. He accused Harold Lloyd, Charlie Chaplin, and Douglas Fairbanks of exerting an immoral influence on the younger generation and on the native population of Java; the movie stars were said to be responsible for the fact that "the little respect they [i.e., the Indonesians] still have for us, is now also lost thanks to the lessons of Hollywood" (B 172; see also 392–93, 531). Walraven thought that the United States, like Canada, was tedious. "Up in a plane you can't tell the difference between one city and another. Streets in straight lines, similar houses, similar people, similar goods, similar thoughts, steaks and onions, chicken pie, apple pie, ice-cream soda, methodist- and baptist churches (a church in every street), and on the corner of the street the Salvation Army with the most naive stories about 'how God saves the sinners.' The blacker your sins, the more amazing is the salvation. America is uniform, uniform in everything, including how one serves God. It's a boring country, a country of sham civilization" (B 260). Since he equates the colonial Indies with the United States, one wonders if he saw any refuge anywhere. He did, but only one: "the west coast of Europe, from Copenhagen to the Pyrenees, but even so, only in the big cities, of course. Anywhere else you die from intellectual malnutrition. You can go and take a look, of course, as long as you make sure that you can get out. If you get stuck in the mud somewhere, like I am, then I'd call you an unhappy man" (B 260–61). It is not surprising that when Walraven returned to Zeeland, he experienced as severe a reaction against his birthplace as he had against the United States and was later to feel about the Indies.

He stayed home less than a year. His dealings with his parents turned from disagreeing with them into hating them. It seems that he was far more wounded by a kind of disloyalty from his mother than by the incomprehension of his father. His mother, Walraven felt, despised him simply because he lacked a prominent position in life. Social status was equated with money: "with those people everything depends on money. Both parental love and the love of one's children are reduced to: 'How much money you got?'" (B 167). In this his parents were no different from anyone else. Walraven characterized their society as one "where one guilder spent on oneself is considered nothing, but one penny spent on someone else is a fortune" (E 41). At the end of 1915, Walraven signed up with the colonial army and left for the tropics.

*

MANY of Walraven's actions seem deliberate attempts to confront his own personality. Volunteering for the military is an example because he was hardly fit to be a soldier. The crudeness of barracks life offended him and he found himself once again faced with a loneliness as profound as the one he had experienced in North America. In the Indies too he was isolated and deprived of congenial companionship, and he felt segregated because he did not speak the language in what was essentially a foreign country.[2]

He was stationed in Tjimahi, a garrison town in the Preanger district of western Java. His first assignment was as a radio operator, but later he became a clerk in the company's headquarters. During this time, as he narrates in the story "The Clan," Walraven often stopped by a *warong*, or small eating stall. A Sundanese girl, called Itih, worked behind the counter. There must have been some rapport despite the language barrier because, after he was discharged, Walraven continued asking about her in his correspondence with a friend. Although it sounds romantic, "The Clan" implies that this friend kidnapped Itih and sent her on a train to where Walraven was living. He picked her up at the station in Banjuwangi on 1 September 1918. Itih lived with him at first as a *njai*. This is a Balinese word for housekeeper, but it was generally used as a euphemism for concubine. In August 1919 Itih gave birth to a daughter. By January 1920 Walraven had married her, although it appears that Itih herself did not see why he bothered (B 45–46).

On the surface, the rest of Walraven's life does not seem very dramatic. He remained in Java from 1915 until his death in 1943. The first decade or so (from about 1918 to 1930) went well. These were Walraven's fat years. He was primarily employed as a bookkeeper in oil and sugar factories and he earned a decent salary. However, he showed a disdain for frugality and what was considered socially acceptable. He took his wife out to dinner, went on trips with her, and brought her lavish presents. He also tried his hand at various businesses, quixotic ventures that all ended in disaster. First he bought a defunct hotel in Pasuruan in east Java, the same little town of his story "Borderline." The problem with this scheme was that no one ever wanted to stay in Pasuruan. As his son reports, Walraven then tried growing orchids for commercial purposes. The flowers thrived in the cool climate of his garden situated at a higher elevation, but when they were shipped to Surabaja to be sold they quickly wilted in the heat of that large coastal city.

When the colonial economy deteriorated, Walraven became a journalist. His letters prior to 1928 make it abundantly clear that his talents as a writer were already fully developed before he decided to live by his pen. He chose to become a free lance, which permitted him to live a life of independence that was so important to him, but this occupation also complicated his last fifteen years. His career provided no stable income and he had a large family of eight children to support.

His marriage to Itih incorporated on a domestic level the ambivalence of colonial society at large. At the head of the enterprise was the *totok,* the European, who felt responsible for the native, in this case his wife. The results of this relationship were eight half-bloods or "Indos." Walraven despised Indo society although, ironically, he should have commiserated with them because they were caught between two worlds as much as he was. The Indos were neither native nor European, straddling a borderline between two cultures, neither of which they could call their own. They were the invisible people of Dutch colonial society. As if a symbolic equivalent of the political reality, Walraven liked his children when they were little but when they developed distinct personalities and rebelled against his authority, he came to distrust and dislike them and began to live past them. The sense of alienation that was so characteristic of his personality and his experience of colonial society soon became a tangible part of his daily life.

At the center of that life was his Sundanese wife, Itih, and his marriage to her graphically illustrates the dichotomy between Holland and the Indies. Socially, Walraven often encountered the barely concealed hostility or disapproval of the Europeans (B 46–47, 152; E 151–57), and, as the two stories translated here indicate, the marriage was not an unmixed blessing for him. Itih, for instance, was careless and lax about the appearance of the house but, like most of her people, she was scrupulous when it came to personal hygiene. This inconsistency did not bother her, but drove Walraven nearly crazy. "Mending socks happens only when you ask for it or order it. A cobweb here or there, well, you better pay no attention to it. Polishing chairs or furniture, absolutely out of the question. I've mentioned this so often, but it was a lost cause. I gave up, nor can I take it so seriously anymore because I'm afraid I might get a heart attack. Let it rot. These people are very clean about their bodies and their clothes, but about everything else. . . . that doesn't matter, as far as they're concerned" (B 358–59). The house was always a mess, what Walraven called a "gypsy camp," and it is telling that he used the same image for his denunciation of tropical society. "The Indies is a kind of gypsy camp. The place where everything is 'more or less' in order, but nothing is ever completely so. A country where everything is always just a little too late. Where death is just in time to come and get you when you were thinking about returning to Holland once more to get some rest from the mess" (B 293). "There's truth in the coarse joke that the Indies is like 'pea soup,' i.e., it's green and hot" (B 294).

But Walraven also understood more clearly than most people that the native woman was quite different from her European counterpart. This seems obvious, but it is surprising how many Dutchmen did not acknowledge this simple truth. The Western concept of love did not exist for the Javanese woman. This, according to Walraven, was due to "the harem mentality, i.e., you come when you're called, and the rest is a mechanical function. . . . The Oriental woman has suffered for centuries from the polygamous notions of her society. She can be cast out, and she might have to share her husband with other women" (B 501). Walraven defended native women against the accusation that they were cold. He felt that they were restrained because they had learned "*never* to believe a man" (B 722). This distrust, which could easily turn into jealousy, was the bane of his marriage. The insecurity that Walraven felt to be characteristic of the native woman may be illustrated by her seemingly frivolous love for jewelry. It also explains, indirectly, why such a woman had little desire to keep house. "The native woman bedecks herself with jewelry that is worth more than the entire house she lives in. She lives on a dirt floor, surrounded by the smoke of her *dapur* [kitchen], but she'll merrily wear diamonds in the midst of that gypsy camp. After all, when you're thrown out you can take your diamonds with you, as well as your beautiful clothes. The rest stays behind, so why get excited about a house and furniture?" (B 505).

Parallels with the colonial dilemma can again be discerned when we read how Walraven repeatedly praised his wife and professed his love for her, while at the same time feeling imprisoned by his marriage and its quotidian realities. "Itih is not an ordinary person. She is quite special and has such virtuous character traits (and yet she is often quite difficult) that you have to respect her. You can't measure her by normal standards. Itih has a fine mind, and since she furthermore lacks the kind of faults most people cling to, you've got to take your hat off to her" (B 280). Nor was his admiration exclusively intellectual. There are some fine passages where he compares Itih to a "Borobudur sculpture." This refers to the sculptured reliefs of the gigantic Buddhist stupa in Java, near Djokjakarta. When Itih sat cross-legged on their bed there was "a striking resemblance to a woman of one of the reliefs of the Borobudur. Her nose and mouth are Hindu, as are her shoulders, arms, and her partially covered breasts. . . . She could have modeled for one of those women sitting at the foot of a king's throne. . . . In every museum of Hindu art I find Itih's portrait in stone, also in every Hindu temple" (B 742).

Nonetheless, one should not assume that Itih was merely an exotic beauty. Walraven was very impressed by her intellectual capacities. Beginning as an illiterate person who could only speak Sundanese, she educated herself until she could read European literature in the original languages, and was soon a match for her husband. Walraven was honest enough to admit that "I haven't learned *her* language! I don't measure up to her who speaks excellent Dutch, Javanese, even Madurese, not to mention, of course, Sundanese and Malay" (B 750). Itih represented the two kinds of Indies the Dutch colonialists had to contend with after the First World War: the old and somewhat romantic colonial realm subservient to the European overlords, and the modern Indonesia that was educating itself and discovering a new confidence in its own worth. "There [i.e., in a museum] are some of those small [sculptures] so beautiful and delicate which remind me very much of Itih, whom I love, and who can sit next to me just as silently as one of those ancient sculptures. Her *kondeh*[3] has sagged and is now in the nape of her neck and her small hands do something which makes no noise. But sometimes she lies on the bed with her glasses on and reads Pearl Buck or Kartini, and then she suddenly looks like a modern Indonesian woman who is just about to start talking about national heroes" (B 744).

There is no doubt that Walraven loved Itih very much, but a sense of loss seems also inherent in the relationship. He warned his nephew that "real love can often be a source of great sorrow. It can change your entire life, change your entire future, can tie you down for the rest of your life to something stupid that you want really nothing to do with. It tied me to this land, though I really have nothing in common with it. It is the reason that I'll have to stay here forever" (B 502). Walraven was a misogynist in some ways, although he was also attracted to the "international Eve" (B 245). He was, in fact, just as much trapped in his relationship with women as he was trapped in the Indies. "Itih always thinks that she'll be the first to die, but she does not understand that I'd be terribly unhappy without her. She also forgets all the time that I'm in the Indies because of her. If she hadn't been part of my life I would have been in Holland a long time ago" (B 365). This feeling of being cornered becomes part of his favorite image for life in the Indies. "When a person goes to the Indies he must also know when he can get out. But people like me are caught in the Indies' mousetrap. We'll never get out of it, except when we die. Then our corpse will be devoured by the white ants" (B 181). He hates the Indies yet he constantly repeats his contention that "once you've been here, it will never let you go. The Indies is dangerous, like a beautiful and bad woman" (B 340). Due to his peculiar character and uncommon sensitivity, Walraven realized something that took the Dutch nation much longer to acknowledge: "We float on top of this Asiatic society like the skin on top of boiled milk" (B 426). Walraven sensed that the Europeans were ensnared. "The Indies means decline, rotting, decay, mouldering, being devoured by sharks, destruction by idiots and greedy people. The spirit of the Indies is always negative, always contrary, especially where Western things are concerned" (B 198).

Walraven was never acclimated to the Indies, but Europe was no longer a habit either. He wrote that if he were back in Holland, he "would return [to the Indies], of that I'm sure. I would long for the Indies, most definitely. Because I was vanquished in my battle with the Indies" (B 525). Walraven never won any battle because he could be satisfied with neither victory nor defeat. He summed up the tragedy of his life in a postscript to a letter from 1939. "A little while ago I was lying on my bed, thinking that for 48 of my 52 years I have really been in exile. That is to say, 19 years in Dirksland, 5 years in Canada, and 24 years in the Indies. This is not true for 2 years in Delft and 2 years in Rotterdam. The rest is exile, and nothing else" (B 498).

FOR such a man who felt always in extremis, the registration of deterioration was second nature. He saw tragedy in his own heart, in his house, in his family, in tropical society, and in Europe as well as in Asia. Walraven never wrote about anything that he had not experienced personally and one will find two favorite subjects in his work that typify his melancholy disposition. He was a master at describing small, dead, doleful towns, backwaters of a crumbling colonial empire. His other fascination was for graveyards. Like a more restrained Baudelaire, or a less baroque Faulkner, Walraven managed to turn his precise descriptions into odes of dejection. One will find a picture of such a town—towns that, as someone wrote, are "too large for a napkin but too small for a table cloth"⁴—in "Borderline," or in the following opening paragraph of yet another sketch.

It rains here every day at an appointed hour. It has already begun by the afternoon and it usually keeps on raining far into the night. *Pajongs* [umbrellas] and wooden shoes are *laku* [in demand] and the chickens make a misanthropic impression. Their tails and other plumage hang down like weeping willows. The nice kid who delivers the paper every day rides through our street on his bike while balancing an open *pajong*. He mumbles something under his breath and shyly apologizes when the paper is a little wet. He looks like a somber character from a melodrama, as do the chickens for that matter. Chickens seldom look happy, but the face of our delivery boy is ten times sadder than the expression of your average chicken. Every day he revolts against the elements. (188–89)

The following two passages describe, first, a Dutch graveyard in Walraven's native town in Zeeland and, second, a Chinese one in Malang, Java.

The Catholics and the Jews mark their graves with headstones and crosses. In so doing they adhere to the old customs of their religious persuasions. But the Protestants, who do not value the flesh but only the soul, still give their dead nothing else to take along on the big journey than a plain wooden casket that is lowered into an earthen grave that will be covered by grass, without anything to distinguish it or to indicate piety. The graveyard is a lawn, planted with trees, where one won't be able to find any individual grave again within a few years. And this may well be the most beautiful and peaceful of cemeteries. In an entirely Protestant village like mine, the grave digger closes the cemetery gate after every burial, and no one sets a foot there again until the next funeral. Visiting a grave is considered an "affectation" because the mortal remains are of no value whatsoever. Only the soul is important, and even the notion of a soul is followed by a big question mark. Only when a stranger was buried did the mayor allow a small pole to be put on the grave, so that possible kin could find the grave again during the first few years. Only the "aristocrats" had reserved a small plot of land for themselves. Even in death they segregated themselves, as they had done in life by means of houses with high stoops and decorative chains. They probably owned their graves. These were usually covered with one of those metal wreaths in iron boxes with a pane of glass. But not even the "well-to-do middle class" dared to contemplate the notion of their own exclusive dwelling after death. After a certain number of years the graves were cleared away to make place for new occupants. . . .

This mentality permeates the entire country. It expresses itself in the straight lines of the roads which cut through the polders as if they had been drawn with a ruler. It expresses itself in the lack of natural beauty, primarily due to the absence of woods. What former landowners may have planted as forest has long been leveled and turned into farmland. Even the poplars along the dikes are disappearing. Wood is worth money, and for money one sacrifices anything poetic, all natural beauty. . . . (E 38–39)

One will see Chinese graves in old shady lawns. Family property of long ago. Here and there a site filled with messy, stone warehouses: a fireworks factory. The solemn and sedate are mingled here with the banal and businesslike. Finally one comes to a section that is enchanting. To the left of the road the terrain slopes down in the direction of the river and on the other side it slowly rises again. And everywhere, but with royal spaces between them, are the neatly kept graves of the Chinese ancestors. Entire generations of Chinese families rest in this vast field of the dead among the finest green of picturesque stands of trees and shrubs. One has to admit that it is impressive.

No European graveyard can compare with this. These places are happily devoid of the dismal and somber character of our own cemeteries, which will always resemble census forms or old archives, their straight paths reminding us of the official orderliness in the world of the living. Here one finds an indication of what ancestor worship means to the Chinese, and how they manage to express it almost with genius, if they have the means and the space. We shake our heads when the Chinese build their ostentatious palaces in the most impoverished neighborhoods, or when they are satisfied with a *klenteng* [Chinese temple] that is not remarkable at all. But here, in this wide riverbed of the Brantas with its gurgling little stream cutting so poetically right down the middle, the Chinese from Malang have found something that is truly theirs, making us see what a city of the dead really should be like.

All of this is, of course, also proof of the enormous wealth these people must hide. Because one is not satisfied here just with graves. One keeps on finding *pendopos,* shelters open on all sides, often impeccably built in Chinese style, with little chairs inviting one to sit and meditate. Here the Chinese can be at one with his dead who, after all, continue to have an important role in his life. And here he can also verify himself of the truth that he has done everything in his power to make the dead person as comfortable as possible. Perhaps he experiences there the best moments of his life. (E 187–88)

It may seem that Walraven apparently prefers the Asian ways. But such sympathies are deceptive, for sometimes he professes to love the tropics and castigates Holland, and soon after he yearns for Holland and mocks his Javanese environment. A French writer summed it up: "l'Europe leur manque et l'Inde leur pèse," or "they miss Europe and the Indies weighs heavily on them."[5] Such ambiguity can lead to unwonted incongruities. He refused to eat rice as long as he lived in the Indies and could not bear the hot spices that many Europeans came to prefer. He ate potatoes, steak, soups, and bread with cold cuts or eggs. He taught his Sundanese wife to cook Dutch dishes, and baked his own bread, cakes, cookies, and pies. His homemade sausage was a delicacy. He absolutely refused to eat margarine and used only butter, which, similar to all the other food he insisted on, had to be imported from Holland as canned goods.[6] Walraven also missed the variation of the seasons. "Nature too is always the same; always green trees, no spring and no fall, and consequently never any spring scents or autumn colors. You only begin to appreciate them when you're over here" (B 94).

While living in Java, Walraven wrote detailed descriptions of Zeeland, inspired by nothing more than an indifferent novel or a dated back issue of a hometown newspaper. Exiles make excellent chroniclers. As Joyce did with Dublin, Walraven could evoke Dirksland better than any native living there, recollecting details people at home were hardly aware of. When Walraven was incarcerated in 1941, he met a young Dutchman

who happened to be from the same town in Zeeland. Walraven noted
with pride that "to his total surprise I knew his entire family background
by heart, going back for about four generations."[7] One senses his nostalgia in a letter to his nephew asking for some cooking herbs, adding that
"they are pieces of a Dutch spring" (B 434). Another passage makes it
clear that these common plants were really metonymies for the land he
had left. "Every animal and plant that comes from a cool climate is more
delicious than those from a tropical climate. Just like those herbs. It's only
my own opinion, but I smell Holland in those herbs. The meadow, the
sides of the road, and the slopes of the dikes. I am even moved when I put
thyme in a pan of food and hold my nose over it. I don't know if you can
understand that, but it is a fact. You can *smell* countries just as much as
you can smell people" (B 449–50). It was not so much Holland he yearned
for, however, as it was a different era, a time irrevocably lost. Only once,
to my knowledge, did he admit as much. Writing to his nephew in 1939,
Walraven mused: "how different was the world at that time, before the
war. I think that I'm really homesick for that time, and less so for Holland
really" (B 318).

WRITING was probably the only activity Walraven loved without reservations. "Everything I write makes me happy, because I really see and feel
it that way. That's probably the reason why others can feel it the same way
I do. I never needed to complain about a lack of readers" (B 748–49). He
was well aware that the greater part of his effort was ephemeral. "Much is
no longer current, much is repetition, and much is too local. All of it was
written from necessity, but it was written with love and with joy for the
work itself, which, I hope, is evident" (B 522).

Walraven lived entirely from journalism for the last fifteen years of his
life, earning what Itih called *uang kepala* or "head money" (B 28). His
son has described his father at work in his room, finally relieved of his
family, dressed in a homemade shirt without a collar or buttons, working
away at his typewriter and sweating profusely: "perspiration," Walraven
told his son, "is inspiration." He often worked at night, when it was
cooler and quieter. He would put a stack of newspapers under his typewriter to muffle the noise, but his son reports that the sound was not that
of the characteristic tapping, but rather a forceful banging, which he attributed to his father's strength and large hands.

War confronted Walraven with political trouble as well as with a severe
curtailment of his journalistic activities. In December 1940 he was accused of being a fascist and a collaborator with the Germans. The incident was, to put it mildly, preposterous, and the formal accusation utterly
ridiculous. Fascism disgusted him, as anyone who knew him or his work

would have testified. Despite his faults, Walraven was a painfully honest man and an individual in need of total freedom—both mental and physical. He would rather do without than submit to any kind of authority. Nevertheless, he was sentenced to one month in prison, and served his sentence in the Sukamiskin prison in Bandung. He recorded his experiences in "Een maand in het boevenpak" (One month in a convict's uniform), an account that was planned as installments in a newspaper in Batavia, but only a few appeared before the Japanese occupied the Indies.

The war drastically reduced his income. Advertising revenues dropped and newspapers were shortened. It is perhaps the final irony of his life that Walraven found it necessary to try his hand at fiction. The stories here translated date from those last two years of his life. Altogether he wrote four, all of them reworkings of earlier journalistic material and all fairly faithful renderings of personal experiences.

The Japanese landed in Java on 28 February 1942. In two weeks the resistance of the Dutch forces was broken, a fact that was far from impressive and that subsequently became a source of inspiration for the Indonesian freedom movement. In July of the same year Walraven and his sons were picked up by the Japanese and put in a camp. Walraven died seven months later, 13 February 1943, a lonely, bitter, and exhausted man who had given up physically and who had retreated into apathy. In 1940 he had accurately predicted: "I am certain that I'll never get back [to Holland] but there is one consolation: it won't freeze when I'm buried" (B 597). Itih survived the war; she went to Holland in 1950 and died there in 1969.

THIS troubled man symbolizes the lack of synchronization that kept Holland from understanding the Indies, and the Indies from appreciating its partner. Walraven lived a limbic existence that did not allow him to be truly centered in either of these antithetical worlds. By his own admission, he was a man of extremes. "I am really someone who can only hate or love, and both intensely, and there's no middle way. Perhaps that's why my scribbling was never a matter of indifference to anyone. They love it or it infuriates them, especially the latter" (B 712–13). One should note that in "The Clan," Itih is drawn with a similar perspective, because what she "remembers the most from her youth are celebrations and disasters, the powerful emotions."

Walraven understood his depressive nature and admitted that he was subject to anxiety (B 210). He once confided to someone that he came from a troubled family with a long history of alcoholism. He did not often refer to his own drinking, but he once wrote: "I have periods when I go sit in a corner somewhere and drink one bottle of beer after the other, until I finally put myself away and wake up the next morning totally disgusted with myself and with a hangover that I can't get rid of for three days. Nor am I the only one in the Indies who is like that. Unfortunately not. You'd be surprised if you knew how much people drink here, especially intelligent people who have all kinds of abilities. It's because of this country. If you're a thinking person here you will look for oblivion, usually you find it with Bacchus" (B 166). His son reported that Walraven could become violent when drunk, but had the compassion to understand that a large part of his father's drunken fury was the result of Walraven's giving vent to his loneliness, to his sense of captivity, to the feeling of being a stranger in his own house.

For Walraven the world was always in the way; reality was an insurmountable obstacle. He was a rebel and an outcast who was exiled from one society and banished to another he both loved and despised. He had married the tropics but felt he had been tricked. He was always on the borderline, a displaced person who did not even have himself for solace. It is no surprise that Heine was his favorite poet.

In the two passages quoted previously, Walraven professed not to like the cemeteries of Zeeland, preferring the Chinese way of death. But in 1939 he seemed to belie both accounts when he wrote about his own death in the land of *tjelaka,* the land of misfortune. It is yet one more discrepancy of a troubled and difficult man who personified the final bewilderment of colonialism in Indonesia.

I would like to be cremated when I die, but that too costs money and we don't even have a crematorium here. I hate the idea of lying in this tropical soil and having the white ants stuff themselves on me. Perhaps it's only an obsession, but I would really like it if nothing personal of me was left behind in the Indies; and I especially don't want to lie in an Indies cemetery. There is no place more ridiculous than a cemetery in the Indies. Circuses of vanity. No one respects you here when you're alive, but once you're dead they adulate you. It seems that only then they become afraid of you because they all believe in "spirits" here, and those spirits can revenge themselves on those who do not sufficiently revere the dead, like by bringing a few flowers or something like that, with their preposterous tombs and the even more preposterous inscriptions on them. I hope I never have to lie in such a display window after I'm dead. The most beautiful cemetery I remember is the cemetery in Dirksland, all grass under the trees, where you will never find a grave again and where the gate is always locked. (B 413)

THE CLAN

Itih, the woman with the little name and the big heart, was born in Tjigugur, a village near Tjimahi in the Preanger district.[8] Although the exact date of her birth is not known, it must have been before the turn of the century because Itih remembers the festivities in honor of Queen Wilhelmina's marriage. She couldn't have been more than four or five years old.

What Itih remembers the most from her youth are celebrations and disasters, the powerful emotions. She remembers the trains which rumbled along the edge of the village, and she still likes to look at a passing train. The many times they moved, due to the fact that her father was a carpenter, are indelibly imprinted on her memory. Her father didn't really belong to the established village hierarchy, though her mother's family did. They moved to Padalarang where she saw a waterfall that burst loose in a powerful wave from a dark hole in the side of the mountain.[9] They moved to Bandung, where the wife of the laundryman who lived next door was hurt by a needle that went right through her fingertip when she was sorting the laundry. A careless lady had left it in a table cloth. The finger became swollen and it turned into a drama which completely absorbed Itih's childish interest. She remembers the wonderful days in the rice fields when along with many other girls she went out to cut the *padi*.[10] Festive days. The meals her mother had prepared they ate at night in the little house by the light of a small lamp, the children sitting in a circle on the floor around the dish. These meals appear in her stories as banquets fit for a king, nor can they be equalled by anything the present may offer. There was also a friend of her own age who faded away when she entered puberty, but he forever remained for Itih the ideal friend who was sweet and innocent, and is loved by her to this very day. Perhaps he still lives in the magnificent Preanger district, though no longer the figure he once was in those happy childhood days.

The end of Itih's youth was marked by a great celebration. It was the most magnificent feast ever celebrated because its occasion was her marriage to Umar. She couldn't have been more than sixteen. Umar came from a prosperous family that had possibly some Arab blood, and owned a large *warong*.[11] When it was time to eat—and it is always time to eat in the Preanger region—the bachelors, and everybody else who worked far from home, went there for their meals. Umar was supposed to have been a handsome youth straight out of *Thousand-and-One-Nights* and, according to those people who could judge it at the time, Itih had made a good match. The respective families had decided on the marriage without her, of course, and Umar was really rather secondary to Itih. She particularly remembered the many presents she received from members of the family, from friends, neighbors, and even from people who, until that day, Itih had never seen or heard about. These generous givers brought an entire household complete with kitchenware, pillows, mattresses, *kains,* and *kabajas.*[12] And in the midst of all of this Itih sat as if enthroned, with her powdered face and with flowers in her hair. They had filed her teeth for just a minute, just barely, because her vehement protests prevented this operation from continuing. Itih is very good at objecting, she is a born nonconformist.

When the big feast was over, real life began. Itih found out about Umar, who demanded his rights, and she also discovered Umar's family and the big and busy *warong* which never stopped making demands on her. There were days when there seemed to be no end to steaming rice, to cooking *sajurs* and *sambalans,* or to washing the dishes.[13] It was too much for Itih's slender and somewhat undernourished body. She also became pregnant and therefore listless and in the end she fell ill. Back home she found comfort in her mother who was probably the only one who, deep down in her heart, understood what Itih was going through. Her child was born, but lived only a short time. Itih never returned to Umar. The flower had been picked, and for the people of the Preanger district things were only now the way they were supposed to be. They don't like unpicked flowers. But thanks to Itih's nonconformity the rest of the story turned out different from what is usually the case. She did not become a *babu* and she did not marry a second time.[14] Nor did she become a vamp. She didn't budge, remained true to herself, and forgot a lot of what had happened. It seemed that she was waiting for a miracle.

I saw Itih for the first time around 1916 when she was working for her uncle by marriage in Tjimahi. They sold things to soldiers in the bamboo stand that was located in the small unpaved yard of a deteriorating and neglected *toko*[15] where an African lived with many children. Inside the *toko* were old cupboards with empty shelves and behind the panes one could see kepis from the time of Van Heutsz, the same model used by the French colonial army.[16] Otherwise the shabby place was filled with old lamps and all kinds of junk no one would ever buy. The inhabitants seemed to have another source of income.

Itih sold cheap coffee made from an extract and condensed milk. It was better coffee than a soldier could find anywhere else. There was also a small rack with jars that were filled with cookies, even with cigars. The roof leaked when it rained, and it rained often, and the water dripped on the jars, including the one that had the cigars in it. It bothered me a great deal, but it was apparently nothing for Itih to do anything about. The latter surprised me, but I was to be often surprised by this same trait in years to come.

Perhaps we got to know each other because I put the cigars in a different place. Or it may have been something else. I came every day and Itih was there almost all of the time. I couldn't talk to her because I hardly knew any Malay, and Sundanese[17] even less. But I had no need for conversation. I sat and mulled things over. I was waiting for a particular date, because on that date I'd be able to leave Tjimahi where I had been forced to stay for almost two and a half years.

My life was bearable, however, especially the last half of my hitch. I worked in a military office that wasn't all that strict. I often had a lot of work, and I worked at all hours of the day. When I was through I walked to the street that was called Pasar Antri and ate something in the *warong* of a Chinese or a Malay, and had a cup of coffee with Itih. It was really a pleasant life, and I never lost my temper. There was nothing that could get me mad because I wasn't really alive. I was waiting until I could resume living again. I wasn't in love and everything passed me by with peaceful monotony. Only later, much later, did I understand the happiness of those days, which I had allowed to slip by unnoticed because I did what I thought I was supposed to do: look for a job that would "suit" me in civilian life.

Everything I have mentioned about Itih up till now I learned much later. At that time I didn't even know her name. She was simply there, small, slender, and skinny. When she stood up straight behind the row of jars in the little rack, it seemed as if her head was too large for her thin neck. She liked to hide behind that rack because then she could smile about what was going on in the street, pulling the corners of her mouth down as if she were mocking somebody. Sometimes she cooked *peujem* on a small brazier. This is a leavened Sundanese cake made from moist, grated cassava that has fermented a little and consequently gives off an odor of alcohol. Sometimes she toasted bread for me on the smoldering charcoal, although I hadn't asked for it. She spread butter on it from a little can that came from Australia. I noticed that she knew the English word "toast" and learned later that, when she was still a little girl in Padalarang, she had helped taking care of the children of an officer who had gone to Australia to buy horses for the army and returned with a wife as well. Because she had a quick mind she had learned a few English words from this lady. And there were times when she silently offered me a candy along with my coffee, but when with my fingertip I touched the part of her breast that curved into a point and that her white cotton *kabaja* had left bare for a moment, she'd say: "Tidak boleh!"[18] It was incredible that she could remain so totally unspoiled in this rather depraved world of a garrison town in the Preanger district. Some rough types came there at times and stayed until late at night. They brought women along and yakked all night and used the filthy language of the barracks and *kampong*. But it didn't seem to bother Itih at all.

She went to the market early in the morning and bought what she needed for that day, then the baker came by to replenish the supply of cookies, and she was ready for business. The money went to her uncle and aunt, mostly to her uncle. She didn't get paid at all but she might get a small present or she'd get a treat when she went to the movies or to one of the many celebrations in the *kampong* with *tandak* and *wajang*.[19]

On the other side of the street was a large movie theater made from bamboo. This was during the early days of film. When they put up new posters I saw Itih shuffle over to them on her tiny, poorly developed feet which made me suspect that she had suffered from rickets in her youth. She admired Zigomar, Eddy Polo, and Maciste, the forerunner of Italy's "strong man," and she wouldn't pay any attention to the coffee stand.[20] I can still see how she worked her way up on those poor little feet to the movie theater on top of the eroded hill of rich Preanger clay, and see her standing there absorbed in the violent scenes on the garish posters. This was Itih's literature. Only much later would she read Kartini, Székely-Lulofs, and Pearl Buck, after she had begun with Ot and Sien. And this was the same person who was to enjoy Daum and know Du Perron personally and chat with him in Sundanese, the language they both loved so much.[21]

My tour of duty was up in June 1918 and I could find plenty of work. I left for Banjuwangi where I got a job as bookkeeper in an oil company.[22] The company provided me with a house and I bought some furniture, the bare necessities, from an auctioneer. I had enough money to live on and employed some Javanese servants, but I worked every day, including Sundays, and I felt strange in that new, almost empty house. Even my servants felt there was something peculiar. I couldn't bring myself to join the typical Indies society because I had lived too long in the tropics without it. I didn't trust those people and wanted to stay free and on my own. I thought I would work all day and read at night. I also wanted to go back to Europe when the war was over. But nothing ever came of it.

I wrote to someone I knew in Tjimahi about my circumstances, and I also asked about Itih, of course. It became clear that she had also asked about me and that she had been kept up to date. This developed into what may be called a correspondence about Itih, until I got a letter one day with the sentence: "Barkis is willin." The famous phrase from *David Copperfield*.

I took twenty-five guilders from my ample supply and sent the money to my correspondent in Tjimahi. I did so nonchalantly, with the smile of a gambler who bets a particular amount on a card, knowing he's going to lose, but also knowing that he won't lose more than that. A telegram arrived: "Left today." They had literally kidnapped Itih in the early morning hours from her aunt and uncle's house and put her on a train that made the connection with the express to Surabaja.[23] Itih, who'd never left her native region, stayed in a Chinese hotel to which she had been brought by the well-meaning driver of a dogcart. Some kindly soul threw her a blanket over the partition that did not quite reach the ceiling of her tiny bedroom. She left Surabaja-Kota the next day for Banjuwangi. I found out later that she had cried a little in the train, somewhere around Kalibaru.[24] On that day, a Sunday, I was waiting for her at the station around half past three. I saw her among the crowd of travelers, small, inconspicuous, yet different somehow: Sundanese. It seemed that she was glad to see me after all those adventures and that long, long trip.

She has never been able to tell me what went on in her mind at that time. Nor have I ever been able to find out how she, who had so much integrity and in consequence protested vehemently against all wrongs, how she was able to decide to make that great journey into the unknown. The miracle she had been waiting for had happened, but she never disclosed how it had come about, not to anyone, nor to me either. For that matter, she could only answer the question "how" at that time, never "why." Nobody in her world worried about the why of things.

She probably felt some guilt as far as her family was concerned, but she was also convinced that she couldn't have done anything else. She had been living there as if she had been indentured to them, a form of slavery which depressed her and seemed dishonorable to her, and which had to end. And she did so with a kind of despair, the way someone who is amok will reach for a knife. She destroyed the life she knew without knowing what the future would bring. She knew only me, and didn't know anything else.

They had given her the money I had sent, but there was still quite a lot left. As soon as she arrived she gave it back to me but I let her keep it. She told me something about the regent and the *wedana* the way *desa*-people do when they come to visit in a different place.[25] Then she borrowed a toothbrush and left to take a bath. When she was finished she said that she was going back the next morning. I gave her some more money and said that I had to go to the factory the next day and would probably not see her again. Before I left the next morning I shook hands and kissed her and told her when the train left for Surabaja. I left her quite calmly. But when I came home that evening she was still there. She'd bought pots and pans and a *kabaja*, and had cooked some rice, and everything that went with it. When she was shopping in the market she met a man who had seen her cry in the train and who had tried to cheer her up. He sold *kains* and other fabrics. And to this very day, when she's faced by a difficult decision, she'd rather follow the advice of a stranger than take my word for it.

And so she stayed with me and so it remains to this day. But the Itih from those days no longer exists, and it seems as if I am talking about a different person.

We lived for two years in Banjuwangi and our first child, a girl, was born there. There were many happy moments but also many unhappy ones. I was already past thirty and wanted a life's companion who wouldn't disturb my private life rather than a woman who wanted to control my existence. Itih was no more than twenty and knew very little about what Europeans call "love," just as Kartini noted about herself and other Javanese women. She only knew the love from a *desa* in the Preanger district, a love with a sting, one that is never assured of itself nor of its adversary. She simply expected that men betray their wives at every opportunity, and no matter what I did to assure her of my affection and, especially, of my esteem for her, and no matter how often I pointed out that I would also wreck my own peace of mind if I were unfaithful, that it wouldn't be in my "interest" if I looked for greener pastures, nevertheless she didn't seem to believe me. For a long time I didn't know what caused those days when she brooded and felt depressed, until finally, during an insane outburst of jealousy, I discovered the reason that had never occurred to me.[26]

That particular misery lasted for years and embittered our lives. It only disappeared much later, when she began to read, along with the children, when she read novels and other books, and I became astonished at her intelligence and her will to understand, especially after she'd met some Dutch friends she could trust completely. But the tragedy of those first few years could never be erased. This woman, who was always true and who would never falter even if it was only because of her pride and profound sense of chastity, this woman was not able to enjoy the fruits of those enviable traits that graced her and made her superior to so many others.

In *Country of Origin* Du Perron writes that the Sundanese woman is cold, but I must submit that this is not true. Her coolness is merely a facade. She forces herself to be this way because of an ingrained distrust of men that many generations have made second nature. She will always consider that a man cannot be trusted as a lover, except in rare cases, and then only after many years have made her fully comprehend the character of the blameless partner, something that probably doesn't happen very often in reality.

We walked a lot in Banjuwangi, especially when the moon was out. At that time a German freighter that had been interned was anchored in the middle of the Straits of Bali, against the background of Bali's rocky coast and its primeval forest. When the moon broke through the clouds it seemed an enchanted ship, one that had only a single watchman on board. Itih had never seen the sea before, but her father was a Buginese,[27] a people of seafarers, and Itih loves the sea and ships. All her trips lead to the sea. We saw the fishermen in their small sailing praos fleeing an oncoming storm in the late afternoon while their women watched anxiously from shore. We often walked through the quiet sections of the little town. She'd shiver from fear if we passed a graveyard, and I was very happy when I finally persuaded her of the obvious fact that dead people are far less dangerous than living ones. And I will never forget some amusing misconceptions she had, and how they were clarified. An *orang bagus* was to her a nicely dressed person, but what my notion of a "good person" was made her happy as soon as she understood what I was talking about.[28]

She always forbade me to write to her family. She seemed to be afraid of reprisals. But when two years had passed in Banjuwangi I managed to get a two-week leave when I was transferred to central Java, and we spent that time in the Preanger district with our baby. This cleared the air, and her mother, an old woman, who really wasn't all that old but was simply worn-out before her time, came often to stay with us for long periods. I hoped that she would stay with us permanently because I wanted to extend her life as long as possible. But her longing for home, for her children, for her region and her language proved always to be too strong and caused her to leave quite suddenly. And one time she left, never to return.

When the telegram arrived informing us of her death, Itih was standing next to me in the bedroom. I read the few words with their pitiless meaning. Itih screamed, sank down on her knees in front of the bed, and cried violently for a few minutes. Then she got up, didn't say anything else, and went about her business. Yet I, a European, will cry months, if not years later, when I think of my dead.

A few years after the old woman died, Itih and I were in the Preanger. I had arrived a few days earlier while Itih arrived in Bandung one evening with the express train. We went to the hotel for dinner and then took a walk along Braga Road and the Great Trunk Road. Then we went dancing and amused ourselves until late at night. But the next morning we were up bright and early and I took her first to Dago, on the small plateau with the tall *tjemaras,* where one has such a fine view of the plain that surrounds Bandung.[29] I was stirring my coffee already, but Itih was still standing near the edge of the plateau and I suddenly saw her burst into tears.

"Why are you crying?" I asked callously and soberly, like a man.

"I'm so happy to be here," sniffled Itih.

I put my arm around her shoulders and took her to our table, and I considered myself lucky to have a wife who appreciated nature and who loved her birthplace. I talked about what we would do that day and we decided to go to her real birthplace, the *desa* Tjigugur.

The *desa* lies just beyond the "*kota*" Tjimahi.[30] Her family on her mother's side has owned land there for at least four generations, probably much longer. One can only get there on foot because no vehicle can get to those little mountain paths. The road is bad and bumpy, and it seems as if they purposely keep it that way to discourage intruders.

It's so safe there and it invokes such peace! In Atim's house, the oldest and most dependable of my brothers-in-law, one can't hear a sound. Atim had a business in building materials. What's more, he lost thousands because of it, and someone who can lose thousands in lime, sand, and cement is an important businessman. I have known Atim since he was a little boy with a little wise face, and he hasn't changed much. He speaks calmly, in a low voice, just as his dead mother used to do. The entire family acknowledges him as the indisputable head of the clan, even Uncle Hassan and Aunt Enèh who also live on the family's property in their bamboo house on stilts, the way they used to build them in the old days. But Atim's house has a cement floor and contains solid beds and furniture, even a modern wardrobe with a mirror. He has no children, but there is a *anak mas,* a little foster daughter, because everybody needs something to take care of.

Atim's wife comes from Cheribon.[31] She speaks Sundanese with a different accent than the people around Bandung. It's faster, sharper, less languid, and less melodious. In the lowlands, life is lived more intensely and far more hurriedly, and this is reflected in the language. The Cheribon woman, childless and perhaps somewhat pessimistic because of it, is clearly not a member of the clan. The same was true of my wife's father, whose grandfather was a Buginese. The land, the family property, comes from her mother's side, and now that the father is a widower, he stays with each of his children in turn, but he is and always will be an outsider. His wife also didn't acknowledge him as a member of the clan, he was and will always be a member of a lower social class, an *orang menumpang.*[32] But he is clean and neat in his old age, almost venerable. He lacks nothing, but he's never present at family councils because they are postponed until after he's left. He could have won himself a place in the clan if he had always made their concerns his own, but he didn't do that. He showed traces of the Buginese love of adventure and desire to roam, which is a horror to the settled *desa* farmers. I'd even say that, though I am a total stranger who barely speaks a few words of their language, I am considered more of a member of the clan than the old man because a few times I offered them money for the common good and once I even defended their interests in a legal sense.

But it is the grave that really shows how much they consider the rather large yard and the adjoining *sawah* as their inalienable property.[33] The grave is located at the center, shaded by a stand of bamboo. The bamboo doesn't grow straight but at a slant, and the wind plays softly with the narrow leaves and makes the long stems creak. The grave is next to the path that goes through the middle of the property, at an angle, as if there were no need for symmetry. But the head points straight in the direction of the Holy City of Islam.

Sick and worn out, the old woman died in Atim's house, on her family property. Only the two brothers and the Cheribon woman were at her side when she died. She remained conscious and said farewell to everybody, including those who weren't present. For Itih and me, and for our children, she said prayers that included Koran texts, over and over again, continually begging the Almighty to forgive us because we lacked the guiding light of the true faith. And now she rests in her grave in the yard, her own yard. No one can cross the yard without passing the grave. Around it are rocks and stones from the river, also cement and other materials, because this grave will be the center of a great mausoleum that will provide space for all the members of the family, even for me, as I was assured quite seriously. I have been loyal to the clan at a distance for over twenty years, and as far as they are concerned I am one of them.

I was quite surprised by this grave. I knew that I had to visit it in order to pay my respects, and I had envisioned a trip to a native graveyard where I would find a small hill, marked off by two wooden or stone pillars, without any other distinguishing marks. I thought to go there with some flowers, roses, *tjempaka* and *melati,* as is customary.[34] But this grave was entirely different. It exhibited a sense of family pride and clannishness which I knew about, but which I saw here tangibly for the first time. And when confronted by this veneration of the dead that had something grandiose and aristocratic about it, I had to quickly suppress the sober notions I had inherited from Calvinism, notions that do not grant much value to the physical elements of life. The grave brought us even closer together and turned the yard into a holy place, a form of *pusaka* which, I felt, would never be touched by profane hands.[35] And I realized that despite nearly a quarter of a century of exile among Westerners, after having been Europeanized in language, dress, customs, marriage, children, and intellectual development, that even so Itih had one dream left: to return one day to this fiefdom among her own people.

The Cheribon woman invited us to dinner. She wore a sky blue *kabaja* with little yellow and red flowers on it. Golden pins glittered on her chest, and she wore bracelets as well. Both she and her entire house were clean and almost painfully neat, and she displayed the manners of a perfect hostess, an Oriental hostess, who never forces herself on anyone. But when the four of us were seated around the table and everyone had been served, the Cheribon woman began to talk. She told us about Mama's death, and everything that pertained to that, and all the things she had done. The vigils at night, the worries, the fears, even how much money was spent. Of the treatment that she, as a stranger, had had to endure from the immediate family. The coolness that the deceased herself had shown—she didn't say this literally, of course, but she hinted at it. One could see that it did her good to speak out for once in the presence of people like us, especially me, who knew everything and knew the family even longer, but who was a stranger nevertheless. She spoke with animation, with broad gestures of her arms, her voice going up and down. She poured her heart out, including even the most insignificant details. Her husband, Atim, sat there silently, saying only a few words now and then to explain things or to give me a meaningful look. After all, I had known the dead person too, and I could bear this apparent "ingratitude" because it made sense in terms of her character and the inner turmoil caused by the past few years, now that all her children lived somewhere else and she could no longer supervise everything and everybody. Furthermore, the daughter-in-law had hardly mattered, and Atim's wife had felt left out, not part of the clan, and she was clearly bursting with grievances.

In the middle of her story the door opened and Uncle Hassan, Mama's oldest brother, came in. Perhaps he had sensed something from his own house, some hundred yards away. He sat down without saying a word and my sister-in-law immediately got up, took a plate, filled it, and offered it to the old man. Her story had come to an abrupt end. Uncle Hassan's sister, Auntie, also arrived a few moments later and the conversation turned to things in general. The usual questioning began, and almost turned into an interrogation.

Auntie was dressed in dark colors which contrasted with her light complexion.

The eyes in her fine, old lady's face were clear and inquisitive. She kept on asking questions about material things, but Atim knew how to mitigate her curiosity very tactfully.

A great deal more was said, also about the other members of the family, and about the in-laws who include many people who want to settle the estate. But the property will be protected by the dead and not one foot, not one inch, of land will be given up as long as a direct descendant of the dead woman lives there and guards the grave. Those in need will be taken care of as well as possible, and the children of poor brothers or sisters will be fed, if necessary. But as soon as the issue of the land is raised, there's no more discussion. Atim's supreme authority, that of the future patriarch, is acknowledged without question.

Just before we left I stood for a moment by the grave and I knew for certain that no one will touch the *pusaka*. As far as that was concerned I could leave without worrying. Their pride would oppose any kind of division or profanation, not only their pride but perhaps the kind heart as well. The heart of the clan.

BORDERLINE

The house was in a fairly wide, usually deserted, street in one of those small, broiling, old harbor towns in East Java which vegetate in the boondocks because there's still a need for a transit depot for a few sugar factories, some mountain plantations, and for the baffling businesses of the Chinese and Arabs.[36] The further you walked in the direction of the sea the more *gudangs* you saw, those squat buildings with their roofs of corrugated iron, until you discovered the sea in the distance, though you were still separated from it by muddy shallows. A wide channel, kept open by the river which disembogued there, cut through the mud flats. Through this channel praos sailed to the steamships which stayed safely anchored offshore and wouldn't dare to get near the silted-up river's mouth. There was a net of fish ponds on both sides for as far as the eye could see. On the mud flat next to the channel lay the wreck of a small wooden ship that had fallen on its side and was now in utter decay. It smashed up once in a storm, within view of the harbor, and after it had been stripped, it was left to its own fate.

But the pier, with its square quay paved with bricks and its small customs office with green shutters, was typically Dutch. When you followed the river back to town, you passed a bridge and came out on a section that had been widened and where the banks had been protected with a layer of stones to prevent erosion. The curve of the right bank immediately betrayed a Dutch construction. It had a quay, also paved with bricks, that had been constructed for the unloading and loading of ships in the shadow of trees, and could have been in one of Zeeland's coastal villages. The low little houses with their windows that looked out over the harbor had been built along a curve similar to that of the quay. The tops of small mooring posts could still be seen sticking out of the pavement. The little houses had an upper and lower door, sometimes a bench on a stoop next to it, and they all had one good-sized window which provided light for the room behind it. The only things needed to complete the picture were transparent curtains, a few red geraniums, fuchsias on the window sills, and some tjalks or boeiers moored near the wall, with deckhouses and gangplanks and a barking keeshond in the gangway.[37] But the old days of sail which must have flourished here once in pure Dutch fashion—including the smell of rope, tar, and tobacco—had vanished when the railroad and trolley lines were built, and only the old decor had survived practically unscathed. When the slanted rays of the setting sun fell on the little harbor in the late afternoon, it made you melancholy just looking at it. It reminded you of a summer afternoon long ago, somewhere in Brouwershaven or Stavenisse.[38]

On the other side of the little old harbor were fences or crumbling, black, moldy walls that surrounded the backyards of the large houses on the street called Gentlemen Street [Heerenstraat], of course. Because here the little town's "Gentlemen" [Heeren] used to live, and they really were the true gentlemen. Such gentlemen no longer lived there, although the word was anxiously preserved. Even in the harbor, in those little houses with their lower and upper doors, were gentlemen living now. To be sure.

Gentlemen Street had rows of gnarled *kenari* and *asem* trees,[39] old-timers that reached down their roots below the stone garden walls and even lifted them up in places, with the result that the pillars were leaning forward and the ironwork was bent.

Quite a lot of the little town was walled in. The dead generations of long ago had not scrimped on bricks, lime, or sand. There were monstrous houses with huge pillars that supported nothing more than a small tiled roof that had partly rotted away and were covered all around with many layers of ancient whitewash, with the result that all sharp contours and edges had been blunted. As if the pillars had been made from a pliable material, a viscous goo, that some messy kid had used by the handful.

The town was old, broiling hot, messy, filthy, with remainders of a past glory and the snobbish structures from a later date. The club had been built with such enormous pillars that one could easily stage Shakespeare's *Julius Caesar* between them without any noticeable change in the sets. The spaces between the pillars were perfectly suited to display Caesar's death litter together with the grand gestures of Antony's funeral speech. The resident's house was really nothing more than a ruin.[40] The walls which encircled the property were crumbling, and the plaster was cracked and falling down. Yet it still had unexpected rooms and "outbuildings" dating from the time when there was unlimited statute labor so that such grotesque piles of stone could be slapped together without any noticeable burden to the colonial budget. And yet Louis Couperus had stayed in this house at the beginning of this century, and had applied the final touches to one of his novels in one of those countless rooms.[41]

There were vague stories about fantastic sums of money which had supposedly been "earned" by smuggling. The coast had not been patrolled because it was thought to be inhospitable due to the fevers from the swamps. Those illegal profits were said to have produced the majority of the vulgar and tasteless houses. The city had been fought over in the days of the Modjopait and Mataram realms,[42] and, even in the days of the Company, important military campaigns had taken place there. The *alun-alun* was still spacious, with a proud and ancient *waringin* tree in its center.[43] The minaret of the mosque reached high in the sky and the graves that surrounded it were considered very sacred. Everything testified to the importance this fortification once enjoyed, when it could rival cities like Surabaja and Semarang, but things had turned into a tragedy. Life had fled and the city now resembled a restored Pompei or Herculaneum.

The mentality of its population was narrow-minded and rather pitiful. A free spirit would never find room there to develop because everyone knew everybody else and people spied on each other and gossiped, consumed by the unhealthy desire to get to know as much as possible about their neighbors' affairs. And if somebody didn't want to be part of it he was declared persona non grata, as if by unanimous agreement, and was forced to capitulate sooner or later. When a prominent citizen on his evening stroll met a European he hadn't seen before, he'd scrutinize him stealthily with his eyes almost closed and ask himself who that could be. What was he doing here? What was his business here? What kind of person was he? What was his income? And the community wasn't satisfied until the stranger had visited a number of people and had justified and accounted for his background and future plans.

All of this went on independently of the lives of the Chinese and the native population, which remained a mystery to the European community. As far as the Chinese were concerned, theirs was a life devoted to becoming rich, consumed by adding a small profit to the other small profits, silent and satisfied, with cool and shiny eyes. And yet this could sometimes alternate with fits of boasting and expansiveness like any other parvenu, as if to catch the eye of the world and blind it. The life of the older natives was centered primarily around the mosque, a little self-satisfied to be sure and somewhat pharisaical when they went to the temple every Friday, the *hadjis* wearing long caftans and holding black European umbrellas.[44] The coolies from Madura lived their sparse existence and saved their money in a moneybelt, sleeping at night in a hovel or in an empty packing crate.[45] Yet there were many among them who got up in the morning, before the sun rose, and gathered with others to pray in the little prayer house in the *kampong*. At first they prayed calmly and slowly and in hushed tones, but gradually they got louder and louder, wilder and wilder until not a living soul could sleep a wink anymore in either the *kampong* or its immediate surroundings. But members of the younger and somewhat more cosmopolitan generation decked themselves out in the latest Western fashions, no matter how eccentric they sometimes might be. And when they got together on moonlit nights they mesmerized each other with such exotic words as "imperialism," "foreign capital," and "nationalism." They squatted next to each other until late at night, and strummed their guitars monotonously while every so often they nasally intoned a line from a *pantun.*[46]

The Javanese were by far the most interesting and sympathetic group of the heterogeneous population. The life of the whites had very little color, all they did was count the days and years. Always preoccupied with "business," and with their eternally chattering, hardnosed wives, whose influence should not be underestimated, behind them, the common Chinese lived as if in a ghetto. And the Arabs hid their mysterious activities behind such barricades as high walls and locked gates, so that only the murmur of prayers could be heard. But the real children of the land, the Javanese, still lived their own natural existence pretty much in the *kampongs* next to the highways, roads which had hardly been constructed for them or by them (unless they had worked on them as laborers). They amused themselves for hours among themselves, especially on Saturday nights. By the glow of flickering lights, among the fumes of oil and *saté-kambing,* the sweet smell of tropical fruit, of cigarettes rolled from tobacco mixed with vanilla, of *bedak* and of hairdos smelling of coconut oil, they enjoyed the noisy *ketoprak,* that popular entertainment from the past fifteen or twenty years, which clearly shows the vulgar influence of the rough slapstick from the early days of silent film.[47]

In other places a tireless *dalang* kept up his endless monologue in front of a white cloth with his filigrain leather puppets, accompanied by the banging and smashing of cymbals and drums.[48] And along with all of this bloomed love, romanticism, and eroticism, though even here the desire for money and the sorrows of passion ruled.

She lived in the large, old, decaying house, in a fashionable street for Europeans. She was called "Mrs.," or *njonja,*[49] but she was one-hundred-percent native. Years ago, while still a little girl, she had begun to share the life of the white man who had become her husband, the father of her children, and whose name she carried with tragic pride. He had died from a neglected case of malaria and influenza, and the children, the boys as well as the girls, had grown up and were scattered in all directions. The boys had unimportant government jobs far away at the other end of Java or in the outer islands, while the girls were living in the enormous city of Surabaja, making livings for themselves in office jobs or European shops. She understood nothing or, at best, very little about their lives, just as in the early years she had understood very little about her husband's life outside the house. The sons, stocky but not heavily muscled, had flown kites, played soccer, and been in the service. The girls had mysteriously blossomed into Oriental beauties, with olive complexions and almond-shaped eyes, displaying elegant legs in silk stockings and, as if life were a play or a fashion show, always appearing in elegant dresses and fancy hairdos, like movie stars. She alternated between amazement and horror. She felt powerless and separated from these children as if by some strange element. If her primitive mind could have conceived of such a comparison, she would have felt like the proverbial chicken who has hatched duck eggs and now sees her brood having fun in the water while she walks up and down the bank scared out of her wits. Her fear gradually turned into estrangement, then acceptance. She had resigned herself and understood that this was the way life was. She had begun feeling this gradual estrangement when the children had gone to school and she had discovered the irrefutable fact that they were becoming part of a sphere that was alien to her, that they belonged to a different world that would always remain a closed book to her, that there were opinions she'd have to accept with true Oriental resignation and with the endurance of a fakir.

But even if the children were scattered to all four points of the compass, and though they lived their own way of life (which she did not understand) in faraway places, yet they did not entirely forget her. They were children of the Indies which meant that, despite their worldly inclinations and frivolous airs, they were graced by that particular trait of the Oriental: reverence, or, at least, a sense of duty, for their elders, for the wellspring of life, for what had cared for them and pampered them in their helpless infancy. And her children also possessed this trait. Not that they wouldn't ask for all kinds of services, nor did they not bother her with all sorts of instructions and requests that came close to sounding like orders, but not a single one of them would ever forget to send her a money order every month. And even if the amount was small, it was nevertheless the first thing that was put aside from their monthly salaries, before all the rest was squandered on useless and vain trifles. Together they made sure that "mama" could live, even if it wasn't handsomely, and even though they criticized her for every luxury (or what seemed luxuries to them) when they visited her sporadically.

And so she lived in that cavernous, old house, together with her grandchild, seven-year-old Gerda, the child of her oldest daughter who very early had married a man who worked on a mountain plantation, far removed from schools and "civilization." And even Gerda was and remained alien to her. No matter how young she was, Gerda saw only the "native woman" in her and obeyed the rules of the boring and deserted house with reluctance. And the grandmother did not recognize her own blood in the child who, until recently, had seemed a surly and contemptuous stranger. But she followed the orders of her married daughter, partly from respect for one of those "bright children" who had outgrown her, and partly for the money order which came every month from that quarter as well.

Gerda called her "grammy" or *nènèh,* and that bothered her. She was, after all, so young. When her husband died and she was left with all those half-grown children, she had no more than finished her first youth, as it were. She had begun life much too early, when she was still practically a child. She had borne her first children, as Hagar bore Ishmael, from a sense of duty and servitude, as if commanded to do so from on high. She had been a child herself when she had given birth to them and now, when all of them, even the youngest ones, were adult or almost grown up, she was left behind not as an old woman, but as a woman in the bloom of life. She hadn't finished yet either with life or with the world. And it sometimes seemed to her as if her life had just begun.

She had taken good care of the large family, and worked hard for it, but otherwise her life had been measured and orderly. Unlike most of her own people, she had gotten used to regular meals and fixed habits of getting up and going to bed. She knew how to use the commonly known medicines such as quinine and boric acid, and she had some notion of antiseptics and general hygiene. She knew what a mild soap did for her face and she had learned to hate the rancid coconut oil in her hair. When she was dressed to go out, her hips and thighs curved gently under the pliant and elegant *kain* from days gone by, and her modest *kabaja* fit tightly over her full bosom and accentuated her small hands very nicely, with their beautifully shaped fingertips and smooth nails. She liked to prance down the street in her slippers, adorned with her flat golden bracelets. And the deference they showed her in the busy Chinese quarter or in the *kampong*, which was her world after all, flattered her, and she enjoyed it immensely.

The *kampong*. That was her life. There she could breathe easy. There were old *kampongs* in the city with quiet corners and picturesque spots which the people living on the avenue would never suspect and had never seen. Immediately behind the European monstrosities of lime and stone the *kampong* began, and it could only be reached through the narrow alleys that branched off from the big road and rarely saw a European. People might say that it was dirty and primitive, but it was also beautiful and pleasant, even poetic. There might be, for instance, a little house that was partly hidden in the shadow of a stand of bamboo, or the spacious and cool house of a well-to-do native with its floor covered with mats that invited you to sit down and where you could chat pleasantly over tea, sweets, or the ingredients of the perennial *sirih* chew.[50] Where they did not address her as "Mrs." or *njonja* but used the respectful, though more informal and cherished, *mas adjeng*.[51] Oh Allà-àh, she sighed, stressing the last syllable of that word, she couldn't help enjoying the silent homage in the eyes of the men. Her own people, her own language, her own *adat*.[52]

She had missed so much in her life despite all the good things from the last few years. Despite being called "Mrs." had it been anything except a life of servitude and slavish submission? And this was still the case. Even in the eyes of little Gerda she read the delusion of superiority inherent in that other race. And the condescending friendliness of the other ladies in the street—which could be either instructive or authoritative, correcting her as if it was almost a command—gave her a chill when she entered the old house again where all her children had been born, but which had never really been hers.

Since the children had left the old house, its hollow spaces seemed to her as so many cavernous graves, and the few pieces of uncomfortable furniture were little more than lifeless memorials of a happiness she had never known or a life that had never been truly intimate, though it had been a time when her life seemed to have known more purpose and warmth. Every morning she opened the three doors that came out into the narrow veranda in front of the house. All the doors were stuck and every lock had its own defect. On each side of the inner veranda she opened the windows with their panes of cheap, lumpy, and wavy glass that showed the world outside as if in a distorting mirror. The old *tukang-kebon,*[53] the jack of all trades who was paid three guilders a month plus a plate of rice for dinner, swept and mopped the floor of red tiles that had been worn down by the many feet that used to walk over them. Against the stark white walls without any paneling stood cupboards from days gone by that were a light yellow, shallow, and had the pointless decorations from the bourgeois era of the nineteenth century. Not a single lock worked, because locks are not really part of the Indies and are therefore always broken. Like any other true native she never understood the proper use of locks, screws, can openers, or whetstones. Nor could she quite comprehend the point of glass jars or tin cans; she always left them open a bit because, if you closed a can really tight, you only had trouble opening it again. And she never sat in a chair, of course. She had her big *balé-balé* couch on the veranda in the back of the house. It was covered with mats and all the kinds of things she might need, such as her *sirih,* her cigarettes, and sometimes a little package wrapped in a green leaf with some food in it. On the front veranda were some rocking chairs dating from the generation that still rocked and which has died out, leaving as souvenirs the shape of the houses and the kind of furniture she had. This generation was described by a certain "Maurits," who was highly praised by Menno ter Braak and others, but who was, as usual, vilified in the Indies.[54] And what became of their black bowlers, their lustre jackets[55] and their batikked pants and white *kabajas?* And one can still imagine them against a dreary background, with their drooping mustaches and their puffy faces swollen from liquor and lack of exercise, grabbing, carousing, building the pompous houses that their children were to laugh at.

She mechanically performed her duties in this environment that was no longer relevant. She helped the child get to school, ate a piece of sticky rice with grated coconut and *gula-djawa,* smoked a Djatirunggo cigarette she loved so much despite the fact that her children looked down on this vulgar habit, and went shopping in the market with one guilder.[56] When she returned after an hour of delicious haggling to get, for instance, *bandeng* fish two cents cheaper, or to reduce the price of *bajem* by one cent, she called for Turi, the woman from Madura who cooked for her and who looked like a skeleton.[57] And Turi squatted next to that marvelous still life from the market. The bright red *lomboks* shone between the light green *petéh* beans, and the silver scales of that fat *bandeng* sparkled. How inviting were the freshly cut slices of *tempeh,* orange between a moldy gray. And the pink meat with an edge of light yellow fat, and two leaves of white cabbage, and the *tèrong* for the *sajur,* and a piece of tripe and, oh, the *trassi,* so enticingly packed in a fresh banana leaf. The ginger root, the *kunir,* the *laos.*[58] Together they went over the prices again and Turi, an old friend who had carried all the children in her *slendang*[59] and who had become a "family piece" as they say in the Indies, Turi the cook opened her crimson *sirih* mouth with respect and amazement when she heard about the *njonja's* talent for haggling. To get the price down even one cent meant a victory over life, over the world.

And then the box with rice was opened, which creaked always in the same way, and the rice was "distributed." And from the square bottle that had contained gin a long, long time ago, the cook poured the required amount of coconut oil, and then Turi disappeared into her *dapur,* her kitchen, which looked like the laboratory of a witch, with its blackened walls and long threads of cobwebs and soot that dangled from the beams. How the kitchen was lit was a mystery. And while Turi rubbed and slapped, scraped and banged all the things that go into making *rijsttafel,* she sat in a corner of her big *balé-balé* and pensively smoked her second cigarette, now and then quietly crocheting an endless bedspread, the only handicraft she had learned and mastered. God knows how, many years ago. She was waiting for Gerda who came home from school around one o'clock.

And after Gerda had come home, hot and crabby from her walk in the fierce sun, they ate *nasi,* the eternal *nasi* of this country.[60] They ate *nasi* the way a horse eats hay, the way a cow puts away grass, the way a prisoner gobbles up his ration. Day in and day out the same menu. And when their stomachs were full they retired to their beds: "Grammy" really to go to sleep because her conscience was clear, while Gerda went only in order to get up again and hang around the yard, or climb in the *djambu* trees looking for unripe fruit, or go in the kitchen and try to mix a *rudjak* on an earthenware dish with the aid of a wooden pestle.[61] Gerda would also get in touch with anybody whenever an opportunity presented itself.

But she always woke up at the same hour, that's how mechanically she lived. Neither howling street peddlers hawking vegetables or fruit, nor tradesmen who wanted to buy empty bottles or cans, nor even the bell of the iceman, were able to wake her as long as she slept like a normal, healthy person. The only one who could wake her up as if by instinct was the official of the orphans' court. When he came it seemed as if she had been pricked with a needle. He was a tall bureaucrat with an affected voice, a twirled and waxed mustache, and a pince-nez in a gold frame. He sometimes came at inconvenient times. The house and the furniture were "in trust" of the court which "represented" the children for as long as there were minors among them, and she was no more than a kind of housekeeper who was barely tolerated. She felt something like fear for the court official who frightened her with his conceited airs and his incomprehensible, authoritarian inspections which were invariably either in the afternoon or late in the evening. He was friendly in an insolent manner and had a way of looking her hungrily up and down when she came out of her room, still sleepy, with a *kabaja* hastily wrapped around what was, after all, still a very attractive figure. Without a *kabaja* she resembled one of the Borobudur statues of a woman, but only the eye of an artist would have appreciated that, not those eyes behind the gold-rimmed glasses. The court official was a powerful man to her and because she was afraid of him she would go to the veranda in the back, where the cook might be, or even Gerda.

But if her siesta had not been disturbed, she got up around four in the afternoon, perhaps half past four, and took a bath in the rickety bathroom at the other end of the yard. She had to walk to it under the covered walkway, carrying her soap and towel. Her chickens and ducks, her doves and cockatoos, all memories of her husband and children, swarmed around her when she walked there, and when she reappeared invigorated from her bath with a fresh cigarette between her lips, she'd toss the feed to her animals very generously and enjoy their greedy pecking and their beautifully plumed shapes. Then twilight and the daily breather from the torrid heat. She rarely drank tea, but she'd have a glass of some brightly colored syrup with slivers of young coconut in it. In the street the stereotypical strolling of the neighboring Europeans began, with their freshly washed faces and anxiously parted and pomaded hair. Their legs looked like wooden ones because of the starched creases in their trousers. And when it got dark she turned her little lamps on. Her children thought that fifteen-watt bulbs were sufficient considering her monthly budget, besides, she didn't do any reading or needlework in the evening anyway. She'd sit down in the pale light of the grotesque veranda in the back where the faded photographs of long dead members of her husband's family shone obscurely on the wall, with his own, enlarged portrait in the middle. The photographer had retouched it so much that all signs of life had been eliminated. At such a time nothing could be heard but the occasional quacking of the ducks in the yard behind the house, or Turi banging in her cave, or Gerda chattering with the children from the neighborhood. After a plate of rice with some sauce and a sliver of meat, and a biscuit for dessert, Gerda went to bed at precisely the hour her oldest daughter had prescribed; went to sleep in the bed which the court had "in trust," the same court that would "represent" Gerda when it came to that. Then she would sit by herself, or with Turi the cook who never seemed to sleep, and listen to the distant sounds of the *gamelan* or the throaty chant of the *krontjong* singer that reached her across the circular wall of the somber backyard.[62] And her lonely heart felt a nostalgic yearning.

On the other side of the *pagger*[63] was light and joy. On this side, in the deserted house, would a young life ever bloom here again? Was she condemned to live this kind of existence until her dying day, waiting for money orders and being always criticized and told to economize, even on the water bill and on the pathetic salaries of the so-called servants who were in fact nothing more than heirlooms from the time when the children were small, people who'd stay even if they weren't paid?

She often thought about this in bewilderment and looked at the old German grandfather clock that was decorated with a little ship on top. A rat had gnawed a piece off because it appeared that it wasn't made of wood but of some sort of hardened pulp that rats found very tasty. She kept an eye on the time and when everything was asleep she sneaked out of the house and disappeared down one of the narrow alleys that led to the *kampong* where she mingled for a couple of hours with what to her was a normal and reassuring way of life. And they accepted her as a matter of course without anyone asking her anything, and time passed very quickly. Then she ran home like a criminal and stole to her room, afraid that she'd wake the precocious child who was always snooping around. But the child had known about it for a long time already, and she'd wake briefly and then fall back asleep again, thinking resentfully: "Grammy is looking for men. I'm going to tell mama when I go home on vacation."

And this is what led to the break. After a fight with her eldest daughter she left in a state of mental amok. It was a decisive moment and she made her choice. Her choice was perhaps not very carefully considered and was rather instinctive. Her past and her marriage appeared to her like some strange dream, with perhaps a bright spot here and there, but one that had faded a long time ago. And she delivered herself to what was calling her and did so willingly, unconditionally, and began her life anew, obedient to a force that was stronger than she was, the authority of her own people, one that knew no rival.

NOTES

1 Biographical material was gathered from Walraven's letters: W. Walraven, *Brieven. Aan familie en vrienden 1919–1941*, ed. R. Nieuwenhuys, F. Schamhardt, and J. H. W. Veenstra (Amsterdam: Van Oorschot, 1966); from his journalistic work: W. Walraven, *Eendagsvliegen. Journalistieke getuigenissen uit kranten en tijdschriften*, ed. F. Schamhardt and R. Nieuwenhuys (Amsterdam: Van Oorschot, 1971); from the description of his incarceration: W. Walraven, *Een maand in het boevenpak*, ed. F. Schamhardt ('s-Gravenhage: Thomas and Eras, 1978), a volume that also contains a bibliography of newspaper and journal articles about his work; and from the moving memoir by his son: Wim Walraven, Jr., *De groote verbittering. Herinneringen aan mijn vader* (Amsterdam: De Engelbewaarder, 1977). References in the text will be cited parenthetically; B refers to *Brieven* and E refers to *Eendagsvliegen*.

2 For Walraven's description of military life in the Indies, see *Eendagsvliegen*, 105–17.

3   *Kondeh* refers to a particular hairstyle. A woman's hair, kept long, was gathered into a bun which was suspended from a loop of her own hair or kept together by hairpins.

4   R. Nieuwenhuys, *Tussen twee vaderlanden* (Amsterdam: Van Oorschot, 1967), 49.

5   Quoted in ibid., 57.

6   His son's report on how his father lived in *De groote verbittering*, 10, 39−41.

7   Walraven, *Een maand in het boevenpak*, 65.

8   *Tjimahi* is the name of the main town as well as the former administrative district in the Preanger region of southwest Java. It was known as the largest garrison town in Java and was described by Walraven in *Eendagsvliegen*, 105−17.

9   *Padalarang* is a town northwest from Tjimahi; *Bandung* is a large city southeast of Tjimahi (see below, n. 29).

10   *Padi,* or mature rice plants, had to be cut by women as *adat,* or custom, dictated. Walraven described it in his letters: *Brieven*, 75−76.

11   *Warong* is both a Javanese and Sundanese word for a "stall" or "booth." Here it specifically refers to a stall where one can eat; it is not a shop.

12   *Kain* can be translated as fabric or cloth, but here it is used as another word for *sarong*. A *kabaja* is a loose jacket of lace or cotton which reaches below the hips. It has no buttons but is closed in front by three brooches connected by little chains, often silver, called *kerosang*.

13   *Sajur* is a general word for a vegetable dish, usually vegetables cooked in some sort of liquid. *Sambalan* or *sambal* is a condiment eaten with rijsttafel, made with a base of hot peppers and a large variety of other ingredients.

14   A *babu* is a female servant who could be either a personal maid or a nursemaid.

15   *Toko* is a general word for shop, and for Chinese shops in particular.

16   The *kepi* is a round military cap with a stiff brim in front, particularly associated with the French armed forces. J. B. van Heutsz (1851−1924) was a controversial general who subjected Atjeh, in northern Sumatra, after several military campaigns. He was governor-general from 1904 to 1909. Under his administration most outlying districts were pacified and brought under direct Dutch control.

17   *Sundanese* is the language spoken in western Java, which is an area that primarily includes the southern portions of what were formerly known as the districts of Bantam, Batavia, Cheribon, and the Preanger region. It is mountain country and some Sundanese refer to their language as *Basa Gunung* or "mountain language." At the time of this story it was spoken by about four million people.

18   *Tidak boleh* means, literally, "That is not allowed."

19   *Tandak* is a Javanese word that became a common term for dancing.

The word *wajang* (or *wayang*) is Javanese (in Malay: *bayang*) for "shadow," hence, by extension, a "shadow play." *Kulit* means "outer skin," "rind," or "peel." *Wajang kulit* designates a shadow play performed with puppets cut from thin leather. *Wajang kulit* is also called *wajang purwa* ("in the beginning") because this is the oldest form of Javanese theater. There is also a *wajang golek,* which is a performance with three-dimensional puppets, and a *wajang topeng,* which is performed by actors with masks. The performer of a *wajang kulit* play is called a *dalang;* he sits behind a screen of white cloth (*kelir*) and moves the puppets across this screen, which is lit by a lamp called a *blenkong.* The *dalang* manipulates the puppets and narrates the texts of various plays. Originally the stories told by the *dalang* were old mythological legends from Java or episodes from such Sanskrit epics as the *Mahabharata* and the *Ramayana.* At first *wajang* was connected with religious or ritualistic ceremonies. A comprehensive discussion of southeast Asian theater (including music and dance) may be found in James R. Brandon, *Theatre in Southeast Asia* (1967; reprint Cambridge: Harvard University Press, 1974) which includes a bibliography. A short popular work in English is Amin Sweeney, *Malay Shadow Puppets* (London: Publications of the British Museum, 1972). One text of the *wajang purwa* repertoire was translated into Dutch, accompanied by an extensive introduction and notes, by J. J. Ras, *De schending van Soebadra. Javaans schimmenspel* (Amsterdam: Meulenhoff, 1976). There are English translations of three of these shadow plays in James R. Brandon, *On Thrones of Gold: Three Javanese Shadow Plays* (Cambridge: Harvard University Press, 1970).

20 *Maciste* was the main character in a series of popular Italian films from the twenties and thirties. Maciste first appeared in the film *Cabiria* (1913), a successful spectacular made by Giovanni Pastrone, which influenced Griffith as well as DeMille. Maciste was played by Bartolomeo Pagano (1878–1947), a semiliterate dockworker from Genoa. Pagano was a huge man with an impressive physique and his role made him so popular that he was featured in a number of "Maciste films," thereby establishing a type of Italian spectacular. As late as 1963 an Italian film was released under the title *Zorro contro Maciste. Zigomar* was originally the character of a popular French "roman feuilleton" by Léon Sazie. In 1911 a French film was made, entitled *Zigomar,* which became a popular series of movies released over a number of years. I have been unable to identify *Edy Polo. Italy's strong man* was, of course, Mussolini.

21 *M. H. Székely-Lulofs* (1899–1958) was a Dutch author who wrote a number of novels about the Indies, especially about Sumatra and the tobacco plantations around Deli. They made her famous in Holland as well as abroad. Her best known novels were *Rubber* (1931), *Coolie* (1932), and *The Hunger March* (*De hongertocht,* 1936).

P. A. Daum (1850–98) was a major novelist who wrote exclusively about life in the colonial Indies. His best work, the first volume of *Ups and Downs,* was published in this series.

E. du Perron (1899–1940) was, after Multatuli, the most celebrated author to write about the Indies in the decade before the Second World War. His most important work, from 1935, is the novel *Country of Origin* (*Land van herkomst*), published in this series.

Ot en Sien was the Dutch equivalent of our Dick and Jane reader. It was adapted for use in the Indies and published in a revised version in 1911. It is an interesting text that shows the different cultural environment in both pictures and vocabulary. A lot of Malay phrases are introduced from the very beginning. A facsimile edition was published recently: Jan Ligthart and H. Scheepstra, *Ot en Sien voor de Scholen in Nederlandsch Oost-Indië,* ed. A. F. Ph. Mann (Alphen aan de Rijn: A. W. Sijthoff, 1978).

22 *Banjuwangi* was the capital of the province with the same name on Java's eastern coast, facing Bali. The city was once an important harbor on the Straits of Bali, exporting rice and copra.

23 *Surabaja* is a large city and harbor on the northeastern coast of Java, opposite the island Madura.

24 *Kalibaru* was a town on the railroad line from Banjuwangi to Surabaja. It is south of the mountain Gunung Andung and due north of the smaller mountain Gunung Terong.

25 *Regent* was the title the Dutch gave to Javanese nobility who ruled over a region. They were, in fact, colonial officials who had been confirmed in their hereditary office. *Wedana* was the title of a Javanese official who was below the regent but superior to the chiefs of individual towns or villages. *Desa* is the Javanese word for a rural village.

26 Itih's different interpretation of love, her distrust of men, and her jealousy were discussed several times by Walraven in *Brieven,* 354–55, 501–2, 791–92.

27 *Buginese* is the name the Malay gave to a people who John Crawfurd, in the middle of the last century, called "the dominant people of Celebes" (John Crawfurd, *A Descriptive Dictionary of the Indian Island & Adjacent Countries* [London, 1856], p. 74). They called

themselves "the people of Wadjo," that is "Wugi," a name the Malay corrupted to the present one. Their original homeland was on the western "leg" of Celebes, bordered on the south by the nation of Macassar, and by Mandar on the north. Like the Malay, the Buginese are a maritime people. They displaced the Javanese and Malay as the marine traders of the archipelago. In the nineteenth century their trading settlements could be found almost anywhere, particularly in Borneo, Sumatra, on the island of Flores, and in the Batam islands.

28   *Orang bagus* can mean either a handsome person or a virtuous person. In Java *bagus* was also a term used for prominent citizens who were not of noble birth.

29   *Bandung* was the capital of the Preanger region in western Java. It is a beautiful city and very popular because of its pleasant climate, which is because it is nearly 2,400 feet above sea level. Tjimahi, where Walraven was stationed as a soldier, is northwest of Bandung. *Braga Road* is a road in Bandung. The Great Trunk Road was constructed by Governor-General Daendels to connect western and eastern Java and ran from Batavia to Surabaja.

Dago, a small town, is due north of Bandung and was noted for its hydroelectric power station. The *tjemara* is a tree. There are several varieties but Walraven is probably referring to *Tjemara gunung* (*Casuarina montana*) which only grows at higher elevations in central and east Java. The wood is used in carpentry.

30   *Kota* or *kuta* is a common word, derived from Sanskrit, originally meaning a fortified settlement or fort. This is the meaning Walraven gives it here. The word came to mean capital, main fort, but it also meant city or village.

31   *Cheribon* is a harbor on the northern coast of west Java.

32   *Orang menumpang* normally means a guest, someone who stays for a long time in one's house. It can also refer to a passenger.

33   A *sawah* is a rice paddy.

34   *Tjempaka* is a kind of magnolia with fragrant yellow flowers (*Michelia champaca*). *Melatti,* also spelled *melati,* is the word in Malay, Javanese, and Sundanese for a variety of jasmine (*Jasminum sambac*). It is a climbing shrub with white, sweetly fragrant flowers, which Javanese women like to wear in their hair and which are particularly associated with marriage ceremonies. The *melati* flower was at one time almost synonymous with the exotic beauty of Javanese, or Malay women in general. The word was adopted as a pseudonym— "Melati of Java"—by a Dutch woman, N. M. C. Sloot (1853–1927) who wrote romantic tales and novels.

35   *Pusaka* (also spelled *pesaka*) is usually translated as "heirloom" but can also mean "family property" or, as in this case, can refer to valuable personal property. The concept of *pusaka*, however, means a great deal more. In many places in Indonesia *pusaka* refers to an object that is holy and that can be inherited. Such objects, said to contain the spirit of people long dead, are often venerated. One could almost translate this common notion of *pusaka* as "fetish." Regal ornaments that belong to a ruler and that he inherited from his ancestors are particularly revered in Java and Celebes. Such objects are often weapons, especially krisses, a *sirih* box, or a sunshade. But in practice a *pusaka* may be any object that has some special significance for that region, ruler, or population. See G. A. Wilken, "Het Animisme bij de volken van den Indischen Archipel," in *De Indische Gids,* vol. 6, part 2 (1844), 56–63. Clifford Geertz gives an example of stories that are "*pusaka* stories," Javanese folk tales about magical objects. He mentions one about a sacred spear and another about a gong that is really a tiger. Clifford Geertz, *The Religion of Java* (1960; reprint Chicago: University of Chicago Press, 1976), p. 301.

36   The old harbor town was in reality Pasuruan, on the northern coast of east Java. Walraven lived there for a short time during an unsuccessful attempt at managing a hotel. Most

of the story is based on fact, except for its ending. In his *Brieven* (721) he wrote: "The end of this sketch was the most difficult part for me. The rest was easy because all of it was a mere copy of daily life." See pp. 162–66 in *Brieven* for his comments on his stay in Pasuruan; on pp. 646–47 he mentions an article he wrote ten years before about the same town; see also pp. 365–66, 721–24.

37 A *tjalk* is a type of Dutch sailing vessel designed for coastal trade and rivers. It has a rounded bow, flat keel, and leeboards. The *boeier* is a boat for river traffic, and its sides, fore and aft, are built higher than normal.

38 Both *Brouwershaven* (on the island Schouwen-Duiveland) and *Stavenisse* (on Tholen) are harbors in Zeeland.

39 The *kenari* (also spelled *kanari*) is a tall handsome shade tree (*Canarium commune*) favored in Java for lining wide streets or avenues. The seeds were eaten raw and taste like walnuts. The *asem* tree is the tamarind tree (*Tamarindus indica*), also frequently used to line avenues.

40 The office of resident was the second highest in the colonial Indies. In Java and Madura there were seventeen "residencies," and the resident was the administrative head of one of these.

41 Louis Couperus (1863–1923) was the great Dutch novelist at the beginning of this century. The novel Walraven refers to is *De stille kracht* (1900), published in this series as *The Hidden Force*. It was the only one of his novels that took place entirely in the Indies.

42 *Mataram* was an ancient kingdom in central Java. The original rulers were Shivaists. They moved their residence to east Java, traded with other islands in the archipelago, and gradually discarded Hindu influences for more purely Indonesian elements. The Mataram realm lasted from 925 to 1222. Modjopait, also spelled Madjapahit, was the other great realm from the Javanese middle ages, lasting from about 1293 to 1389. The beginning of this realm coincides with the arrival of the first European, Marco Polo, and the beginning of the spread of Islam. Under the brilliant rule of Prime Minister Gajah Mada, who died in 1364, there was for some time a unified Indonesian realm under the hegemony of Java.

43 An *alun-alun,* which now means no more than a village square, originally referred in Java to a large, square field of grass in front of the residences of nobility. It was surrounded by *waringin* trees and one or two of these trees were also in the middle. These wide spaces were once used for tournaments and for staged battles between tigers and water buffalos. Waringin trees were considered sacred. These trees, *Ficus benjamina,* could grow to impressive heights and circumference, and are similar to the banyan trees of India.

44 *Hadji,* a term from Arabic, indicates a person who has made a pilgrimage to Mecca.

45 *Madura* is an island off the northern coast of east Java opposite the large harbor of Surabaja. Since it was overpopulated many Madurese went to Java to find work.

46 The *pantun* is probably the most common and popular form of poetry in Indonesia. A pantun is a quatrain. The first line rhymes with the third, and the second with the fourth. Assonance is a favorite device. The pantun is somewhat similar to a sonnet in that the first two lines present an event or subject and the last two lines meditate on it.

47 *Saté* resembles a miniature shiskabob of small pieces of meat skewered on a little stick and roasted over an open fire. *Kambing* is goat meat. Cigarettes made from a mixture of tobacco and vanilla were not very common, as far as I know. However, Indonesian cigarettes are often made from local tobacco spiced with cloves, the so-called *kretek* cigarettes. *Bedak* is a cosmetic face powder, made from rice flour and other ingredients. *Ketoprak* is a Javanese term for a popular form of theater, *not* wajang.

48 The *dalang* is the man who performs a wajang play.

49 *Njonja* was only used for the wives of prominent citizens.

50 *Sirih* refers to the leaves or the fruit of the pepper plant (*Piper betle*), which is the main ingredient of *sirih* chewing, known in English as betel chewing. The other ingredients were lime, some *gambir* (an extract of the plant *Uncaria gambir*), and a piece of the *pinang* nut.

51 *Mas adjeng*. *Mas* is a Javanese title for someone of hereditary nobility, and is used as well for the wife of such a person. It also means gold. Now it more often refers to a person of the middle class. With the addition of *adjeng* (*mas adjeng*) it indicated the wife of a man of standing.

52 *Adat* generally refers to the particular customs of the various ethnic groups in Indonesia. It is a complicated principle, one that also included *adat* law. For a description of the latter in English see B. ter Haar, *Adat Law in Indonesia* (New York: Institute of Pacific Relations, 1948).

53 *Tukang-kebon* means gardener; *kebon* is garden, and *tukang* means a man skilled in some handicraft.

54 *Maurits* was the psuedonym of P. A. Daum (see n. 21 above).

Menno ter Braak (1902–40) was a Dutch critic and man of letters, a member of the influential group of writers associated with the journal *Forum*. For an introductory article on Ter Braak, see E. M. Beekman, "The Critic and Existence: An Introduction to Menno ter Braak," in *Criticism: Speculative and Analytical Essays*, ed. L. D. Dembo (Madison: University of Wisconsin Press, 1968).

55 *Lustre cloth* is a thin, light clothing material. The warp was once silk or linen, then more commonly cotton, and the weft was wool. Lustre cloth has indeed a shine to it.

56 *Gula-djawa* is a brown sugar from Java. *Gula* means sugar and *djawa* is the Javanese word for Java. *Djatirunggo* was a cheap brand of Javanese cigarettes made from Javanese tobacco.

57 The *bandeng* is a marine fish (*Chanos chanos*, of the family *Clupeidae*) which is raised commercially in fish ponds (called *tambaks* in Javanese) along the northern coast of Java. *Bajem* can be thought of as a kind of tropical spinach (*Amarantus tricolor*).

58 *Lombok* or *tjabe* is the fruit of *Capsicum annuum*, the so-called Spanish pepper. *Peté(h)* refers to the pods of the *Parkia speciosa* tree. This tree, about forty-five feet high, is grown in Java for its seeds. These seeds have an offensive smell but the native population eat them either raw or toasted. *Peté* is also used in *sambal* or as a vegetable. *Tempe(h)* refers to cakes made from fermented soybeans. *Tèrong* is eggplant. *Trassi* is a shrimp paste with an offensive smell; it is almost indispensable for native cooking. *Kunir* or *kunjit* is the *Curcuma longa*, the most widely used kind of *temu* plants, i.e., plants raised for their roots. The roots of the *kunir* plant are mashed or grated to produce the Indonesian variety of curry. *Laos*, or *langkuwas*, is another indispensable spice in Indonesia. It refers to the powdered roots of *Alpinia galanga*. The white roots are used in cooking; the red variety (*langkuwas merah*) is used for medicinal purposes.

59 The *slendang* is a cut of cloth women wear over one shoulder and across the chest with the lowest point at the hip. It is used for carrying an infant.

60 *Nasi* refers to the staple food of the Indies, cooked rice. Walraven hated rice and insisted on eating potatoes.

61 *Djambu* refers to a fruit tree of the *Eugenia* family. There are a number of varieties, but perhaps the reference is to the *djambu bol* tree (*Eugenia malaccensis*) which has red juicy fruits. *Rudjak* is a spicy fruit salad.

62 *Gamelan*, a Javanese and Balinese word from *bergamel*, means "to make music." It refers to the Javanese orchestra used for *wajang* performances and ritual dances. Some of the instruments of a *gamelan* orchestra are the *rebab*, a kind of violin with two strings, a *suling* or bamboo flute, drums, gongs, varieties of an instrument resembling a vibraphone

such as the *saron,* the *gambang gangsa, gamnang kaju,* and so forth. The Javanese *gamelan* music and instruments have a complicated history and ritualistic significance. See J. Kunst, *Music in Java: Its History, Its Theory, and Its Technique,* ed. E. L. Heins, 3d enl. ed., 2 vols (The Hague: Martinus Nijhoff, 1973). *Krontjong* music was a popular kind of music in the Indies, especially favored by the Eurasians (called Indos during the colonial days). It is neither entirely Indonesian nor quite European. It seems to have derived from Portuguese music. A typical *krontjong* band has a violin, a guitar, a five-string guitar, a flute, and a tambourine. The music is slow and sounds somewhat like popular Hawaiian tunes. *Pantuns* were often used as lyrics. See R. Nieuwenhuys, *Oost-Indische Spiegel* (Amsterdam: Querido, 1978), 305–7.

63 *Pagger* (Dutch spelling of Malay *pagar*) can be a hedge or a fence around a house, made of bamboo or shrubs. It can also be the wall of a room made of mats.

Acknowledgments

The publication of *Fugitive Dreams* marks the completion of the twelve-volume series entitled the Library of the Indies. I am grateful to the various individuals who, over a period of seven years, have helped me bring this project to fruition.

Three institutions in particular have been intimately involved in this endeavor: the National Endowment for the Humanities, the Foundation for the Promotion of the Translation of Dutch Literary Works (Amsterdam, the Netherlands), and the University of Massachusetts Press. My gratitude goes particularly to the people connected with those institutions, especially Dr. S. Mango, director of the Translation Program of the National Endowment, and Mr. Joost de Wit, director of the Foundation for the Promotion of the Translation of Dutch Literary Works in Amsterdam. The transatlantic cooperation of these two individuals made the Library of the Indies a reality.

I am also indebted to the following individuals whose contributions cannot be more fully documented here. First of all, Ms. E. Sturtevant-Qualm for the selfless and cheerful support during the daily grind of getting the manuscripts ready; at the University of Massachusetts Press, Ms. P. Wilkinson, Ms. Leone Stein, Mr. Bruce Wilcox, Ms. M. Mendell, Ms. B. Werden, and Ms. E. Kearney; the staff and directors of the Prins Bernhard Fonds in Amsterdam, the Ministry of Welfare, Health, and Culture in The Hague, and the Royal Netherlands Embassy in Washington, D.C.; and Professors J. Wijnhoven, S. Flaxman, Th. D'Haen, E. Phinney, H.C.D. de Wit, A. Lewis, and William Jay Smith.

But the greatest support and inspiration came from Dr. Rob Nieuwenhuys. He knew why this work had to be done. Terima kasih Rob.